I0588854

Kelly Jennings

and

The Golden Knight

ANISSA PAPADAKOS

Copyright © 2023 Magic Walls & Canvas.

ISBN: 978-0-6484235-2-2

First Published in Melbourne Australia 2023

Anissa Papadakos has asserted her right under Copyright, Designs and Patents Act 2023, to be identified as Author of this work.

All rights reserved. No part of this production may be reproduced or transmitted in any form or by any means, electronic or mechanical, including photography, recording, storage in an information retrieval system, or otherwise, without the prior written permission of the publisher, unless specifically permitted under the Australian Copyright ACT 1968 as amended.

A catalogue record for this young adult fantasy novel is available from the National Library of Australia.

NATIONAL
LIBRARY
OF AUSTRALIA

Written By Anissa Papadakos
Text Copyright © Anissa Papadakos
Cover design by Anissa Papadakos
Back cover design by Anissa Papadakos

Anissa wishes to thank her wonderful editor, Kat Pagan, for her extraordinary work in transforming her manuscript into a poetic piece of art.

Facebook: Pagen Proofreading
Instagram: Kat _m_pagan

BOOKS BY
ANISSA PAPADAKOS

Children's Books

The Adventures of Mr C

Self Help Books For Adults

The Brochure Lied

Superdad

BIG THANK YOU AND LOVE TO:

My *brother David for writing
an amazing poem when he was a little boy.*

*The Oak Tree opened a door to imaginable
magic and creativity.*

*Mr P, Annabella and Lulu for always keeping me
on the right track and for helping me to believe in
myself and in the magic.*

*George and Karen for always taking the time
to listen to my crazy ideas.*

*To my Hubby Peter aka Superman, Thank You for
encouraging me to undertake this project and for
being there, especially during the hardest of times.*

*My Four Frogs (Zabe): Ivana, Niko, Teresa and Ellen
for always showing me what true magic is.*

*Last and not least, Thank You to you all
out there for all your support and love.*

This book is dedicated to all the Lovers of Magic.

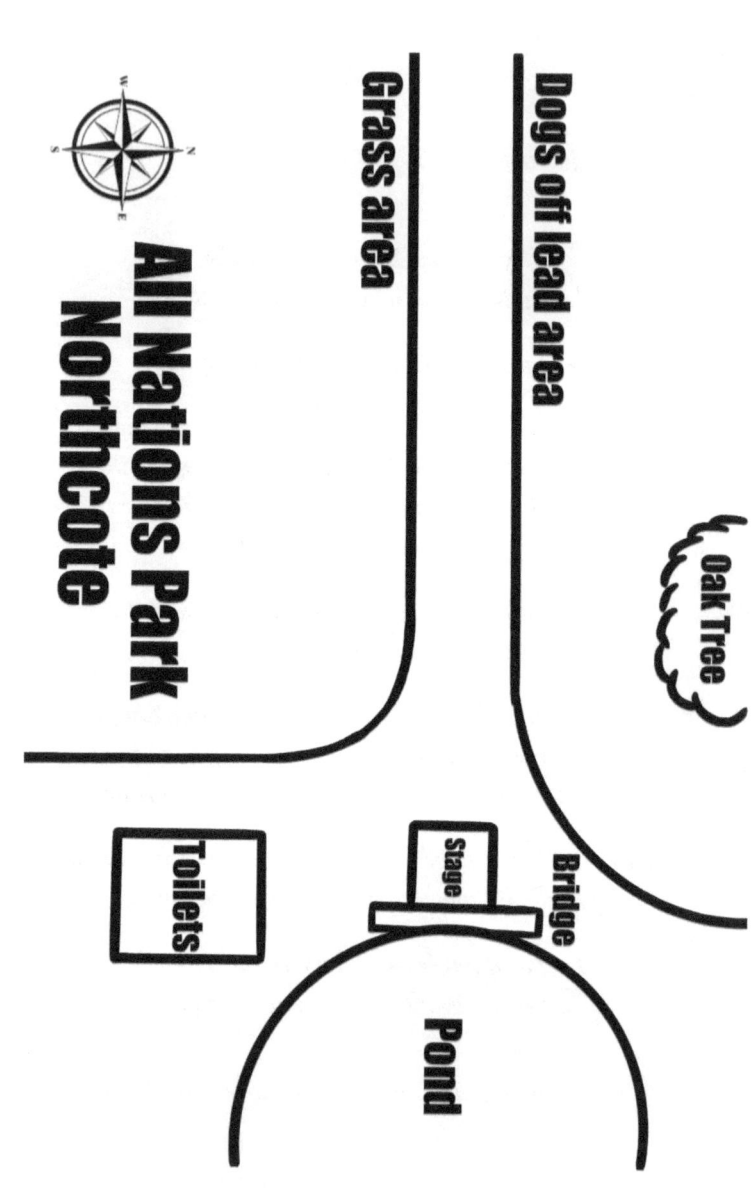

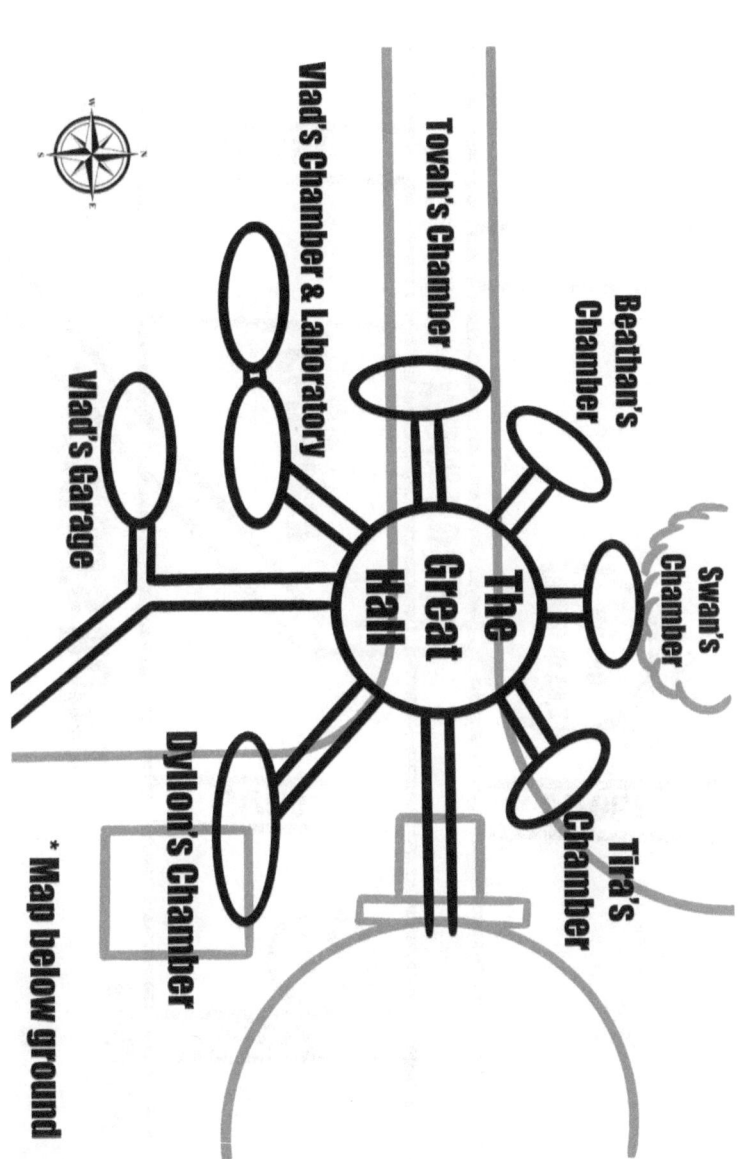

Vlad's Chamber & Laboratory

Vlad's Garage

Tovah's Chamber

Beathan's Chamber

Swan's Chamber

The Great Hall

Dyllon's Chamber

Tira's Chamber

* Map below ground

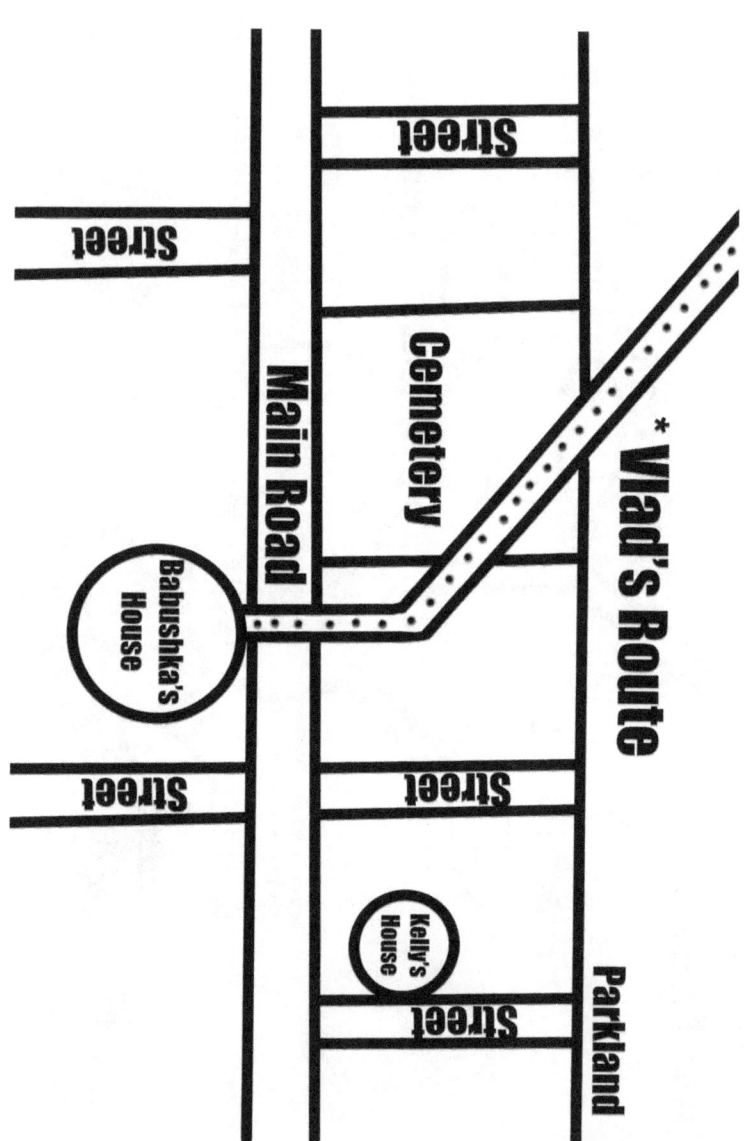

STUDENT OF THE WEEK ENDING 16.11.90.

Grade Prep	Brad
Grade 1	Ramay
Grade 2	Christian
Grade 3	Melody
Grade 4/5S	Marcin
Grade 4/5H	Bidong
Grade 6	Melanie
ESL/Miss Kelly	David

POEM FROM DAVID   GRADE 6

The oak tree,
So old and mighty,
You look so strong with
the swift wind flowing through your leaves
Your powerful branches fork out so high,
You are so tall and I am so small.
You tower over me and I know that I am really small,
compared to you

PRELUDE

THE STONE WAS cold as the turbulent waves continued to lap against the city walls. No voices sounded in the distance. No laughter either. What was once a busy and flourishing city now lay silent. Windows remained shut; merchants ceased singing their songs of sales. There was nothing. There had been nothing for many years. All that could be heard was the howl of the wind and the cries of the crows, the new tenants of Saphira, which had been a jewel in its glory days.

It was an ancient city, ruled by a just king. A king who loved and cared for his people, and in turn, received that same love and care back. He was a king who was respected. Now that very same throne has sat cold and empty for countless seasons. Generations have come and gone, but still the city remained dormant.

Leaning heavily on his walking stick, the old shepherd stopped at the city gates and sighed. A tear trickled down his cheek and he quickly wiped it away, shame replacing his sadness.

Has it been so long? he wondered. *Has it been so long since the end of the kingdom? Has it been so long since he yielded his sword as a strong, young knight? Has it been so long since he watched the fine, shining steel become tarnished by the blood of the king's enemies?*

"Yes, it's been so long and yet death never pays me a visit. A visit which I deserve. It's me who should have died in that throne room, on that horrible day. It's me who should have been slayed. Yet, I was not." Bowing his head in shame, as if asking the long-dead king for forgiveness, the old shepherd continued on his way, stumbling along the cobblestone road leading towards the hillside where his flock of sheep awaited his return.

He eagerly counted them. Nine, ten, eleven, twelve... Yes, they were all there. Exhaling with relief, he cursed under his breath, chastising himself for being away from his flock for so long. He slapped a palm to his face in wonder. He just didn't understand why this strange force was pulling him to the gates of the old city. Was it guilt he felt? The guilt that kept him awake at all hours of the night while staring at the ceiling of his hut. Or was it the voices that haunted him? The voices that belonged to the stone statues scattered all across the city.

Once, these statues were men and women. Breathing men and women, who lived within the city walls. Brethren who had children, who had voices and smiles on their faces. Who sang songs under the starlit skies. Now they were nothing more than crumbling rock. Their souls taken. Their bones frozen. Their voices silenced, forever.

At that moment, he whimpered and clutched at his chest, his breaths swift and quick. Was this the end he hoped for? The end he had been praying for, for so long. But his heart eased and bounced back into rhythm. He cried out in pain and yelled to the sky. "Damn you, Ba'al. Damn you to the seven hells." The shepherd fell to his knees and sobbed uncontrollably while his sheep scattered in all directions. He didn't care.

Go, run, take your chances with the wolves, he thought. The anguish he felt in that moment for his old kingdom, for his brethren, and for his king was far more excruciating than the scattering of his small flock.

Gradually, the tears slowed, the sobbing subsided, and he cleared his head and concentrated on his breathing. The old shepherd spotted some rosemary growing by a cluster of rock. He lifted himself off the ground with the aid of his crook and grabbed a handful of the herb. He needed to visit the tomb. He needed to pray for strength so that he could press on and continue this wretched life.

At the back of his hut was a hidden cave, leading deep into the hillside. At one time, it was a fully functioning mine but now it was nothing but a long black labyrinth of chambers, passageways, holes, and pits. Steadying himself with his crook he descended into the darkness. Light was not required; he knew his way well. To a stranger, this journey would lead to a painful death, but not to the old man. The way was clear. He could walk with his eyes closed and still find it.

At the cross roads, he stopped and sniffed the air, searching for a scent but there was none to be found. *Good,* he thought. No one would know that he was here. No one would find him and desecrate or burn *him*. Turning to his left, the old man took the familiar passageway without hesitation. It wasn't long before he saw the faint, purple, glowing light. And he knew that it was not much farther. Hope spread in his heart and the strength he yearned for began to grow within him. His burden, for just that split-second, somehow felt lighter.

The guardians appeared before him. They stood their ground as protectors. Strong and tall with their jaws agape. Sharp rows of teeth surrounding a long, serpentine tongue. They were vicious and seemed life-like. To the unwelcomed visitor, they spread bone-rattling fear. A cold, panic-inducing sensation through the body and the mind, but they reminded the shepherd of the old days, when glorious beasts flew through the skies and stood beside mankind, protecting it from all evil. That protection was gone. The dragons were gone.

Entering the tomb, the shepherd bowed and placed the fresh bouquet of rosemary at the armoured feet. He whispered the word "vivant" (long live) and stood in silence watching *him*, hoping he would awaken from his long slumber. But he did not.

They laid him to rest in this modest tomb on a stone-carved altar, covered in rosemary, with his sword in his hand and his shield resting above him. When the old man looked up, the imprinted golden dragon with its rider at its centre shimmered in the purple hue of the light.

I

IT WAS A beautiful and sunny day in Northcote, no different from any other. Park Street was busy with the hum of buses and cars. It was that time of day when frantic people were rushing to pick up their children from school or out quickly shopping for the night's dinner.

The bell rang at Santa Lucia High School—it was time to go home. All the students were excited as it was the beginning of the weekend. It meant freedom, no rules, and no teachers.

Kelly shut her locker with a sigh of relief and said goodbye to her friends. Home was not too far away, only a ten-minute walk from campus. She preferred to walk as she didn't like to be picked up by her mother. It was just too embarrassing, you see. Sometimes the mean girls would tease her and call her names. They would say nasty things such as: "Oooh, does Mummy need to wipe your bum too?" Comments like that made Kelly sad and angry. All she wanted was to fit in with the cool gang—to be normal.

As she exited the school grounds, Kelly thought that since it was a nice day, she would walk through the park. Take her time and enjoy the weather. She could even go visit the ducks at the pond and maybe sit in the sun for a while before heading home. That idea put a smile on her face. Kelly loved the parkland; it was her favourite place, and her favourite spot to sit was under the old oak tree.

There was something special about that tree. Yes, it was old, but it was also majestic. No one really knew how long it had been there or how it got there. It had a huge, thick trunk. And its bark was full of various shades of browns, greens, and greys. A tan rainbow embedded into ancient wood. It was magical and it drew you into being in its presence. It felt like it rejuvenated you while you sat beneath its shade and under its protective branches. The branches seemed like they were mighty arms belonging to a giant—a protector. But there was no giant, just an oak tree, which somehow stood the test of time and against all odds.

For you see, this beautiful parkland was not always green and lush. It used to be the old local community tip. It was the dumping ground where the neighbourhood trash got swallowed up by the earth, where old cars came to rust and die, and where cheeky children went in search of adventure and treasure.

Kelly was very young when the tip was transformed into the beautiful green parkland that it is today. She couldn't remember what the tip looked like, but she could never forget the smell. It was disgusting. The odour much like rotten eggs. Her mother always made sure that the windows at home were closed on the hot summer days, as the smell was much, much worse. No amount of air fresheners or incense could rid the air of that putrid smell.

~

It was beautiful in the parkland. The sun was shining and it felt like a happy place. There were lots of people walking their dogs and children were flying kites or riding their bikes. Laughter could be heard all around. It was simply magical. The magic could be felt in the breeze, heard from the songs sung by the birds, from the howls of the wind in the sky, and the rustle of the leaves in the trees. Kelly was in awe.

She reached the pond and looked over the rail.

Where were the ducks and the swan? she wondered. "Hmmm." *Maybe they were hiding from all the noise the children were making.*

Kelly felt a little bit disappointed because she wanted to feed them some stale bread she had brought from home. Kelly's parents never threw anything away, especially bread. "Why throw out yesterday's bread when it can be made into breadcrumbs or it can be used to feed the ducks?" her mother would say. It was these types of teachings that influenced Kelly to start her once a week Friday ritual of feeding the animals at the pond.

"Ahh, I know what might lure them out," she said, getting all excited.

Kelly unzipped her schoolbag and took out the bread. Slowly and gently, she broke the bread into pieces, small enough so that the animals would find it easy to eat. She threw a few scraps into the water and watched the ripples spread, hoping that it would attract the ducks and the swan. But there was nothing. Not a sign and not a sound.

This was strange. This had never happened before.

Something didn't feel right. Kelly started to get worried. *Did someone or something hurt the animals?* she thought to herself. *Did a dog jump into the pond and chase them away?* She hoped the latter was not true either.

There had been many occasions when Kelly watched the nightly news and saw what damage a dog could do to a small child, but to a helpless duck? The damage would be catastrophic...

"Get a grip, Kel. You are going crazy," she said to herself while she shook her head. As she threw the last pieces of bread into the pond, from the corner of her eye, she saw a little grey rat with a long tail scurry out of a hole and enter the water. It picked up some of the bread, and as he swam back to shore, he lifted his hand and waved thank you. Kelly rubbed her eyes in shock. "What in God's name did I just see?" she mumbled to herself. She quickly grabbed the rail and lifted herself up to get a better look at the rat. But the rat was no longer there. He was gone. "Nah." She was being ridiculous.

Rats didn't do that. They didn't wave thank you to strangers. Well, then again, they didn't wave thank you at all.

After a few minutes of looking for the rat, Kelly came back to her senses and started feeling embarrassed. Who had seen her hanging off the rail like a want-to-be monkey?

Then she thought, *Oh my God, everyone must have seen my blue underwear!* Jumping down off the rail, she grabbed her bag and started walking towards the oak tree, all red-faced.

~

"Did ye go out again in broad day light? How many times do I have to tell ye not to do that?" grumbled the toad. Vlad the rat stopped in his tracks and just stared at Dyllon, his mouth agape, trying with all his might not to say something that would anger the toad even more.

For some reason, Dyllon had been on edge for the last few days, grumbling at everybody and everything. To be honest, he got like that every now and then. The clan believed that he missed his home and more importantly his battle axe: Fearbreaker. Others believed that he missed having a pint or two of ale down at his favourite inn. But when he got like this, everyone stayed quiet and out of his way.

Vlad decided it was best to continue walking to his quarters, still holding the moist bread in his hands. He didn't bother answering the toad's questions as he knew that either way he would get yelled at again. It was only a matter of time.

"Don't walk away from me when I am speaking to ye, ye stupid vermin," yelled Dyllon.

Immediately Vlad stopped in his tracks and turned around, anger spreading all over his face. "What did you call me?" he snarled, staring Dyllon right in the eyes.

"I asked ye a question and I expect ye to answer me. Not walk away like I am some dirty dog in the street," said the toad with his head held high.

The rat stared at the toad without flinching. He took a deep breath and began to speak, exhaling the frustration that he felt a moment ago. "My old friend, I know what is troubling you and I feel pity for you. But stand strong and be patient. The time will come when you will see your beloved home again. The time will come when you will yield Fearbreaker and your enemies will fall at your feet," said Vlad with all the humility and care that he held in his heart for his old friend. Putting a hand on the toad's shoulder, he continued. "But this is not the way. You must not exert yourself or your heart will give. Then who will I have the pleasure of arguing with all day long?" Vlad ended his speech with a great big rumble of laughter.

Dyllon sighed and bowed his head. "Ye are right. I don't know what has come over me. Think it's the sleepless nights I have been having. This may be our home for now but I miss my starless sky. I miss the mines and the smell of the steel being forged in the depths of the earth and the sweet symphony of my anvil. I miss my home."

Tears began to well in the old toad's eyes and Vlad noticed. "Are those tears I see in your eyes?" The perfect opportunity arose for the rat to stir the toad. After all, that's what friends are for. "Are you growing soft, my friend?" laughed Vlad while slapping Dyllon on the back so hard that it nearly knocked him off his feet.

Dyllon trembled and shook at the remark made at his expense. He felt his face turn red, and with sheer embarrassment, he stomped his foot and yelled, "I am not soft. If I had me battle axe, I would strike ye down with one swift move." Dyllon pretended he was holding his prized weapon. He raised it high above his head, paused for just a minute to admire it, and then brought it down, swinging hard and fast. "I would crack ye head open and feed on ye brains to see if you truly ever had any sense." But Vlad continued to laugh so loudly that he keeled over and started rolling on the floor. This outraged Dyllon even more. "Bah, to the seven hells with ye."

He sighed and stormed off towards the pond, leaving Vlad rolling on the floor in a fit of laughter.

"Why? What has happened, Sir Vlad?" asked a sweet voice out of nowhere. "Is Master Dyllon all right?" continued the voice, belonging to none other than Princess Annora of Saphira. "I heard a lot of commotion going on down here."

Vlad immediately stopped laughing and jumped to attention. He bowed low to her, looking down to the ground with glowing red cheeks. "Your Highness, please forgive me. I sincerely apologise for my behaviour." He did not know what else to say and just stood there twiddling his thumbs. He wouldn't dare look into her beautiful eyes. After a moment of silence, Vlad lifted his head, about to apologise once again, when the swan princess held up her large, crisp-white, feathered wing to stop him.

She looked into his big brown eyes and said, "Come, walk with me, Sir Vlad."

"Why yes, Your Highness," he replied, still embarrassed. Together they turned and started walking through the tunnel towards the Great Hall. The swan grabbed Vlad by the arm and they walked together like equals, side by side.

"Please, Sir Vlad, call me Annie. I don't like these formal names, as I am not a princess here. The home I was told about—Saphira—is a long way from us. We are here together, looking after each other. Let's leave the formalities for another time, in another place, where they belong. Even after all these years, surrounded by all of my beautiful friends, I do not consider myself a princess. I am not royalty. I am just your Annie." Princess Annora's voice was so soothing.

As he gazed into her beautiful eyes, Vlad didn't know what else to say. "Yes, of course, Annie. As you wish."

"Now, tell me, Vlad, what happened today to our good friend Dyllon? How has he upset you today? What is that old toad grumbling about?" asked Annie.

While exhaling a deep sigh, Vlad said, "It's always the same with him, Annie. He misses his home. He has been here in this world for far too long. To be honest, I don't know what we are going to do and I don't know how we can help."

"Perhaps we should just let him be," replied Annie as they entered the Great Hall, which was quiet and empty for a change.

The Great Hall was where the clan would gather as a group and discuss any concerns or issues affecting them as a whole. Here, they would spend hours debating what was the best way to tackle and solve problems, patiently listening to each other on most occasions. On other days, it was also a space that would often be filled with laughter and joy. Each member of the clan enjoying the other's company, reminiscing with stories of the old days or sharing the latest joke. But at this very moment, it was a room that felt cold and empty. And in that cold and empty space, a faint sound could be heard in the distance. It was Tovah the priest chanting.

Vlad and Annie continued their walk towards the southern tunnel, which led to Vlad's laboratory. Back at Saphira, Vlad was an inventor. He spent many hours and days locked up in the highest tower of the castle working on his latest invention. He hated to be interrupted and all he ever wanted was to be left alone, to go about his business, and to create new and wonderful things. If he couldn't be found in the tower, then he was somewhere lost in the beautiful lush forest not too far from the castle. The forest was a mysterious place filled with mysterious creatures. It held a strange energy and that energy felt powerful.

Vlad wasn't scared to venture deep into the forest as there was always something new to discover out there. And with new things, there was limitless possibilities that always got him very excited.

Suddenly, the chanting stopped and out popped Tovah. In this world, he was a wise old owl, but back at Saphira, he was a priest. Sometimes, when Dyllon was really upset, he would tease Tovah and call him Hooty. Tovah hated that. He would run after Dyllon with a bottle of Holy Water, hoping to sprinkle some on him. Tovah was convinced that he had the power to purify the old toad and get some well-needed manners into him.

But Dyllon was too quick for Tovah and he always managed to jump into the pond and swim away while he shouted, "Come and get me, Hooty. Come and jump into the water and cool your fiery tail feathers."

Of course that never happened. Tovah never jumped in after the toad. All he did was stand at the edge of the pond and yell with all his might, "One day I will catch you, Dyllon. You'll see!"

"Ahh, have we come for a confession, Vlad, my son?" asked Tovah with a smirk on his face, while he turned and bowed to the swan. "Good day, Annie, my child, how are you?" He beamed.

"Good, Father Tovah, how are you today? We could hear your mesmerising chanting from the entrance of the great hall. It delivers a feeling of peace, and I quite enjoy listening to it, I must say."

He beamed ever so brightly at Annie, and then, without warning, he abruptly turned to Vlad and asked again, "Confession, my son?" Vlad looked at Tovah in frustration. He slapped his hand on his head, thinking how many times must he apologise for all the noise he made in his laboratory. He was an inventor and his duty was to invent, which meant he would definitely make some noise and also a bit of a mess. Besides, all that racket was for the greater good of animal-kind. Vlad didn't mean to make that explosion happen the other night; it was an accident. He was experimenting with new materials that he found in the park during the day. Boy, were they some great finds! He found a paper clip, a battery, a copper coil, and a gold coin and he was up all night experimenting, welding, banging, cutting, slicing, etc. until there was an awful loud noise that shook up the entire burrow.

It knocked poor Tovah from his perch, making him think the end of the world was near. The great owl came flying out of his quarters, screaming and yelling at the top of his lungs, ordering everyone to get in line so he could douse them with holy water just to make sure they could enter Heaven when the end came. Only Annie could bring Tovah back to his senses and when she did, he was really embarrassed so he cried. Since then, Tovah and Vlad's relationship was still on shaky ground. If there ever was a chance for one to upset the other, it would happen. Vlad apologised to the owl many a time but it was no use. Tovah would never forgive Vlad.

"Father, when are you going to stop punishing me for the accident?" asked Vlad. "I didn't mean to cause you or any one of us harm," he continued. "Please, my friend, let it go and give me and yourself some peace."

"Peace! Peace, you say?" piped up the owl. "We have not

yet had any peace since you and that witch started watching that dreadful show," he snarled.

"Babushka Lilliana is not a witch," cried Vlad in defence. He paused for just a moment and cleared his throat. "Well, yes, she is a witch but she is a white witch—a good witch."

There, he thought, *it is true and I have said nothing wrong.*

But the owl continued his piece as he felt he was the wisest and the most intelligent of them all. He knew better than everyone else. "She is a witch, nonetheless, and she is the one who introduced you to that television show—*Mac-Gyver.* You think that you are like him, but let me tell you, you are not. He creates things; you make things explode!" shouted Tovah at the top of his lungs. "And that thing that you call Bubble Bee is an evil contraption."

"You mean Bumble Bee," corrected Vlad cheekily.

"Oh, do not interrupt me when I am speaking, my child. I will bring down the wrath of God upon ye," he spat, shaking his finger at the rat. Tovah looked at Vlad in utter disgust.

How could anyone interrupt a man of the cloth? he thought. *How!*

It just didn't make any sense. But he wasn't in the mood to find out as he wasn't finished delivering his sermon, so he straightened his robes and his stole, making sure they were sitting perfectly, took a deep breath, and continued. "Like I said, this Bumble Bee, you shouldn't be using it and only God knows what harm it will bring to the burrow and to us all," stated the owl firmly. "Someone will see you and start poking around." He turned to Annie and pleaded with her, "For years, we have been lying here, hidden and safe under this mighty oak tree, no one to bother us." He pointed at Vlad. "If he keeps taking that machine he calls a transformer out in public, someone will see him and then he will give us all away. Oh, Annie, what are we going to do."

Annie stood there and watched them both. Watching all the stress and concern that was written across each of their faces. One was trying to help the burrow, while the other felt it would get destroyed. She was caught in the middle and she loved them both. They each treated her like a daughter.

"Father Tovah and Sir Vlad, I love you both very much. We all love you both very much, but this madness needs to stop. We are here together, surviving together, and we all need each other." Annie grabbed a hand from each clan member and continued. "Forgive each other and move on with love and compassion. Let it go… I beg you."

Tovah took a deep breath and sighed. "Ah, my Annie, you are right. God would not want it, not at all." He squeezed her hand, raised it to his lips, and gave it a quick kiss. Next, he turned to Vlad and said, "I am sorry, my friend. Let bygones be bygones. Let old dogs sleep, and let there be peace." He turned away and started to walk towards his chamber. But just before he entered, he turned back and said, "Good day to you both. I am off to pray to God to bring mercy upon the soul of my son Vlad, so that he can be forgiven for the sins he continues to make." And with that final statement, Tovah pivoted on his heel and disappeared into his chambers, leaving Vlad and Annie frozen in their tracks.

2

KELLY DROPPED HER bag and sat down with her back leaning against the big oak tree. The tree looked old to Kelly and it seemed like it had a story to tell. A secret. But it was just waiting for the right confidant to come along. She rubbed the palm of her hand against one of the roots. It was her way of saying: *hello, I'm back and it's so good to see you*. She closed her eyes, exhaled, and began to relax.

What a day it had been, she thought.

School was okay and there were no problems today. No bullying. The *bad girls*—as Kelly called them—didn't bother her because they were too excited about their dates tonight. Why tease poor little Kelly when their minds were preoccupied by which pair of shoes to wear out of the hundreds they owned? Sometimes Kelly wished she had those types of problems; they sounded more fun and exciting.

Even the teachers were lenient and didn't allocate too much homework for the weekend, which made her happy.

This meant that she had a little bit of freedom, some time to do whatever she wanted. So Kelly and her best friend, Gemma, decided to go for a long-deserved coffee tomorrow afternoon down at their favourite café: Black Bean. She was excited and couldn't wait.

Kelly opened her schoolbag and took out her diary, eager to organise the little bit of homework she had. Looking down her list, she realised that the only pressing thing on her agenda was the poem she needed to write for English. It had to be a creative piece and there was no word limit. It could be about anything or anyone. She recalled how some of the girls in her class were going to write about their latest boyfriends, "the love of my life" as Sandra said while batting her eyelids at her minions.

Sandra was the school sweetheart and everyone loved her. Well, not quite everyone as she also had a bit of a reputation for being a bully at times—a mean streak that the teachers were known to turn a blind eye to, on occasion.

Sandra came from a very wealthy family. Her father owned one of the largest law firms in the city and was a big contributor to the school's building fund each year. Without those funds, the school couldn't develop and grow. So, in exchange for the financial support, the principal made sure that Sandra was kept happy and always got what she wanted.

Kelly let out a sigh, wondering why she couldn't come from a family who was so influential. A strong family, with a strong name that allowed her to get whatever she wanted too. Instead, she had to be ordinary; she had to be a nobody.

Taking a pen, she ticked off all the things that needed to be done by Monday. Luckily it wasn't much and it was quite easy.

Maths could be completed tomorrow night and that shouldn't take long, she thought to herself.

They were just some basic algebra calculations that Mr Zang assigned to introduce and ease the class into the topic. He didn't allocate anything more difficult as he didn't want to scare the girls. Mr Zang was a very caring teacher, and this made him quite popular amongst the students at Santa Lucia.

Science was next on her list.

Again, too easy, she thought.

All that was required of her was to collect some snails from the garden and place them in a plastic bucket. That wouldn't be a problem. You see, Kelly's father kept everything. And by kept everything, it meant HE literally KEPT everything you could possibly think of. If everyone in Kelly's class needed a plastic container, her father wouldn't find it difficult to supply each student with one. And to make it even more interesting, he would be able to give them one in the colour of their choosing. That's how versatile he was. He simply found a use for everything. Nothing plastic, wooden, or tangible found its way into the rubbish pile (including the recycle bin) unless it was approved by him. In fact, there were instances where her mother would have to hide the rubbish next door, so that Kelly's father didn't sift through it and store the dirty, smelly items in the garage.

"Oh no," he would say. "You can't throw that out. There are plenty of things that can be done with it. In fact, I have been looking for something just like that for a while. I need it to fix this." He would gesture. "Oh, and that thing that makes all the noise can be fixed using this right here," he would say, while giggling like a schoolboy.

Kelly just smiled at the thought of her father. He was a

dork but a very lovable dork. He was her favourite dork and she thought the world of him.

Her attention returned to her English assignment, since it was something she could handle in the present moment. "This poem is going to be the death of me," she said out loud.

Kelly had no idea what she should write about. Should it be something personal? Should it be something funny? Should she talk about her feelings or describe something that she really liked? She just didn't know what to do. English wasn't her favourite subject but she knew that she still had to try to get the work done. Why couldn't they be allocated a book to read? That type of thing she thoroughly enjoyed. But it was when words had to be written and sense had to be made of those words that she found herself struggling. What didn't help her either was how her English teacher, Miss Scully, always criticised her work, and this affected Kelly's confidence.

"Come on, Kel," she mumbled to herself. "Surely it can't be that difficult." Leaning back against the trunk of the oak tree, she stared into the lush green leaves high above. The beautiful sunshine kissing her face, and warming the quickly pinkening skin there, lured her into a sense of peace.

The oak tree...
So old and mighty...

She began, and slowly but surely the rest followed until she stared down at her sheet of paper and her assignment was complete.

You look so strong with...
The swift wind flowing through your leaves...
Your powerful branches fork out so high...
You are so tall and I am so small...

You tower over me and I am really small...
Compared to you.

She spoke her poem out loud again and could not believe what she was hearing. Where did these words come from? How had she thought of them, let alone verbalized them? But the words were beautiful and they made her smile. They made her feel good. Kelly closed her eyes in awe and drifted off to sleep, feeling so proud of herself.

~

Annie finally reached her quarters and closed the door firmly shut. Leaning against it for comfort, she sighed, feeling drained.

What am I going to do with those two next time? she thought.

Deep down, she knew there was not going to be a next time. Because next time meant all-out war and she would be torn. "This constant bickering needs to stop. It's unhealthy and starting to affect the other members of the clan. God, please give me strength. Please give me peace," she pleaded. Peace was something she craved.

Being a princess in this world was beginning to take its toll. There were days where she thought it was a mistake; they must have gotten it wrong. Surely, she wasn't a princess. Annie felt she wasn't strong enough to be a princess. *Their* princess. The survivors of the Great War back in Saphira.

The swan didn't remember that world. She didn't remember her birth parents—the king and queen of the lost kingdom. She had no memories of that time or that place. All she had was the members of her clan and the stories of what once was. Stories of a beautiful kingdom ruled by a just king. A king who was loved and adored by his people. And stories of dragons, powerful and majestic creatures loyal to the crown. These dragons were tamed by a legendary dragon whisperer: Millard Drakon. The Drakon family was one of legend. A bloodline that dated back to the creation of the swan's world. But those were stories, fairy tales, and they didn't feel real. What felt real was the love she had for her clan. These survivors were all that she had. They loved her and she loved them all equally. But how could she be a leader to them when she felt weak. She didn't understand what it meant to lead.

I know what I need to do to lift my spirits, thought Annie. *I need to play my harp.*

And she went and sat beside her beautiful instrument. Taking a deep breath to clear her mind, she ran her fingers over the taut strings. The music was majestic. It filled her heart and soothed her soul. The cobwebs and the strain of the day just melted away. Love came and replaced all fear. The music travelled into the open space of the room, along the corridors, and vibrated through the wood of the old oak tree. Up and up, it went along the branches, through the twigs, and out to the sky—released by its lush green leaves. Annie felt at ease and her heart felt full. She began to hum and the humming soon turned into words. Beautiful words, speaking of a mother's love for her baby. It echoed and filled the air with magic.

~

Outside, Kelly began to stir in her slumber. Visions of a great and bloody war appeared in her mind. Sounds of weapons clashing and banging. Voices screaming and pleading. Women and children running from a dark army. Kelly didn't understand what was happening. It seemed so real. The screaming, the crying, the bloodlust. So real in fact that she felt like she had been there.

What is happening? Where am I? she thought.

The vision of the battle faded, and she was now standing in what appeared to be a cottage. There was a man holding a baby. Beside him lay a dead and bloodied body. She sensed that the man's arrival was too late—it was tragic. He suddenly turned and looked at Kelly. She knew him. There was something familiar about him, a connection. It was strong. They stared at each other.

God, he looks so beautiful, thought Kelly.

His big blue eyes were hypnotising. Then, out of nowhere, he reached a hand towards her, as if wanting to communicate somehow. But as he tried, a sword was plunged through his heart and he released an agonized cry.

"Argh." Blood spurted from his mouth as he fell to his knees, and with his last breath, he pleaded, "Come home."

Kelly woke in a fright, sweat dripping down her forehead. She felt disorientated. "Where am I?" she said. Her heart was racing a million miles an hour and a bout of nausea turned her stomach. "Oh my God, what was that? Who was that man?" She grabbed her water bottle and gulped down the contents, the cool liquid rehydrating her and making her feel better. Calmer. Kelly remained seated with her back propped against the tree trunk, deep in thought, while slowly coming back to her senses and whereabouts.

Wow, she thought, shocked by how real her visions felt.

The blood and the screams seemed so real. That man seemed real. His eyes were incredibly blue. Mesmerising. The colour was just magical.

She looked at her watch and realised she had been asleep for a very long time. Too long in fact. Standing, she grabbed her schoolbag and gave one final long rub to the belly of the great old oak tree. It was her way of saying thank you.

Thank you for keeping me safe in your shade while I slept.

3

CLANK, CLANK, WOOSH, *smack, bang* went the pots and pans in the kitchen sink at the Jennings' household. Woosh, splat!

"Oh damn," said Joyce as the soapy water splashed and dripped everywhere, several drops landing on her beautiful silk blouse—her *favourite* blouse. "Oh, double damn," she cursed under her breath as she looked down at herself and saw the damage. "Now I am really angry."

She huffed, tossing the pot back into the water without thinking. The cookware landed smack-bang in the centre of the sink, causing the biggest splash the world had ever seen—at least that was how it felt at the time. The dirty, soapy foam leapt into the air and crashed right in Joyce's face. Bullseye. Some even went into her mouth and the taste was horrid.

"Pfft, pfft! Oh my God," she screamed. With one eye barely open, Joyce grabbed the nearest tea towel and started rubbing the muck away. She took a gulp of fresh water from the tap and cleaned out her mouth. "Pfft, pfft, ew," she spat. "Honey, what time is it?" Joyce yelled out to her husband, who was sitting in his favourite recliner chair in the lounge room, reading the day's paper and oblivious to what was happening in the kitchen.

There was no response, so she called out again—this time even louder. It was more like a shriek, a sound only dogs could hear. Surely it would register. *Bam!* His head popped up like a meerkat. "Ha, w-what did you say, baby?" yelled Mark. "I'm having trouble with my hearing today."

"Geez, you have trouble with it every day, my darling," she mumbled. "I keep telling you to go get your hearing checked, but *no*. It's just too damn hard," she continued, all the while mimicking her husband sarcastically while she cleaned up the mess she'd created.

Something was telling Mark to go to the kitchen and see what his wife was trying to say. His gut was urging him to go, so he folded his newspaper, placed it on his little coffee table, and bounced off his chair and out of the room. "What's wrong, my darling—" He stopped in his tracks with his mouth ajar. "What in God's name happened here?" he asked.

There was gunk everywhere. All over the floor, on the walls, and covering his wife. Her blouse was drenched, looking more like the colour of dog doo than the luscious blue he'd witnessed this morning.

"Oh, don't ask," she replied.

"Why didn't you wear an apron? Aprons help keep you clean at least," he stated, an eyebrow arched in confusion.

Joyce stopped cleaning within an instant to stare her

husband in the face. If looks could kill, the man would be dead right about now. "You're joking," she said, raising her arms in protest. "Why didn't I wear an apron? Well, because I thought I wouldn't need one, darling." She rose from her crouched position on the floor and threw all the damp paper towels into the bin. Turning back to Mark, she continued, "I had a fight with a pot and the pot won—TKO."

"Well, I can clearly see that, honey. Did you at least go the distance? You know, fifteen rounds?" Mark lifted his hands like a boxer and started to shadowbox all around the kitchen. "Did he give you a jab, jab, cross? Or was it a jab, jab, uppercut that got you right smack-bang in the face?" He clapped his hands together to make a loud noise.

"No, my darling, he did a face-buster," replied Joyce.

"Oh no! Not the good old face-buster move! *Damn!*" And he fell to his knees in mock agony, holding his jaw in feigned anguish. Mark was breathing hard and fast. "Oh, you poor woman. If only I were there to see it!" he exclaimed. "It's a very difficult move to do properly, and only the elite can do it, you see." He pushed to his feet and plucked the pot from the depths of the sink. He dried it with a towel and held it up high.

"What are you doing?" asked Joyce between giggles and chuckles.

"I am Copper Pot. The king, in all his glory. The victor of the battle. The champion!"

Joyce broke out in full laughter. "Stop! You are going to make me pee my pants and then I will have more to clean."

"What are you doing with that pot, Dad?" came a little voice from nowhere. Everyone stopped dead in their tracks and turned towards the newcomer.

"Hello, my darling. You have come home just in time for the ceremony." There was a huge smile plastered across Mark's face. Kelly began to smile along with him, because she loved her dad's humour. He always tried to make a bad situation into a funny one.

"And what ceremony would that be?" she asked, still grinning while suppressing a large giggle.

Mark continued to explain the situation at hand. "Well, you see, you missed the greatest fight since Muhammad Ali and George Foreman. And it happened right here, in our kitchen." He pointed to the sink, then at his wife. Everyone in the room was completely silent, which meant he had his audience in the palm of his hands. "Ba-ba-baaa!" He mimicked a trumpet sound, holding a pretend microphone, and announced the match. "Ladies and gentlemen, what a colossal fight we have witnessed. In the blue corner, weighing in at 110 pounds, we have Mumma Chef. And, in the right corner, weighing in at 5 pounds, we have Mr Copper Pot—the winner by a *knockout*!" echoed Mark.

Kelly looked at her mother, her clothes drenched and dishevelled. "Oh, Mum," she said. "I am sure you fought dirty, but that pot was just too dirty for you." She giggled.

"Ah-ha-ha-ha, that's a good one, hun. High-five," said Joyce, raising her palm in the air.

Kelly walked up to her mother and gave her a big hug and kiss instead. "You okay, Mum? Can I help you clean up?" she asked.

"No, darling, it's all good. Why don't you go upstairs and get ready for dinner. Your dad and I will finish up, and then you can tell us all about your day." She caressed her daughter's cheek, to show her how much she appreciated her offer of help.

"Okay, Mum, I will be back in just a minute."

"Wow, wow, where is everyone going?" asked Mark. "We have a ceremony to conduct and the crowning of the champion," he pleaded. He stood in the kitchen with his hands on his hips, his eyebrows drawn in disappointment at his audience. Mind you, he was trying to keep a straight face as well. But his complexion was getting redder and redder by the second, until he could not suppress the laughter anymore. He let it out, keeling over, and slapped himself on the knee. "Just joking, my darling. Come over here and give your old man a hug. I missed you today."

Kelly ran into her dad's arms and got a great, big bear hug. God, it felt good to be loved. Hugs from Dad were the best. They were the ultimate balm and the greatest medicine. It was what every daughter needed in order to feel better—a hug from her dad.

"You okay, Kelly Bear?" asked Mark. He noticed that their embrace lasted longer than usual, and this made him a little concerned. Kelly just continued to hug her dad in silence, her eyes closed and her face pressed into his chest. "Kel, what's wrong, darling? You know you can talk to me about anything. I won't get upset. You know that, right?"

Kelly opened her eyes and released her dad. "Yeah, I know, Dad. But I'm okay. I'm all good. Just a little tired. It's been a long week and I'm so glad it's Friday." She walked up to the fridge and opened the door, peering inside while searching for something to give her a bit of sugary comfort.

"Did something happen at school today. Did someone tease you, darls?" he asked, crossing his arms. He noticed that her behaviour was a little off. She wasn't her normal bubbly self. To him, the decrease in *bubble* meant that something had unsettled her.

But what could it be? he thought.

He hated seeing her like this; it hurt so much. Mark walked over to the fridge and leaned against the kitchen cupboards, trying to act cool, instead of like a protective parent. "So, what happened today at school, kiddo? What went down?" he said, in gangster-style rapper mode, trying to bring himself to the teenage level.

"Nothing much, Dad. You know, the usual: English, maths, science, et cetera, et cetera," Kelly stated quickly, looking at her dad and bopping her head back into the fridge. "God, where did Mum put the chocolate?" she continued. *Bang, shake, rattle.* "Damn, I can't find it for the life of me. I just want a very small piece," she pleaded in frustration.

"Now, now, Kelly, there will be none of that," Joyce interjected as she walked back into the kitchen with a fresh blouse on. "Close the fridge door, go upstairs, and change out of your uniform. Dinner is in five minutes, kiddo," she ordered.

Kelly sighed and did as she was told. She paused for a split-second at the fridge and turned to her dad. Their eyes connected—blue on blue. "Dad, don't worry. I'm okay. Just tired. It's been a long week. That's all," she reiterated.

Mark looked at her. Looked her dead in the eyes, trying to find some hidden answers. A clue perhaps? But there was nothing. Just two beautiful eyes staring right back at him. After about a minute of silence, he finally spoke and assured her, "Okay, Kelly Bear, I believe you." He unfolded his arms and raised his right hand. "Give me a high-five, kiddo."

"Sure, Dad." And they slapped their hands together, showing each other that they were cool and that an understanding was reached: the conversation was over. There was nothing more to be discussed, nothing further to be added.

But before she could walk away, he replied, "And down low, kiddo," holding out his palm for a second time.

"Absolutely, Dad." Kelly gave him a good, hard slap—just the way he liked it. It showed him she wasn't afraid to offer up a bit of power and brute.

He surprised her by grabbing a hold of her hand at the very last minute. "Gotcha," he said with a smirk. "You're still not faster than your old man, kiddo."

Kelly laughed in response and shook herself free. She turned away and headed towards her bedroom upstairs. As she approached the first step, she yelled out, "True, but one day I will be," and she quickly disappeared.

He stood there, still slightly concerned about his daughter. She didn't fully understand what he was implying with the "gotcha" and that was okay. He just hoped that when and if ever there came a time, she would understand that he had her. He had her back, no matter what.

4

"WOW, MY DARLING, dinner looks amazing as usual," said Mark as he placed his napkin on his lap. He turned to Kelly and whispered, "We are so lucky to have Mum cook for us, because she always adds a secret ingredient—something you can't find at the supermarket. Do you know what it could be, Kel?" he asked, winking at her.

"Hey, silly sausage, I can hear you, you know," said Joyce while she spooned some beautiful and fluffy mashed potatoes onto her plate. Without taking her eyes off her meal, she continued, "And, by the way, Sherlock, I'd love to know what that ingredient is, if I may ask?"

Mark winked at Kelly, trying to encourage her to have a go at guessing. "Well, Mum, I reckon it's onion salt—yep," she chirped, feeling confident about her answer. "It's definitely onion salt."

"Onion salt?" said Joyce. "That's an interesting guess. I never knew that existed. Sorry, darling, I don't use that type of salt but you definitely have given me a new idea." Which Joyce quickly added to her mental shopping list. She didn't want to hurt her daughter's feelings by saying that her answer was wrong, so she decided to turn it around and make it into a positive—a good idea type of thing.

Mark raised his hand in that instant and started making noises like a monkey at the zoo. "Oh, oh, oh, I know what it is!" he said, surprising everyone at the table by acting all childlike, as if he were at school trying to get the teacher's attention.

Joyce decided to put him out of his misery. "Yes, my darling, please tell me what the secret ingredient is because I'm surely going to explode from the suspense." She giggled to herself as she spooned mash into her mouth. "Oh, and darling, can you please pass me a piece of the roast first." She pointed to the sizzling rack of lamb sitting just in front of Kelly.

"Sure, darling," he replied. But before he could do anything, Kelly grabbed the plate and handed it to her mum, making it easier for her to help herself.

"Oh, thank you, Kel." Joyce grinned. "So, tell me, darling," she continued, rolling her eyes, "what is this secret ingredient?"

There was a pause at the table, and then Mark cleared his throat and said, "Love." Kelly and Joyce looked at each other and burst out into laughter. Distress was written all over Mark's face as he watched the two people he loved most in the world laugh at him. He felt so embarrassed and all he wanted to do was crawl under a rock and never come out.

"Oh, sorry, darling," Joyce said between gasps of breath. She nearly choked on her lamb when he told them his answer. "I am sorry for laughing. It's just that you can't bottle love, and in that split-second, I got this image in my head of a cow. And that cow had my head on it, you see, and she was being milked just like an ordinary cow. But they were milking me for my secret ingredient: love, not milk."

As soon as she finished saying it, Kelly and Joyce broke out into hysterical laughter once again, each slapping the table in amusement. Mark just looked at them, absolutely aghast at their behaviour. "You know what, Mum?" Kelly stated, then paused with a mixture of snorts and chuckles. "That is the same exact image that popped into my head too! Imagine if that really happened to people!" She doubled over at the idea.

"I know!" said Joyce, sharing her daughter's hysterics. "God, that would hurt but imagine how much money we would make!" They both sat there and continued to laugh, wiping tears off their faces.

"Come on, guys, it wasn't that funny," said Mark sheepishly. It was obvious he was still upset and embarrassed—it was not the reaction he was expecting to get.

Kelly turned to her dad and placed her hand on his. "Sorry, Dad, I didn't mean to upset you." She felt bad. "Why don't you tell us about your day at the zoo. You always have interesting stories to tell us," she pleaded, trying to make him perk up a bit. He always lit up like a candle when he spoke about his job and about all the things that happened behind the scenes, out of view of the general public.

"Oh, Kel, I don't feel like it today, hun," he said, his voice and demeanour deflated.

"Come on, Dad, you always have a cool story to tell.

Please," she pleaded for a second time and added some eyelash batting in hopes of luring him in.

"Well, okay, sweetheart. You always melt my heart when you stare up at me with those blue eyes of yours." He cleared his throat, cutting into a piece of lamb as he recounted his tale. The excitement had returned to his voice. He loved the spotlight, not for attention but because he loved telling stories.

Stories are full of magic and wonder. When you step through that magical doorway, you are transported into a world full of imagination, colourful characters, and enchanted, far-away places, with plenty of fairy dust for everyone to share.

You see, magic is all around you. All you need to do is open your eyes and look. It's in the trees, in the leaves, in the air... It's everywhere.

Next time you are outside, take your shoes off, and plant your bare feet in the ground. Close your eyes and inhale and exhale. Focus on your breathing and just listen. Listen from your soul. Allow yourself to hear and feel the pulse of magic running from the soles of your feet, right up to your crown. Allow the magic to flow through you, and when you are ready, open your eyes and see for the first time that magic has been around you all along.

"We got an interesting phone call today," began Mark. "There was a hostage situation."

"A hostage situation," Kelly piped up in shock. "What do you mean, Dad?"

"Well, a little old lady rang us and needed our help ASAP. She had cornered a black king cobra in her kitchen and was terrified."

"Oh, wow, darling, that is absolutely insane," said Joyce.

"But how was the old woman a hostage?" she continued in confusion. "She wasn't the one in the corner of the kitchen, was she?"

"Oh, no, no, no," said Mark, giggling at his wife's question. "She wasn't the hostage, my dear. The hostage was the snake."

"Ohhh!" said the two girls in unison.

"But, Dad, that snake is dangerous," Kelly reminded him. "If it bit her, then that little old lady would be dead."

"Yeah, that is true," said Mark. "But she had that snake in that corner, all good and proper. The little guy wasn't going anywhere, hence it was a hostage," he explained with a giggle.

"Ha-ha-ha-ha, good one, Dad," said Kelly. "So, what happened in the end?"

"I had to dust off my cape and fly to the rescue. It didn't take long to get there, and luckily, she had the front door unlocked. I found them in the kitchen of course. I calmed Old Gran down and reassured her that everything was going to be okay. I showed her my snake catching kit and then I got to work."

"Wow, Dad, that is so cool," said Kelly in amazement.

"Yeah," replied Mark. "Hmmmm."

Silence suddenly descended upon the table and onto everyone seated around it. Joyce decided to speak first. "What's wrong, hun? Did something happen to the little old lady?"

"No, darling, nothing bad happened."

More silence followed. "Mark, what's wrong?" Joyce continued to press, the concern evident in her voice, while Kelly sat there, staring at her dad and not daring to speak or make a noise. She was starting to feel a strange sensation in her stomach. Something was out of whack.

"I don't know what to say, honey," stated Mark. He clasped his hands together and rested his chin on his knuckles. He was thinking about what had happened in Old Gran's kitchen. Something was telling him that he was going crazy. You know, *hallucinating*. But another part was telling him that what he saw was no daydream. He took a deep breath and began. "I had my foldable snake tongs ready and I opened my hunting bag, making sure there was a good clean slot so that the snake could be placed inside without a hitch." He paused and took another breath, steadying the anxiety while calming his sudden urge to projectile vomit all over the table.

Kelly took a big gulp of air as her stomach continued to twist. She too was starting to feel nauseous.

But why? she thought to herself.

"Must be the gravy—yep, that's it. It's definitely the gravy." It always gets her. And it gets her good. In that *run, run, run, I have diarrhoea*—volcanic eruption, going to kill a small village diarrhoea—kind of way. She took a sip from her icy cup of water, hoping it would settle her stomach. "So, Dad, was there a hitch?" she asked.

"No, no," he replied, feeling a bit frustrated. He ran his hands through his hair. "There was no hitch, and it was a perfect job," he stated matter-of-factly. "Everything went smoothly."

"That's good, Dad," Kelly said. "Then what are you so uptight about?"

In that instant, Mark broke down with tears and all. They just came gushing out, like the floodgates had broken.

"Oh my God, Dad, I'm so sorry. What did I say?" Kelly got up and ran to her dad. She grabbed him and threw her arms around his shoulders, squeezing him tight. Mark continued to sob. "Dad, come on, what's wrong?" Kelly asked in concern. Her stomach started to rumble, the bile rising in her throat.

"Here, darling, have a drink of this." Joyce handed him a glass of fresh ice water from the fridge. He took it happily and gulped it down within seconds while his wife rubbed his back.

"Thank you, girls. I feel better now," he stated, the colour slowly returning to his face. Kelly and her mum went back to their chairs and sat in silence, Joyce staring at her husband while Kelly stared at the floor, hoping the nausea would subside. Mark took a deep breath. "You see, I must have gone mad, because I swear I saw the snake look me dead in the eyes, bow, and then slither right into my bag. I didn't need to use my stick to handle it, and to be completely honest, I didn't do much of anything. I just stood there like a statue," he stated in complete bewilderment.

"Maybe you just can't remember correctly, darling," Joyce assured him. She grabbed his hand across the table and gave it a squeeze, trying to ease his discomfort.

"Yeah, Dad," said Kelly, still looking at the floor.

Joyce continued, "Sometimes we're so stressed in a moment that our body simply performs on autopilot, and our mind just switches off. Like it has gone to sleep and we don't remember a thing."

Kelly's stomach started to churn even more; the bile bubbling farther up her throat, as if looking for a way out.

"In fact, it happens to me all the time, hun," concluded Joyce.

"No, my darling," said Mark. "It doesn't happen all the time." He exhaled in frustration and went silent for a moment, glaring at his plate of food in front of him. Taking a deep breath and exhaling again to settle his nerves, Mark turned to his wife and continued. "Look, sweetheart, I know you are trying to make me feel better…"

Kelly started to dry retch.

"But the sort of thing you are talking about…"

Kelly then raised her hands to her mouth, trying to provide a block.

"Doesn't happen to anyone, because it doe-sn't ha-ppen at *all*," emphasised Mark. "SNAKES DO NOT BOW!" he yelled, as vomit spewed across the table in every which direction.

It leapt over the plates of food; it bypassed the salt and pepper before it reached its peak. Everyone stared in horror, the current conversation forgotten as chunks of lamb, bits of potato, slivers of gravy, and mashed up morsels of broccoli and carrot all mixed and entwined together started to make their descent.

The initial climb into space was a steep one, and according to Newton's Law of motion, what goes up must come down. And down it came. No one could foresee where it was going to land, but the collision was absolutely spectacular—a once in a century occurrence. It landed smack-bang on Joyce's clean blouse. *Splat, crunch, and plop.* Where it rolled off her chest and landed with a flop right in her lap.

Making matters worse, bits of goo ricocheted off on impact, landing right in her mouth—much like the incident with the pot. Joyce was appalled, and in that split-second, she gnashed her teeth down hard in response, hoping to prevent entry. But it was too late. Her body reacted reflexively and she swallowed with a gulp.

And that's when she started to scream. "Oh my God, my blouse!"

She jumped up from her chair. And *splat, glop* went the pool of vomit from her lap, drenching her feet and her slippers. She ran to the kitchen and turned on the tap, washing her hands. Mark followed his wife, concern written all over his face as he left Kelly alone at the table. Kelly couldn't believe what just happened. She was flabbergasted.

What caused the nausea? Surely, the story about the cobra couldn't make anyone react in that way. It was just a cobra, she thought to herself.

She wiped her mouth with her serviette and left the table, embarrassed by the aftermath of her family dinner. She ran upstairs to her room and slammed the door shut, breathing heavily. The nausea had stopped but she sensed a headache coming on, and it was coming on fast. Kelly wobbled to her bed and changed into her pyjamas, stopping repeatedly to steady herself and rub her temples and forehead.

"God what is happening to me?" she said out loud. "I don't feel good." She pulled back her doona and lowered herself on the bed. As soon as her head touched the pillow and she closed her eyes, there was darkness and Kelly was fast asleep.

5

THERE WAS A soft *tap-tap* on the chamber door and an ever so soft whisper coming from the darkness of the shadows. It was Tira. "My lady, we are set for the night. All is calm."

"Ah, oh my goodness," yelped Annie, startled from her thoughts. She grabbed her chest, her breaths coming out in quick pants. She giggled with embarrassment. "Ha, you surprised me yet again, Tira," she said while gasping for air.

Tira stepped out of the shadows and bowed to her princess in apology. "I'm so sorry, my lady. Are you all right?" she asked with genuine concern.

Taking a deep breath to settle herself, the swan responded, "Yes, yes, everything is all right. Tira, come sit with me for a moment." Annie gestured towards the empty chair sitting opposite her.

Tira felt scared and uncomfortable at first, but it only lasted for a split-second. She didn't allow her emotions to rule her head nor her heart; she brushed the negativity aside.

Tira moved with such grace. She was part of the king's arsenal, his own private elven bodyguard back at Saphira. The king trusted her not because of her natural powerful abilities or her skill with the sword and bow, but because of her honesty. Tira was incredibly honest. If someone—king or pauper—asked her for advice or an opinion, she would give it wholeheartedly and without ulterior motives. Her one rule in life was to speak the truth, no matter the consequence, as only the truth could set you free. It was her belief.

But here, in this world, she was a cat. And her strength, highly attuned senses, and super-quick feet were priceless to her companions and the residents of the burrow.

Annie watched as Tira sat opposite her. The princess admired the feline. She admired everything about her: her strength, the respect she had not just for herself but also for every living creature, and also her beauty. She was unbelievably beautiful. Her emerald-coloured eyes shone a bright luminescent green. It was the most incredible shade ever created and those eyes were magical.

Plus, Tira was one of the reasons everyone had stayed safe and hidden for all these years. She was a valued member of the clan, and Annie felt that her services had not been shown enough gratitude, hence the invitation to come and join the princess for a chat.

"I'm so sorry to keep you from your duties, Tira, but I just wanted to grab a quick word with you," said the swan, hoping to sound warm and inviting.

As was typical with the cat, there was no response but a subtle nod of her head to show acknowledgement and compliance. Annie started to feel uneasy as she was hoping for a much more engaging interaction. She was hoping to learn about Tira: who she was, where she came from, and what made her tick. Tira was a mystery to the princess. She didn't know anything about her, yet Annie was fascinated by the king's long-time confidant.

Annie pushed on with the conversation. "I just wanted to thank you for always looking after us all and for making sure that we are safe," stated the princess. "We all owe a lot to you, and I just wanted to reassure you that you are doing an impeccable job."

I bet I'm incredibly red-faced, the swan thought to herself, following her little speech. There was silence and Annie didn't know what else to say. Where to look. She simply continued to twiddle her thumbs.

"My lady, I may not speak often but I understand and feel your appreciation," said Tira in a soft and sensual voice—much like a purr.

Annie glanced up from her hands, and Tira caught her stare. Those green eyes were captivating, and it was so hard for Annie to turn and look away. Tira could sense Annie's unease. Perhaps this time the princess needed some comforting for a change, so the cat decided to open up and return the reassurance.

"The king, your father, bestowed a great honour onto me and it is my duty to fulfill that honour," said Tira with pride, before continuing, "Long before you were born, my life was headed on the wrong path." she paused, contemplating what to say next, what to share with the princess. "Your father found me... well, to be honest, I'd been caught and thrown into the dungeon beneath the castle."

Annie listened with piqued interest. Tira's life story was incredibly fascinating. It was rare to see an elf living amongst humans, and she hoped to find out why the cat had chosen to leave her homeland and swear allegiance to the king. "You were a prisoner, oh my," said Annie in response.

"Yes, I was very young and I was trying to survive. Everything I learned stemmed from my need to survive. My instincts kept me alive," she said. "But when you live on the streets, eventually, your luck runs out and mine certainly did—I got caught."

"What were you doing?" asked Annie, slowly creeping to the edge of her chair in anticipation of the answer.

"I was stealing bread from the bakery within the castle walls," explained Tira. "I hadn't eaten for days and I was so weak from the fatigue and hunger that I got sloppy and I was caught."

There was silence and the two ladies just stared at each other. Annie was shocked. *Wow*, she thought. Tira grew up on the streets, and the streets were deadly. From the stories the swan had been told about Saphira, those same streets where a different world. A world filled with crime and seclusion, a place where you had to learn quick to survive or you wouldn't.

Annie found it absolutely amazing that a younger version of the Tira sitting in front of her grew up on those same streets, learning and surviving. Well, not just surviving but thriving. The skills the cat must have acquired from all those dangerous bandits, thieves, and *possibly* murderers would have made for one hell of an experience—scary but thrilling at the same time. In that moment, the swan wished that could have been her. Instead of wearing a crown, she wanted to wear a hooded cloak. She wanted adventure and action and yearned for thrill and excitement. The princess had been born into a role that was meant to give her all she desired, yet it delivered none of that. She did not want to be royalty. She wanted to be like Tira: brave, courageous, skilled, and beautiful...

"My lady," said a distant voice. "My lady, my lady, are you all right?" asked Tira.

Annie laughed, lost in a daze.

"Are you all right, my lady?" Tira repeated, placing one paw on the swan's wing.

"Why yes, yes, I am fine. Thank you, Tira, and I am sorry. I drifted away," she whispered, not looking at Tira as she answered.

"Are you sure, my lady?" the cat pressed softly, demanding an honest answer in a gentle voice.

Annie took a deep breath, to steady her nerves, and exhaled—feeling much calmer than she had a moment ago. She responded firmly, "Yes, I am perfectly all right, Tira."

"All right then, my lady." Tira stood from the chair and walked to the door, but before she left the princess's chamber to do her nightly patrol with Beathan, she turned and faced Annie one last time. "My lady, the honour that was bestowed on me was to protect Saphira at all costs."

Silence fell upon them once again. Annie didn't know what to say in that moment; she was confused, as Saphira was gone. There was no kingdom to protect. Tira could sense the confusion and, thus, elaborated on her statement.

"You are Saphira, my lady. We are all Saphira. I protect you and the clan, so that we may keep Saphira alive in our hearts and in our minds. One day, we will return and reclaim our homeland. But, for now, we hang tight—*together*," she emphasised. "And you have kept us together just like a true leader would." With that final remark, the feline bowed to her princess and disappeared into the shadows, leaving Annie feeling lighter and much warmer in the heart.

6

BY NOW, YOU *probably have several questions running through your mind. What is the burrow? Where did it come from? What does it look like? Where is it located?*

Rest assured, all your questions will be answered in due course.

Let's start with the burrow, which consisted of a small network of tunnels that were built by a family (or skulk) of foxes long ago. Foxes were a regular sight within the neighbourhood as well as common within the suburbs. If you went out late at night, chances were you would have crossed paths with one casually walking the streets in search of food.

However, over time, the fox population grew and before anyone was the wiser, their numbers had doubled—tripled. They could be found everywhere within the community and were unfortunately becoming a menace.

They would dig up veggie patches, chase cats, wrestle with dogs, and steal chickens from backyard coops. The worst reported case was when one of those unwanted furry intruders snuck into someone's home (via a forgotten open window, mind you) and slept in front of an open fire all night long. In the morning, the homeowners woke to a fright, and as a result, they alerted the authorities and the local council. Thus, the witch hunt was born.

You see, a price was put not on the head of the fox but the tail. The local council stated that they would pay five dollars for every tail brought to their offices. And did they pay, you may ask? They sure did.

Over a period of time, the government-issued cull caused the numbers and sightings to decrease. There were less and less reports, meaning less and less rewards were distributed. Backyard chicken coops were no longer targeted. Cats were still chased, but now only by other cats in the neighbourhood—the kitty street bullies. Dogs stopped wrestling and some became fat and lazy. And the good old band of local foxes disappeared, their burrows left vacant.

When the companions came to our world, they came through the oak tree. Babushka used her magic to open up a portal in Saphira at The Great Orac Tree (*orac* meaning *oak* in the ancient tongue of Saphira). The Orac was a sacred tree, situated in the heart of the enchanted forest. Then the old croon used her powers to save the princess and her companions from the forces that had already killed the king, the dragon whisperer, and many, many soldiers and townspeople. The Great Army was crushed and Saphira fell.

When the survivors stepped through the portal, they exited into another mighty oak tree. The trees may have been separated by dimensions and time, but they both oozed magic and ancient secrets.

Disorientated by their sudden passage, the companions landed in a park, in the dead of night. Local folks said the weather changed instantly. Within a flash. The black night sky turned a crimson red, the winds howled, and the heavens lit up with a brightness. Great beams of lightning came thundering down to the earth from above, which were said to have struck the oak tree not once or twice but several times over. And just as suddenly as it began, it stopped. Order and peace befell the quiet neighbourhood, while anyone who had witnessed the phenomenon certainly did not hang around long enough to see the finale. The portal opened up, and one by one, the companions passed through.

First, a rat was flung through the air like a beanbag. Bounce, bounce, somersault, face-plant, and a *kaboom*. The force was so great that when his body had finally stopped moving, his tail hadn't received the memo, and it smacked him right in the face, cracking the poor rodent like a whip. It knocked him out cold and left a nasty red mark across his little snout. Even someone who hated rats would feel sorry for him—the scene was that heart-wrenching.

The winds picked up again, the clouds above the oak tree swirled, and *pop...* another creature was flung through the portal. This time, the skies rained a puff of grey feathers. Tiny, soft, and beautiful feathers. And they were everywhere. It was the very image of the aftermath of an overenthusiastic pillow fight.

Upon closer inspection, there appeared to be a baby swan lying on the cold, wet grass. She lay not far from the rat, shivering amidst her lost plumage. Somehow, the portal had stripped her of all her feathers, leaving the cygnet completely bare, with her little bum exposed to the elements.

Poor darling. She sat there with her wings wrapped around her body, hoping to stay warm on that cold night.

"Croak," went the toad as he flew through the portal. Yep, you heard that right; it was a *croak* and not a *ribbet*. The fat, slimy toad, all bloated and warty, floated through the air like a big balloon. But when he landed on the spiky grass, he didn't explode into pieces. No siree. Upon impact, the old toad let out a colossal fart. It was so loud that it temporarily woke up the rat. The drowsy rodent lifted up his head and slowly opened one eye.

Where… where are we? he thought to himself.

"What… what happened?" he asked aloud, rubbing his eyes with his tiny paws, stroking his snout, and realizing it was still tender to the touch. But wait… "Why do I have a snout?" he asked, his voice panicked. He looked down at his hands and was absolutely bewildered. "Fur! I have fur on my hands," he continued, incredulously. "And claws on each and every finger!" He peered down again. "Claws," he repeated the word, as if he hadn't understood it's meaning the first time.

And then he smelled something horrific. Something worse than the odour of rotten eggs, worse than mouldy cheese, worse than spoilt milk, worse than any bog that he'd ever smelt before. It crept into his tiny nostrils and wrapped its stench all around his throat, squeezing the life out of him like a boa constrictor looking to eat its next meal. The poor rat didn't stand a chance. He dropped to his side and fell unconscious.

"Bahaha, croak," said the fat toad. It was all too amusing for him. He was the cheeky one back in Saphira, and it seemed as though that *cheek* was not lost along the journey.

However, much like there had been in his homeland, there was also a strong force at play—a force known as karma. So he sort of deserved what happened next...

The wind changed once again, and as another companion (a sleek cat) was flung through the portal, the stench carried with the breeze and hit the toad right in the face. This time, it was a double whammy, seeing as his mouth remained open from laughter. The sudden, bright, jarring brilliance of the portal made the old geezer gulp up the stench, taste it, and swallow. Down the hatch it went. The foul stench deposited in the pit of his stomach, where it started to rumble. The toad felt sick instantly. He grabbed his big brown belly and rubbed it in slow, circular motions—round and round. But there was no use. His head was aching and beads of sweat came pouring down his face. He grabbed his head with his free hand and closed his eyes. The pain was excruciating. He tried to move, to scurry away from the stench, but the odour was too overwhelming.

However, this old toad was stubborn, more stubborn than a mule. So he focused, took a deep breath, and with all his might, he stood upright on his webbed feet.

Oh, oh, bad idea.

Out flew the vomit. Litres and litres of multicoloured vomit. It cascaded like a giant waterfall, leaping out of his mouth and crashing down onto the grass. It splattered everywhere: sloppy, juicy, thick in some spots, rainbow-coloured vomit. It splashed all over his feet, ricocheted onto his legs, and created a pool right in front of him. The expulsion had been so forceful that the last convulsion caused the toad to ball over, pass out, and land face-first in the puddle. This poor toad may have copped a beating but Lady Luck was definitely on his side. Tira pounced upon him and rolled him onto his back.

She checked his vital signs. Check.

Made sure his air passage was clear. Check.

And that he was breathing without a hitch. Check.

For an old toad, his pulse was strong, which meant his heart was still good. His brain may have lost all its sense but his cardiac muscle was beating loud and clear.

Tira stepped away from the toad. The stench was becoming a little too much to bear now, and she looked around. *Where are we?* she wondered. *What is this place? Oh no! The Princess, where is she?*

She lifted her head in the air and took a big whiff, searching for the girl's scent. "Phew! that stench is horrific," she said after gagging and then coughing up a big furball— though the lump of hair didn't shock her as there just wasn't time to think about herself. She was fine, so no need to fuss. Her motto was: *I can breathe, I can walk, I can arm myself, therefore I am fine.*

She moved upwind to get some clear air, hoping to pick up the princess's scent. And finally she did. The girl was close. Tira followed the scent, using her incredible feline senses. A leap and a bound later found the child all curled up. The cat's sensors confirmed the baby swan was okay, naked but okay. Her long white whiskers tickled the sleeping babe and it made the cygnet stir. She cried out to her father but there was no reply. Tira nuzzled up to the princess, hoping her fur would keep the child warm, that her purr would give the girl some comfort, make her feel safe.

"You are safe, my lady. You will always be safe and I

will always protect you like I promised your father, the king. Shhhh, shhhhh," she continued to soothe.

It was the third time Tira allowed someone into her heart. The loss of her parents at such a young age had nearly destroyed her, while the path that followed was hard and bitter, especially for an orphan. It was also cruel and isolating. There was no one to hold her at night. There was no one to whisper sweet nothings into her ear. There simply was no one, and no one cared. Until she met the king, a memory she thought she had long since buried.

Seeing the princess now, bare and all alone, sent her spiralling in the past as she recalled a night she thought she had forgotten.

She saw herself in the princess and the comparison broke her heart. All that fear she felt as a child came rushing back and it scared her. Fear was a weakness; it was a cancer. Once you let fear in, it would be your undoing. She didn't know how she survived for so long, all alone on the streets, but she knew very well that fear nearly killed her. The numerous scars on her body were enough to remind her to reject the negative emotion. She didn't want the same fate for the princess, especially now.

When Tira was captured as a child, the king was kind to her. Instead of leaving her in the dungeon to rot, he had listened to her. He treated her like a human, not an animal, and when he found out that she was of elven kind, his treatment did not change. The king was compassionate and Tira never forgot that day. It was a day that changed her life and her destiny. And it was all because of one man. A king who treated an outcast like a daughter.

Now, looking down upon the swan princess, Tira swore

to protect the babe with her life. It was her duty and honour. The king had once protected her and now the tides had changed. "Nothing will happen to you, my lady," she whispered. "Nothing," she repeated and she began to purr.

Kaboom! Bang! Shake, rattle, and bam!

The noise was so loud that a few car alarms were set off in the distance. "Ahh!" everyone screamed, human and animal alike.

It was one big mess as the entangled bodies flew through the air and out of the portal. Arms hung here, legs hung there, paws sticking in the eye sockets of others, and beaks embedded in hairy, smelly armpits. They all flew through the air together and landed smack-bang on the grass in front of the oak tree. It was a very clean landing. No one was harmed in the quick expulsion. No bones were broken, and no egos were bruised.

"Oh, my head," moaned Babushka. "What happened?" she questioned, still lying on the moist grass while facing the beautiful starlit sky. She felt lost, and for a split-second, she couldn't remember a thing, as if all her memories were wiped out. She stared into space, looking at the unfamiliar constellations and at the occasional shooting star blazing its way across the galaxy. Until images flashed in her mind. There was a great battle, a city fell, and thousands perished to the evil.

What was that evil? she thought.

Babushka pressed harder, searching her brain for answers. "The king! Oh nooo!" And the truth finally hit her.

She couldn't save him.

"Ahh!" she shrieked, propelling herself to her knees. She knelt and grabbed her hair, pulling at the ends with all her might. The pain was excruciating, but she didn't care. She felt she deserved more. The king was dead and it was all her fault because… she couldn't save him. She was meant to protect him but her magic hadn't been strong enough. She failed him, and she shrieked with agony, howling like a wild animal in the dead of night in hopes of forgiveness.

Wymann stirred from his slumber, heard the shrieks, and jumped up—ready to defend himself. But his hands found no sword at his side. There was no weapon and there was no dagger. He ran to her.

"Lilliana," he yelled. "Lilliana!" He grabbed her by the shoulders and tried to shake her out of her hysterics. But it was no use. She continued to scream, oblivious to what was happening in front of her, so he raised his right hand high above his head, closed his eyes, and gave her a good old-fashioned slap right across the face. *SMACK!* The force was so strong that he worried her head would turn 360 degrees, like some possessed zombie.

But, no, that didn't happen at all. What did happen was a large amount of spittle and a booger or two flew right out of her mouth and nose and landed on Tovah. The owl instantly jumped three feet into the air in fright.

"Woohoo," he sang at the top of his lungs. His feathers were all ruffled and they were standing on end like he was electrocuted. But as soon as his talons touched the ground once again, he grabbed his rosary and promptly did the sign of the cross, prepared to purify and eradicate all evil.

Beathan, who was a champion wrestler in Saphira—and now stood a big, strong pit bull in this world—grabbed Tovah with his equally big, strong arms and bear-hugged him, squeezing the owl tight and not allowing him to move.

"Stop, my dear priest," he yelled. "Grab hold of yourself," he pleaded. "No one is harming you."

Tovah continued to wiggle, trying to escape the dog's firm grip to no avail. The owl was no match. "Let go of me, sinner," he shrieked. "I'm doing the Lord's work," he said, all high and mighty. But Beathan didn't heed the priest's warnings.

The owl continued to wiggle, and Lilliana continued to shriek, and this was becoming too much for Wymann to handle. Too much to digest. The journey through the portal, travelling from one dimension to another, was quick but it was bumpy. Now, here, on this new world, it was beginning to feel even bumpier, with a dash of frustration thrown in the mix. Wymann just stood there and stared at it all.

Tovah decided to seize the opportunity. He lifted his beak, embedding it right into the dog's enormous bicep. The poor pooch yelped in agony and released his grip, the bird dashed away, and the chase was on.

As Tovah fluttered through the air, dodging Beathan, he held his rosary and began to pray. "Lord Almighty, Father—*ahh!*" he gasped as he took a sudden sharp turn, just missing the closing jaws of the hound. "Please purify the souls of these poor—" *Smack! Bang!* A roll and a scream. Pluck, out came all the feathers in his tail. Tovah gasped but he flew on. He felt as though he must finish his prayer and save the damned.

Beathan spat out the irritating plumage and cleaned his tongue with his paw. It felt horrible, like there was an enormous hair in his mouth, and he couldn't get it out.

Better to ignore it, he thought, *and get that bird.* He returned to the chase.

"Ahh, please forgive me, my king," Lilliana pleaded. She screeched so forcefully this time that tufts of her hair were ripped out, leaving a red raw bald patch in its place. It looked incredibly sore, but she didn't care as the emotional agony was far worse than anything physical.

"Phew," Tovah said. "I just made it away from the jaws of that beast," he panted as he stopped to take a breath and examine his bare bum. He turned his head and looked closely. He stared and stared, wondering how on earth his back had feathers—feathers that certainly weren't there before. There was a lot of hair but not feathers.

I must be going mad, he thought.

He turned to his rosary, attempting to make the sign of the cross, but he stopped midway. He noticed that his hands weren't hands anymore. They were feathered fingers.

Oh my, he thought in shock as his heart began to race.

He reached for his face, his limbs trembling, a little scared to see what he might feel. And what he felt was an enormous solid pit bull running at 100 kilometres an hour, colliding right into him. The poor bird didn't see it coming. On impact, Tovah—rosary still in hand—flew five feet into the air and then landed back on the ground like a sack of potatoes. *Splat!* It knocked him out cold and poor Beathan started to howl once again. He thought he had killed the priest. Accidently, as all he'd wanted to do was catch the owl and hold him until he calmed down.

The pit bull grabbed the bird and turned him over. He placed his big sloppy ear on the bird's chest and listened. At first, he couldn't hear anything, and he let out a sorrowful howl. "Noooooo! Priest, priest, wake up!" he demanded, hitting the ground with his solid paws. "Wake up, I say!

Awoooo!" he cried, tears running down his face in streams, temporarily blocking his vision. "I-I-I am so, so sorry, my friend," cried Beathan. "Pl-please fo-fo-forgive me," he whimpered.

He nestled his wet nose on Tovah's head and sniffed him. The feathers started to tickle his snout and the sensation irritated him. He raised his paws high and pummelled them down upon Tovah over and over again. He wasn't angry; he was hurting. The feathers triggered his pain and Beathan exploded. And good thing he did, because the pummelling started something in motion: Tovah's heart.

The priest stirred. "Ohhh," he hooted very, very softly. "Oh, my head. Dear Lord, bless me with your light so that I may enter heaven," he preached.

Beathan stopped crying and listened. *Am I hearing things?* he thought.

He lowered his snout, inching ever so slowly towards Tovah. Watching carefully for any movement of eyes or feathers. Nothing. He must be going mad for sure. Beathan decided to move closer, sensing something was out of whack. But what? He couldn't put his paw on it. Closer and closer, he crept until they were touching beak and snout. Cold, wet, slimy snout against cool and bony beak.

Snap, snap, snap went Tovah's beak. "Woohoo," he yelled. "Take that, you filthy animal! Now that's karma, my boy, straight from the hands of God," he cheered, jumping up and down while waving his rosary all about—as though he were creating a shield of pure holy protection.

"Awoo!" screeched the pit bull. His cries were so loud and so intense that it matched Lilliana's, and together, they offered the night air a sympathy of agony and despair.

Wymann couldn't take it anymore. This was over the top. *Too much.* His hands, which were hanging limply beside his hips, started to pulse.

Squeeze, release, squeeze, release. *What is going on?* he thought. Squeeze, release, squeeze, release.

"This is madness," he whispered. Squeeze, release, squeeze, release. But his friends didn't relent. Wymann grabbed his head with his hands and started to squeeze that too. "Dear Lord, make it stop. Make this madness stop. I beg you," he spat in desperation, spittle flying everywhere with remnants cascading down his chin. He closed his eyes, trying to block out the noise but it was no use.

A faint siren could be heard in the distance. As each second ticked by, it was becoming louder, clearer, and it was approaching fast. No one, none of the companions, heard it because they were either knocked out cold or screeching too loudly. But this siren was important. It was the local authorities, the police, and they were going to be here any minute...

"Ahhh, my Lord," screamed Lilliana.

"Awooo," yelped Beathan.

"Wee-oow, wee-oow," went the police siren. And then it happened...

"Ahh, shut up!" screamed Wymann and he pulled hard on his hair in frustration. He was so angry that his eyes bulged out of their sockets and the veins in his temples stood proud, looking as if they were going to burst. All of a sudden, there was silence. Everyone and everything stopped. All that could be heard was the wind, the rustle of the trees, Wymann breathing heavily, and the fast-approaching police siren.

Wymann fell to his knees, exhausted. He didn't lift his

head to look at the companions. He just stared at the moist ground and all the different coloured pebbles in front of him.

This ground is our new home, he thought. *If we're going to survive in this new world, we're going to have to be stronger and wiser. The madness cannot overtake us like it has tonight.*

He stretched out a hand and touched the ground. It felt cool and inviting, and all he wanted to do was lie down on it and close his eyes. "Sleep. I need sleep," he whispered. But there was no sleep, at least not for now.

Instantly and unexplainably, the winds picked up and the ground started to tremble. A light appeared in the centre of the oak tree. It grew brighter and brighter and then it stopped. It disappeared. It didn't fade away; it just simply vanished as if it were never there.

Wymann, Lilliana, and Beathan looked at each other, not knowing what to say or do. They remained still, wondering what was going to happen next. Minutes passed and still the light did not return. The oak tree remained dark. But the wind blew and the ground continued to rumble— rumble like something was trying to escape, as if it were trapped, and it wanted to get out. And out it came. The oak tree lit up like a massive Christmas tree, with an array of dazzling lights. It had finally reached its crescendo and this was the final show.

"Pfffttt!" Out flew the final companion, followed by a shrivelled stick. The newcomer was the son of Millard, the dragon whisperer, and the stick was the once majestic staff of Evermore used to open the portal.

The sleeping boy was catapulted right over the companions, over the grassy field, where he landed safely and soundly in a cluster of evergreen shrubs. The landing was not hard but the child did wake up on impact, unharmed, and started to cry.

The shrivelled stick did not have to travel far; its journey ended just in front of its wielder, though a little worse for wear. Lilliana picked up her stick and held it gently in her hands, feeling the rough surface. The once smooth and beautifully ornated staff was gone. In its place, stood a shrivelled, ugly, and grey stick that resembled more of a bare, uneven, dead tree branch than anything else. The magic was gone—she couldn't feel it in her heart—and now she couldn't feel it in her once-so-powerful staff. Even the threads were gone; she could no longer see them. All she felt was sorrow and emptiness. She grabbed her chest where the pain felt the greatest, looked up into the starlite sky, and vowed to never use magic again.

It was over. She was done.

"The babe," Wymann cried. He jumped up onto his feet and started to make his way to the young boy. He could hear him. He wasn't too far, and he didn't sound too distressed.

It will be okay, he thought. *We will all be okay.*

But things weren't okay. The sirens, which could be heard in the distance, turned into heavy boot steps. *Stomp, stomp, stomping* rapidly through the park. "Over there," said a mysterious voice. "I can hear a baby crying," the stranger continued.

"Okay, partner, let's go," replied the second man.

Wymann stopped in his tracks. Where were the voices coming from? They sounded like they were here, there, and everywhere. He just couldn't pinpoint their exact location. *Click, click.* Flashlights shone brightly. Wymann saw them and they found the babe. In fear, he ran. He ran away from the strangers, back in the direction of the oak tree. He knew he would regret his decision. He knew what he was doing was wrong, but he was scared and he panicked.

Lilliana saw him first. His face was whiter than a ghost. "What's wrong, Wymann?" she asked in concern.

Huffing and puffing, and with absolutely no energy left, he answered, "Grab everyone, quickly. I heard voices in the shadows and those same voices found the babe."

"Ohhh," Lilliana gasped. "Nooo, we must get him back, Wymann," she pleaded. "He is one of us and we must protect him."

Solemnly, he answered, "We can't, Lilliana. He has been taken, and now we must hide, or more of us will be separated." He looked her dead in the eyes and said, "We will find him. I don't know how but we will." He grabbed her hand, squeezed it, and turned away—not only to round up the others but to not show her the uncertainty in his eyes and the tears beginning to streak down his cheeks.

For the decision he'd made in that moment would affect each of their fates forever.

7

"DA-DA-DA, DA-DA-DA, DA-DA-DAH!" screamed Vlad as a sharp claw jokingly pinched him on the bum. He turned around and glared at the culprit—well, what could be seen of the culprit in the shadowy corridor. Vlad stared into two incredibly beautiful, green, almond-shaped eyes. It was Tira and she loved to play cheeky games with Vlad. Especially since, in this world, she was a cat and he was a rat. "Oh, Tira, grrr. Stop that, you crazy puss," he spat. "You know how much I don't like it when you creep up on me," he pleaded, shaking a frustrated hand in the air.

"Oh, come on, mousey, mousey, you know I don't mean any harm by it." She batted her lashes at the rodent in jest.

Vlad put his hands on his hips, took a deep breath, held it for a minute, and exhaled. He had a very strong urge to keep arguing with her but thought better of it. Time was of the essence and he needed to get his little hairless tail to Babushka's house. "Aren't you meant to be out patrolling the park, puss," asked Vlad with a cheeky grin. "Why are you bothering me?"

Every Friday was *MacGyver* night, his all-time favourite television show. Vlad and Babushka watched it together religiously and always danced and clapped when the theme song came on. It was so much fun.

Vlad loved *MacGyver*. The fictional character was the rodent's idol. He loved everything about him. All his tricks, his inventions, his creations, everything. Sometimes Vlad would get good ideas from the show and spend countless nights experimenting in his laboratory. Unfortunately, things didn't always go according to plan, and occasionally, there was a bit of a *bang*. On really bad nights, a minor tremor or two could be felt throughout the burrow, which would send poor Tovah flying right off his perch. The old owl would shout that Armageddon was once again upon them. And by now, it should be evident how much he loved using his holy water.

"Sorry to be a bother, my dear small, juicy morsel—oh, I mean *friend*," grinned the cat. "I was on my way to meet up with Beathan, to start our patrol, but my stomach rumbled," she explained, rubbing her belly in the shadows.

"I'm not a snack, you silly feline," growled Vlad. "And S-T-O-P baiting me." He held up is hands, pretending that he was reeling in a fishing rod. He looked her dead in the eyes and held her stare without blinking.

"Ouch, mousey, mousey," replied Tira, though her demeanour was calm and collected. "Just having some fun. That's all." Her voice hummed a friendly tune while she offered Vlad a cheeky wink. But the rat would not partake in any of it. He had better things to do—things like get to

Babushka's house ASAP. So he continued to hold his stance, refusing to move a centimetre, let alone drop his glare.

Tira got the message and decided it was time to move on to her duties. Night watch always seemed very long and, on most nights, very boring. A little bit of a joke here and there made the whole ordeal a bit easier to endure.

She didn't apologise to Vlad for stirring the pot. She just melted back into the shadows and disappeared like magic. Vlad stood there a minute or two longer, ensuring the rest of the burrow understood that their games wouldn't be well received. The last thing he needed was for someone to ruin his day completely. It was bad enough that he had to deal with Tovah's wild antics about the Armageddon and Dyllon's constant mood swings, but missing an episode of his favourite show would be disastrous for everyone—mankind, animal… ALL. So they all better move aside, move along, and stay out of his way.

"Finally." Vlad took a breath and released it with relief. He couldn't hear anything in the corridor and he couldn't sense anything either. He was alone, and very excited. The spring, which had originally been in his step, had returned and he continued towards his garage.

Now, Vlad's garage was like nothing anyone had ever seen before. It was truly a remarkable place, housing many, many amazing functioning and not-so-functioning creations, all varying in shapes and sizes. These creations were his robots and everybody knew how much Vlad loved robots.

The rodent had created robots with four legs, robots with two heads, robots with wheels, and robots that could be strapped to your body, offering capabilities such as flight.

The latter one was still in the prototype stage, and it needed more work.

Vlad loved using his prototype. He named it Iron Eagle, after a famous 80s movie he watched regularly with Babushka. He loved watching those beautiful jets on the screen—the way they manoeuvred, the dips and somersaults, and the speed of which they did it all was mesmerising. To him, the jets were powerful, iron birds without the limitations of ground animals, and the rat wanted a pair of iron wings of his own. He wanted to be among the clouds and closer to the stars, just like he witnessed in the movie.

The only problem was, for some reason or another, his prototype malfunctioned mid-flight. And by malfunctioned, what he really meant was that it just stopped working, and he plummeted all the way down to the ground. Sometimes the landings were smooth, but other times it left him quite bruised and battered. No broken bones, as of yet, but definitely a scratch or two and a few deep-purple bruises.

One time, he landed in a tree and smacked his face right on a branch; the incident left him with a big shiner. The poor little rat couldn't see through that eye for weeks, but it didn't stop him. Nothing ever stopped him from doing what he loved.

He'd first come across robots on one of his adventures in the park, while scavenging for lost items picnickers may have left behind or dropped while they were playing with their children or walking their dogs.

That particular day was an exceptional one, with an exceptional find. It was the day that started his love for all things robotic. He found a lost, solar-powered walking bot.

When he came across it, the poor little rat nearly had a heart attack. He had never seen anything quite like it; nothing of the sort existed in Saphira.

The bot had four legs but it wasn't an animal. It had a giant head but it was smaller than an owl and there were no feathers. Instead, it had these smooth, rectangular, solid panels on its back—which were warm to the touch. They weren't sticky or gooey, so they couldn't be fish scales.

So what could they be?

Vlad later came to learn that those were in fact solar panels and they could do some amazing things. But what had scared the rat the most was the creature's face. He only noticed it when the sun shone directly onto the canine-looking bot, illuminating its wild, unearthly stare. Though he had been truly terrified when the thing began to move. The poor little rat screamed in horror, nearly peed himself, and fainted—all at the same time. Now that would have been a horrific experience, if he'd collapsed in a puddle of his own pee. But rest assured, that didn't happen. The bot dog didn't move for long. As soon as the clouds covered the sun, blocking the much-needed power source, the creature was dead once again.

Vlad had been frozen to his spot, too scared to move a muscle or even a whisker. He was worried that the mysterious creature would come alive again and this time eat him or tear him into millions of pieces; thankfully it didn't. The bot just remained there, motionless, with the same scary, unblinking eyes and sharp teeth.

Seconds passed and then minutes. Vlad was still too afraid to move but he knew he couldn't stand there all night either. Sooner or later, he was going to have to find the courage to head back to the burrow. His stomach did a small gurgle and he rubbed it soothingly. He was starting to get hungry, and the sudden thought of food made his tiny little mouth salivate. He grabbed his snout in embarrassment as drops of saliva began to seep out between his lips. He quickly licked them away, trying to hinder their flow.

"Raaaaa!" said the unblinking, jagged-toothed robot dog.

Vlad held his breath and didn't move. *Jeepers creepers*, he thought. *It's alive and this time I'm going to die for sure!*

The little rat was sweating, beads of perspiration pooling on his forehead and snout. "Please, please, don't move, Vlad," he murmured to himself. "Please, please don't make a sound. One wrong move and we're dead."

"Raaaaa!" said the dog bot again—it seemed angrier than before.

Vlad let out a little whimper and quickly covered his mouth, hoping that the horrible creature didn't hear or see him in the grass. He was breathing so heavily and so quickly that his throat was making a wheezing noise, little bits of spittle flying through the gaps between his fingers.

"Who goes there!" screamed the beast.

"Ah!" yelped Vlad, quickly re-covering his mouth and clasping his snout shut with his fingers. He was shaking from the top of his head all the way down to the tip of his toes. Shaking like a leaf blowing in the wind. His poor little heart was beating uncontrollably. It was racing so hard and so fast.

"Who goes there!" repeated the beast, its tone nearly a growl.

"Hmm, hmm," squeaked Vlad, his limbs shaking uncontrollably. "Please don't eat me," he mumbled more to himself than to anyone else.

"Answer me, you snarly vermin—ahh!" yelled the dog bot as the sun's rays struck it, and the creature became mobile once again. It thrashed and kicked in the grass, like a bull in a rodeo. "Ahhh!" it yelled. The head popped forward and then it popped back, while the rest of the body continued to kick and bounce around in the vegetation.

Vlad could not believe what he was seeing—it was spectacular! Like a performance at a show. He didn't move from his spot, so fixated by the scene in front of him. Vlad did, however, unclasp his fingers from his snout. Which helped him to breathe better and easier.

The dog bot continued to thrash and kick. "Ahhh!" it screamed. It thrashed so hard that it lost its balance and fell onto its side right in front of Vlad. What followed was a loud "ahh" and a *kerplunk* with a slight *splat* from the small, fat, and wart-covered mass known as Dyllon the toad.

He landed right on his back, just a couple of centimetres from Vlad's feet. And when he did dare to open an eye, all he saw was a pair of very evil-looking, angry eyes positioned above a snarly mouth filled with sharp, fanged teeth. The only difference was that those eyes and teeth didn't belong to the robot. They belonged to Vlad and he was livid.

8

THE RAT SLOWLY walked up to his prize possession. It was hidden in the back of the garage, covered by a huge piece of ultra-soft fleece. The material was the same colour as the burrow so that it would remain camouflaged. Not that anyone would come into his garage and steal his toy. It was more to ensure it wouldn't attract any unnecessary attention—an out of sight, out of mind type of thing. Mostly for one person he was not interested in dealing with when it came down to his creations: Tovah.

The owl hated everything Vlad loved. To Tovah, all of the rodent's creations were an abomination. *Evil.* If they couldn't be understood by the priest, then they were wrong. Science wasn't Tovah's forte.

It annoyed Vlad when Tovah would run out of his chambers, dousing the rodent with holy water and shouting at him *to go repent his sins.* It annoyed him because it always happened when he was deep in thought, or in the middle of some important experiment, and all he needed was for everybody to just leave him alone. But, for some reason, the priest just couldn't resist.

When Vlad didn't bite at Tovah's provocations, the priest would turn nasty. He would call Vlad's best buddy a "witch" and that angered the rat to the point of madness.

Now, Vlad was a very patient and diplomatic kind of rodent, but when push came to shove, there was no room for diplomacy. He didn't care what anyone thought or said about his work. But when they attacked his buddy for no reason at all, it was uncalled for, unnecessary, and completely wrong. All they wanted was to get a rise out of him. And, to be honest, it worked… and it worked well.

Vlad always defended his good friend Babushka, as he loved her not only because she was a good person but because she always encouraged him to try. As a result, Vlad shared all his ideas with her, including his failed experiments, hoping she would be able to see where they went wrong or what he could do differently next time. Plus, she had been through more than enough herself, and now all she needed was love, compassion, and a good friend.

It broke Vlad's heart how Babushka never forgave herself for not being able to save the king. After all this time, it still bothered and affected her. He wished he could take away her pain but he just didn't know how. He noticed if he spent time with her, it lifted her spirits and she smiled. Sometimes she would even laugh but those occasions were rare.

Hopefully they would have some fun together tonight, while they watched their favourite show.

Vlad removed the fleece from his prized toy and smiled. Things were going to get interesting—he could feel it in his bones. His Bumblebee had been dormant for far too long. It was time to awaken the beast.

He looked down at his wristwatch but this was no ordinary timepiece. It was a special, remotely controlled GPS, which told him exactly where Bumblebee was at all times as well as how much power she had left, including her reserves. It also allowed robot and controller to speak to each other. Bumblebee was his refurbished dog bot, the same dog bot he found abandoned in the Parklands so long ago.

She was no ordinary dog bot anymore. In fact, she didn't look like the dog bot at all. Vlad had put countless hours into his creation: chopping, cutting, welding, wiring and rewiring, making her smarter, faster, and sleeker. She was his Bumblebee, named after his all-time favourite Transformer. He loved Optimus Prime nearly as much, but he chose Bumblebee in the end.

It suited her better for two reasons. One, he gave her a pair of iron wings, offering the rat the ability to fly when he was safely strapped in place. However, these wings weren't ordinary either. There were two on each side, a forewing and a hindwing, meaning the bot could zig and zag and weave in and out in a blink of an eye. One minute, he was there, buckled to his seat, and the next minute he was gone. Superfast, just like a bee.

And two, he decided to paint her totally brown with one exception: her wings. They had streaks of yellow running through them and the design made her look badass. Brown was the colour of the burrow and, once again, Vlad wanted her to be camouflaged. To blend in and not be seen. When he was outside in the park, he found that she fit seamlessly amongst all the autumn leaves and also with the colourful flowers of spring. The added bonus, which he later learned while watching an episode of *National Geographic*, was that yellow was one of the warning colours in nature. It explained why he was never attacked by a bird or any other predator when traveling outside the burrow.

And so, he'd concluded that her name was fitting and perfect in every way. But, deep down (just between you and me) no matter Vlad's logic or reasoning, in the end, he would have always named her after his favourite Autobot of all time.

Beeeeeeep went Vlad's wristwatch and without delay—*whirft, bonk!*

"Good evening, Vlad," said Bumblebee to her trusted friend.

Vlad looked at his precious toy with such fondness. "Good evening, Bee. So glad to see you and speak to you," he said, running a hand gently over the side panel. She was cold to the touch but so incredibly smooth and clean too. The fleece had done its job well; there wasn't a speck of dust on her exterior.

Beep, beep, burp. "Where are we going tonight?" hummed Bee.

The rat opened the door and jumped inside, and the small screen in front of the steering wheel lit up immediately with a pair of eyes, a nose, and a mouth. It was Bee herself. Vlad put his hands on the steering wheel and gave it a quick squeeze.

God, he missed driving his car, he thought.

The gadgets and numerous buttons along the interior were lit up too and waiting. All they needed was for the driver to press go and they would be on their merry way.

Beep, beep, burp. "Where to?" Bee repeated, and the question startled Vlad out of his daze.

"Oh, ah, er, sorry, Bee. I was deep in thought," said Vlad, his cheeks pinkened with a hint of embarrassment.

Beep, beep, beep. "You all right? Anything wrong?" asked Bee. She may have been a robot without tangible feelings, but she knew when her friend wasn't acting like himself.

Vlad took a deep breath and exhaled slowly, relaxing his nerves. "No, no, Bee, it's all good," he replied. "Just a hard day. Hmm…" He smirked. "You know, the usual. There's never a dull moment in this burrow, my friend," he stated matter-of-factly.

Beep, beep, beep, burp, laughed Bee. "I know, Vlad," replied his bot. "You just have to keep going, one day at a time, and keep your nose out of other people's business."

"That's the thing, Bee. I already do that but, for some reason, trouble seems to find me," he tried to explain. "Hmm…" He rubbed his snout with his hand, hoping to find the reason for his dilemma.

Beep, beep, burp. "So where to, my friend?" asked Bee, yet again, hoping to switch her creator's mood from gloomy to excited.

"Oh, yes, let's head down to Babushka's house using the usual route, shall we?" replied Vlad, perking up a bit. "We have an episode of *MacGyver* to watch and we can't miss it. Time is of the essence, my friend." The rodent pressed a few buttons on his console, adjusted his mirrors, double-checked his buckles—safety was number one in his book—and was about to press go when Bee interrupted.

Beep, beep, boop. "Shall we rock it tonight, or what?" ask Bee, her illuminated display offering him a wink.

Vlad hesitated for a minute, considering all the possible repercussions. His mind was swamped with hundreds of images. Images of Tovah getting mad, Dyllon making fun of him for days on end, the princess having to get involved yet again to smooth things over, the burrow stinking of burnt rubber and God only knows what else... Ah! And the holy water! He couldn't forget the holy water.

There would be lots and lots of holy water thrown his way. And right now, Vlad hated holy water with a passion. If even the minutest droplet somehow found its way onto him, he would explode. Not melt like the witch in *The Wizard of Oz*, but explode like a volcano of rage and fury. It would be Armageddon, and no amount of pleading would stop the flow of anger that had been bottled up for so very, very long.

However, before he could respond, it was as if the universe was trying to answer for him, in the form of Bee's prompt coaxing. "Yes, let loose. You deserve it." A small compartment just right of the digital screen opened automatically. Vlad stared at it in wonder, racking his brain for what could be inside.

Did he leave something in there the last time he drove Bee? he thought, but his stomach told him differently.

"Oh, you are up to something. I can feel it," stated Vlad. He dropped a hand to his hairy belly and gave it a rub, trying to calm the unease. Bile was building up in his throat. Surely this was a warning sign. A little tray within the compartment started to eject. The movement was smooth, absolutely soundless. Like the pivotal scene in a movie. The plot twist. The deciding moment and climax. "Bee, what are you up to?" Vlad pressed, a little more urgently this time.

Beep, beep, boop. "Nothing, my friend. I just have something I cleaned, prepared, and looked after for you. It's something special," she stated with another robotic wink.

Vlad tilted his head and looked at her suspiciously. "Something you've cleaned, hmmmm…." He thought for a moment. "What could that be?" Vlad stated, his gaze far off as he wondered.

"Voila!" said Bee. "Take a look, my friend." She nudged her head in the direction of the now fully extended compartment.

Vlad turned and froze in shock, his eyes wide and his expression gobsmacked. He blinked hard and took another look. Nope, they were still there. But he just couldn't believe it. He decided to rub his eyes with his hands. He rubbed and rubbed and rubbed until they were red and watery. He took a final peek and, yep, still there. His mind was not playing tricks on him.

"Bee, oh my God, are you for real?" he asked, his eyes locked on the prize.

Beep, beep, beep. "For real, my friend," she said. "Take them. They're yours."

"Oh, Bee!" said Vlad.

He grabbed the item ever so gently and placed his favourite "T2" sunglasses on his face. Now he was complete. All missing parts had been found and returned. Vlad sat there for a moment, motionless and unflinching. He didn't make a sound nor utter a word. He was reminiscing about all the good times he and Bee had together. And, eventually, those memories made him smirk. Something awakened within the rodent.

"Bee," said Vlad, all of a sudden. "Yes, we shall rock it!"

And he smiled his big, cheeky grin. "You know what to do when I hit go."

Beep, beep, burp. "Absolutely, ready when you are," she stated with an odd undertone of excitement, especially for a robot.

Vlad took a deep breath, did the sign of the cross, and punched the button before he could change his mind. It was all systems go. Bee lit up and revved her engine. Off she went, cruising out of the garage and through the tunnel.

Tonight was extra special. She played the driver's favourite song: "Bad to the Bone." It was a fitting choice because of those sunglasses. When Vlad first watched *Terminator II*, he fell deeper in love with science and robotics. He wanted to learn even more, so he could create bigger, better, and smarter bots. But the part that hyped him up the most was one of the early scenes in the movie, when the T100 left the bar with exactly what he asked for: clothes, boots, and a motorcycle. Though the cherry on top was when he helped himself to the barkeep's sunglasses. The very same sunglasses Vlad now wore. And just like that scene in the movie, "Bad to The Bone" started blaring through Bee's speakers. The rodent felt cool, badass—perhaps even a little *bad to the bone*—and Vlad loved it. He was nearly euphoric, as he sat behind the wheel of his own personal robot.

They cruised together right through the tunnel. It was a very smooth drive with no issues or obstacles. Babushka's house wasn't too far from the burrow, and the tunnels they used led them beneath the park and under a section of the old cemetery. There was a sharp right with slightly a little more travel beneath some houses, across the main road, and voila!

X marked the spot: Babushka's house.

Babushka lived in a small, rundown shack. In its heyday, so very long ago, it was beautifully painted with intricate patterns all over the exterior. Upon closer inspection, some of these patterns appeared to be a series of familiar celestial constellations. But others looked like squiggly lines that made no sense. Perhaps they were an ancient language or coordinates to a lost world.

The town used to joke that Babushka was an alien from another planet, dumped here on earth as punishment. Everyone knew her but no one knew *about* her. No one knew her story: where she came from, when she was born, who her parents were, or even what her favourite colour was. All they knew was her name and what she did for a living.

Babushka was a naturopath, meaning she helped people by using herbs. And boy did she know her craft. She knew about ever herb that ever existed, what its capabilities were, and how it was best used. She was amazing and even grew her own collection in her backyard. She didn't like the store-purchased kind because she could smell all the preservatives and the additives inhibited their potential. Therefore, when it came time to fertilise her crops, Babushka would jump into her favourite car—her red banged-up Kingswood station wagon—and head into the countryside for the day. Not to picnic or go on a stroll but to collect magic pies.

Which were really just mounds of cow poo. She would put her gumboots on, tie her straw hat underneath her chin, grab her roll of garbage bags (extra large to be exact) and her favourite shovel. Off she would go, slowly collecting her magic pies, bagging them one after the other, and she loved it. The fresh air, the serenity, and most of all, the peace. Here she could connect with mother earth, listen to her stories, teachings, and guidance. It was simply magical. The whole experience would help uplift her spirits and recharge her batteries.

But when she returned home, back to the city, her work was not yet done. Babushka would lock herself up in her shed and concoct her potion, which made her herbs the best in town. This potion created magic. It made everything grow in an extremely fruitful manner. If you thought a bush or a tree was dead or dried up, sprinkle some of her magic potion on it and *BAM!* The plant would bounce back to life right in front of your eyes.

No one knew exactly what the ingredients were in her magic potion, but it sure had a pong to it. It was worse than Seasol and dead carcass put together, but it got the job done without luring in a single blowfly. Babushka would often tell her customers that there was no secret ingredient and that it was *all in the wrist*. That would leave her visitors confused, though no one ever asked her what she meant. They would simply nod their heads and say, "Ah, yeah, gotcha." And walk away, too embarrassed to question her further.

So, what did Babushka mean?

Well, that depended on if you had the stomach for it. When Babushka would lock herself in her shed, she would get out her big deep bucket (not a cauldron) pour some lukewarm water inside, drop in a magic pie or two, roll her sleeves right up to her shoulders, and stick her arm in the mixture. All the way up to her elbow.

Next, she would grab a hold of one of the moist pies and flick her wrist to break it apart. She couldn't complete this exercise with both arms inside, as one was needed to hold the bucket down. The flicking could be an arduous process, depending on the stiffness of the pie.

Once the pies were broken down, Babushka would use her entire arm like a giant wooden spoon. She would stir and stir and stir until the floating bits of digested grass and dandelions were dissolved and all that was left was a thick, runny, smelly, brown stew. AKA her magic potion. Her job was done. The contents of the bucket would finally be poured into individual bottles labelled: *Babushka's Magical Potion*. Ready for use.

And boy did she use them. She would fertilise her hedges as well as her rose bushes in the front yard. The hedge, which acted as a perimeter around her property, was incredibly luscious, green, and very, very tall. It was rumoured to have been there even longer than Babushka herself, but it was the magic potion that transformed it into what it was today. From a tiny shrub, to a beautiful hedge.

And the roses were to die for. They were the richest, reddest roses that ever existed. The colour was so deep and luscious that it would make the rose in the *Beauty and the Beast* look like a weed. And the aroma? Well, it was in a league of its own. It was the sweetest of smells, fragrant but not overpowering. There was a hint of freshness and a dash of springtime. It was the smell of beauty and it was breathtaking. No florists could replicate the flower nor its scent. It could only be found in one place and that was in Babushka's front yard.

People all over town would come to Babushka's house, asking for a stem or two, and she never disappointed them. Without fail, she would cut stems and gladly part with them. Seeing the delight on her visitors' faces made her heart sing. It was this generosity and kindness that endeared the townspeople to their elderly resident. Even though they didn't know much about her, they trusted her, because she simply cared about others more than herself. She was selfless, always giving where it was needed and offering a helping hand without thinking twice.

As a result, many, many townsfolk turned to her, seeking her help to look after their children while they went to work. The funny thing was not one child ever complained or made a bother of being in Babushka's care, no siree. Every child in her presence was as happy as Larry. And even that was an understatement. From the cheekiest of children to the best behaved, they all loved being with her. In fact, parents had a hard time getting the children to return home at the end of the day—that's how much they loved her.

There were no issues when it came to getting up in the morning either. The children were up and dressed well before Mum and Dad were awake. No one could explain the effect that the old crone had on their children, but it didn't matter. All that mattered was their child's happiness, which was found in spades.

You see, children built special and unique bonds with Babushka, and many of those bonds were still going strong today. There was only a handful of families in town who didn't have a child in Babushka's care at some point in time. And as each generation grew up and moved on to school and beyond, they always returned. Back to Babushka's house, with their own children in tow, hoping that the old crone would also be their children's fairy godmother. Just like she had been for them so very long ago.

9

"OKAY," SAID BABUSHKA to herself while she busily ran around her kitchen, getting things ready for her guests. "Popcorn, check. Milk warming on the stove, check. Tin of bickies loaded, check." She stopped in her tracks and looked around the kitchen. "Hmmm."

Something was missing but she just couldn't remember what it was. She decided to go through her list of provisions again, hoping something would trigger her memory.

One by one, she recounted her list, pausing on each. "Damn, no, I still can't remember what I've forgotten," she said to herself, her tone clearly agitated. "Grrrrrr!" She slammed her fist hard on the bench, hoping to release her frustration.

If only my magic worked here, on this planet, she thought.

When she came through the portal, everything changed and she felt different. As soon as she landed on the moist ground in front of the oak tree, she knew something was amiss. The connection she felt with her magic was gone. The tingling sensation that flowed from the heart of her home planet, up into her feet, through her body, and out her hands and head was *gone*. It was her connection with Gaia, Mother Earth as we know her, and it was magic.

Gaia was part of every living thing. Be it tree, beast, person, earth, ocean, soul, heart, or gesture. Everything was connected, and through these threads, the energy flowed. Some felt that connection more strongly than others, Babushka being the former.

From an early age, she knew she was different from everyone else. She could see the light and the energy that flowed— the threads that connected one thing to another. This came in handy, especially when she would play hide and seek with her friends. She could find everyone with utmost ease. No hiding spot was too difficult as she would follow the threads. Since they were all connected to each other all she had to do was trace the energy.

No one ever understood how she did it. Her friends simply thought she was skilled at the game. But Babushka was all too happy to share her secret. And on one occasion, she did. She told them that she followed the threads. Everyone went quiet, not understanding what she meant. So she asked her friends if they could see them too. The connections. She described them as appearing like spider webs. Everyone laughed at her and thought she was tricking them, just playing a nasty joke. But Babushka pleaded and reassured them that there were no tricks. No jokes.

To be honest, it didn't bother her and she never felt hate for anyone who judged her. She simply hoped that one day they too would see the magic that flowed through and connected each of us. Just like a spider's web.

But here, on this new planet, the connection was gone. The spider's web was gone, and so Babushka spent the next forty years trying to work out why the magic had left her. No matter how much she thought about it, no matter how much she replayed her last hours on Saphira, she could not come to any other conclusion than that it was her fault. The king was dead, and it was all her fault. She didn't save him, and as a result, the universe had severed her connection with Gaia, with every living thing, with energy, with magic.

Blurp, blurp, blurp went the little pot of milk warming up on the kitchen stove. The liquid was now bubbling and fizzing. The fat on the surface was thickening into white foam.

CRASH! BANG! The trap door in the fireplace suddenly burst open and in came Vlad with his trusted sidekick, Bee.

"Honey, I'm home," sang the rat.

"Ahhh!" yelled Babushka, throwing her hands in the air and grabbing a rolling pin in reflex. The baking utensil was all she could find—better that than a knife.

"Babushka," said Vlad. He took off his T2 sunglasses and stepped out of Bee, concerned about the state of his dear friend. He looked down at his wristwatch, flicked a button, and made his way towards the old crone.

In the meantime, Bee instantly transformed into a full-fledged robot and began to do her thing, which consisted of organising all the seating and the pillows while making sure that everything was in place in the lounge room. Comfort was her main priority, and you definitely needed to get that sorted before any movie or show started. The last thing anyone wanted was to scourge around, tossing and turning, making noise, and potentially ruining the experience for everyone, including themself.

"Babushka, it's me… Vlad," the rat yelled. "Are you okay?" He waved his hands in the air, trying to snap her out of her shock.

She was breathing heavily—her chest heaving up and down, up and down. Even though she was looking at him, she seemed like she was miles and miles away. Vlad decided to yell out one more time. Maybe he would finally get through to her and help her snap out of this sudden trance.

This wasn't the first time Vlad had witnessed his friend in such a state. In fact, it had happened on many occasions, but not as frequently as it had been lately. The rat didn't have the heart to tell the rest of the clan, as it felt like a betrayal on his behalf. Babushka was always there for him, through thick and thin. He'd shared all his concerns about anything or anyone with his dear friend, and it always stayed between them. Now it was his turn to repay the debt.

Vlad made his way to Babushka. Closer and closer, he came. She may have been holding a rolling pin, which could potentially flatten him like a pancake, but he wasn't afraid. He knew he could still get through to her. Babushka remained glued to her spot, unmoving, her arms raised with her make-shift weapon in hand. Like it was batter up, ready to swing, and Vlad was the baseball.

The concoction on the stove had turned brown, nearly evaporated. The smell of burnt milk wafted throughout the house. Bee was already on top of everything. She understood what was going on and headed straight to the stove, to turn the flames off. Once that was done, she made her way back to the lounge room and continued to finalise the seating arrangements.

"Babushka!" yelled Vlad. He stood only a metre away,

but he still couldn't grab her attention. He decided to climb the kitchen cupboards so that he was in direct view. Eye to eye. Once he was firmly situated at the top, he made his way closer to her, and this time he didn't have to yell. "Babushka, are you all right?" he asked, attentively.

He stood there, patiently, and waited for her to respond. But there was nothing. She just remained a stilled version of the friend he knew, her gaze fixed and her chest heaving.

God, Vlad thought. *This one is a very bad one. What are we going to do?*

He ran some scenarios through his head, but everything seemed ridiculous. Every possible option seemed to the detriment of his dear friend, and that was just no option at all. He took another step, and now he knew he was in clear reach of the rolling pin. It was either get through to her, or rodent pancake. But he had to at least try.

Why won't she answer me? he thought. He crossed his arms, trying to work out the puzzle.

The other thing Vlad had been doing in his spare time was a lot of research about the human body. His interest, in particular, focused on diseases of the brain. He noticed that Babushka had started to forget things about a year ago. On one occasion, she'd left the stove on and had gone to the shops. Luckily, Wymann had stopped by at lunchtime to deliver some books Vlad had requested. Wymann turned off the stove and made sure that everything else was in order before he left. He didn't mention it to Babushka, but he certainly did tell Vlad. He was concerned and the last thing he wanted was for Babushka or anyone to get hurt.

Then there was the odd occasion when Babushka started to repeat things. And by repeat, he would note how she would tell the same story two or three times in one conversation. This was unusual and out of character.

Now, you were probably thinking that those things mentioned above were all normal. And, yes, they certainly were. They could be caused by many things, one being stress. But what you might not have realised was that, even though Babushka couldn't do magic here on this planet, her mind was still sharp, her wit even sharper. She was like a machine that didn't stop, didn't forget a single thing, and always remembered what you said and when you said it.

It appeared as though being here, on earth, was slowly making her human. And being human meant she was mortal and susceptible to the same diseases as any other inhabitant of this planet. Vlad, therefore, believed that his dear friend was sick. He wasn't a doctor, so he couldn't give the disease a name. But from what he read, he knew that she was deteriorating and the signs were showing that she was getting worse.

Vlad inched towards Babushka, stopping right next to her torso. He placed his furry little hand on her belly without any hesitation, knowing she wouldn't hurt him. She flinched at his touch but didn't lower the rolling pin, continuing her laborious breaths. Vlad closed his eyes and took a moment, his hand maintaining contact with his old friend.

He exhaled and called her name ever so gently, like a whisper, "Lilliana." There was no reaction. So, again, he called her name, "Lilliana." And he held his breath, waiting and hoping, but still there was nothing. He didn't open his eyes; he refused. Something was telling him to call her name one more time, that he would and could get through to her, so he tried. "Lilliana, it's me, Vlad, your friend."

Vlad did not move. He stood there, waiting for his friend to return to him. And she did.

"Oh," Babushka said, the rolling pin hovering above her head. She lowered her arms, as by now, they were painfully numb and tingling. If she held them up there any longer, surely her muscles would give out and God knows what would have happened. She could have dropped the rolling pin on her head and knocked herself out. She looked at the wooden utensil questioningly, her brows furrowed and confusion written all over her face. She turned the rolling pin over, hoping for some kind of explanation but found none. "What happened?" she said to herself.

"You blacked out, my dear friend," replied a voice out of nowhere. Babushka jumped, but she recognised the speaker; the sound was familiar. She looked down and there stood Vlad, with his furry little hand on her belly.

"Oh, Vlad," she said with relief. "What do you mean I blacked out?"

The rodent removed his hand and took a couple of steps back, so that she could see his face without straining. "You had another episode, Babushka. And this time, it was for much longer than before," he stated, calmly and slowly, so as not to worry her.

She stared at him with concern, took a deep breath, and exhaled, calming her nerves. She raised her free hand and gestured towards the rolling pin. "What is this?" she asked.

He looked at her, dumbfounded, and responded, "It's a rolling pin."

"I knooooow *that*," she said, her tone sarcastic and her expression a bit annoyed. "I meant why do I have it in my hands? Clearly, I haven't been baking." She gestured to the clean, tidy kitchen. There were no dirty pots or pans anywhere. "Oh my god!" she screamed suddenly. Vlad fell backwards, landing *splat-bang* on his back. He remained motionless as he watched Babushka jump into the air, do a 180-degree turn, and run to the stove. "My milk!" she cried. "My milk! There goes the hot chocolates!"

She reached the stove and took in the scene. The milk was brown and burnt, having leaked over the edges of the pot. It looked horrible. Babushka started to cry. Streams of tears flowed along her cheeks, down her chin, and dripped onto her blouse. She sobbed and sobbed and sobbed uncontrollably, not bothering to wipe her nose either. The nasal mucus mixed with her tears, and together they flowed downstream into the endless ocean of snotty water pooling on her beautiful blouse.

Babushka wasn't crying over the spilt milk—no, she cried because she realised her condition, whatever it was, was getting worse. She cried because she could have burned down her house and even hurt someone other than herself. She cried because she didn't know what the future held.

"Damn," she said, giggled for a split-second, then went back to crying. "Damn, damn, damn," she spat. She didn't wipe away the tears or snot and just stood there, staring angrily at the stove.

Beep, beep, beep, said Bee.

"I know, Bee," said Babushka, not pivoting to address the bot. "Thank you for turning off the stove. I greatly appreciate it."

Bee spun around and made her way back to the lounge room. This time, Babushka pulled a handkerchief from her bosom and wiped her face and her chin clean. She even dabbed at her blouse, trying to soak up the sticky, goopy, snotty water that had settled there and started to solidify.

"Oh, to the seven hells," she murmured in frustration, raising her hands and flailing them about as if she were swatting a fly.

Vlad laughed ever so loudly. He laughed and laughed, so hard that he had to grab hold of his stomach, as it was starting to hurt.

"What are you laughing at?" Babushka asked. But Vlad didn't answer her; he continued to laugh and roll on top of the kitchen bench. "Stop that," she said. "You're going to fall." And she too started to giggle.

Laughter was contagious. Once you heard someone laughing, it was highly likely that you too would start laughing along—it was the best medicine, really.

"Ha-ha-ha," continued Vlad. "Hiccup, haha, hiccup."

They continued to laugh and giggle.

"Oh, oh, oh my God," Vlad said, inhaling and exhaling in rapid succession. His eyes were overflowing with tears and he let them stream down his cheeks and soak his fur. He was paralysed. He lay there on his back, staring at the ceiling. He felt a million times better. Lighter. The laughter was what he needed; it soothed his soul. Vlad could not remember the last time he'd laughed. It felt like it had been forever.

"Are you all right, Vlad?" asked Babushka. She stood next to the rat, leaning on the kitchen bench with her hands clasped together, watching him.

"Yes, yes, haha! I'm all right," he said. "You just reminded me of Dyllon there for a second." He rolled onto his side and picked himself up. He felt a little weak from all the laughter but he didn't care. It was worth it.

"Dyllon," said Babushka, confused. "How did I remind you of him?" She looked at Vlad questioningly. "Speaking of, how is the old geezer these days? It's been awhile since I've seen the likes of him," she added.

Vlad turned to her, his brown fur somehow reddened and his beady eyes somehow beadier. "Oh, Babushka, don't ask. He's a lost cause and getting more lost as each day passes," he stated. "Come on, let's go sit down and watch *MacGyver*." He gestured to the lounge room, where Bee was waiting patiently for them. "What's the time anyway?" he asked. Vlad looked down at his wristwatch and his eyes bulged out of their sockets. "No, no, nooo!" he screamed. He climbed down from the kitchen bench and ran to the lounge room. "Bee, Beeeee! Turn the TV on to channel ten," he demanded.

And what they saw next left robot and animal alike crying. It was the credits.

They missed the entire episode, and to make matters worse, they even missed the closing theme song. Vlad loved that song. He needed to hear it at the beginning of the show and also at the end, and it had to be in full. Not one second, one sound, was allowed to be missed; that was how much it meant to him.

Watching the very last part of the credits roll by, with a split-second of blackness before it moved on to the next scheduled show, made Vlad turn a new shade of white. They sat there motionless, Bee dropped the remote control—at a loss—and neither knew what to do.

"Oh, stop that sulking, the both of you," said Babushka. "It's not the end of the world." She sat next to Bee and grabbed the remote.

"W-h-a-t d-o y-o-u m-e-a-n i-t-'s n-o-t t-h-e e-n-d o-f

t-h-e w-o-r-l-d?" asked Vlad, grabbing hold of the hair on his head and giving it a pull, to relieve some of the frustration. He rubbed his eyes and then began to rub his face, hoping it would calm his panic. It didn't.

"Well, since my episodes have been happening a lot more frequently recently," explained Babushka, "I asked Wymann to show me how to use the record function on my TV."

"Record function?" both Bee and Vlad piped up in hope, their full attention on Babushka.

"That's what I said," the old crone hissed in frustration. "Stop interrupting me when I'm speaking *please*." She paused, lifting a finger to her temple. "Now, where was I? Oh yes, the record function. Wymann has been such a dear, to show me how this record function works. It allows me to set a timer, lock it in, and schedule and record as many shows as I would like—never missing a single thing." She pointed the remote at the TV, pressed a few buttons, scrolled around, and found what she was looking for. "Ahhhh, here we are, ladies and gentlemen," she stated proudly. "The latest episode you thought we missed."

And there it was, highlighted and ready to go. All they had to do was press play.

"Woohoo!" screamed Vlad and Bee simultaneously. They jumped and danced on the spot with newfound energy and excitement. The night was saved. "Oh, Babushka, I can't believe it," said Vlad. He turned back to the TV and stared at the recorded episode with glee.

Is this a dream? he thought.

"Thank God for Wymann," he said out loud, clapping his paws and rubbing them together. "And thank God for your smart thinking, Babushka," he quickly added, throwing her a thumbs-up and a wink.

"You are welcome, my dear friend," she replied. "Everyone, come, sit, make yourselves comfortable while I go heat up some nice hot chocolates for us." Babushka made her way back towards the kitchen, where she once again saw the burnt milk and messy stove. "Take two, hey?" She laughed, feeling a bit embarrassed.

"It's okay, Babushka," soothed Vlad. "I bet those hot chocolates will be your best yet." He was trying to make light of the whole situation. He didn't want his friend to feel bad for what had happened earlier, so he attempted to distract her. "So how is Wymann? How is the bookshop? Is he any closer to finding information about opening the portal and getting us back to Saphira?" asked Vlad.

"Unfortunately, not at the moment," sighed Babushka with a sense of dread. She was refilling a clean little pot with milk and placing it on the stove to warm up. She had a thought, and added, "He did say that he has been reading a lot of books about Norse mythology. Some very, very old and some new."

"Oh, yeah?" pressed Vlad with great interest. The rodent had recently finished rewatching the Thor movies. He loved all of the Avengers. Iron Man in particular, mainly because of the gold titanium alloy suit Tony Stark got to wear. Vlad hoped that one day he too could develop something similar; he couldn't begin to imagine all the fun he would have. "So, what did he find out about Thor? Does he know where his hammer is?"

Babushka stopped what she was doing and turned to face

him. "Have you been watching your Avenger movies again, young man?" she asked with her hands on her hips.

Vlad's cheeks reddened as he started to mumble, "Well, ohhh, erm, just a little. You know how much I love Iron Man, Babushka. He's my favourite." The rodent started to fidget on the spot.

"No, dear, he doesn't know where Thor's hammer is, but he has been telling me all about Norse mythology and it's really interesting, to tell you the truth. You should read it when you get a chance. I have a feeling you will enjoy it." She winked at him. "And who knows? Maybe you will be able to find Thor's hammer yourself, hey?"

Bubble, bubble, crackle, pop went the milk in the little shiny pot. It was ready to be poured.

"Ahh, we're nice and warm," stated Babushka in reply. "Not burnt or brown this time," she added with a giggle. She took the pot over to the sink and slowly poured the warm milk into the mugs. She gave each a gentle stir and inhaled the sweet aroma of the chocolate—*it was divine*. With a *ting* and a *thump*, she dropped the spoon into the sink. "Ahhhh," she said out loud and stopped in her tracks.

"What's wrong?" asked Vlad. "Did you burn yourself?"

Babushka took a deep breath and exhaled in frustration. She hit the bench with the palm of her hand and shook her head. Vlad jumped to his tiny feet. He was ready to leap off the couch and go help her if needed. If there were to be another episode, he would stay with his dear friend tonight for as long as it took.

"I remember," Babushka said.

"Remember what?" Vlad asked, his voice heightened in alarm and his hands raised in despair.

What could it possibly be now?

"I remember what I forgot just before I had my episode."

Vlad stared at her questioningly. He didn't know what to say or what to think.

"The marshmallows." She gestured to Vlad. "I couldn't remember the marshmallows." She slapped a palm on the forehead for being so silly and forgetful.

"The marshmallows?" the rodent repeated.

"Yes," replied Babushka. "You see, I was getting everything ready for tonight: the biscuits, the popcorn, the hot chocolates… But for the life of me, I could not remember the marshmallows. It made me so upset and I think the anger may have brought on another episode," she explained.

"Hmm," hummed Vlad. Maybe the incidents were stress-induced. The rodent crossed his arms in the usual *Vlad is thinking* way and began to analyse Babushka's theory. "Interesting," he said to himself.

"So how many would you like?" asked Babushka while holding a packet of marshmallows in her hand.

"How many? How many of what?" he questioned, lost to his own thoughts.

Babushka showed him the pink and white packet and gestured to the sugary delights inside.

"Oh, now I understand, Babushka!" Vlad jumped on the spot and giggled like a schoolboy. He loved marshmallows; they were one of his all-time favourite foods and they were a must with his hot chocolate. "May I please have two?" he asked, holding two fingers up to reiterate his point.

"Sure," said Babushka. She reached into the packet and extracted two puffy, bloated, sweet-smelling, sugar-coated marshmallows and quickly dropped them into the cup of steaming hot chocolate. Voila! The perfect hot beverage was ready. She did the same for herself, and when no one was looking, she quickly rammed one into her mouth.

Oh my God!

The flavour was exhilarating and the texture so smooth, light, and soft. It was like biting into a fluffy cloud, all the rays from the sun oozing into your mouth and filling your belly with rainbows. It was spectacular and incredibly addictive.

"I'm so excited," said Vlad to no one in particular. He made himself comfortable on the couch, ensuring the pillows were in the right spot and that there was enough room for the popcorn and hot chocolate. "Are you excited too, Bee?" he asked. "You've been awfully quiet."

Beep, burp, burp. "Just waiting patiently," said Bee. "Besides, I'm very comfortable and I don't want to move," she added with a robotic giggle.

"I'm coming!" yelled Babushka to her guests from the kitchen, knowing they were likely growing impatient. "Just placing everything on the tray. I don't want to get up once I sit down." Babushka set the tray on the coffee table and distributed the bowls of popcorn, mugs of hot chocolate, and plates of biscuits so they all were within arm's reach. "Okay, here we go." She sat down in her favourite armchair and covered herself in her crocheted rainbow blanket. She was ready. "Execute, my dear friend," she said while holding her hand out and giving the Vulcan salute.

"Aye, aye, captain," replied Vlad, returning the gesture with one hand while pressing play with the other.

10

A BABE LAY NEXT to a lifeless mother, crying and screaming for her comfort, but there was none. The infant pulled at the fabric of his mother's dress, hoping this was all some sort of trickery. A game. And sooner or later, Mama would pop up and say peekaboo.

Slowly and clumsily, he rolled over and sat upright. *Smack, smack, smack* went the little hands on Mama's belly—surely, now, she would stir and move. The child waited but nothing happened.

A glimmer from above suddenly caught the babe's attention. It was a bright flash that only lasted a second. He stared. Before him was a beautiful, exquisitely decorated sword. The craftsmanship was simply breathtaking, even to a toddler. The boy continued to stare in wonder, his sobs diminishing to quiet whimpers.

The sword slowly rose, and the babe watched it with his big blue eyes traveling up and up, looking and examining as they went. At first, the child noticed a pair of strong, stained hands with white knuckles gripping the hilt. The hands lifted higher, the babe's gaze following suit and meeting a set of grinning yellow-stained teeth, surrounded by brittle stubble and sweaty whiskers. The hands bypassed an ash-smudged nose, caked with a hint of dried blood. The blue eyes lingered for a moment but decided to move on, catching up to the hands, which had stopped. The ascent had ended and two pairs of eyes locked. One belonging to those of innocence, and the other belonging to sin incarnate.

The sword-wielder licked his lips hungrily. Hatred had consumed his soul long ago and now bloodlust filled his veins. He'd been waiting for this for a very long time. He prepared for the kill, excitement bubbling in the pit of his stomach. He gripped the hilt of his sword and adjusted his fingers ever so slightly, taking his time and savouring the moment.

"Traitor!" screamed a voice. The yellow-toothed man pivoted towards the sound, and the babe startled and cried out.

"*You*," hissed the swordsman with spittle sliding from his mouth.

"Get away from my son, you traitor." Millard, the dragon whisperer, drew his sword while his boy continued to wail. The child shivered, his skin reacting to his fright, and nestled himself deep between his mother's shoulder and neck. Right into her beautiful, sweet-smelling hair. For now, he felt safe.

"Argh!" yelled the swordsman, his arms raised and his weapon at the ready as he barrelled towards Millard.

The dragon whisperer stood his ground. He wasn't afraid of what was coming. He knew he had to remain calm if he was to save his son. He maintained eye contact with the traitor and, at the very last possible second, he sidestepped. With one swift move, he blocked the blow with his sword— *kablam*.

The impact was powerful, each opponent taken by surprise at the sheer force of the collision. The block sent both antagonist and protagonist tumbling backwards. The two men quickly and gracefully regained their composure, staring each other dead in the eyes, ready for the next round.

The traitor laughed, his belly bouncing with the action. "You are no match for me, brother! I am not what you think I am..." He shook his head mockingly while grinning from ear to ear. He was baiting the other man, egging on his opponent with his taunts.

Millard remained calm. "Oh, I know exactly what you are, brother. A murderer and a traitor." He paused for a split-second. "And you are my brother no more." He hesitated. And, this time, his words hit home. Striking his heart. He closed his eyes and cleared his head, shaking the pain away. Taking a deep breath, he reopened his eyes and stared at the man in front of him. "You are dead to me."

The swordsman flinched, surprised by his body's reaction. Those words hurt; they cut like a knife. *You are dead to me.* The sentiment rang in his ears. *You are dead to me.* Over and over again. Like a broken record. *You are dead to me.* Why did it bother him? *You are dead to me.*

"Argh!" He screamed out his frustration, his pain, his anger. The sound jolted the babe from his nap. "Dead to you?" he repeated, ignoring his distraught nephew and taking a step forward. He tossed his sword to the ground, leaving himself defenceless, but he didn't care.

Millard watched on, keeping one eye on the traitor, the other on his beloved son.

"I was dead to you long ago, brother. Long before the king loved you, long before our parents died." Taking another step forward, he continued. "You never loved me as your equal. You never accepted me as your equal!" The traitor raised his fists and pounded on his chest, as if trying to remove the pain in his heart.

The dragon whisperer didn't move a muscle, let alone a whisker.

The traitor took a deep breath. "I cannot speak to the dragons like you can, meaning my blood isn't pure like yours." He pointed at Millard. "I am and never was a true descendant of the Drakon family, brother." He smiled, his chest convulsing with uncontrollable laughter.

Millard continued to watch the swordsman. His defences up, and his muscles coiled and ready for any surprise attack.

"But…" The man gestured to the veins on his neck. "Brother, I'm very powerful." He held Millard's gaze and licked his lips in excitement, as there was an unveiling to be had. He grabbed his helmet by one of the horns and removed it in one swift pull.

"Oh my God…" Millard dropped his guard and stared in horror. "What-have-you-done?" The question left him in one long, rushed breath of air.

His brother laughed in reply, the sound growing louder, more grotesque, and more disturbing by the second.

∼

Beep, beep, beep went Kelly's alarm clock.

"Ohhh, ahhh!" She woke with a fright. Drenched in her own sweat. Her heart racing.

Beep, beep, beep continued the clock.

"Ohhhh," she groaned. The muscles in her neck and her back were stiff, sore. Kelly felt as if she'd survived an arduous battle. "Ha…? Battle…?" She shot upright and searched her brain. "Battle?"

Beep, beep, beep.

Kelly grabbed her head and took a deep breath. Her temples were pounding. Another headache was coming on and fast.

Beep, beep, beep.

She squeezed her eyes shut, trying to remember her dream. "Battle? There was a duel… between two men." She thought hard, searching her mind.

Beep, beep, beep.

"A baby lying on the floor, next to its dead mother." She closed her eyes even tighter, trying to block out the pain and the noise.

Beep, beep, beep.

"Millard." Kelly spoke the name aloud. And in that moment, she realised that the face she'd envisioned at the oak tree had a name—*Millard*. That familiar face and those blue eyes.

Beep, beep, beep.

"Argh! Enough!" she screamed and, without looking, slammed her hand on top of the clock. Abruptly ending the piercing noise. She flopped back down on her pillow and covered her eyes with her arms, attempting to obscure the harsh lighting. "God, my head hurts…" She exhaled a deep breath and focused on her breathing, trying to relax both her body and mind.

You are dead to me. The phrase resurfaced, and she wondered who this brother was and what he did. Something awful must have happened in that room. She pondered the idea.

"Oh!" She startled herself with the realization. "What about the baby? What happened to the baby?" Kelly clasped her mouth with her hands and stared at the ceiling, dreading what the answer could be. "No…" she whispered, shaking her head in disbelief. "No, please don't let it be true…"

She was trying to reassure herself. She thought long and she thought hard. The two men duelled but nothing happened to the baby.

"Yes, that's right," mumbled Kelly, analysing what she could remember of the dream. "Phew," she sighed in relief, the anxiety slowly leaving the pit of her stomach.

But what did Millard see? she wondered, the curiosity getting the better of her.

"What was it?" she asked aloud. "Damn!" Kelly hit her mattress with her fist. She didn't see anything because the dream ended. She turned and looked at her alarm clock, her eyes narrowed at the object of her contention. "If that stupid alarm clock didn't wake me up, I would have seen more. I would understand more…"

Kelly grabbed the pillow beneath her head and smothered her face with it. Screaming like a wild animal. Letting all her frustrations out. However, that only intensified her headache.

~

Crunch, crunch, crunch, slurp, slurp, slurp went the sounds at the kitchen table. Mark and Joyce were enjoying their breakfast in peace. There was no chitchat early in the morning for those two—well, not before coffee at least. You see, coffee was a magical drink and when the right amount was consumed at the right time of day, it could prevent the ogre within from arising and pillaging the land. And when that cup or mug, whichever you preferred, was drunk, only then could a reasonable conversation be had. The horns would retract and the green tint appearing on the skin would simply fade away. Once again, *like magic.*

"Good morning, Mum and Dad," grunted Kelly as she made her way into the kitchen.

"Ah, there's my girl," said Mark. "How are you today, darling?"

"Oh, Dad, erm," replied Kelly, her gaze averted as she moved fast towards the cupboard.

Mark watched his daughter closely. Something was wrong. "What's up, buttercup?"

Joyce placed her coffee cup on the table and turned to her daughter. "You okay, honey?"

Kelly remained focused on her task. She grabbed her favourite mug out of the cupboard—it was handmade and it was blue, her favourite colour. Kelly made this mug one afternoon long ago when she went to visit Babushka Lilliana. At the time, Babushka was teaching pottery on the potter's wheel at her home. That Saturday was when Kelly learned how to centre clay and throw pots. Her design ended up being very small so she decided to make it a mug instead, and she enjoyed her choice ever since.

"Oh, it's Babushka's mug," said Mark, trying to start a conversation with his daughter so that he could find out what was troubling her.

"Yes, Dad," Kelly huffed in response. She walked up to

the percolated coffee machine and poured herself a generous cup. This worried Mark and he looked at his wife for help.

"Honey, you okay?" asked Joyce again. She got up from the table and went to Kelly. Placing a hand on the girl's shoulder, Joyce looked at her daughter's face, gently caressed some of the stray hair out of the way, and kissed her on the forehead. "What's up, buttercup?" she repeated with a smile.

Kelly's eyes were bloodshot and there were huge dark saggy bags. She looked pale. "Nothing, Mum," she replied, sipping her coffee. "Just have a really bad headache today."

"Headache?" piped up Mark. "Whoa, have you been drinking, young lady?" he asked with a smirk. He jumped up from his chair, typical Mark style, and pranced to his daughter's side. "So, what was it, kid? Too much wine or too much Scotch?"

"No, Dad." Kelly rolled her eyes. She grabbed her temple and gave it a good rub, hoping it would relieve some of the tension.

"Ohhhh, I see," said Mark, crossing his arms but still smiling. He pointed his index finger at the girl before adding, "You mixed your drinks. Yeah, that's what you did, my girl." He nodded his head in understanding while his daughter and wife just stared at him. He was attempting to lighten the mood with his antics, but Kelly was not up for it this time.

She lifted a palm in his direction. "Dad, stooooop. I just have a headache and it's a really bad one." She paused and took a breath. "Nothing is wrong, so please stop."

Joyce draped an arm over her daughter and held her close. Mark didn't say a word as he allowed her plea to sink in. After a moment, he hummed in response, raising his hands in mock defeat. He took a step closer to Kelly and lowered his face to eye level. "Sorry, kiddo, I was just trying to make you laugh." He stood upright again, stared at Kelly for a split-second, and then looked at his wife. His cheeks were reddened in embarrassment. Joyce gave him a reassuring wink. "I just hate seeing you sad, kid," Mark admitted with a palm to his heart.

"I understand, Dad." Kelly stepped forward and gave him a big hug. Mark kissed her head in return.

"So, guys…" said Joyce, trying to break the ice and liven up the atmosphere. "What're your plans for the day?" She began to clear the table of breakfast dishes, stacking and scraping food scraps from one plate to another. She grabbed her coffee and gulped down the last of the magical liquid.

"Do you need some help with those, darling?" asked Mark. "Here, let me grab those from you." He took the dishes out of Joyce's hands and headed towards the sink. "We don't want a repeat of what happened the other day, do we?" He winked at his wife, referring to the pot incident.

"I'm meant to go catch up with Gemma this morning," said Kelly. She sat down at the kitchen table while her parents cleared up after breakfast.

"Oh yeah?" said Joyce. "What are you going to do? Is she coming here or you meeting her somewhere?"

Kelly closed her eyes and massaged her temples when her mother spoke. "God, my head is going to burst. Hmmmmm." She looked at her mum and replied, "No, she's coming here, Mum. We will go together. It's nicer that way."

Joyce peered up at her daughter while she wiped down the table. "Lift your cup, love," she instructed before adding, "Well, that sounds like a good idea, going together." Joyce stopped what she was doing, her expression serious. "But, honey, if you don't feel up for it, cancel—stay home and rest." She held Kelly's gaze, so the girl understood her meaning.

And similar to how she'd responded to her father, Kelly lifted a palm. "Mum, I understand. Please, I'm not a baby anymore, God." She let out a sigh and continued to rub her temples. Joyce didn't drop her glare, while Mark remained tight-lipped at the sink. "Mum, I'm okay," said Kelly sternly. "It's only a headache and it will pass. I promise. Besides, there's nothing better than getting out of the house, some fresh air, and a change of atmosphere."

Joyce continued to stare at her daughter, trying to digest what the girl was saying. But like all parents, she was beginning to realize that there came a time and a place when your babies aren't so little anymore and they stop listening to your advice. She took a deep breath and exhaled. "All right," she said as she turned away from the table. And from her not-so-little baby.

The tension in the kitchen was not any lighter, much like the tension in Kelly's head. This was all too much, the dream and now her parents. She needed to escape and she needed it now. With one huge mouthful, Kelly downed the remnants of her coffee, got up, and ran upstairs to get ready. She left the mug on the table and didn't say a peep to her parents. To be honest, she didn't want to.

"I hope she's okay," said Mark. You could see the worry written across his face. Joyce knew how concerned her husband was for their daughter. She also knew that his silence meant he was at a loss and didn't know what to do. She turned to her husband, smiled, and rubbed his back while he finished off the last of the dishes.

"She will be okay, hun," she said. "She will be just fine."

Mark looked at his wife and smiled back. His face may have been expressing relief, but his gut was telling him something totally opposite. And he didn't like it one bit.

~

Ding-dong went the doorbell.

"Ahhh, I'll get it, hun," Joyce called out, and off she went towards the front door. She straightened her blouse and gave herself a quick once-over in the hallway mirror, making sure there was no food stuck between her teeth.

No, all clear.

Kelly took the stairs two at a time and bypassed her mother. As she was running towards the door, she turned her head slightly and shouted, "It's okay, Mum. I got it!"

Joyce halted in her tracks, fearing she would get bowled over. "Stop running in the house, young lady!" she yelled after the girl.

Well, some things never change, Joyce thought to herself, *even at almost sixteen.* Her daughter may have been a teenager, but part of Kelly was still a little girl at heart.

Kelly reached the door with a thud. She was huffing and puffing, but she didn't stop to take a breath. She just wanted to get out and away from the house. She opened the door with a grin. "Gemmaaaaaaaa!" she sang.

"Kellyyyyyy," Gemma sang back, and the two girls embraced each other in a warm hug. "Good to see you, Kel."

Kelly stepped across the threshold and out of the house. "So good to see you too," she said in a hurry.

Gemma looked at her friend and sensed something strange was going on. She placed a hand on Kelly's shoulder. "Babes, what's wrong?" she asked. "Why're you in such a hurry?"

"Yes, darling," asked Joyce. "Why *are* you in such a hurry?" Kelly's mum appeared at the entrance and opened the door wide. "Hi, Gemma." She smiled. "How are you, sweetheart?"

"Hi, Mrs Jennings. I'm good, and how are you? Lovely to see you," she added.

Joyce loved Gemma because the girl was always polite and respectful. She was also very authentic and had a mind of her own. Gemma was different from the other teenagers her age because she always did what she wanted and never cared what others thought. And Joyce loved that sort of confidence. "Lovely to see you too, darling," answered Joyce with a very wide smile. "So where are you going today? Kelly was telling us at breakfast that she was catching up with you. Anything fun planned?"

Gemma looked at Kelly and turned back to Joyce. "Well, we're going to the Black Bean Café to discuss ideas for Kelly's sixteenth birthday next weekend," said Gemma.

"Oh," said Joyce, surprised. "I didn't know she wanted to do anything." She looked at her daughter and continued with a shrug, "I presumed it was going to be a quiet one, at home."

Gemma felt terrible, fearing she had let the cat out of the bag and told a very big secret.

"Well, Mum, to be honest, I have been thinking about it," piped up Kelly. "I thought it would be nice to do something this year. You know, sixteen being a huge milestone and all."

"Oh…" said Joyce again. The three looked at each other and smiled. Silence fell upon them.

"Errr, would you like to join us, Mrs Jennings?" Gemma offered, thinking it was the right thing to do in the situation. Kelly's gaze shot up at her friend and then at her mother, concern and dread written all over the teenager's face.

"Thank you for the invite, darling, but today I can't, unfortunately," said Joyce with genuine sincerity. "I would have loved to come to hang out with you young ladies, but this old chook has a million and one things to do around the house." She laughed and clasped her hands together.

"Okay, Mrs Jennings, next time then," said Gemma, her tone suggesting her disappointment.

Kelly huffed her relief, thinking no one heard it. But her mother had, she'd heard the message loud and clear, and it stung. She didn't understand why her daughter was acting so strange. Normally, Kelly would have been more than happy for her mum to come along, but for an unknown reason this time was different.

"Well then, I won't keep you guys. Go and have an awesome time, and I look forward to hearing all about it." Joyce smiled awkwardly at the girls and went back inside the house, closing the door behind her.

"Seriously, are you okay, babes?" asked Gemma, her brows knitted. "Why didn't you want your mum to come with us? She always comes with us?"

"It's nothing, babe." Kelly shrugged. "I just wanted it to be us two today, you know? Like the good old days."

Gemma looked at her friend for a split-second. Then she smiled and hugged Kelly one more time. She giggled. "Good to see you outside of school for a change, hey?"

Kelly laughed. "It sure is. Hey, let's go grab a hot chocolate and chat."

"Let's," said Gemma. They held hands and slowly made their way to High Street, towards Black Bean Café.

II

THE WALK TO the café was beautiful. Even though they walked along a main road which was busy and loud, that Saturday it was simply blissful. There weren't too many people about and that included cars. Kelly and Gemma walked hand in hand and laughed, sharing stories, including the latest gossip at school. They might have been best friends but best friends didn't always have the same classes. And being separated some of the time meant that they saw the different goings-on on the campus. And by different goings-on, that included the good, the bad, and definitely the ugly. There was never a dull moment at Santa Lucia High School.

Even though Kelly and Gemma had different likes and interests, there was always one thing they had in common, and that was their love of books. Both girls loved to read and they each read absolutely everything they could get their hands on. It didn't matter what it was; they simply consumed it and then spent hours talking about it, dissecting it, and finally digesting it. It was so much fun for them and they loved doing it together.

Having different likes and interests didn't bother the girls. Their friendship was strong and a long one. The two girls met at the local kindergarten at the age of four and had been best friends ever since. They'd played together over the years. Having sleepovers, sharing secrets, and always being there for one another when a helping hand was needed. Their differences meant that there was always something new to learn about the other. It kept things interesting.

Kelly loved subjects such as art, textiles, and graphic design, and that intrigued Gemma. She found it absolutely fascinating how her best friend could have a blank piece of paper and turn it into a masterpiece. Or say a piece of fabric… Do a little cut here and a little cut there, add some thread, a button or two, and voila! A stunning dress. Gemma was always in awe of Kelly and how creative she was. She loved hearing about her latest sketches and sewing projects.

Whereas Gemma was the opposite and loved all things science and mathematics. She was incredibly smart. So smart that she never needed to use a calculator when she did maths. The teachers at school were amazed by her ability and even encouraged her to do year 12 maths in year 10. But her true love, besides books, was science. It was all science, science, science. She loved learning about the forces in physics. She loved the periodic table—mind you, she knew the chart back to front and front to back. She loved learning everything about space and dreamt of one day going to the moon in her very own rocket.

Kelly loved hearing Gemma speak about space. She loved watching her best friend's face light up with her big vibrant smile when the subject matter was about the universe and everything in it. Sometimes the girls would watch *Star Wars* together and, my God, if only you could see Gemma then. To be honest, her joy was out of this world.

There was one promise they made to each other when they were kids, and it was that Gemma would take Kelly in her spaceship to the moon. And when they landed, together, they would write their names in the soft dirt: Kelly and Gemma, BFFs forever. This way, the whole universe would know how much they meant to each other. The bonus was, since there was no wind on the moon and no ocean, nothing would blow or wash away their names in the sand. The words would last forever, just like their friendship.

Gemma hit the pedestrian crossing button, signalling for the little green man to pop up and make it safe for them to cross the main intersection. She rubbed her hands together and turned to Kelly with an idea. "Hey, HB, do you want to grab a takeaway coffee instead and go check out that old secondhand bookshop that we've been meaning to visit for God knows how long?" Gemma was excited; she was jumping on the spot and flapping her arms like she used to do when she was little.

Kelly laughed at her friend. "You are so cute, babes," she said, attempting to rein in her giggles. "Nothing ever changes with you and I love it."

"Come on, HB, it will be fun, *please.*" Gemma joined hands in prayer, pleading for her best friend to agree to the idea. She grabbed Kelly's palm and held it tight, her expression serious. "Imagine the treasures we could find," she said in bewilderment, with one hand on her heart.

"Ohhhh," said Kelly, nodding her head. "And these treasures need homes."

"Good homes, dare I say," added Gemma matter-of-factly.

Kelly grabbed both of Gemma's hands in that instant and said, "Then we must go and rescue these fine treasures and bring them home."

Both girls cheered and did a little dance at the crossing, oblivious to anyone who may have been watching them.

Beep, beep, beep. The little green man lit up, and the girls crossed the road, laughing and dancing at their brilliant idea.

"Hey, HB," said Gemma as they approached the other side.

HB was Gemma's favourite nickname for Kelly. It was perfect for her, because Kelly's favourite medium when she sketched was an HB graphite pencil. She had boxes, upon boxes, upon boxes stacked in her room. Sometimes Gemma would also call her *Speedy*. There was this one time in year 9, when Gemma didn't complete her textiles homework. The assignment had been to finish sewing their kimonos at home. Gemma panicked because she got the dates wrong and only realised it the night before it was due. She didn't know what else to do but call her favourite seamstress: HB. And that night was the night she saw how amazing and skilled Kelly was with a sewing machine.

Her friend breezed through it, and before Gemma could even finish her cup of cocoa, the kimono was done and perfectly sewn; hence, the nickname *Speedy*.

"Yeah, Pi," said Kelly in return.

Gemma laughed. "I haven't heard that in a while." Pi was the name given to Gemma because of her brilliance in mathematics. Everyone, besides Kelly, would tease her and call her a walking calculator. It used to make Gemma very sad, but that all changed one day when the teacher asked the class what Pi (π) was. Gemma, like always, flung her hand up into the air, ready to answer the question. She not only defined the term but also got up from her chair and wrote it on the whiteboard: 3.1415926535 and another 90 digits. She explained how Pi was an irrational number, meaning that it never ended.

The teacher could not believe what he saw, nor what he heard. He just stood there and stared at the whiteboard for what felt like forever. Even the class was silent; no one moved nor made a sound. When the teacher did break away from his trance, he grabbed his phone and Googled Pi. What he did next was unexpected. He started to cheer and clap and yell out, offering a "woohoo" and calling Gemma a "superstar." It was so infectious that it made the whole class join in too. When the cheering and clapping ended, the maths teacher told everyone how amazing Gemma was. He said from that day onwards, Gemma would be known as Pi. And Pi she was. Everyone called her Pi.

"You know what I am going to do in that bookstore?" said Gemma.

"No," said Kelly, giggling at her friend. "Do tell me, Pi. I just have to know."

"Well, when I find all those treasures, I'm going to hug them and pet them and squeeze them and name them George," said Gemma, in her best Hugo the Abominable Snowman from the Looney Tunes impersonation. Both girls exploded into laughter. They laughed so hard tears were rolling down their cheeks. Kelly even snorted like a pig, and that drove Gemma to laugh even harder.

"Stop, stop, Pi," said Kelly. "I can't breathe! It hurts!" The girls continued to giggle, each holding the other upright. Somehow, amongst the theatrics, they managed to walk up the road, a good two hundred metres, to Black Bean Café. "Oh, we're here," said Kelly, wiping at the tears on her face.

Laugh, laugh, hiccup went Gemma. "Oh my God, that was so funny, HB. My stomach is so sore now." She placed her hand on her belly and gave it a rub.

Kelly blew her nose. "What would you like, Pi? Hot chocolate or a latte?" she asked.

Gemma took a second to think about it before she answered, "I reckon today I will go for a hot mocha, the best of both worlds."

"Ohhhh," said Kelly. "Now that sounds like a great idea. You stay here while I quickly go inside and order."

Gemma tried to take her purse out of her bag so that she could give Kelly some money to pay for the beverages. She felt like it was her turn to pay. Besides, the trip had been her idea so it was her shout. But Kelly was too quick, and within a flash, she flew inside and placed the orders.

"All done, Pi," said Kelly when she returned a few moments later. "It won't be long and the lady will bring them out to us."

"Thanks, HB, I appreciate it."

"No," said Kelly, "thank you for getting me out of the house today."

Gemma looked at her friend, her eyebrows drawn in concern, the conversation from this morning coming to mind. "Hey, Kel, what's going on with your mum? Is everything okay?"

"Yeah, everything is fine," she replied. Gemma listened

patiently to her friend while she spoke. "It's the usual at home. Nothing's happened," said Kelly, shrugging her shoulders.

But, for some reason, Gemma didn't fully believe her. Something just didn't feel right; something felt like it was out of whack. "Then why did you say thanks for getting me out of the house? Plus, your mum looked really worried about you. And your mum never ever looks like that, not about you," added Gemma, trying to get her point across.

Kelly didn't know what to say. She didn't want to continue to lie to her best friend; more than that, she didn't want to keep secrets from her. They always shared everything with each other, no matter how bad it was.

Gemma watched her friend and her heart went out to her. Her gut was telling her that something wasn't right; she just knew it. But what was it? She turned and looked Kelly right in the face and said, "You know I won't judge you, HB. You know that, right?" She laid a hand on Kelly's shoulder for reassurance.

"Yeah, I know, Pi," said Kelly. "But…"

"But what? What's the *but*?"

Kelly took a deep breath and exhaled.

"Is it the birthday party?" said Gemma, thinking that must be what was troubling her friend.

Was she worried that no one would come if she had a party? thought Gemma.

"Nope, Pi, it's not the party." Kelly sighed, and then fell silent again.

Gemma held up her hands in defeat and said, "Then what's up?"

Kelly felt embarrassed. *Get a grip, Kel,* she thought to herself. *Just tell her. You will feel better for it.*

"I have been having these weird dreams," she said. "They feel real, Pi, like really real. And familiar, like somehow I am connected—*ahhhh,* I can't explain it." She huffed in frustration, stomping her foot on the floor and punching her fist into her palm.

"Well, what do you see, Kelly?" said Gemma. She could see how much these dreams were affecting her friend and she was starting to worry.

"I don't know. It's... it's weird. Like a battle. Yeah, a battle has happened, bodies lying everywhere," replied Kelly, her eyes glazed over. She was a million miles away. "There were many wounded, many, but there's this man..." She stopped speaking for a split-second, remembering the beautiful blue eyes. "There is a man with beautiful blue eyes. He's appeared twice to me."

"Twice," said Gemma, in surprise, bringing Kelly back from wherever it was that she went. "So these dreams have happened more than once?"

"Yes, they have. One yesterday, after school, when I fell asleep at the park under the oak tree."

"You fell asleep at the park?" asked Gemma. "Did anyone do anything to you or take your stuff?" She was beginning to sound panicked. But before she allowed Kelly to answer, Gemma threw another question her way. "When was the second time?"

Kelly took a deep breath and exhaled. She placed her fingers to her temples and gave them a quick massage. "Last night," answered Kelly, and she suddenly turned white as a ghost.

And that spooked Gemma. "Hey, listen, Kel, they are only dreams. It's nothing and probably means nothing either," she assured her friend.

"But it felt so real, Gemma," she pleaded, before yelling out in annoyance.

Ding, ding. The door to the cafe chimed to life and a lady walked out, holding two cups of mocha. "Kelly," she said.

Kelly spun around and smiled at the woman. "Yes, that's me."

"Two mochas, extra hot?" asked the lady, confirming the order.

"Oh, yes, that's perfect." Kelly grabbed the cups and handed one to Gemma.

"Okay then, enjoy, ladies," said the woman, and she walked back into the café.

Kelly took a sip from her cup—*oh, the sweet luxurious liquid was so exhilarating*. It tickled her mouth and warmed up her stomach. It was sheer bliss, and exactly what she needed.

"HB," said Gemma softly, trying to get her friend's attention without making her even more upset. Kelly turned but didn't say anything; she just continued to sip her mocha. Gemma grabbed her shoulder and gave it a squeeze. "I understand that dreams feel real. I get that." She took a second, pausing to think of a way to verbalise what was in her head. To word it right, so there were no misunderstandings. "To be honest, when I dream, it does feel real and scary too, especially if someone is chasing me or if I am free-falling," she continued.

Kelly just stared and listened.

"Um, the good thing is, when we wake up, we realise

it's going to be okay because we have woken up, you know?" Gemma took a sip of her mocha, feeling stupid. What she wanted to say and what she actually said didn't quite line up. "What I am trying to say is, when we have a dream that shakes us up a bit, we sort of just need some time to shake it off." She smiled at Kelly, attempting to reassure her friend that what she was feeling was normal. That everyone goes through it at some point or another. "It will be okay, HB. I promise." *There*. That's what she wanted to say. Gemma felt better, relieved. The last thing she wanted to do was upset her best friend even more. She loved her too much.

"Yeah, you are right, Pi," answered Kelly. "Yeah, I agree. Thanks for helping me work it out. I'm grateful, my friend." She opened her arms wide, signalling that it was time for a hug. The girls embraced each other for a minute or two, feeling relaxed and even relieved.

"Hey, HB, how good is this mocha? Oh my Goddddd," said Gemma, breaking free.

"I knowwwwww! Oh my God," said Kelly in return. "Hey, let's go find this bookshop you mentioned and…" Sticking her index finger up for silence so that she can grab everyone's full attention, she continued. "Find the treasures," she concluded with a cheeky smile.

"Oh yessss," said Gemma. "The *treasures*."

Gemma grabbed Kelly's free hand and spun her around. "It's this way, not far. Hmm, about a block away, methinks."

They started walking up the street, Gemma leading the way. Kelly followed her best friend, feeling excited and genuinely joyous for the first time today. "How did you find this place?" Kelly asked, trying to keep up with Gemma while finishing her mocha.

"I found it by accident one day with my mum," she explained. "We were out shopping in this street for a birthday present for my aunt."

"Oh yeah?" said Kelly.

"And my mum parked right in front of it."

"Oh, wow, did she?"

Gemma looked back at Kelly and offered a smile. "Yeah, she did. And at first, when I got out of the car, I didn't notice it." She gave Kelly a little bit of a tug, signalling to stop drinking her mocha and to keep moving. When Gemma had her mind set to go somewhere or do something, she didn't stop until it was done.

"Whoa, slow down, tiger," said Kelly, nearly tripping on the sidewalk.

"Come on, HB! We're almost there!" replied Gemma, determination written across her face. She continued to drag her friend up the street, pulling and tugging until finally she stopped. "Here we are, HB! What do you think?"

Kelly stared at the shop front and finally understood what Gemma had meant. "I didn't notice it."

It was an old building, brown brick and beige mortar. Some of the mortar was missing in certain sections, and there was moss and graffiti on others. It looked like it had been there for a very long time. Even the signage was plain and drab. Written in bold black letters were the words: *Wymann's Bookstore, Already Read.*

Kelly looked at the bookstore and shivered. "Pi, this place looks creepy."

Gemma laughed in reply. "I know, but wait till you see what's inside." She smiled and the expression was enticing.

There was one large window in the shop front with a

door adjacent to it. The wooden frame looked like it needed a good lick of paint, whereas the door itself looked grimy from the years of graffiti left behind by the neighbourhood delinquents who roamed the streets. The whole building appeared drab and in much need of an uplift or renovation.

"So, what made you go inside? Because I certainly wouldn't." Kelly shrugged. "Well, at least not on my own."

Gemma finished off her mocha and shook it, checking if there was any more inside. *Nope. Damn, it was empty.*

"I saw this awesome book on astronomy right in the window and I had to have it." Her eyes lit right up as she recalled the memory. "The book was so old but it was in great condition and it wasn't too expensive either."

"Oh, wow," said Kelly.

"You should meet the owner, Wymann. He is a very beautiful man, and very kind. You'll like him."

"You reckon, Pi?" she responded quizzically. Kelly was a shy girl and she mostly stayed quiet around people she didn't know—it was a habit she was trying to grow out of. It frustrated her at times because there were heaps of cute guys at school who she really wanted to talk to but just didn't have the courage to approach. Her mum encouraged her and told her on numerous occasions to just go up to them and talk as if she were talking to Gemma. But Kelly couldn't do it; the anxiety was too much.

"Come on, let's go inside and see what treasures we can find." Gemma winked and grabbed Kelly's hand, pulling her friend towards the door.

~

As soon as they stepped over the threshold, it felt like they had stepped into a giant old library. There were bookshelves everywhere. There were old books and new books; books having belonged to libraries that had closed down long ago. There were picture books for children, comic books, rare books, pop-up books and many, many more. The variety was immense, and Kelly loved it. She stood at the entrance, closed her eyes, inhaled that awesome old bookshop smell, and smiled from ear to ear. She felt like a kid in a toy store.

"See what I mean?" piped up Gemma, all of a sudden. "I told you, you would love it, HB." Kelly opened her eyes and grinned at her friend, not knowing what to say next. "Wymann must be somewhere at the back. Do you want to say hi now or later, HB?" Gemma asked.

Kelly's heart skipped a beat, she blushed a bright-red colour, and she stammered her words when she spoke, "H-how a-about w-we h-have a l-look a-around first." She cleared her throat and swallowed hard, trying to regain control. "I want to have a look around first and see what treasures I can find before I ask for assistance," she said, her tone firm but friendly.

"Sure, sounds great, HB. Let's look and find, my dear friend. There are lots of books in need of a new home." Gemma giggled as she finished her statement, turned, and walked towards the second aisle. Before she entered, she spun to Kelly and said, "How about you start in that aisle, and I will start here, and then we can just work our way towards the back of the shop."

Kelly looked down the long row of bookshelves. *Geez, this bookshop was definitely big.* It was deceiving from the front, and no one would truly know how big it was unless they stepped inside.

Gemma saw the wonder on Kelly's face and smiled. "Hey,

HB, there's also a basement," she added. "We definitely need to go down there and have a look. You will love it, guaranteed." She winked, and before Kelly could protest, Gemma disappeared down her aisle, leaving her friend all alone to search for treasures.

Kelly looked around. She didn't know where to start and she definitely didn't know what to dig for. She scanned one of the shelves, pulled out a very old shabby-looking book, and flipped through the pages.

God, so old, she thought.

"To whom did you once belong?" she said out loud, curious as to what the former owner may have looked like. She didn't bother reading the title, placing it back where she'd found it. Not much dust was unsettled in the process but a tiny bit somehow made its way up her nose. "Ah-ah-acho." She rubbed her nose with the sleave of her jacket. The dust made her face itchy. "*Achoo,*" she said this time, even louder than before.

From somewhere within the walls of the bookshop a mysterious voice said, "Bless you."

She was embarrassed because someone had heard her— then again, who hadn't? She rolled her eyes at herself. *God, I probably sounded like a big out of key elephant,* she thought. Her face turned a bright shade of red.

"ACHOOOOOOOO!" Another sneeze came rushing out of nowhere, some spittle too, with a little booger landing on her palm. "Oh God," she said in response. Kelly took out a tissue and blew her nose loudly, hoping that was the end of it. "No more," she said.

"Bless you," said the mysterious voice again. But, this time, it was closer than before.

Despite her embarrassment, Kelly sheepishly responded, "Thank you," quickly turning back to the books on the shelves, hoping the voice would not come any closer.

Hmm, what would I like to read? she thought.

"This looks interesting," she said to herself as she pulled out a book about Audrey Hepburn—it was her memoir. She flipped through the pages and glanced at the photos of the Hollywood starlet. She was a true beauty and oozed elegance and class.

Kelly loved vintage clothing, especially evening gowns from the 1950s-60s era. They were to die for and simply breathtaking. Even the hairstyles were elegant, and so different from today. She preferred that style above everything else, as it made her feel more feminine and stylish.

"Ohhhh," she hummed, a lightbulb moment. "I would love to sew a dress like one of these," she mumbled under her breath, still looking at the beautiful photos of Audrey Hepburn.

She stopped and took a moment to think, trying to remember when the school holidays were. It would be the perfect opportunity to start her project, as nothing would disturb her. There would be no classes. And no homework, hopefully. It would be something she thoroughly enjoyed, and in the end, she would have a beautiful 1960s dress of her own. And that was something she'd wanted ever since she watched Breakfast at Tiffany's when she was a very little girl. Kelly smiled to herself. She was excited.

How much is this book anyway? she thought.

She turned the book over and looked at the back cover. Nothing, no price was listed. "Oh," she said. Maybe on the front? Kelly turned the book back to the front, but again there was nothing.

Where could you be? she thought.

"Hey, girl," came a voice from behind her, and it startled her. Kelly jumped and yelped. It was Gemma, giggling while she covered her mouth. "Sorry, HB, I didn't mean to scare you. You okay?" she said sincerely.

"Oh my god," said Kelly, her limbs still shaking. "You scared the bejesus out of me, *girl.*"

"Sorry, HB. I didn't realise I would do that. Oh, by the way, I heard you all the way down there, sneezing three times. Bless you, babes," said Gemma with a big, cheeky smile.

Kelly closed her eyes. "You're joking, oh my God." She covered her face with the book, hoping she could hide behind it forever.

"Oh, wow, what treasure have you found there?" asked Gemma, reaching for the book to have a look. She pulled it away from Kelly's grasp. "Audrey Hepburn." Gemma examined the front cover and stared at the starlet in wonder. "God, isn't she beautiful, HB?"

Kelly turned and took a good look. Wow, how could she have missed it? On the front cover, in black and white, was a side profile of the goddess herself. Her hair was elegantly pinned up and she was wearing some sort of white evening dress with a high collar. "I love what she's wearing, Pi," said Kelly. "You reckon it's a dress or a shirt?"

Gemma stared at the photo, trying to make out what the garment was. She shook her head. "I don't know. I can't tell." She frowned. "Yeah, definitely a dress, HB."

"You think?" said Kelly, grabbing the book to examine it for herself.

"I don't ever recall seeing any of those beautiful women

from the golden era of Hollywood ever wearing a shirt for a photoshoot like this." Gemma pointed at the portrait.

"Hmmmm, you might be right, Pi," said Kelly, not looking up at her friend, her focus fully absorbed by the photo.

Ka-ching went the old-fashioned cash register, and the noise caught Gemma's attention.

"I have an idea, HB. Let's go ask Wymann if he has other books on Audrey Hepburn. Perhaps some with more photos, and hopefully one of those photos is of her wearing that exact white dress." She grabbed Kelly by the hand and started walking towards the cash register. Kelly didn't hear a single word Gemma had said. She just stumbled her way while Gemma led her.

Wymann had his back turned to the girls and didn't see them coming. He was busy sifting through a boxload of books someone had donated to the shop.

"Ahhhh," he said as he pulled out a very rare book on Norse magic. He smiled to himself as his heart skipped a beat.

Perhaps I can find some of the answers I'm looking for in here, he thought.

He opened the front cover, and read the year: first print, edition 1, 1785.

Wow, a beauty, authentic, and old.

"Oh, what," he said suddenly, noticing a faint blue glow emanating from under his shirt. "This can't be…" He touched his necklace, a very special magical necklace given to him by the king of Saphira so very long ago. He took off his glasses in disbelief and gave them a quick clean with his handkerchief. He also gave his eyes a deep rub, thinking that they were playing tricks on him. He placed the glasses back on his face and gasped. The glow was even brighter. "Dear Lord, this can't be…" he repeated in astonishment.

"Ehem." Gemma cleared her throat. "Excuse me, Wymann, can we bother you for a sec?" She didn't look at him as she spoke, trying to grab the book out of Kelly's hands.

Wymann turned around slowly, and as he did, the necklace emitted a more luminescent glow. The light was so spectacular that he caught the attention of both girls instantly. Three pairs of eyes connected.

"You…" said Wymann, pointing his finger at Kelly. "You… I've found you!" He ran around the counter towards Kelly. He grabbed her by the arms and stared at her. "This can't be," he said yet again. "How can this be?" He shook her, more out of shock than anger. "We all have waited so very long for you…" He salivated, some spittle flying out of his mouth and landing on Kelly's cheek.

She screamed. "Stop, let me go. You are hurting me!"

But he didn't hear her pleas. He continued to hold her by the arms, refusing to release her. "I have to take you to the others," he said suddenly. "Yes." He shook his head. "They have to see this with their very own eyes. I don't even believe it myself!" He laughed.

He grabbed Kelly by the wrist and started walking towards the door. The girl pulled back in protest, refusing to go anywhere with him.

"No, I'm not going," she yelled. She turned to her friend for help. Gemma stood like a deer caught in headlights, her eyes unblinking and lost. "Gemma, snap out of it," Kelly shouted. But it was of no use. Wymann kept on pulling her towards the door.

Kelly wasn't going to give up without a fight, however.

Images of her dad flashed in front of her eyes. Recent images, of him shadowboxing around the kitchen, teasing her mother. Mum versus the pot.

Left, left, right kept on playing in her head. *Left, hook, uppercut.* More patterns. She looked at her free hand—the one holding the Audrey Hepburn memoir—instinctively raised it, and slammed the book into Wymann's shoulder. He released her instantly, yelled out, and grabbed for his arm. Thankfully, the book was thick and heavy enough to cause some pain, and in this case, a bit of distraction for Kelly to make her final move.

Kelly stepped towards him, automatically getting into a boxing defence position, fists raised and ready. She gritted her teeth in anger and made the first move. The jab was light, hitting the assailant on the injured shoulder while causing him to open up and face her head-on. She didn't linger for long. She went all in, landing a mean right jab on his nose and finishing him off with an uppercut.

BAM, BAM. She danced like a true champion.

Wymann went flying backwards and landed on the floor like a sack of potatoes. *KERPLUNK.*

Kelly peered down at her hands in surprise.

My God, she thought. *My hands did this?*

She looked back at Wymann, then at her hands again, her eyes widened in disbelief. He groaned and grabbed his face in agony. Kelly reacted quickly, without thinking, and while running on adrenaline. She spun around, grabbed Gemma by the hand, and bolted out the door, leaving Wymann and Miss Hepburn to keep each other company on the floor.

12

"OH, MY HEAD, ohhh," said Wymann from the floor. He tried to get up but he felt dizzy. He took a couple of breaths, hoping it would help settle him and alleviate the stars he was seeing.

Oh, what have I done? he thought.

Wymann whimpered not because of the pain he was feeling but because he hurt that poor girl, and he hadn't meant to. He raised his bruised arm and slapped himself on the forehead.

"Ahhh!" He released a painful groan, not just from his head but also from his injured shoulder. Double whammy. He decided to lie on the floor for just a minute longer to steady himself. "Come on, Wymann, you are the king's hand, a knight. Get a grip, soldier," he said to himself, trying with all the strength left in him to pump himself up. But all he could think about was *her*, the girl with the bright, clear blue eyes just like Millard's. The resemblance was uncanny.

Those eyes… they were like looking at Millard himself after all these years. A tear ran down his cheek and nestled into his beard. "God, how much I miss you, my dear friend," he said.

As he lay there next to Miss Hepburn, he wondered who the girl was and where she came from. He touched the necklace around his neck, worried that it may have come off during the struggle. But, no, it was still there and it was still glowing its iridescent, bright-blue light.

"Ohhh!" He sat up and realised that he had to tell Babushka.

Yes, yes, yes, yes, he thought. *Lilliana needs to know that I've found her—those blue eyes and this glow from the necklace will prove it.*

He giggled for the first time in a long time; he was so excited. He lifted himself off the floor, forgetting about his pain. He couldn't wait to share the good news. The news they had all been waiting for, for forty long years.

Wymann ran to the cash register and locked it shut with his keys. He normally would take a walk around the bookshop, checking for customers before he locked up for the day. But today he couldn't wait—no siree.

He decided to shout out instead. "Hello, is anyone in here?" He stood at the counter and listened for a sign. Nothing. He removed his weathered coat from the old-fashioned wooden coat stand and quickly rushed to put it on. His sore arm got caught in one of the sleeves and he cursed under his breath. "Oh, damn." Wymann took some calming, though agonised breaths. He was angry at himself for rushing. "Whoa, Nelly," he said. "Slow down. Nothing ever gets done right when you rush."

He worked slowly and steadily, untangling the sleeve and then slipping his arm through, being mindful of the pain. And then, *slap*, the coat was on.

"Hello!" boomed his loud voice. "Shop will be closing early today, three minutes." Still there was no response.

He decided to slowly walk towards the front entrance, looking down each aisle as he passed, and noticed they were empty. No one was there. Wymann instinctively removed his beanie from his coat pocket and placed it on his head.

"Ahh!" He flinched. He'd forgotten about the pain. Even though he was jabbed in the face and received an upper cut to the chin, his entire head hurt and his skull throbbed. "Hello, I'm closing now," he warned. But there was no one listening. Taking his keys, he turned towards the door, releasing it from the magnetic door stop. As he pulled it forward, he noticed a reflection in the mirror behind the door. "Oh!" He was taken aback. "Wait a minute," he said, gently rubbing his chin. "That face looks very familiar."

He stared hard at the image. At first, he thought it was someone behind him and was frightened because he hadn't heard them coming. Besides, the face appeared familiar but also unrecognisable.

Who could this be? he thought. But then he realised that the puffy face he was looking at was his own reflection in the mirror.

His eyes had black bags and his nose was red and swollen. His lower lip was slightly cut and swelling fast. He looked hideous. Never during his time as a knight had he ever been so brutally beaten. And the most ironic thing of it all was that it hadn't taken much to get him into this state.

He looked at the man in the mirror and smirked. "No

time to lose. There is much at stake. Hurry on." And hurry on he did, all the way to Babushka's house, located on the main road.

Knock, knock, knock, smash, smash, smash went Wymann's hands on Babushka's front door.

"Lilliana!" he shouted. "Are you home?"

Knock, knock, knock, smash, slap, slap went his hand. *Ring, ring, ring.*

"Lilliana, it's me... Wymann," he said in frustration. "Quickly, open up the door. I have to show you something. QUICKLY!"

The door opened with a whoosh. "Stop making that racket. What is it, Wymann?" she yelled. "Can't a woman ever go to the toilet in peace?" she added, not caring if the statement had embarrassed him.

Wymann ignored her and barged straight through the door, nearly bowling the poor old lady over. Luckily, she was still quick. She grabbed on to a small chest of drawers positioned in the corner of the hallway, allowing it to steady her. Her grip was still very strong, even after all these years.

"Wymann, stop this madness!" Babushka yelled. "What are you doing?"

"I've found her, Lilliana," he said triumphantly. Wymann was so overjoyed that he jumped on the spot with glee.

"Found who? What are you talking about, Wymann. I don't understand..." She stared at him, confused.

Had he gone mad? she thought.

"And what in God's name has happened to your face?" she said in horror. Babushka walked right up to him and stood on her tippytoes, grabbing him by the shoulders and pulling him down towards her, so that she could get a better look.

Wymann was not a very tall man, but he was too tall for Babushka as she only reached his armpit. He would tease her from time to time by resting his arm on her head while pretending that the old woman was a bench. This made Babushka really mad and she would huff and puff at him, threatening to turn him into a toad *or worse*. But all Wymann would do is laugh.

"Oh, stop that, Lilliana!" yelled Wymann. He removed her hands from his face but she refused to give up without a fight. So she tugged him by his long beard and pulled him towards her with all her might. "Ahhhhh!" he screamed.

"Stop resisting," Babushka said with frustration, pulling the beard a little harder.

"Stop, *please,* I beg you," he cried out in agony.

"All right, you big baby," answered Babushka. She let go of the beard and Wymann grabbed his face and rubbed his chin.

"God, woman, why do you have to be so rough," he whimpered.

Babushka rolled her eyes at him. "Why do you have to always resist? So are you going to tell me what happened to your face or not?" She stared at him, waiting for a response.

Wymann ignored her and changed the subject. "Lilliana, get ready." He curled his fingers around the zipper of his coat.

"Get ready for what?"

"Oh, get ready to be blown away. I'm going to show you something amazing," he said as he started to hop on the spot, from one foot to another, once again.

"Well, what is it then? Did you bring me something amazing?" she pressed, clearly not feeling the same level of excitement as her friend.

Wymann pulled hard on his zipper. *Zip.* And with one quick motion of his arm, he dropped his coat on the floor and used his hands to frame his magical necklace, trying to bring all attention and focus to that very spot. "Voila!" he said.

Babushka continued to stare at him. She glanced at the necklace and back to his swollen face. *He must have fallen over at the bookshop,* she thought. She turned her head sideways and looked at him through one eye, studying the man in front of her.

"Hmmm," she said. "You definitely fell over, didn't you? You fell over in your bookshop, probably down the basement stairs. That's why your face is like that, and that's why you've gone mad."

Wymann just looked at her with his mouth agape. He couldn't believe what he was hearing. "Have *you* gone mad?" he said. "Do you need your glasses to see the light?" Wymann was in complete shock. His magical necklace was glowing for the first time in forty years and his friend hadn't even noticed it.

"What would I need my glasses for? My eyesight is perfectly fine," she said to him.

He couldn't take it anymore. He was about to explode. "Look," he said, pointing at his necklace. "Look at it!" he roared.

"I *am* looking at it," she yelled back, holding her hands up in frustration.

"For God's sake, Lilliana, it's glowing." He unbuttoned

his shirt, revealing his chest and the shaggy clump of white hair. The necklace was sitting proudly just below his collarbones, glistening in the light of the hallway. But it wasn't glowing anymore.

Babushka didn't know how to respond. She just stared at her friend, feeling sorry for him. *The fall must have rattled him, and now he was not just confused but also seeing things that aren't real,* she thought.

"Why aren't you speaking?" Wymann asked. "You never stay silent for long. But Babushka continued to stand there in silence. Wymann looked down at his chest and his heart skipped a beat. "Oh no! This can't be!" he cried. He grabbed the necklace with both hands. "No! No! No!" A tear rolled down his cheek.

"It's okay, my dear friend," said Babushka. She stepped up to the bookshop owner and hugged him. He placed his head on top of hers and cried, hiccupping between sobs.

Finally, the crying subsided and his breathing slowed. "I can't take this anymore, Babushka," he said. He stood up and buttoned his shirt, but not to the very top, leaving his necklace visible.

In that moment, Babushka truly felt for him; she wished she could take away the pain. "Come, let's sit and talk over a nice cup of tea. That will make you feel better." She looked at him tenderly and smiled. Wymann smiled back. He looked exhausted. "Come," she said again, and this time she extended her hand. He grabbed it and they both walked together towards her kitchen.

Wymann exhaled as he sat on Babushka's comfy couch. He adjusted the pillows, making sure they supported his back.

Crunch, crunch, crunch.

"Oh, popcorn. Did you have popcorn last night?" He picked up a few stray kernels and placed them on the coffee table.

"Popcorn?" said Babushka. "Oh, popcorn, yes. Vlad and I had popcorn last night while we watched *MacGyver*."

Clank, clank went the teakettle as she filled it up with water and placed it on the stove to boil.

"Oh, was last night *MacGyver* night?" said Wymann in surprise. "You two still watching that show together?"

Babushka took two mugs from the cupboard and placed them on the bench. "We sure do and we love it," she said. "That show is so fascinating, Wymann. Even you would love it if you gave it a chance." She winked at him.

"No, not for me," he said. "I have my books and I love reading them. There never seems to be enough time for anything else." He sighed and rubbed his eyes ever so gently, grimacing from the pain.

"I know you think the answer is in one of your books, but you also need rest and a little fun."

Wooo, wooo. The water was bubbling loudly. Babushka turned off the stove just before she removed the kettle. Her biggest fear was that she would forget and then accidentally burn down her house.

"Any sugar, Wymann?" she asked.

"No thank you, Lilliana. I have to watch my diabetes," he responded.

Lilliana took two teabags out and placed one in each mug. She poured the hot water and then added some milk. *Clink, clank, clink, clank* went the spoon as she stirred.

"How is your blood sugar?" she asked as she walked towards the lounge area with the cups of tea.

"Oh, you mean how is my new machine?" Wymann lifted his shirt just above his waist and showed Lilliana his new diabetes pump.

"Wow," said Lilliana. "Does it hurt?"

"No, it doesn't hurt. It's just annoying."

Lilliana handed him his tea.

"Thank you." Wymann took a sip. "Mmm, lovely." He sighed. "I hate this thing because it feels strange sitting on my belt all the time."

"Like a mobile phone," piped up Babushka.

Wymann looked at her and rolled his eyes. "I don't have a mobile phone so I don't know what it feels like having one attached to my belt. I just don't like it; it's uncomfortable." He huffed. "Just like this damn necklace now." He placed his tea on the coffee table and grabbed at the buckle of his necklace. He hesitated and looked at Lilliana. She didn't say a word as she slurped her tea.

Wymann had not taken off his necklace since they came through the oak tree and that was a very, very long time ago. His biggest fear was that the day he took it off would also be the day when Millard's long-lost child would walk into his bookshop, and he would be none the wiser. The necklace was the key and all they had left after Lilliana lost her powers. He placed the necklace on the coffee table with a *clank* and leaned back on the couch.

"Are you all right?" asked Lilliana after a while.

He turned to her with a huff. "No, I'm not all right. I feel so empty, Lilliana. "I-I-I feel like a failure." He cradled his face in his hands and sobbed.

"You are no more a failure than I am," said Babushka. "I have failed the king and all of us."

"I-I don't… don't know how we are ever going to get back home, Lilliana," he said between sobs. "I just don't know anymore." He used the sleeve of his shirt to wipe his tears and the snot that was now flowing freely out of his nose.

Babushka's heart broke into a million pieces. She felt sorry for her friend, for the pain he was feeling and the burden he was carrying. "I wish I could see the cords of energy." The old woman perked up a bit. "Then I could find him, Wymann. You see…" She moved to the edge of her armchair as she spoke. "If my magic were alive, I would follow those cords and find him." She shook a frustrated fist. "But I can't, Wymann. I just can't…"

He breathed deep, trying to calm himself. "Do you know what I regret, Lilliana?" Before she could answer, Wymann continued. "I regret not taking that chance in the park with the police." Tears welled up in his eyes again and he started to rock himself on the spot. "I regret cowering away and turning my back on the babe," he sobbed.

"You can't punish yourself, Wymann. That's what I'm trying to learn, even after all these years. You can't punish yourself," she repeated sternly. She didn't know how to tackle the matter at hand. "Look, you don't know how it could have turned out even if we approached the police that night. We could have been sent to jail for kidnapping or much worse… locked up in an asylum. It was a hopeless situation and no one, not even me, could have foreseen it."

Wymann blubbered into his hands.

"Stop that crying this instant, you hear?" she said, hitting the armrest with her fist.

"I can't," he said. *Sob, hiccup, sob.* "I can't. The necklace was wrong. A girl walked into the shop and my necklace glowed."

"A girl?" gasped Babushka.

"Yes, a girl."

Babushka looked at Wymann and then back at the necklace. "It must have been a glitch, because the child we lost in the park that night was a boy not a girl, remember?" But Wymann ignored her and continued to cry. Babushka was feeling beyond frustrated. No matter what she said, this stubborn old knight just didn't want to listen. "Listen to me, we have it easier than the rest. We came through the portal as we were in Saphira, minus my magic." The old woman pointed to the necklace on the coffee table. "That necklace saved you, just like my staff saved me."

"How could it have possibly saved me or you?" he cried. "The magic doesn't work."

"Oh, you cheeky bugger," she said, shaking her tush in her armchair while gritting her teeth. "It prevented us from changing into animals. We aren't animals like the others, dear knight. We're still the same." But her friend was lost to his misery and didn't seem to understand her point. "If we went through that portal without the staff and your necklace, we would be in a deeper hole than we're in now. A hole like the burrow with the rest of the clan."

"We *are* in a deeper hole, Lilliana. That's what you don't understand," he cried. She stopped and stared at him, allowing him to release all the pain and anger he'd been carrying for a long time. Wymann started to speak but his words came out muddled and wonky. He took a deep breath, swallowed, and tried again. "The necklace deceived me."

"How could the necklace have deceived you? It's *magic*."

"I believe it's this damn machine I'm wearing." He shook his head and rubbed his hands together. "Yes, it's this pump. It must have caused the glitch somehow, and the necklace glowed. It deceived me," he repeated.

"It couldn't have deceived you, Wymann!" yelled Babushka.

"Then explain the glow I saw, woman, the glow brought on by a girl!" he yelled back, huffing and puffing, his chest heaving as he stood his ground.

Babushka held up her hands, trying to calm her friend and deescalate the situation. "Stop," she said. "Stop. I can't explain the glow. I can't." She looked at him tenderly. Then she placed her hands in her lap and took a minute to think.

"I-I am... sorry, Lilliana. I'm sorry," he said. "I don't know what happened to me today. I think I'm going mad." Their eyes connected and Babushka smiled. Her gaze reassured him that everything was going to be okay. She was here for him.

Today was too much for everyone. And being here, on earth, for so very long was taking its toll. The stress and anxiety on Wymann to find a way back home was becoming a burden, and Babushka could see it now. Her friend looked old and he looked worn. His spirit seemed broken. Babushka picked up the necklace and handed it to him. "Here, take it back and wear it."

"I can't, not today, Lilliana." He pushed her hand away ever so gently. "I can't bear its weight anymore..." And he jumped up and walked towards the back door.

"Wait... Where are you going?" Babushka asked, shocked.

"I need air and I need to clear my head." He kept on walking and didn't slow down.

"But your necklace?" She held it up so that he could see it. "You need your necklace."

Wymann didn't stop. He didn't turn back to place the necklace around his neck, where it belonged. He kept on walking, straight out of the lounge, out the back walkway, and out the door. He just kept on going, on autopilot, to wherever his legs were taking him.

Babushka sighed. She held the necklace in her hands, examining it. It was so beautiful and intricately made. The relic was old, and all she knew of it was that it had been passed down to the king by his father and his father before him. She remembered touching it once in Saphira and the energy she felt was extraordinary, but now it felt cold in her hands. She didn't know if they all would be trapped here forever, never to see their homeland again. She didn't even know if Saphira still existed, but one thing was certain. They had to keep trying, looking, and searching. And it was only a matter of time.

"Hmm, don't worry. He'll come back for you." She stood and placed the necklace back on the coffee table, where Wymann left it, just in case.

13

SWORDS CLASHED. VOICES *screamed.*

Kelly tossed and turned in bed, calling out in her dream-like state.

"Get the women and the children. Take them through the catacombs," yelled a knight.

"Where is Millard?" yelled another.

Kelly flounced about, sweat rolling down her face and onto her pillow. Her bedsheets were drenched. "Millard," she shouted. "Someone…" She breathed heavily. "Someone, please," she begged. "Please help him." Tears were streaming along her cheeks. "Please help him before it's too late."

But no one heard her pleas.

Kelly was running. *Squish, squish, squish.* Running barefoot through moist grass. She stopped and looked around. She was in a beautiful grove and there were thousands upon thousands of tiny white daisies. They covered the grass like a weed but at the same time made the grove appear magical.

It felt peaceful here. She picked one daisy and held it tight between her fingers. It reminded her of her childhood, especially the springtime.

Kelly would go to the park with her dad, and together they would sit on the grass and make daisy chains. It was so much fun. There was this one time when her dad made a crown of daisies. He'd placed it on Kelly's head, pretended to blow a trumpet, and then declared her queen of All Nations Park. He bowed to her and said, "At your service, my Queen." Kelly had laughed so much and so did her dad. It was the best day ever.

"Ahhh!" There was a loud scream.

"Oh," Kelly said in alarm, snapping out of her memory. She turned her head towards the sound and noticed a cottage. It looked familiar. "I've seen that before." She stared at the small structure a little longer, trying to remember before it dawned on her. "Millard." She dropped the daisy. "The baby, no!"

With her heart racing a million miles per hour, she ran. The trees in the grove along with the daisies became a blur. She saw nothing but the cottage, and feared nothing but the worst. She reached the door and it opened easily. As she entered, everything went dark.

"What's happening? Millard!" she called out loud, but her voice only echoed. Kelly looked around. She felt disorientated. The cottage was gone, the daisies were gone, and so were the trees and the moist grass. "

What to do? What to do? she thought.

As if on autopilot, her legs started moving. First, she walked and then she broke into a slow jog. Still nothing appeared. All around her, there was nothing. Only darkness. Kelly panicked, her breathing laborious.

"No…" she said. "Nooo!" she screamed this time.

"Ahhh!" That voice cried out again, it frightened her, and she started to run.

Crunch, crunch, crunch. "Ouch!" she yelled and grabbed her foot. Kelly examined her toe, which was now bleeding. Not badly but enough to give her pause. She looked at her foot, confused.

How had she stubbed her toe? There was nothing out here, she thought. But there was…

A path had appeared, a path made of earth and pebbles. She bent down and touched the ground. It felt rough and cold. "Cold earth, hmm," she said to herself. "I must be in an underground cave." She looked closer, and there were tree roots sticking out here and there. "Yes, this must be a cave. It explains how I stubbed my toe. Damn it, why can't you ever wear shoes when you dream?" Kelly looked at her toe and then at the tree root, frowning and rubbing her injury. By instinct, she decided to follow the path. Everything else led to nothing, so this must have been the right way. This must have led to the way out. Kelly crossed her fingers.

The path was long. There were many tunnels veering off into other passages. Some tunnels had been completely caved in by large boulders, whereas others were covered in a veil of webs. Kelly shuddered at the sight of those, wondering what type of creature resided beyond.

"Better to not find out." She reached a crossroad. "Oh God," she said, rubbing her head. "What now?" Kelly stared at the tunnels, not knowing what to do, which one to choose. She yelled out in anger, pulling her hair. She began to pace, left and right, hoping something would happen.

Crunch, crunch, crunch. Crunch, crunch, crunch went her feet on the gravel.

"This is so frustrating—*ahhh!*" Everything was too much. Kelly felt like she was in a real-life nightmare, and she couldn't get out. She continued to stand and stare at the two tunnels. "Aha!" An idea popped into her head. She narrowed her eyes because she knew she was onto something. "This will surely work." She shook her fist and egged herself on. Taking a deep breath, Kelly raised her right hand and slapped herself across the face. Hard.

SMACK.

"Whoa, whoa, whoa!" she yelled as she lost her footing and fell onto her back, seeing stars. "Ow!" The pain. Kelly didn't move from the ground. *TKO.*

She laughed to herself. If only her father saw her now, he would be either very proud or very upset. Two brawls in a matter of hours, one with Wymann the bookshop owner and another with herself.

"God, what are you doing, Kelly?" she huffed. "Get up." But getting up meant she needed to deal with the nightmare she was stuck in, and she didn't have the energy anymore. Her tank was empty. She stared at the nothing above her. The endless darkness. The floor might have been cold and prickly in certain spots, but at least it was making her body numb. "Maybe if I lie here, I'll wake up," she wondered aloud. "Yes." She shook her head. "The cold will wake me up." She wiggled a little to move a pebble sticking into her spine. "Ah!"

She got up to see what had suddenly pricked her out of nowhere. Rubbing her back, Kelly dislodged a small dried-up leaf. She turned it over in her hand, examining it.

"What… what is this?" She touched the end of the dried

leaf with her index finger. "Ouch!" She shoved the digit into her mouth by instinct. "What type of plant are you?" She looked at it closely and decided to rub it between her fingers. It broke apart into millions of tiny, dust-like particles. The particles took flight and scattered with the force of her breath. "Oh!" she said in surprise.

Kelly brought her fingers to her nose and took a small sniff. She rubbed her fingers together, hoping the heat might help lubricate the smell and make it stronger. Recognisable.

Rub, rub, rub. Sniff, sniff, sniff.

"Ohhh! Rosemary." Inhaling one last time, Kelly smiled, proud of herself. "Yes, this is rosemary." But that feeling didn't last long. "What is dried rosemary doing down here?" Kelly looked around and didn't see any more of the herb anywhere. She stopped to recall her journey on the path, and again, no rosemary bushes. Nothing. Scratching her head, at a total loss for a reasonable explanation, she stared at the two entrances again, her decision not any clearer.

Time passed. How much? She wasn't certain.

"Wait, stop, Kelly. The floor. Look at the floor," she said out loud, and this time with a touch of hope. This must have been the key. Kelly got down on her hands and knees and examined the floor leading to each tunnel. The right side had no dried leaves scattered anywhere. "This must not be the right tunnel." To make sure that her theory was correct, she looked on the left-hand side. Slowly, she searched, taking her time and making sure every square inch was covered. "Yes!" she yelled in triumph. "I found one."

She searched for more. *Another one, awesome!*

"Yes, that's three now…"

Kelly stood up, dusty and dirty from crawling on the

floor. She counted her dried rosemary. One, two, three, four, five, six, seven, eight... She looked up at the left entrance, and without hesitation, she entered. The trek down this tunnel was the same. Dirt, dust, pebbles, and tree roots. She continued anyway, knowing this was the right choice.

Crunch, crunch, crunch.

"Oh, light! There's purple light up ahead!" she screamed in relief. "It must be sunset." Kelly hastened her pace. Light meant an exit was not far. Kelly's spirits lifted and she was feeling excited. The nightmare was going to end and then she would wake up.

Crunch, crunch, crunch. Without warning, the path veered left and Kelly happily followed it around the corner. *Crunch, crunch, crunch.* The light was growing brighter and brighter and so was Kelly's spirit when suddenly...

"Ahhh!" She screamed a chilling, mind-blowing, window-breaking, earth-shattering scream, stumbling backwards and falling onto her bum. "Ouch." Kelly covered her face with her arms, protecting herself from the horror in front of her...

Before her, standing at a colossal height, stood two ginormous golden dragons. Motionless. Their eyes open and jaws frozen in the scariest of snarls imaginable. Beneath the purple hue of the tunnel, they looked so real. So frightening.

Kelly breathed in and out, her chest heaving up and down, up and down, with her pulse racing and sweat running over her cheeks. She didn't drop her arms, and she didn't move a muscle, too petrified to do anything.

"Oh, please wake up," she cried, tears welling in her eyes and her body beginning to tremble.

"Come forward," whispered a voice.

Kelly's ears shot up like a puppy hearing a dog whistle.

A familiar scent slowly wafted through the tunnel towards her. It drifted up her nose. "Mmm, rosemary." The smell was fresh, calming, and it helped to soothe her fears. Kelly lowered her arms slowly.

"Come forward," said the voice again.

She recognized it. "I've heard you before," she muttered under her breath as she stood. Her heart began to rise from her gut where it had plummeted, as she fought the curiosity building within. "Don't look up at them. Don't look up!" But the pull was too strong and she cast her eyes on the two dragons again. This time there was no fear.

The statues were amazing. Kelly stared at them in wonder and imagined what sort of magic moulded them out of earth and rock. The craftsmanship was exquisite. The details were mind-blowing, and every inch appeared as if it were carved to perfection. Almost lifelike.

Kelly raised her hand to one of the dragons. It was warm to the touch. "God, that's impossible. How can this be?" She shook her head in disbelief. "No, no, you aren't real. You are earth and rock and nothing else."

"Come forward," said the voice for a third time. "Come, have no fear."

Kelly obeyed, drawing closer and closer to the source, the scent of the rosemary thickening. As she passed the two colossal dragons, a doorway appeared. She looked around, worried that she may have missed something. But there was no alternative route, nothing else out there.

"The voice did say to have no fear." She placed a hand on her chest, wondering if she should trust the voice, and noticed that her heart was beating at a steady pace. All her anxiety was gone. That must have been a good sign, so she decided to trust her instincts and entered the passageway.

As she walked towards it, the scent of the rosemary became even stronger. Whatever the source was, it lay beyond the entrance. Taking a deep breath, Kelly stepped over the threshold leading into the small corridor, only two metres long.

Crunch, crunch, crunch. The scent was more powerful with every step. At the end of the corridor, Kelly could see the light. The purple hue was breathtaking; it called out to her. "Not far now," she assured herself. "The end is near."

Crunch, crunch, crunch. With her last step, she entered a small room. She was slightly blinded by the purple light and instinctively raised her palm to shield her eyes, in order to see past the brightness. And what she saw took her breath away...

A tomb. Against the wall carved out of pure white marble was an altar. And upon that altar was a knight dressed in the most beautiful and intricate golden armour that had ever been crafted.

Kelly stared. "Am I dreaming?"

Above the altar hung a magnificent golden shield and the source of the purple light. Once Kelly's eyes had adjusted, she could see its full beauty. The shield possessed an incredible 3D relief, which covered its entirety. It depicted a mighty golden dragon in flight and on the hide of the beast rode a warrior armed with his sword.

"Wow..." Kelly stepped closer, not just out of curiosity but in sheer awe. "Who is this knight?" she wondered aloud.

From what Kelly could see, surprisingly, he wasn't bug-eaten nor a skeleton. The questions kept building in her mind. The sword he held matched the image on the shield. It was just breathtaking. Kelly looked up at the shield and back to the sword.

"Yes, you're one and the same," she whispered. "You must be that warrior riding the golden dragon. God…" Kelly felt dizzy and placed her hands on the altar to brace herself. "This is all too much. This can't be real."

She inhaled a deep breath, trying to clear her head.

"Oh, rosemary, here you are." Bouquets upon bouquets were laid at the knight's feet and others by his side. Some were long dried-up and brittle, whereas others seemed freshly picked. "Hmmm, how strange."

But the scent was fresh and soothing, and Kelly inhaled another deep breath. She was so lost in thought she didn't notice when a golden hand lifted from its resting spot and touched her on the arm. Kelly choked on the rosemary-scented air as the armoured hand grabbed her forearm and held firm. Kelly tried to push the hand away but it was so strong. Solid.

She screamed out, images of the incident in the book-shop flooding her mind. "No!"

"Go see Babushka," the voice boomed but Kelly continued to wiggle in the golden warrior's grasp. "Babushka…" the voice echoed. Then the hand was gone. It released her, and Kelly flew backwards, landing on her back and knocking her head on the ground.

KERPLUNK.

"Ahh!" She sat up suddenly. In bed. Trembling.

Instinctively, she grabbed the back of her head, searching for any traces of blood. Nothing. She was sweaty, her clothes drenched and her hair plastered to her face. Wet.

"Oh, my arm." She examined her wrist, where the hand had been, turning it over this way and that way, making sure she hadn't missed anything. No, not a scratch anywhere. "Phew, only a dream," she said, falling back on her soaked pillow. Kelly untangled her bedsheets and covered herself, feeling slightly cold.

God, what a dream. What is going on? she wondered, rubbing her face, her mind exhausted and her body drained. She shut her eyes, willing sleep to come, but it didn't. So she lay there, pondering over who that golden knight was and what he wanted with her…

"Babushka…"

14

THE BIRDS WERE chirping, and the sun was shining. It was Sunday morning.

"God, please shut up!" Kelly screamed at all the noise outside her window. She threw the pillow she'd been using to cover her face towards the sound, hoping it would scare the birds away.

Chirp, chirp, chirp they continued, as if they didn't have a care in the world.

She covered her face with her arm this time, as the sun was way too bright, but the rays found a way through. Rolling onto her stomach, Kelly pulled her doona over her head, creating a makeshift cave. It was pitch-black under the covers, offering a moment of reprieve.

"Finally, some peace," said Kelly, closing her eyes. An image of the altar appeared before her, the beautiful golden knight forever asleep upon it on a bed of rosemary. "Hmm, rosemary…"

She wiggled in bed, gently rubbing her back on her bedsheets. Her shoulder blade was itchy. In the exact spot where the dried rosemary had pricked her in her dream.

"The shield." Kelly exhaled, her shoulder all but forgotten. "God, that shield was beautiful." She recalled the details and the shield reappeared in her mind. "So exquisite, wow."

Whoever fashioned that shield was a true master craftsman, thought Kelly. The intricacies were mind-blowing.

It was then that she remembered her shoulder. Opening her eyes, she threw the doona onto the ground and jumped up. Kelly tried to scratch the irritated spot but she couldn't seem to reach it, too stiff this early in the morning, and yelled out in frustration.

She scanned her room, looking for something to use, before her eyes landed on a ruler. "Yes!" Grabbing the wooden utensil, she reached over her back and rubbed her shoulder with all her might.

Rub, rub, rub but the itch didn't dissipate.

Throwing the ruler back onto her desk, Kelly sat on the edge of the bed, gave herself a bear hug, and closed her eyes. Fatigue had enveloped her. She wiped at her eyes and then her face. Today was going to be a very hard day and the lack of sleep didn't help. Kelly was irritated in her own skin, and she didn't know what to do or how she was going to get through the day. And, to make matters worse, she still had to finish her homework.

She looked at all the books piled on top of her desk. "God," she sighed, and decided she couldn't be bothered. The homework wasn't hard; her heart just wasn't in it. Her dreams kept playing and replaying in her mind.

"Who was the golden night? How did he die? Where is his tomb located?"

There were too many questions without answers.

"Babushka…" said Kelly again. She raised her arm in shock and examined where the golden knight had reached out and grabbed her. She grasped the very spot with her free hand; it felt surprisingly warm. She could still feel his touch.

How can this be? she wondered. *It was only a dream.* She shook her head, trying to convince herself.

"Grrrr." The itch on her back grew stronger, and now it was beginning to throb. Wiggling her shoulders and twisting her waist, Kelly tried to shake it off—along with her frustrations. But nothing was working or helping. It seemed to be getting worse and worse as the minutes ticked by.

Coffee. It was time for coffee. *Coffee fixes everything.*

"How silly of me to forget," announced Kelly triumphantly. This would solve all her problems. She grabbed her dressing gown, threw it on, and headed downstairs.

"Good morning, my darling," chirped Joyce as her eyes landed on Kelly.

"Hey, Mum."

Joyce was making some raisin toast for breakfast and pouring herself a cup of black coffee from the percolator when her daughter walked into the kitchen, the teenager's expression dull and gloomy. "What's wrong, hun?" she asked gently. "You didn't sleep well?"

Kelly ignored her mother's questions, as usual, and helped herself to a large mug. She walked past her mum in silence and placed the mug on the bench, waiting for her turn. Tight-lipped and without a second glance, she turned her back on the kitchen bench and leaned against it, all thoughts focused on the golden knight who evaded her dreams.

Joyce stood there, shocked and confused by her daughter's recent behaviour. She could see Kelly's mind was not here; she was preoccupied by something. However, she didn't know what it was. Joyce continued to watch her daughter's tense posturing. Kelly didn't seem relaxed or carefree. The girl fidgeted with her hair and bit her nails, spitting a piece across the kitchen on occasion.

Hmm, Joyce thought. *And the wiggling… What's going on with the wiggling?*

"Honey, are you okay?"

No answer.

Okay. Joyce sighed to herself. *Let's try again then.*

"Darling, are you okay?" This time, her voice was a tad louder, in an attempt to get an answer. And this time, there was still silence.

Kelly continued to wiggle and fidget, her mind fixated on the golden knight.

This is beyond a joke now, thought Joyce. She placed the jug of coffee back on the stand and, in frustration, reached out and grabbed her daughter by the arm to get the girl's full attention.

Kelly screamed at the top of her lungs, and Joyce immediately released her grip and took a step back in alarm. Kelly held on to the kitchen bench to steady herself. "Oh, sorry, Mum." Placing one of her hands on her chest to calm herself, Kelly took a couple of deep breaths, her cheeks pinkened by embarrassment. And, slowly and surely, her body relaxed— though she continued to fidget in place.

Joyce poured coffee into Kelly's mug, making sure it

was a generous serving. Something was telling her that her daughter needed it. "Here, darling." She passed the teenager the steamy cup.

"Thanks, Mum." Kelly grabbed the mug of pure black magic and gulped it down. After a few swigs, she slowed down and sipped, still ignoring her mum's presence.

This worried Joyce. It was unlike her daughter to be so cold. She cleared her throat and asked again, "Kelly, are you okay? What's wrong with your back? You haven't stopped wiggling since you walked in here."

Slurp, slurp, slurp. Then the message finally got through.

"I don't know, Mum, but my back is *so* itchy." Kelly wiggled while she spoke, attempting to reach behind her back and scratch her shoulder. But, for some reason, she just couldn't hit the spot. So she decided to open the kitchen drawer and pulled out a fork before quickly sticking it down the back of her pyjamas.

"Nooo!" yelled Joyce, yanking the fork back in a flash and tucking the utensil away, where it belonged. "Best we don't do that, hun. We could seriously hurt ourselves. Besides, that's not what forks are for." Joyce smiled.

"But, Mum, it's driving me crazy! I don't know how to make it stop."

"Okay, well, let's have a look. Come here." Joyce gestured for her daughter to slide over. Reluctantly, Kelly complied.

Desperate times call for desperate measures.

Joyce pulled out a chair and patted the seat, indicating for her daughter to sit. Kelly lowered herself on the chair, with her back facing her mum, and unfastened the button at the top of her pyjamas, allowing her mother to get a better look.

"Oh goodness, Kel. Take off your top!" Joyce demanded, tugging at the fabric.

"Mum!" Kelly grabbed at her shirt, hugging the material against her body. "I'm not doing that."

"Well, why not?" asked Joyce, crossing her arms in shock. "I'm your mother. Besides, I've seen a lot more than that before." She winked, grabbed the top again, and started to pull.

"Mummm, *stop*," Kelly huffed. "FORGET ABOUT IT." And immediately pushed off the chair to stand.

"Darling, it looks really bad. We need to do something about it." Joyce walked over to the kitchen table and picked up her phone. "Let's see… How about we make an appointment to go see the doctor this afternoon? Who's available?"

"Mum, no one is available. It's Sunday," said Kelly in a matter-of-fact kind of way. "Every clinic is closed. Besides, I'm not going to see a doctor today or any day." She stood her ground, crossing her arms in defiance.

"Young lady, your shoulder looks terrible and I don't like your attitude either." Joyce aimed an irritated finger at her daughter.

"What attitude?"

"The present one. Enough of it."

"Hey, girls, what's going on? Enough of what?" asked Mark out of nowhere. He'd been out for the morning and seemed to return in the nick of time. There was never a dull moment in that household, whether it was good or bad.

Joyce and Kelly both jumped in surprise. They were in deep conversation and hadn't heard the front door open or close, let alone noticed Mark when he walked into the kitchen.

"Hi, Dad. Where have you been all morning?" Kelly went up to her dad and gave him a big kiss and a huge bear hug.

"Oh, that's a good one, Kel. Thank you. I needed that, hun," said Mark, his face reddened by blush. He held his daughter for a second longer, enjoying the love and the warmth. Hugs like this were very rare, so it was better to enjoy them while they lasted. "So, girls, what's going on?" asked Mark, his expression sombre.

"Well, Daddy Dearest, your daughter has a very bad rash on her shoulder and, from what I saw, her middle back too," explained Joyce.

"Mum, it's not that bad," Kelly was quick to interrupt. She looked at her dad with those puppy-dog eyes, hoping to win him over. "Dad, it's not that bad at all." She shook her head to further argue her point.

"No, it *is* bad and it will get worse if we don't do anything about it, Mark," stated Joyce firmly. And when she used her husband's name in a sentence, it meant serious business.

Mark looked from one girl to another. He stood there, in silence, thinking and analysing each possible outcome. He was torn and didn't know what was the best thing to do. If he chose his wife's side, then his daughter would get upset and everything would fall apart. It would go back to no kisses and no cuddles, and he couldn't handle that. Besides, he'd been really worried about his girl lately, concerned about her sudden mood swings and change in attitude. On the other hand, if he chose his daughter's side, his beautiful wife would go nuts. And she probably wouldn't talk to him for a bit.

Well, that wouldn't be too bad, he thought to himself, because then he could sit and read in peace or go out to his man cave and work on one of his projects. *Oooh*. The idea was exhilarating for a split-second, but then he realised that he probably wouldn't get far into his book or with his project—guilt would make it too hard to concentrate.

Mark walked over to the kitchen table, pulled out a chair, and sat down, each of his girls waiting for him to decide. To speak. "Well, this morning, I was visiting Babushka." He opened his jacket and pulled out a small velvet pouch, placing it on the table.

"Why did you go there, Dad?" asked Kelly. "I haven't seen Babushka in a very long time."

"Funny you say that, kiddo. She said the same thing about you." Mark pushed up from his chair and went to the kettle. He flicked the switch and turned back to face his family. "I've had some stomach pains lately and I don't know why, considering I eat really well."

"Darling," said Joyce. "Are you okay? Why didn't you tell me?" She eyed her husband warily. She walked up and grabbed his hand, comforting him. "Is there anything I can do, darls?"

"No, no. Nothing to worry about here," he assured his wife and daughter at the same time. "I just didn't want to worry anyone, so I thought I might go see Babushka. That's all." He nodded his head.

"How is my Babushka and what did she say?" piped up Kelly.

"Oh, Babushka is great. It was really nice to see her. We had a good chat about things, caught up, and yeah…" Mark shrugged.

"Oh," said Kelly.

Swish, woosh, pop went the kettle. The water was nice and hot.

Mark turned around and grabbed the kettle and a mug. He walked back to his chair and placed everything on the table, like he was getting ready to do an experiment. He picked up the velvet pouch and held it in his palm, for everyone to see. "See this, girls," he said. The girls stayed silent and looked at the pouch. "This is magic."

Mark opened the pouch delicately and took out a pinch of herbs, placing it into the mug. He repeated the process twice more before looking up at his audience.

"Now, you must be thinking why three pinches?" No one answered. "Well, your body was designed with your needs in mind. For example, your feet are proportional to your height, your hands are proportional to your face, et cetera, et cetera. So, a pinch, according to Babushka, is the best way to determine how much your stomach needs. A pinch is the perfect measuring tool."

"Really?" said Kelly, surprised.

"Really," Mark confirmed with a wink. "So, in this case, we need three pinches." He picked up the mug and showed it to his girls. "Now we add hot water and mix, mix, mix." Looking around the table, Mark realised he'd forgotten to grab a spoon. "Spoon, spoon, spoon, damn…"

"Here you go, honey," replied Joyce as she handed him a silver teaspoon.

Mark stirred his concoction. *Ding-a-ling-a-ling.*

He brought the mug up to his lips, took a whiff, and poured it down the hatch. "Hmm, yum." Mark wiped his mouth with the back of his hand. *Burp.* "Oh." He rubbed his belly in what appeared to be satisfaction. "Feels better already, wow."

"Really, Dad? Is your stomach better?"

"It sure is, kiddo." He patted his belly one more time with an enormous grin. "Now, this is what we're going to do: Kelly, you're going to go to Babushka's, and you will show her your rash."

"Oh, Dad, come on. I have homework to do," the teenager whined. "Oooof."

"Now, now, don't be like that, kiddo," said Mark. "You saw the miracle that just happened." He pointed to the velvet pouch and then to his stomach. "That magical potion cured me and all it took was a short and pleasant trip to Babushka's and back. That's it." Kelly stared at her father, her expression cross. Mark noticed his daughter's sour attitude and decided to ignore it as well as the anxiety that was building inside him. He looked at his watch and continued, "If you go now, after you get changed of course, you will be there and back in say... thirty minutes max."

"Oh, Dad, really?" pleaded Kelly.

"Really. Now chop, chop. Otherwise, it's a long wait in the emergency department, and I'm not going to sit there for seven hours. And I don't think you'd want to either, since you have homework to do."

Kelly looked at her dad—she sure as hell wasn't going to look at her mum because she already knew what side Joyce was on and it wasn't hers. Without saying a word, the teenager pivoted on her heel and went back upstairs to her room to change. Stomping, huffing, and puffing the entire way.

This better take less than thirty minutes, she thought to herself, *because I have better things to do.*

Mark sat at the kitchen table and grabbed his belly, agony written all over his face.

"What's wrong, darling?" asked Joyce for the second time that morning.

"Can you please get me some orange juice, hun. I'm about to dry retch. Those herbs were disgusting and now my belly really, really hurts." Mark keeled over in pain. Joyce handed her husband a glass of cold orange juice and he gulped it down within seconds. "Ah, much, much better." Licking his lips, he upturned the glass once again, trying to gulp down the last remnants of the fluid.

"I thought you said you felt better?"

"I did," said Mark. "But I lied about the taste. I had to." He stopped speaking abruptly and checked to see if anyone in particular was eavesdropping. Thankfully, no one was within earshot so he continued. "Look, darling, I overheard your entire conversation with Kel, and I figured the only way to get her to see someone about her rash was to play a trick or offer a little white lie." Joyce didn't say anything in response; she just stood there and listened. "I'm worried about our daughter and I don't know what to do." Mark looked at his wife and then at his belly, shifting in his chair in discomfort.

"Me too, darling," said Joyce. "I've noticed a change in her and I don't like it."

"Then better we don't butt heads with her and argue, otherwise things could escalate very quickly and take a turn for the worst." Mark rubbed his belly vigorously. "Ohhh."

"You okay, hun?"

Mark shifted in his chair again, rocking from cheek to cheek. He continued to rub his belly, clockwise then counterclockwise. Something was brewing inside. He rocked left and he rocked right. He swayed a little bit farther, leaning more to one side than the other and then… without any warning…

BRAP.

The volcano erupted. First came the vicious pong of noxious gases, which wafted through the air like the Angel of Death, killing even the most innocent of bugs found hovering within the airspace. *Kerplunk.* Dead on arrival. Once the deadly fumes were all released, then came the fireworks. And, boy, were there fireworks in Mark's pants—the man himself stopped to thank the gods at this point, grateful that he was wearing brown.

As the "lava" started to spill, the pants absorbed the brunt of the carnage, meaning that any innocent bystanders wouldn't have noticed what was happening, the fabric serving as the perfect camouflage,

"Ah, oh, ah," cried Mark in both agony and relief, holding tight to his belly. Joyce stood there in utter shock, unable to move. There was silence. The show was over and Mark breathed a sigh of relief and content. "Phew, oh my God," he said. "Wow, I feel so much better." He attempted to rise from his chair but Joyce stopped him.

"Nooo, do not move!" she screamed and ran out of the kitchen. Within a second, she came back with a tarp, gloves, safety goggles, and a garbage bag. Placing the tarp on the floor, she gave her husband strict instructions, telling him step by step what he was going to do. She repeated herself, making sure everything was crystal clear, before the delicate operation began. "Oh, God," she muttered under her breath.

Mark noticed her frustration and he vowed to make it up to his beautiful wife... *somehow*. He smiled to himself, chuckled a little, and said, "See? Babushka can fix anything, hun." And then he stood up.

~

Ding-dong went Babushka's doorbell.

Kelly stood outside the old woman's front door, feeling angry and frustrated, much more than she had before.

God, why do I need to do this, she thought.

Ding-dong. She pressed the buzzer again, wiggling on the spot to try to shake out the itch on her shoulder and back.

"Grrr." She was becoming impatient, and everything was starting to affect her. She looked down at her watch and sighed. "At this rate, I'll be here for thirty years not thirty minutes." She was about to ring the doorbell again when suddenly it opened. And there, standing before her, covered in flower and dough, stood Babushka.

"Sorry, dear, but I'm covered in goop and now look what I have done." Babushka turned and pointed down the hallway. "I've left a trail of havoc, and guess who's the silly duffer who has to clean that up?"

Kelly peered down the hallway, then back to Babushka. The teenager was embarrassed and didn't know what to say in response. "Arrr, aw, arrr..." She shrugged her shoulders.

"Baaaa," said Babushka. "It's me. I'm the silly duffer." And she let out a huge rumble of laughter, which made her belly wobble and the black hairs on her chin shimmy and dance. "Well, look at you, my dear." She eyed Kelly with her good right eye, smirked, and held out her doughy hands— some dough dislodging and crumbling to the floor.

Kelly didn't know what to do. All of a sudden, she felt like that scared little girl who was sent to this mysterious old lady's house for the first time, and she trembled at the thought.

Jeez, that was so long ago, she thought to herself.

"Well, come here, child," said Babushka, losing patience while shaking her outstretched hands.

Kelly looked at the hands in front of her, hesitated for a split-second, then dove into her fairy godmother's arms. The sensation was instant. Warmth, love, and many, many happy memories rushed back. All the fun and laughter. Those were some of the happiest days of her life, and she smiled.

"Well, there she is! My child has returned to me," said Babushka, wiping a tear from her eye. "You're so grown up, dear." She patted Kelly on the arm. "And beautiful too," she added with a wink.

"You are beautiful also, Baba," said Kelly, smiling at her favourite fairy godmother.

"Oh, dear me, look at what I've done now." The old woman grabbed Kelly's jacket and started to rub away the flour and some of the goop. "Oh!" Babushka stomped her foot. "I've made it worse now. Come, come inside and I will get that cleaned up." She ushered Kelly into her house and closed the door behind them. Squeezing by, she asked Kelly to follow her into the kitchen. "Ignore the mess, my child." She waved her hands about. "I've been making cookies and muffins for one of the local primary schools." Babushka picked up a few dirty bowls scattered about the kitchen and placed them neatly into the sink. She grabbed a wet rag, wrung it out, and started wiping the bench. "The school is having a raffle tomorrow and needed some donations from the community." She placed the rag into the sink when she was finished. "So, you know me, darling. I'm always happy to help in any way that I can."

Bing went the oven.

"Perfect timing!"

When that oven door opened, the most incredible, sweet, luscious, and aromatic smell filled the room. It was so scrumptious and inviting that Kelly closed her eyes and inhaled. Fireworks erupted in her mind, fairies danced around her head, and she felt as light as a feather. Babushka pulled out the freshly cooked muffins and placed them on mesh trays to cool.

"Beautiful," she said.

When Kelly opened her eyes again, she was so excited and her mouth was watering. "Baba, these look absolutely amazing. You haven't lost your touch." She salivated uncontrollably and licked her lips at the sight.

"Ah, thank you, my child." Babushka smiled at her girl. "Tea time!" She picked up the teakettle, filled it up, and placed it on the stove. "So, darling, did your daddy send you?" she asked with a cheeky grin.

"What? How did you know that?" Kelly questioned in shock.

"Oh, honey, I'm your fairy godmother. We always know everything. Now, tell me what brought you here?" The old woman got straight to the point. With Babushka, there was never any beating around the bush. Everything was always black and white, and she always said it how it was.

Kelly leaned against the kitchen bench and placed her hands in her jacket for comfort. "Well, Dad said you could help me, Baba."

"Of course. Always happy to help."

The kettle started to boil and it rattled a little on the stove, signalling that it was almost ready. Babushka took out two mugs from the cupboard and gave them a little wipe, making sure there was no dust inside.

"Herbal or black tea, darling?" she asked Kelly.

"Ah, may I please have peppermint?"

Babushka didn't respond to her request, only nodding while waiting patiently for Kelly to explain her appearance today.

The girl fidgeted a little, wiggled her back, and quickly twisted her waist from side to side. "Mum says I have a very bad rash on my back, and Dad reckons that you could probably give me something to sooth it."

Errrrrr, bubble, bubble, bubble went the kettle.

Babushka picked up the kettle and mumbled under her breath, "Turn off the stove, check." She filled up the mugs with warm water and handed one to Kelly, along with a spoon and a canister of sugar. "Help yourself, dearie," she added. Walking back to the stove, she opened the oven, quickly looked inside, and muttered, "Oven fire off, check."

"What are you doing, Baba? Are you all right?"

"Of course, my dear, just taking extra precautions. That's all, my child." And no further explanation was given. Babushka grabbed her mug of tea and took a sip.

Kelly stared at the muffins, finding it very difficult to concentrate. Babushka noticed and handed the girl a small dessert plate with a wink, which Kelly eagerly accepted. And, without thinking twice, the teenager helped herself to a mouth-watering sweet delight. It was still warm to the touch but she didn't care. She couldn't wait a second longer, so she grabbed it, opened her mouth wide like a python, and took a humongous bite. If she could, she would have swallowed it whole—that's how good it was.

"Mmm," Kelly moaned, her mouth full. "Sooo good. Mmm." *Hiccup, hiccup, hiccup.*

Babushka stopped sipping her tea. "Slow down, child. There's plenty."

"Sorry, Baba, it's just that it's so good," said Kelly, wiping her face and shoving large crumbs back into her mouth. "It's been such a long time since I've had your muffins. I've forgotten how good they truly are. Mmmm."

Sip, sip, sip.

"Okay, I have a rash on my shoulder and my back, and it's extremely uncomfortable, Baba." Kelly placed her mug on the kitchen bench and took off her jacket. Draping it over her chair, she turned around and lifted her T-shirt, no longer embarrassed or shy.

Babushka cleared her dirt-flecked glasses with the hem of her skirt, making sure she would be able to examine the rash thoroughly. The last thing she wanted to do was give the incorrect potion. "Ahhh," she said. Gently touching the rash, she squinted her eyes a little, the bright kitchen lights obscuring her view. "Come and stand here in the sunlight, by the window." It was important to know the true colour of the rash in natural light, so that nothing would be hidden and anything sinister would be visible. "Such an unusual rash, hmmm," said Babushka after a couple of minutes. "I've not seen one like this here."

"Here? What do you mean, Baba?" asked Kelly in alarm. "Where have you seen one of these if not here?"

Babushka lifted her head in disbelief. She wasn't thinking properly, and with all the episodes with her memory of late, she'd forgotten where she was for a split-second. She thought she was back on Saphira, not on earth. "Ah, err, arr," she replied in a panic. She grabbed Kelly's T-shirt, pulling it back down. "Oh, nothing, child. Nothing at all.

Kelly noticed Babushka's strange behaviour all of a sudden. She turned around and stared at the old woman questioningly.

"Go sit on the couch, child, and I will grab some special ointment that I keep in the fridge." Babushka ushered Kelly into the lounge room. The girl did as she was told while Babushka opened her fridge and stuck her head inside. She exhaled, pretending to riffle through some jars and plates in an attempt to buy some time. "Now, where is that ointment?" she intentionally said out loud.

Kelly sat on the couch and rubbed her eyes. It had been an eventful morning, and it seemed like more events were unfolding. She took a deep breath and exhaled. Removing her hands from her eyes, she opened them to an incredible sight. On the coffee table, in front of her, sat an intricately and stunningly crafted gold and blue bejewelled necklace. It wasn't the workmanship that caught her eye; it was the bright-blue glow emanating from it.

"Nearly there, child!" yelled Babushka, still pretending to shuffle items around the fridge with her head buried deep inside.

But Kelly didn't hear anything. Not a word, nor a peep. She was mesmerised by the beauty of the glow. She picked up the piece of jewellery and stood, holding the necklace delicately in both hands with her back turned to Babushka.

"Ah, here it is," lied Babushka. She took a deep breath,

pulled her head out of the fridge, shook off the cold, and shut the door. She was on a mission. While her head was submerged in the fridge, she'd concocted a plan. She was ready. She knew exactly what to say and off she marched.

Stomp, stomp, stomp, stomp.

"Look what I've found, child," she said to Kelly, who'd yet to face her. "This ointment will help that rash. Turn around, child. I want to show you." Babushka removed the lid, dipped her fingers into the glass tub, and rubbed the cool texture between the tips. "Now, there are many incredible ingredients that go into this, child," she continued. "Some I won't mention… Babushka giggled anxiously while she continued to babble.

Kelly realised that Babushka was behind her and slowly turned, still staring at the gemstone as she did so. When she finally faced the old woman, she raised the necklace to her oblivious fairy godmother and said, "What is this?"

"…It has dead bat wing. Well, that isn't too gory, I'd say. And a touch of ox blood—yes, ox blood," said Babushka, looking up to the ceiling as she ticked off the ingredients on her fingertips. "Also, some—oh!" The bright-blue light had finally caught her attention. She looked at the necklace and stared in wonder, instinctively extending her hand while not believing what she was seeing. "How… how can this be?" She looked at Kelly and then back to the necklace.

This was all too much to handle and her mind started to reel. She was feeling dizzy and faint. Grabbing her head, Babushka took several quick breaths, trying to steady herself, but it didn't help. The room began to spin. Quicker and quicker, it went. Babushka was sweating and her heart was racing. Her legs buckled and she fell.

Kerplunk.

The last words she spoke to Kelly before she hit the floor were: "He was right. He found you."

And then there was darkness.

15

KELLY DROPPED THE necklace back onto the coffee table. "Babushka," she screamed. "No!" Instinctively, she lowered herself to the floor and took charge. Her heart was racing like a wild animal but she knew she had to stay calm. She had to save her beloved fairy godmother.

And thank God they spent a couple of days at school learning all about CPR and what to do if someone needed help.

"Okay," said Kelly to herself. "The first thing is: stay calm." She took a deep breath and exhaled, steadying herself. "Stay calm, Kel," she repeated.

Kelly examined the area to make sure it was safe. Thankfully, there was nothing close by that could harm Babushka while she lay unconscious on the floor.

"Babushka, Babushka!" There was no response. "No!" she yelled out. "Please, Baba." Tears started to well up in her eyes. It hurt Kelly to see Babushka on the floor. This wasn't her fairy godmother; it couldn't be.

Kelly always remembered her Baba as a happy, full of life, strong, and resilient lady. She was tough but she had a heart of gold. And she was invincible. Seeing her now, unconscious, felt like a bad dream. A nightmare. And all she wanted was for Babushka to wake up. Kelly gently grasped Babushka's shoulder and gave it a squeeze, hoping it would stir the old woman. But there was no response.

"Damn," she cried. She grabbed her mobile from her jacket and dialled triple zero. The phone rang once and straightaway an emergency consultant answered. "Please, I need an ambulance at 23 Crammer Street. Hurry!" screamed Kelly, with tears running freely down her face.

"Calm down, miss," said the person on the other side. "Tell me what happened?"

While Kelly recounted the events to the consultant, she checked Babushka's mouth and throat, making sure they were clear. The great news was that Babushka was breathing and this made Kelly's heart skip a beat, so she rolled her fairy godmother over and placed her in a recovery position.

"Great job, young lady," said the consultant. "An ambulance has been dispatched and will be arriving within a minute."

"Thank you," said Kelly, and she hung up her mobile. Kelly exhaled and rubbed her forehead. It was starting to really throb. She was relieved that she remembered what to do. She often wondered if learning CPR and first aid was worth it. She always thought that she would be one of those people who'd freeze in such a situation or wouldn't remember what to do. But she proved herself wrong and thank God for that.

In that moment, Kelly felt proud *and* relieved that Babushka seemed to be okay and breathing fine. She just wished the old woman would wake up.

Ding-dong went the doorbell.

Kelly ran to the front door and opened it. "Quick, quick, please," she pleaded, ushering the paramedics into the house. She ran down the hallway, leading them to Babushka.

"Okay, step aside, miss," said one of the men. Another dropped his medical bag on the floor and started to examine the patient, checking her pulse while asking Kelly questions every now and then. "Who are you, miss, and what are you to the patient?" asked paramedic one.

"My name is Kelly and Lilliana is my f—godmother," she stammered as she corrected herself.

"Okay, Kelly, do you know if your godmother has been sick lately or if she suffers from any illnesses?" asked paramedic number two as he attached a pulse oximeter to Babushka's arm.

"Ah, err, I don't know," said Kelly. She shrugged her shoulders and shook her head. "I haven't seen her in a bit…" Kelly's face turned red. "But today she seemed fine to me."

Both paramedics continued to do their work as Kelly answered anything they threw her way. They worked quickly and thoroughly.

"Vital signs are all good," said paramedic one, reading off the machine. "Blood pressure is okay, a little low, but still okay."

"What about O2 saturation?" asked paramedic number two.

"Yep, O2 saturation is also normal," responded his partner.

All this information was gibberish to Kelly; it didn't make any sense. If everything was normal, then why wasn't

Babushka waking up? The teenager curled her hands into fists; the frustration deep inside her was starting to bubble and it was going to explode.

"What's going on?" asked Kelly. "Why isn't she waking up?" She ignored the paramedics instructions to remain out of their way, ran to her godmother, and knelt beside her, not caring if this angered the paramedics or not, as her heart hurt and she felt helpless. "Oh, Baba," she said in a breathy whisper. Kelly swept aside some of the stray hairs that covered Babushka's face. She stroked her head, hoping the old woman would open her eyes. "Come on, Baba. It's me, Kelly. Open your eyes," she pleaded.

The paramedics could sense the girl's pain. "Miss, everything will be okay. Look. Her vital signs are good and there is a pulse," said paramedic number two as he placed his hand on Kelly's shoulder, trying to give her some reassurance and hope.

"Let's get the stretcher and transport her," stated paramedic number one.

"What!" screamed Kelly in alarm. "No!"

"We can't do any more for her here. The hospital will help her wake up, so we need to move her," explained paramedic number two, distracting Kelly as his team member slipped out the front door to collect the trolley.

"Oh, okay." Kelly continued to stroke Babushka's hair.

Trrrr, woop, trrrr went the wheels of the trolley.

Kelly didn't watch. She just sat there on the floor, staring at her fairy godmother, terrified that she was never going to see her smile again or hear her beautiful voice.

Gently, paramedic two asked Kelly to move aside.

"Come here. Let us help your godmother. I promise to take good care of her."

The teenager pushed to her feet and moved out of the way. After that, everything was a complete blur. Within seconds, Babushka was strapped on the trolley and loaded into the ambulance with Kelly by her side.

"Okay, is everyone buckled in? We're about to head off," said the driver.

"Oh, wait!" yelled Kelly. "I forgot my phone."

She quickly ran inside the house and grabbed her phone, which she'd left on the floor. She was about to rush out again when she realised people would be wondering where Babushka was, as her house had been left in a shemozzle. The muffins were tossed on the kitchen counter, now cool. And dirty pots, pans, and trays were piled up in the sink. That wasn't like Baba. Plus, with the raffle tomorrow, the school would probably want to know where the muffins were.

What should I do? thought Kelly.

"Ah, I know! I will leave a note." She rummaged through the nearest kitchen drawer, found a notepad, and quickly scribbled a summary:

> Babushka is sick. She fainted and couldn't be revived. I called the ambulance to have her taken to hospital. If you need more information, please call Kelly at 0408 123 456.

"Perfect," she said after she reread the message. She placed her pen down with a *thud* and ran out the front door, locking it behind her.

～

"Is she going to be okay?" asked Kelly as Babushka was

wheeled into the emergency department. Doctors flew from all sections, coming out of rooms she didn't even notice. They swarmed like vultures on a dead carcass.

Electric devices were attached to Baba's chest, a blood pressure device was applied, and they even checked her eyes with a bright torch. But none of the noise nor any of the commotion helped to wake the old woman. Kelly stood there, frozen like a dear in headlights, doctors weaving in and out all around her.

A nurse embraced Kelly by the shoulders and gently walked the girl to the waiting room. "Come and sit here, honey. It's better you don't see all of that," assured the kind nurse as she led Kelly to a comfy chair.

"What will happen to her?" asked Kelly. "Will she wake up?"

The nurse held Kelly's hand and gave it a slight squeeze. "They are great doctors, my darling, and they will do everything they can to help your grandmother."

"She's my fairy godmother," blurted Kelly, without thinking twice.

The woman smiled and winked. "Well then, she is magic, so I'm sure she will wake up. Is there anyone I can call for you? To come and keep you company, my dear."

Kelly liked this lady as she seemed warm, kind, and caring. Her concern helped ease the pain; the teenager started to feel calmer and hopeful. "No, thank you," said Kelly. "I just want to sit and wait for some news before I call anyone. I don't want anyone to panic and worry."

The nurse patted Kelly on the knee and stood. "Okay, honey, if you change your mind, don't hesitate to come and ask me." The woman pointed to her name badge. "My name is Blanche."

"Thank you, Blanche. You're very kind. Oh, my name is Kelly, by the way." And she extended her hand politely as she felt safe and comfortable.

Blanche gently accepted her greeting and shook the girl's palm. "Nice to meet you, Kelly, even though it's under unfortunate circumstances." The nurse smiled at the girl one last time and walked back to her station.

Babushka lay very still on her bed while all the doctors ran around her like chooks with their heads cut off. She could hear them, but they all sounded muffled and felt like they were miles and miles away. She tried to open her eyes but they seemed to be glued shut. To be honest, she didn't mind it, because she felt extremely tired. Worn out. All she wanted to do was to sleep. Sleep forever…

Where was she? Whatever this place was called, she didn't care that she was there. For the first time, in a long time, Babushka felt at peace. Everything she'd been holding in, every tear and every single ounce of pain, didn't matter anymore. She felt free.

Oh, what about the companions? she thought. *And what about my dear friend Vlad?* Her heart began to ache, and immediately she felt guilty.

Babushka loved her friend Vlad, her mini MacGyver. She loved watching that show with him, watching all the cool ideas and groovy things the main character, Richard MacGyver, would make out of nothing. It was so inspirational, and the best part of all was how it made Vlad come alive. His whole face would light up like a Christmas tree, and his eyes would shine ever so brightly, like they were the star that topped it all off. You could see that his mind was ticking, thinking, analysing, wondering what he could try next as the possibilities were endless. Babushka loved that. It made her heart sing, to see her dear friend so happy.

Happy… Ah, the good old days when all of us were truly happy—when was that?

Their arrival here on earth was abrupt. But it had to be done. If they all didn't escape through the portal, who knows what would have happened? They'd be dead. Or worse…

A tear ran down Babushka's cheek. The pain of that day felt raw once again, like it all happened yesterday.

It's all my fault. It's all my fault… My powers were not strong enough to save him. I'm a fake. I'm a fraud. She whimpered in her half-conscious state, slamming her hand down on the bed. *And here I have no powers at all. I'm nothing… I was nothing and now I am nothing.*

The rage she felt deep inside her erupted. It had to come out; it needed to be released. So, with all her might and all her anger, Babushka balled her hands into fists and started pummelling again and again, each blow harder than the last. The frustration was bubbling and the anger was boiling, and it all erupted like a massive volcano. It was so relieving. And for the first time, in a long time, she was starting to feel better. Lighter. Her legs joined in and danced; they didn't want to miss out on the party. Babushka kicked her legs high up into the air and then brought them down hard and fast.

"Hi-yah!" she called out and it felt good. Cathartic. "Let's shake all the cobwebs out once and for all." She decided to bang her head on the bed. The only downfall was that there was no pillow, and by the sixth time, her head hurt a little but it was worth it.

"Oh, watch out!" said one doctor. "We might be seizing. Everyone step back for a second…"

"We're going into a full-body cronic seizure! Rails up on the bed and be ready to steady the patient," yelled out the head doctor in the emergency department, as they all watched Babushka hitting the bed viciously with her fists and kicking her legs, flailing like a wild animal. She bashed her head against the pillow-less mattress as if she were possessed by the devil himself.

What a sight it was. They all stood there, with their mouths open, bewildered by the scene before them. They'd never seen anything quite like it…

Babushka continued to wiggle like a madman. She huffed and puffed, but she didn't care. It hurt but she didn't care, as the pain of the last forty years was much greater than the pain she felt now. Living with the image of the dying king haunted her and a little pain while she wiggled, hit, flipped, and banged her body was nothing compared to that memory. Fatigue eventually kicked in and Babushka slowed down. Her breathing was heavy and her heart raced—it felt like it was going to explode.

Go ahead! she thought. *Explode, end my misery.*

And she hit her chest, hoping that was the final blow needed to end her existence. But it wasn't her time. Not just yet. And, deep down, Babushka knew it. It hurt because all she wanted was for the pain to end. She wanted her heart to stop hurting. She wanted her friends, the companions, to stop hurting.

Oh, Wymann, my dear friend, I understand your pain and your loss of faith. I understand… I feel it too and have for so long.

She sighed and laid very still on the bed, looking straight ahead. Into nothing.

"Okay, the seizure has stopped and it was a long one," said the doctor in charge. He turned to the nearest aide. "Nurse, let's administer some anti-seizure medication and run some blood tests. We need to get on top of things and see what's really going on here."

The aide nodded and took action. "Yes, doctor."

It was mayhem in the emergency department that day. There were countless patients who'd been brought in by ambulance. Some were unconscious, like Babushka, but others were either screaming in pain or crying from shock. But one thing was certain; they all would receive the help they needed in order to get better.

The head doctor grabbed the phone at the nurse's desk and dialled number three. He looked out at the waiting room, scanning all the people waiting for news about their loved ones.

"Hello, MRI department," said a voice on the other end.

"Ah, yes, hello. This is Dr Brown, and I would like to schedule an emergency MRI for an elderly patient who was brought in by ambulance. When can you do this, please?"

This doctor did not muck around. He did everything within his power and knowledge to help people straightaway. He was also very polite. And most of all, Dr Brown relied on his gut. His gut never lied to him and it wasn't indigestion or gas. His gut gave him hunches and these hunches had saved many, many lives in the past, and right now his gut was telling him that problems lie within Babushka's head. And the only way they were going to get an answer was by doing an MRI.

"We can do it right now, Dr Brown," said the voice.

"Wonderful, I will get the little old lady wheeled up to you right now. Thank you." And he hung up the phone.

Little old lady, thought Kelly. She immediately perked up like a meercat, head popping up. *POP.* And she propelled herself right off the chair she'd been sitting on for the past hour and flew like a rocket straight up to the nurse's station.

"Doc, Doc," yelled Kelly. She banged her hands on the bench, trying to get the man's attention.

Bang, splat, bang went her palms. The doctor turned around and looked in her direction, his eyebrows furrowed at the noise and commotion. He pointed to the sign against the wall.

No noise please or you will be escorted out.

Kelly read to sign and halted her hands midair. She looked at the doctor and smiled nervously. "Please, Doc, I overheard you saying something about a little old lady. That has to be my fairy godmother."

"Is this a joke, kid, because I don't have time for jokes," the doctor said, clearly unamused.

Kelly waved her hands, trying to reassure him that this was no joke. "Please, Doc, my godmother was brought in by ambulance and I need to know if she's all right," she pleaded.

The doctor looked at his chart and then at Kelly. "What's your godmother's name?" he asked, unsure if this girl was related to the patient he'd been treating.

"It's Lilliana, and she has long grey hair and a mole on her left cheek." Kelly thought about what else she could say about Babushka's appearance. "She has the greenest of eyes and she is very short... shorter than me."

The doctor looked at his paperwork once again, confirming that the details on the chart seemed to match. There was no licence on the patient, so they couldn't verify the old woman's identity. But because the teenager could describe her godmother, he believed this girl was definitely her family. This satisfied the doctor. "Okay, young lady, we have stabilised your godmother. She's had a very bad seizure while in the emergency department."

"Seizure?" said Kelly, placing her hand on her chest in shock.

"Yes, seizure. Did you know she suffered from seizures?" asked Dr Brown.

Taken aback by this news, Kelly didn't know what to say. "Ahh, err, ahh..." she stuttered, shaking her head.

This must be a joke, Kelly thought. *Baba is not sick. She can't be sick. We all need Baba.*

The doctor could see the distress on Kelly's face. "Where are your parents, young lady? I need to speak to them about your godmother." He looked down at his watch and back to the girl. He felt a little guilty as he needed to return to the emergency department, so he could continue to help the sick.

"Look, Doc," said Kelly. "My parents aren't here yet, but I have called them and they are on their way," she lied. "Tell me what's going to happen and I will fill them in when they arrive. Please," she added for politeness, clasping her hands in prayer.

The doctor knew it was best to speak to an adult, in order to properly relay what was happening in the emergency department. But, at the moment, time was of the essence. And to be honest, his heart went out to the girl. "We don't know exactly what's happening to your godmother," said the doctor. He glanced down at his chart, read a couple of facts, and continued. "We've stabilised her by giving her some anti-seizure medication for now. Her vital signs and oxygen saturation appear normal and stable."

"So what's happening to her?" asked Kelly, still confused.

"We're going to take her up to level three to have an emergency MRI done of her head and brain."

"MRI…?" said Kelly. "That full-on? Oh my God… is she going to die, Doc?" The tears started to well in her eyes and a lump grew in her throat, forcing her to stop verbalising the questions she was desperately trying to ask.

The doctor reached out and held Kelly's hand. "Young lady, I know this is hard, believe me. But your godmother is in the best place possible," he assured her. Kelly looked away and down at her shoes. She felt helpless. "There are specialists here, with state-of-the-art equipment that can help her." He smiled gently. "Is there anyone I can call, until your parents arrive?"

Kelly sighed. "No thanks, Doc. I'll just sit here and wait. Thanks for your help though." Kelly smiled back at the doctor and returned to her chair. There was no way she was going to leave Babushka's side—*no way at all*. She would wait here as long as it took. All Kelly wanted was for her fairy godmother to wake up and be okay.

⁓

The doctor returned to Babushka's bedside. She was all alone. No one was there with her; no one was poking and prodding her. He made sure she was safely secured before one of the orderlies came to collect her.

Check, all good.

"Knock, knock. Doctor, are we ready to go?" said the orderly.

"We sure are. Thank you for coming down."

"No problem at all. Once all the scans are done, we will transfer the patient to recovery and get the results straight to you," said the orderly as he wheeled Babushka out of the emergency department.

Babushka continued to lie still as she stared into nothing. She felt like she was floating, even though there was no water. And she felt warm, even though there was no fire. Odder still, she felt safe, even though this place was unfamiliar.

Dear me, what's going to happen? she asked herself. *What's going to happen to us all?*

Flashes of the companions appeared before her. Her friends, who'd stood beside her ever since they'd been flung out of the portal she'd created. Friends who'd helped and supported her no matter what.

What's going to happen to you all?

The hospital bed popped out of the elevator on level three—the MRI department—as planned, the orderly ensuring Babushka was okay and kept warm while properly covered by her blanket. He had a soft spot for her as she reminded him of his grandmother. He extended his security tag on his retractable pocket clip and flashed the barcode under the red censor. The door automatically opened, allowing him access into an *authorised personal only* area. Then he wheeled Babushka through; they had arrived at their destination.

"Knock, knock. Patient 505173 has been delivered for an emergency MRI," he stated to the tech at reception.

"Oh, hi, Seb. How are you today?" greeted the tech in a cheery voice.

"Good, mate, how are you? Busy day?" asked Seb, always happy to have a quick chat with a fellow staff member.

The tech punched a few keys on a computer and signed some paperwork before he took the patient in for her MRI. "Nah, not busy today." He walked over to the trolley and had a look at Babushka. "Righty-o, I will take it from here and thanks for bringing her up." He gave a nod and a wink of gratitude.

Seb nodded in return and headed back down to the emergency department, hoping that this lovely little old lady would be okay. She somehow pulled on his heartstrings, and he made a mental note to call his grandmother during his lunch break just to make sure she was okay.

Tears filled Babushka's eyes as the images of her friends continued to appear. It hurt seeing them. It hurt because she now felt like she had failed them too.

She screamed internally. *Sniff, sniff.* And cried.

I'm sorry for failing you. I'm so sorry…

The tech wheeled Babushka into the MRI scanning room; the machine was ready to go. Along with a colleague, he gently rolled Babushka onto her side and placed a wooden plank on top of the hospital bed. This plank was going to aid the techs so that they could safely transport the patient from one bed to another. And it did just that.

Babushka continued to blub, the tears falling down her cheeks like waterfalls.

The techs placed Babushka head-first onto the motorised bed. It was her brain that needed the scan, so it was her head that was going to enter the large magnetic tube first.

"Okay, everyone ready?" asked tech number one.

"Affirmative," said tech number two.

"Good, then we are ready to go." He flicked a couple of switches, pressed a few buttons, and the machine came alive while the motorised bed slowly entered the magnetic tube.

P-please, f-forgive m-me, my dear friends, Babushka cried out to the void, stuttering from the pain and the anguish of failing her friends.

Zew, zew, whoosh, whoosh went the MRI machine as it swallowed Babushka's head. Even though the techs were behind a wall of plasterboard and glass, the noise emitting from the machine was still incredibly loud. But, of course, it would be even louder for the patient lying on the motorised bed. It was so loud, in fact, that it sounded like a rock concert.

The whooshing continued. The magnet was on in the tube, working and doing its magic. A powerful magnetic field was charging and growing stronger and stronger with each whoosh.

Sniff, sniff went Babushka, the snot dribbling down her nose and into her mouth. But she didn't care. In that moment, she didn't care if she swallowed it and vomited all over herself.

Woosh, whoosh, whoosh went the machine. The magnetic field was strong. It was charged and it was ready.

Babushka cried. *Ah, I'm so sorry, my dear friends. Please end all this pain. Please end all the agony!*

Sniff, sniff, hiccup, sniff.

Oh, Wymann, I'm sorry I doubted you. I am so sorry. Babushka's eyes were blurry from the tears, as they were rapidly filling her eyes and streaming down her cheeks.

"STOP!" boomed a loud voice. "It was not your fault."

It was firm but gentle, and the speaker had piped up out of nowhere within the nothing. It frightened Babushka, halting her cries.

Was this the end? she wondered. *The end she'd hoped for, for so long.*

"Wake up, Lilliana," said the voice. "You must believe again."

Believe? Believe in what?

As if reading her mind, the stranger replied on cue, "Your magic. Believe in your magic."

"Oh, I can't. It has failed and left me." She swallowed hard and then continued, afraid to admit the truth. "I never deserved the magic and I don't deserve it now," she whispered in her mind. A freak gust of air rose from nowhere within the nothingness while sparks of energy zapped here and there. It seemed like some sort of portal was forming. Babushka opened her eyes wide.

What is happening? This must be a dream—no, a nightmare, she thought.

"We're ready to take the images," said tech number one. "Let's do this and then go on our break."

"Great, let's," said tech two.

Tick, tick, tick went the keys on the keyboard as images of a Babushka's brain and head materialised on the screen.

"Beautiful," said tech number one.

More sparks and energy began to appear. The gust blew stronger and Babushka's hair flew wildly, whipping her cheeks again and again. It was painful. She covered her face with her hands, shielding it against the blows. Energy crackled loudly in the distance, thunder rumbled, the wind blew and blew. And then, as it reached its peak, *KABOOOM*. A fiery portal exploded right above Babushka's bed, some ten meters from her head.

She screamed, too scared to even take a peek, and didn't remove her hands from her face, her breaths short and frantic. Suddenly, a beautiful, white, majestic light appeared. It glowed ever so brightly, taking away all fears and all pain as it spread throughout the nothingness. It engulfed Lilliana and smothered her with its radiance.

"Oh!" she said without fear, feeling the warmth. She removed her hands, no longer afraid. But the beautiful, iridescent light was too bright for her eyes so she squinted. Luckily, her eyes adjusted. There was something special about this light. And when her gaze settled upon the portal, she knew exactly why—it belonged to the Sage of Light.

He stood in the centre of the portal and he was radiant, divine, and dressed in his ceremonial golden robes. Babushka stared at him. After all this time, he hadn't changed at all.

"I've found you, Lilliana, thanks to this magnetic field, and I am here to deliver a message."

My God, was the Sage of Light beautiful, thought Babushka.

She was just a girl, running away from the children in the village. They were all taunting her, teasing her, and calling her names. Cruel names. And some were throwing rocks, yelling for her to go jump into a river to be washed away. All evil should be washed away is what the children chanted. They chased her into the woods, thinking that the ugly and dangerous creatures who lived there would eat her up. Or better yet, that she would get lost forever, never finding her way home again. But Lilliana knew the woods better than anyone else. Upon entry, she hid, safely tucked away from the cruel children, and that's when she met the Sage of Light for the first time.

He appeared to her while she was hiding and trembling deep within the hole of a mighty oak tree. He urged her to come out, as it was safe. The children had gone. She'd trusted him instantly. When she came out, he smiled at her and she saw the energy that flowed around him. The magic.

"You are special, Lilliana," said the sage while wiping away all her tears. "Be strong and feel the energy within. Embrace it and let the magic flow through you."

Lilliana smiled and her whole heart filled with joy. She felt the energy and she truly felt special. The sage held out his hands and Babushka took them. A *buzz* and a *whoosh*, then a gust of wind blew all around them and sparks of energy crackled through the air. A vision appeared in her mind and what she saw was a beautiful woman with the whitest of white hair. She wore a golden crown of ivy upon her brow. Delicate, silky, white robes adorned her body, covering her from head to toe. She held a powerful staff in her left hand, and atop that staff was an orb glowing brightly. Emitting magic. And in her right hand, suspended on a chain of pure gold, was the medallion of light.

Babushka blinked, and the vision was gone. She looked at the sage, confused and clearly not understanding the significance of what she saw. She trembled.

What does this mean? she thought.

The sage squeezed her hands, Babushka caught his eyes, and they stared at each other. "One day you will understand. Don't be afraid, my child, when that day comes."

Babushka pinched herself on the arm, worried that she was imagining this moment. Now, here, within the void.

Pinch. "Ouch," she whispered to herself. A small smile of hope appeared on her face.

No, this is all real, she thought. The sage was here; he'd found her like he did when she was a child.

"Saphira needs your help. Wymann needs your help. The companions need your help," said the sage. "And, most of all, Kelly needs your help. She's the chosen one."

"Oh, Kelly…" Babushka said out loud. "The chosen one. Why? How can this be? How?"

"When you opened the portal through the oak tree, you came through to a world much different from your own, a world without magic. But, Lilliana, the magic was always within you." The Sage pointed to Babushka's chest. "There, in your heart, is where it lies and where it always has been."

Babushka instinctively placed her right hand on her heart, rubbing it gently. Trying to feel the magic again. Her lips trembled as she fought back the tears.

"Forgive yourself so that your heart can heal. Forgive yourself for what happened. It was not your fault," continued the sage.

Tears flowed down Babushka's face. "Ah, I cannot forgive myself. It's my fault the king is dead." At those words, the light extinguished and the sage vanished. Pitch-black. Babushka caught her breath and held it. "The lights, who put out the lights?" she screamed and panicked. "No!" Her voice echoed within the void.

Crack. Thunder rocked and rumbled, the ground shook, and the hospital bed rattled, jiggling Babushka wildly like she was riding a bull at a rodeo.

A pulse began to ring throughout the nothing. *Dew, dew, dew.*

It became faster and faster and louder and louder. Babushka shivered and her teeth clattered. She grabbed her jaw and held it tight, stopping the rhythmic dance inside her mouth. The temperature dropped dramatically, and you could see the dragon breath coming out of Babushka's lips and nostrils as she breathed.

What's happening?

She whimpered. The noise was loud and it hurt not only her ears but her mind too.

Pulse, pulse, pulse, dew, dew, dew. Crackle went the air above. The atmosphere was now supercharged and the voice reemerged.

"Forgive yourself," said the sage, and his face reappeared in a sea of light, right above Babushka's bed. He was huge! Much larger than he'd been the first time. And he was still beautiful. But, as quickly as he'd come, he was gone again and Babushka was alone in the void. In the darkness.

"The lights, who put out the lights again?" she called out in rage. "No!" she screamed, and her pleas echoed.

CRACK. The thunder rocked. *RUMBLE.* The ground shook and the hospital bed rattled, jiggling Babushka wildly. Just like it had before. But more intense.

"Forgive yourself. Your time has come," boomed the sage, and the vision she had as a girl reappeared. "Heal your heart so that you can rise from the ashes stronger, wiser, and more courageous."

Babushka trembled from the shock and from seeing the vision again. *Who was that beautiful woman?* she wondered.

Without being given a minute to contemplate, the image of the sage illuminated. "Believe in the magic and rise." The face grew brighter and brighter as each second past. Babushka closed her eyes, trying to block out the overwhelming light. "*Believe*," echoed the voice.

"Ah!" Babushka screamed.

"*Believeee…*"

And *KABANG!* The sage's entire face, including the portal, exploded, the force knocking into Babushka and her bed. She flew ten metres, like a rocket through the nothingness, eventually slowing down.

Kerplunk, kerplunk, kerplunk. The wheels hit the ground and screeched to a stop. The ride was thrilling but scary, knocking Babushka out cold. She was unconscious within the void.

"Okay," said tech one, wheeling Babushka out of the MRI room. The orderly was back, ready to take his patient to level four. "She is ready to go. Thanks again, mate," said the tech as he signed the last of the paperwork on the patient's chart before he handed her over.

"No, thank *you*. I got it from here," he said as he grabbed the hospital bed and took control. Seb looked at Babushka caringly for a split-second and his heart went out to her. "I hope you will be okay," he whispered.

Little did he know, something deep within Babushka's heart was beginning to stir…

16

"HOOOOOO," BREATHED KELLY as she slumped down on her bed in her bedroom, exhausted. It was early, 6:30 in the evening, but she didn't have an ounce of energy left in her body to do anything. Her parents had left a note on the kitchen table, saying that they'd gone out to do some grocery shopping and they would be home very soon.

Kelly was relieved when she'd read the note because the last thing that she wanted was to talk to her parents or answer all of their one hundred and one questions. She preferred to be alone right now. On her own.

Kelly plopped down on her bed and placed her arms behind her neck, her gaze shooting upwards. "Hmmm." She smirked to herself. "I've been staring at the ceiling a lot." She rubbed her eyes and massaged her temples. Then she jiggled in place, trying to relieve the persistent itch on her shoulder and back. "God, so annoying, grrrrrr," she growled.

Kelly found that the more she jiggled, the worst the

rash felt. There wasn't any reprieve. With her right hand, she reached over her left shoulder, shoving it down her back and stretching as far and hard as she possibly could.

She huffed and puffed. "Nearly there." Her right shoulder popped a little under the strain but it wasn't painful, so she kept on pushing her arm, hoping to hit the spot. "Damn!" She released herself from the awkward position and threw her body back on the mattress.

How bad is this rash? she thought.

Kelly jumped up from her bed and ran into the bathroom. She opened the vanity drawer and rummaged through it. "Band-aids, no. Vitamin E cream, no. Vaseline…"

Rummage, rummage, rummage.

"Ah! There you are."

Hidden right behind the bars of soap was a small handheld, compact mirror. It was the same mirror she'd played with when she was a young girl, pretending to put on makeup just like her mum. Kelly grabbed the mirror and went back to her bedroom. Even though no one else was home, she still shut the door because *you never know.* Anyone could come home at any minute. Kelly pulled off her jumper and also her T-shirt. She positioned herself in front of her bedroom mirror and turned around, so that her back was exposed.

"Okay, let's see what you look like," she said, preparing herself for impact. She took a deep breath and gently and slowly lifted the small compact mirror until she could see the reflection of her back. "Oh my God!" Kelly stopped instantly. "What in God's name is that?" she asked herself, shocked at the sight of her rash. She jiggled around a little more, turning here and there while changing the angle of the handheld compact mirror to get a better look, but it didn't work. "God, what's wrong with my skin?" She panicked. Kelly's eyes fell on a large patch of what looked like red, scaly skin, currently the size of a football. "How did it get so big?" It was so red and incredibly hideous.

BANG went the back door, and Kelly dropped the mirror and quickly got dressed.

"Kelly!" yelled her mum.

"You home, hun?" called her dad as he brought in all the shopping, like a pack mule.

"Yes, I'm home!" Kelly yelled back to her parents, hoping this was the end of the conversation while praying to God they wouldn't come upstairs to her room to check on her.

"Wonderful," said Mark to his wife. He looked at all the groceries in front of him. And, boy, was there a lot. There were bags of fresh colourful veggies and fruit. Mark always believed it was important to eat the rainbow. The rainbow gave you the vitamins and minerals your body needed to function properly. So, if you ate the rainbow—five servings of veggies in a day and two pieces of fruit—then there was no need to pop an artificial multivitamin.

Now, Mark did also love his sweets. He enjoyed a teddy bear biscuit (chocolate-coated of course) with his afternoon coffee. He swore it perked him up at work and gave him that extra buzz he needed to get through the afternoon. But his wife believed otherwise—wink, wink. He simply had a sweet tooth and couldn't live without his chocolate-coated teddy bear biscuits.

However, there were also plenty of bags containing healthy cereals, yoghurts, fresh meat and fish, toiletries, cleaning products, et cetera. There were just so many bags.

"Darling," said Mark cheekily. "I'm going to go check on Kelly. You get started and I'll be right back." He winked at his wife and quickly left the room.

"Ah," breathed Joyce in annoyance. "He does this all the time." She opened the first bag and got to work, sorting and storing. She knew that she shouldn't hold her breath as he wouldn't be back to help her with the groceries. She decided that, next time, she was going to do the same thing to him, just to see how he liked it. And giggled at the thought.

Knock, knock went the door.

Kelly was sitting at her desk, pretending to do her homework. Her hunch was right; she knew one of her parents would come and check on her. Mark opened the door and peeked inside. "Hey, kiddo, how are you? How was it at Babushka's house?" he asked, hoping for some really good news.

Kelly hesitated for a split-second, pretending to read her maths book. *Here we go,* she thought. *One hundred and one questions.*

She looked up at her dad. "It was okay. Great to see her after all these years," said Kelly, trying to act all cool and collected.

"Oh, sorry, hun, you're studying. I didn't mean to disturb you," said Mark, throwing a quick glance at Kelly's books, trying to see what she was working on.

"It's okay, Dad," said Kelly, suppressing her frustration.

"Did she give you something for the rash?" he quickly asked. Mark was really concerned about his daughter and wanted to get a feel of how it went today. He was hoping Babushka and Kelly would have a chat about all the things that were bothering the broody teenager. If she didn't feel comfortable talking to him or her mother, then perhaps she would find some security in an old friend. He crossed his fingers at the thought.

Kelly looked up from her textbook again. She was starting to feel uneasy and didn't like the game of twenty questions, as it wasn't the right time, especially with the day she'd had. Baba was in hospital in a coma and Kelly had sat there for hours waiting to hear some good news. She was even hoping to go sit with her godmother and hold her hand, but the doctor said no. They told her that no one would be able to visit with Babushka today. Kelly pleaded through tears, begging them to let her at least go see her godmother, but they refused. They did, however, inform her that Babushka had an MRI scan of her head and they were awaiting Dr Brown's assessment. At that time, the main doctor was preoccupied by a trauma patient, who'd been rushed into hospital by ambulance. Kelly felt incredibly helpless and sad while sitting in the waiting room. When she realised what time it was, she decided to go home. It was all too much and she needed to think things through. And, right now, her dad was not helping.

"Look, Dad, so sorry to do this, but I have a lot of work to do tonight." Kelly pointed at her desk. "Baba did look at my rash. She said she would make an ointment for me, and I could come over after school tomorrow to pick it up."

Mark didn't know what to think. It wasn't the answer that was the problem; it was the delivery of the message. Short and blunt. This was not his girl speaking and he didn't like it. But to prevent her from slipping farther away from him, he smiled his huge cheeky grin in response. "Well, that's great news, Kel." He offered the teenager a thumbs-up. "I will leave you to it then." Mark turned his back and closed the door behind him, feeling terrible about whatever it was his daughter was not telling him. He just hoped that she remembered she could always come and tell him anything—anything at all.

Kelly slammed her maths books shut and tossed her pen at her desk. It ricocheted against the wall and flew off somewhere, never to be seen again. She didn't care about her maths homework, and she didn't care about algebra. Right now, she didn't care about anything. All she wanted was for Baba to wake up and for everyone to leave her alone.

"Oh, I can't take this anymore!" she yelled, slamming her fists hard on her table.

Kelly started to cry; the tears were uncontrollable. They just kept on flowing and flowing, down her cheeks and down her chin. A small amount ended up pooling on her desk. She just sat there and watched each tear gently drip into the puddle, creating a ripple. After a while, her face got itchy. But she couldn't be bothered to dry it or the snot that was oozing out of her nose. It was all too much. Kelly got up to lie on top of her bed. She grabbed the pillow and covered her face, hoping the plush material was enough to help her hide.

"Oh, why is this happening?" she asked the universe, praying someone, anyone could answer her question and release the burden she'd been carrying for the last day or so.

Crunch, crunch, crunch went the tiny pebbles below her feet. *Crunch, crunch, crunch.* It was cold and Kelly shivered.

Looking around, Kelly realised she was back underground and she knew exactly where the path led.

Why am I here again? she wondered. Her stomach was

knotted and she was incredibly anxious. Something felt different this time, but what was it?

She rubbed her hands together, hoping it would bring some warmth and ease some of her anxiety. She was of two warring minds. A part of her wanted to follow the path again, but another was reluctant to move. She just didn't know which to listen to. Looking down at her arm, Kelly remembered how the golden knight had grabbed and held her. It was a shock to her system.

Would that same thing happen again? *Or would it be much, much worse?* She shivered at the thought.

Kelly turned around and looked in the opposite direction. Behind her there was nothing, just pitch-black nothingness. No dirt, no roots, and no tiny pebbles. Absolutely nothing.

If there's nothing, she thought, *then this all must simply be a dream—a bad dream. And, eventually, I'll wake up again.*

She stood there, analysing her thoughts. And nodded her head, happy with her conclusion. "Well, come on, feet. Let's go and see what we will find this time." And off she went down the tunnel. As she travelled, she remembered her way. She easily skipped over protruding tree roots, not stubbing her toe twice in the same spot, and ignored dark, cobwebby passages that veered off the path. "Better to keep your eyes focused ahead," she reminded herself. "Oh!" said Kelly, stopping abruptly and holding her breath, while trying desperately to convince herself that she wasn't hearing things. She exhaled, and as she was about to move, she heard the noise again.

Someone else was down here, she concluded. Panic rose

in her chest and she felt like running back in the direction she'd come from, getting as far away as she possibly could.

Sniff, sniff went the nose. *Shuffle, shuffle* went the noise.

Kelly decided it was not wise to run. She might alert whatever this was of her presence. It could be a bear—a grizzly bear in fact.

Don't bears hibernate in caves? she thought.

Ahem went the noise, followed by a hacking sound, then a *splat*.

What? thought Kelly, feeling foolish. *Bears don't do that.* She scratched her head.

Shuffle, shuffle, shuffle continued the noise. It was moving.

Intrigue kicked in, which had Kelly's legs moving forward. Without thinking or hesitating. She had to know what this "thing" was. *Surely it wasn't a bear?*

Slowly and very quietly, Kelly treaded forward. Her footsteps were as light as a feather, and she thanked her lucky stars that she'd been here before. The second time around was so much easier, as she felt she could walk the same path blindfolded.

Crunch, crunch, crunch went her feet. *Shuffle, shuffle, shuffle* went the noise.

One at a time, they each approached the intersecting paths, choosing the correct tunnel of course. At first, Kelly thought that perhaps the noise had gone through the opposite tunnel, the one that didn't lead to the golden knight, but echoes coming from behind her told her differently. So she decided to head down the same path and see, once and for all, what this noise was—bear or otherwise.

As she continued, she knew it wasn't far to the tomb, and that knowledge was confirmed by the two colossal dragon statues position just ahead. Viewing them now for a second time was as equally awe-inspiring. They were massive structures, appearing incredibly beautiful and incredibly lifelike. The fear Kelly felt during the first interaction was now nonexistent. She was overcome by sheer fascination.

Who was this incredible sculptor? she thought to herself as she moved on, gently touching the flank of one of the dragons as she passed. *Hmmm, still warm to the touch*, she noted.

The purple hue was there as well. Just as bright and just as radiant. Her heart skipped a beat and her stomach did a somersault. The tomb was up ahead. Kelly covered her face slightly with her arms, blocking some of the light. It was just too bright for her eyes.

Through the narrow passageway, she went ever so quietly. She noticed the shuffling had ceased and wondered if she'd missed something on the way here. Perhaps the bear or "thing" had found another tunnel and carried on that way.

No, she concluded, *there is no alternative path. This is the only way.*

Crunch, crunch, crunch went Kelly's feet.

Finally, she stepped into the chamber where she'd first lain eyes on the magnificent shield, glowing with its purple hue. "God," Kelly said under her breath. It looked even more beautiful and radiant the second time around.

Instinctively, she moved closer, wanting to see it again. The desire pulling her in. But Kelly stopped dead in her tracks, her gaze landing on the figure in front of her. Kneeling before the golden knight was a man clad in dirty, tattered robes. Beside him, on the floor, was what looked like a long wooden crook with a metal hook attached at the end.

A shepherd, realised Kelly. *What is a shepherd doing all the way down here?*

Sob, sob, sob went the shepherd. He wiped his face with the edge of his robes, blowing his nose with all his might.

"I'm so sorry, my lord," he cried and convulsed in pain as he kneeled.

Slowly, Kelly moved forward, curiosity getting the better of her. One tiny step at a time, edging closer and closer, while holding her breath.

Who is this shepherd? she wondered, trying to put some of the pieces together. *And this knight must have been a powerful lord once...*

Nothing made any sense, however. In fact, things were getting more complicated and confusing. First, there was a great battle, then came the man with incredible blue eyes. Next, there was a tomb with a golden knight, the same man depicted on the glorious shield. And now, all of a sudden, a shepherd was thrown into the mix. With each thought, Kelly inched towards the altar, not realising how close she was actually getting.

"And last but not least," said Kelly out loud. "What does this all have to do with *me*?"

Within a flash, the shepherd picked up his crook with his right hand and propelled himself up and off his knees with ease. *JUMP.* Then swung around to Kelly, his face still fully covered by his tattered robes. The teenager jumped backwards in fright.

"You can hear me?" she said, dumbfounded. "How can this be?"

"Who are you?" yelled the shepherd, pointing his crook at Kelly. "Who sent you?"

Kelly instantly paled, as she couldn't believe what she was seeing and couldn't comprehend the trouble she'd gotten herself into. Her legs trembled while her feet felt warm and wet. Looking down, she realised why. She'd peed herself.

"Who. Are. You?" bellowed the shepherd, this time even louder. He aimed his crook at Kelly and started to run in her direction, not allowing her to answer and not caring. The only thing on his mind was protecting his lord's eternal peace.

Kelly instinctively held her hands up, ready to go fifteen rounds. Mohammed Ali style. She looked at her fists and back at her incoming assailant. "This is not a good idea, Kel," she muttered to herself. But for some unknown reason, her legs didn't move. She was frozen on the spot with a maniac running towards her. She closed her eyes, not wanting to watch.

The shepherd continued to rush forward, crook poised. *Run, run, run… slip.*

"Ahh!" His robes got tangled up with his feet and he was airborne. Kelly opened her eyes just in time to see a flying, dirty, smelly, tattered man sailing straight towards her. She ducked at the very last minute, rolled headfirst underneath the flying mass, sprang up, and ran towards the altar.

Grab the sword, she told herself.

KERPLUNK. Splat. The shepherd's face was plastered on the floor.

Kelly reached the altar, noticing the aroma of the rosemary was stronger than the last time. She inhaled the soothing scent. Looking around, she now noticed fresh bouquets laid at the golden knight's feet, and realised who had placed them there.

"Pfft, pfft," the shepherd spat the age-old dust out of his mouth. He was angry now. Very, very angry. Not at the intruder, but at himself. "How could someone have found him? He's been hidden for so very long." He grabbed his crook, feeling the effects of time on his body while realising he was no longer the young and agile knight he once was. "No!" he yelled as his heart sank. The intruder was at the altar.

Kelly turned around. The shepherd was back on his feet. He screamed, running towards the teenager with more gusto than before, his mouth open and spit flying everywhere. Luckily, his robe still covered his face as it absorbed the free-flowing spittle. Kelly grabbed at the golden knight's sword but it wouldn't budge.

"What?" And she screamed. The shepherd was getting closer. She pulled at it again. And again, nothing. It just didn't want to move. Kelly turned and grabbed the sword with both hands. "Ah, move, goddamn it," she yelled in frustration, gritting her teeth. The maniac was upon her. He swung his crook, raising it high above his head, and then brought it swiftly down.

Down, down, down it travelled towards Kelly's head.

"Try something smaller," said her gut instinct, so she pulled the golden glove off the dead knight's hand and lifted it above her head. And just in the nick of time, because the weapon and glove collided.

KABANG! The sound filled the chamber with the loudest high-pitched ring, knocking them both off their feet before sending them flying to the ground.

Kelly screamed as she flung herself off her bed and landed on her bedroom floor, drenched in her sweat once again. "Oh…" She raised her hands midair, protecting herself from a fatal blow. She didn't flinch or open her eyes, anticipating the *whack* of the crook.

But nothing happened.

Slowly, she opened her eyes, daring to grab a glimpse of the maniac running straight at her. And sat up, breathing heavily. "What?" she said out loud and scrambled to her feet. Her legs trembled like jelly. She grabbed on to the side of the bed for support. "What's going on?" Kelly looked around her bedroom, not understanding what she'd witnessed. "Was it a dream or was it real?" She turned a full 360 degrees, searching for the maniac.

Was he hiding? she wondered.

She looked under her bed. Nothing. She opened the sliding wardrobe. Nothing in there. And childishly, she looked behind the curtain but there was no one hiding there either. Sitting on the edge of her bed—feeling like a big, stupid, childish girl—Kelly exhaled with relief, smirked to herself, and let out a small giggle of embarrassment.

"Geez, Kel, you're losing your mind, girl." She rubbed her face and massaged her eyes, as it was much needed and helped soothe her troubles. What a hell of a weekend it had been, and it had definitely taken a toll on Kelly. She was incredibly tired and drained. Looking at the time, she realised she had been asleep for four hours. Four long hours, yet she didn't feel refreshed at all. Not one bit. She must have dozed off after she got mad at her dad for coming to check on her.

Dad, she thought, guilt churning in her stomach.

She felt guilty for speaking rudely to him and for pushing him away. She knew that she could always go talk to her dad, no matter what, but this time seemed different. As if it were way above her head, and she could only imagine what an adult would think. How was she meant to explain the dreams she'd been having, and the things she'd been seeing? Especially to him. They felt so real, as if she'd truly been teleported to wherever she went. Kelly didn't know where the tomb was but it definitely felt real. If she told her parents everything, they would laugh at her for sure.

She shook her head. *No, this is my secret and only mine. No one needs to know about it.*

Taking a deep breath, she exhaled and plopped down on her bed. It was nearly one in the morning, and she knew she should change into her PJs but she didn't care.

Too tired and it's too late, she thought to herself. Tomorrow was school and she needed to get some rest, otherwise the lack of sleep was going to make the day super, super hard.

Kelly grabbed her doona and covered herself with it. All she wanted to do was sleep and have some nice dreams. She switched off her bedside lamp and rolled onto her stomach. For some reason, the dark was scary, and she didn't like it. It had been a very long time since she was afraid of the dark, and that was when she was very, very young. In primary school.

Her parents could not convince her that there was no such thing as monsters. They told her goblins weren't real and the bogeyman was a Hollywood invention, meant to scare people using something called special effects. That there was nothing sinister living under her bed, waiting to grab her. And, most of all, that dragons weren't real. Eight-year-old little Kelly didn't believe them. So she spent many, many nights sleeping with her night-light on.

As she shuffled around, trying to find that spot in her bed, she wished she still had that night-light. Not knowing how to make herself comfortable, or how to relax, Kelly decided to lie on her stomach, her favourite position. She could cover her head with her doona as it was the only thing she could think of that would make her feel better, more relaxed. She knew that by the morning, she would be incredibly sweaty, and her hair would be really frizzy from the sweat but she didn't care.

Breathing wasn't a problem because you could mould the doona in a way that created a cave or tent-like opening. When she slept, she just had to place her nose within that cave or tent. Fresh air would then flow into the opening, allowing her to breathe. And no one would be able to see her nose—this included any monsters that happened to be in her bedroom while she was sleeping. As a result, she'd feel safe and get a good night sleep.

Kelly smiled at the idea. "A good night's sleep." She placed a fraction of her arm under her pillow and froze, dead-still. "Oh, something cold,"

What is that? she wondered. She stopped for a minute, trying to remember if she had placed something under her pillow earlier. *Nope, nothing at all. So what is it?*

With all fear replaced by curiosity, Kelly switched on her bedside lamp and lifted up her pillow. "No!" she said to herself, bewildered by the sight. "No!" She shook her head in denial. "This can't be!"

Slam went the pillow onto the mattress. Kelly sat up in her bed, staring straight at the thing lying under her pillow. Every single hair on her body stood up; she was covered in goose bumps. Her back itch kicked into overdrive, and she instinctively lifted a hand to scratch it, not taking her eyes off the pillow.

Am I going mad? she thought. *This can't be real!* But there was only one way to find out if she was going crazy or not.

Kelly slowly reached for her pillow, her hand trembling as she grabbed one corner with her fingertips and started to lift it up. At first, the item looked like a small piece of jewellery, golden in colour. But as more and more of the pillow shifted out of the way, Kelly realised this was not just some trinket. Yes, it was golden in colour, but it definitely was not jewellery.

She flicked the pillow out of the way. It landed on the floor but Kelly didn't notice where. Her gaze was fixed on the golden "thing" lying on her mattress. Her eyes were watering and she whimpered. Her lower lip started to tremble as she tasted her salty tears. "No," she said to the golden thing. "No." She shook her head.

She wiped her cheeks dry, hoping what she saw was only an illusion…

No, it was as real as can be, and a part of her still didn't believe it. *Well, there's only one way to find out,* she thought, then hesitated.

If this thing was real, then everything she had been dreaming was real too, as real as can be. A part of her wanted to know for sure, because then she wouldn't feel crazy anymore. But another part wanted her to pluck her pillow off the floor and cover the object. Ignore it and maybe it would go away by the morning. Kelly stared at it a little longer. One thing was certain; it was incredibly beautiful and alluring. It called out to her, inviting her to touch it. She reached out, as she could not withstand it any longer, brushing it with the tip of her index finger.

It was real. The golden object on her mattress was real. Kelly couldn't believe it. *How can this be?* she wondered.

"The golden glove is real, and it's right here in my bedroom…"

17

CHIRP, CHIRP, CHIRP went the birds in the tree outside Kelly's window. Their morning song was so beautiful. Soothing. To everyone but not Kelly.

She groaned. It was too early. She felt rotten, tired, completely drained and didn't want to get up to go to school. All she wanted to do was hide under a rock and stay there forever. But Kelly knew that wasn't going to happen anytime soon.

She stretched under the doona; her body needed it. All night long, she'd slept in a foetal position and stayed there, not moving a muscle nor budging. It'd brought her some comfort and helped her to drift into a dreamless sleep, but rest was not on the cards that night...

Kelly felt just as tired and as drained now as she had when she found the golden glove under her pillow. Somehow, she'd managed to find the strength to pick it up with her hand and instantly felt an electric current running through her fingertips and up her arm. It continued to travel and spread throughout her torso, to her neck, and down towards her hips. It tingled as it went and the hairs on her body stood on end with the sensation.

Kelly couldn't handle the intensity, which was both strange yet familiar. She quickly opened the bottom drawer of her bedside table and threw the glove inside. Without thinking twice, she covered it with some of her underwear and bras, knowing her parents wouldn't rummage through the drawer if they saw her personal stuff in there.

Slamming the drawer shut, Kelly jumped back into bed, covered herself with her doona, and tried her best not to think or move. She closed her eyes and wished for sleep to come. Sleep without dreams, sleep without the tomb, sleep without the crazy robed shepherd. Just sleep and rest—the two things she desperately needed. Sleep did eventually come that night, but it was without the rest…

Kelly peeked from underneath her doona, her eyes shooting to her drawer. *The glove was in there… unless this was all just a bad dream?* she thought. Her brain felt frazzled, and she wasn't sure what was real and what may have been a result of her sleep-deprived, overactive imagination.

Reluctantly, she extended an arm and touched the handle of the drawer. "Should I?" she asked herself. "Or should I just ignore it, get dressed, and go to school?" Kelly didn't know what to do. Ignoring it ever existed would make things much, much easier. But living with the curiosity would be horrific. Her rash began to tingle on her back and she wiggled in her bed. "Nah, I need to check and see with my own eyes." And she jumped out of bed and kneeled in front of the chest of drawers. She grabbed the handle, took a deep breath, and held it, steadying herself. Her heart was racing. She wasn't sure what she would find, and doubt clouded her mind. "Come on, Kel, you need to do this," she egged herself on.

She breathed in and out, trying to slow her heart rate. Her grip tightened around the handle. The suspense was all too much, so she closed her eyes and quickly pulled with all her might, huffing aloud with the action. *BAM*. The drawer flew open, and she slowly found the courage to open one eye, peeking ever so slightly, worried that it actually wasn't a dream.

"Oh!" she said in shock. "Nothing here, *phew*." The relief came in waves but her gut rumbled, disturbing her temporary peace while nudging her to look deeper, underneath her underwear. She trembled, reluctant to dig deeper, but she had to do it. She had to find out.

With a shaky hand, she grabbed and lifted the underwear gently and slowly. It was so slow that the movements of a sloth would have seemed lightning fast in comparison. Up and up, each piece of clothing rose and there, beneath all the underwear, sat the golden glove glistening brightly once again in the morning rays of the sun.

"Oh my God," whispered Kelly in shock. "You are real and not just a dream…"

"Kel, you up, hun?" called Joyce from the bottom of the stairs.

Kelly looked up suddenly, in a panic. "Oh no!" Without thinking, she re-covered the glove with her underwear and bras, and slammed the drawer shut. *BAM*. She was shaking in her slippers.

"Oh, drats," she said, looking at the clock. Time was running out. She needed to get dressed and get her bum downstairs before the swat team (AKA her parents) made their way upstairs to her bedroom. She screamed and threw her hands in the air. Running to her wardrobe, she pulled out her school dress and, in one swift move, took off her clothes and replaced them with her school uniform. *Shazam.* Ready within an instant.

She looked in the mirror. *Eek! Hideous*, she thought. *Hair needs a good brush and look at my eyes—oh my God.*

She touched her face gently, fearing the black bags would turn even blacker. Her skin was pale and pasty, like she was getting sick. Kelly took a step back from her mirror and examined herself from head to toe. Besides the school uniform, she realised she looked like a giant-sized panda. White face and black around the eyes. She smirked at herself and had a little chuckle. She needed it.

"Kel, are you ready, hun?" called her mum once again. "You are going to be late for roll call."

"Coming, Mum," she yelled back instantly. Taking a deep breath, Kelly looked into the mirror one last time and gave herself a wink and a pep talk. "Let's go kick some ass. Woohoo!" Then she grabbed her schoolbag and headed down the stairs to tackle the day.

~

Ding, ding, ding went the bell at Santa Lucia High School. It was the signal to get to homeroom for roll call.

Kelly walked into the corridor and headed straight to her locker. "Hey, Kel," said a couple of her friends as she passed. The teenager nodded and kept on going as she was on a mission and she wasn't going to stop, not even for the Pope if he were here on campus. She might pause for a visit from Elvis but there was a fat chance of that happening.

And not just any type of Elvis. It would have to be the King himself and not an impersonator—no siree.

She arrived at her locker and dropped her bag on the floor. "Phew." For some reason, her bag felt extra heavy today, like she was carrying a bunch of rocks. She unzipped it and took all of her books out, leaving only her diary and her English exercise book.

English was always a double period after homeroom on Mondays, so she didn't have to bring many books with her. To be honest, right now she was grateful for that. The lack of sleep and energy, following what felt like a disastrous weekend, meant that the last thing she wanted to do was lob around a sack of rocks from one room to another.

Ding, ding, ding when the second bell.

"Oh!" Kelly had no less than twenty seconds to get into class before her homeroom teachers arrived. If she didn't make it there before them, then she'd be considered late, which meant a letter to her parents and more *questions*. And Kelly wasn't going to have any of that.

SLAM, BANG went her locker. The door was shut and it was time to go. Kelly picked up her bag and bolted into her class, followed by the homeroom teachers five seconds later.

"Good morning, girls. How are we today?" said Mrs Richards. "I trust everyone had a good weekend?" She smiled at the class.

Mrs Richards was the nicest out of the two homeroom teachers. She was sweet, funny, and caring. If she caught you doing something naughty, so to speak, she wouldn't get cross and she wouldn't yell. She would just frown at you, call you *her darling*, and explain why she was disappointed. On the other hand, if Mr Lunateri caught you doing something bad—and depending on what cycle the moon was at—he would either yell at you at the top of his lungs, making sure you were severely embarrassed. Or he would drag you out of homeroom by the ear and straight to the principal's office. Mr Lunateri was a weirdo with an extremely short fuse. And by short, think of the shortest piece of string you could possibly imagine and then shorten it by 99%. *You get the picture.*

All the students in the entire school were petrified of him and his nickname was Wolfman because, when the moon was full, he was a ticking time bomb. Anything, absolutely anything, could set him off. You could be walking through the corridor, minding your own business, and pounce! Mr Lunateri would jump right at you, grab you by the ear, and drag you to the principal's office for doing a-b-s-o-l-u-t-e-l-y n-o-t-h-i-n-g. And no matter what you said, or how you pled your case, you just couldn't win. So, if you saw Mr Lunateri coming your way, you made sure to quickly turn around and get the hell out of there ASAP.

However, when you had that man as a homeroom teacher—well, that was just another kettle of fish. And he was even harder to dodge. Kelly was lucky because her desk was in a good spot, the second row from the back, and she was positioned right on the end of the row, next to the windows. Today, those windows were open and letting in some much-needed fresh air. Kelly was starting to feel green after the restless night and lack of breakfast this morning. The slight breeze helped her: a) not to projectile vomit all over the person seated in front of her, and b) not pass out face-first on her desk.

"Okay, girls," said Mr Lunateri, getting a little impatient with all the commotion in class. "Quickly find your seats and settle please." He stood front and centre in the classroom and stared down viciously at the students who were taking too long.

Geez, Kelly thought. *If looks could kill, all those girls would be dead.*

After a minute of silence, Mr Lunateri opened his roll book. "You know the drill. If I call your name, I want you to yell 'here.' Let's go." He slowly read out each name in alphabetical order.

"Here!" flew out from every corner of the room, one after the other, and Mr Lunateri placed a tick next to that name, confirming they were present for the day.

"Kelly!" he called out next, not looking up from his book.

Kelly quickly sat straight in her seat and yelled, "Here!" Mr Lunateri paused for a second and looked up at her. Their eyes connected, and Kelly started to sweat profusely. "Oh God," she whispered under her breath. "I'm dead for sure…"

"Kelly, are you okay?" asked Mr Lunateri, his eyes now laser-focused on her face.

She swallowed a big lump that had risen in her throat and wiped away the sweat on her forehead. Kelly was starting to feel clammy.

God, what is happening to me? she thought to herself, panic rising in her gut.

"Kelly?" said Mr Lunateri again. He was beginning to get mad as his question wasn't getting answered.

"Ah, ah, ah," she said in response, unable to find any words to respond. And making matters worse, everyone in class turned to face and stare. Some of the nasty girls were snickering and pointing at her too. It was horrible and she felt like a little worm on a great big hook. While the rest of the class, including Mr Lunateri, were the fish waiting to pounce.

Once again, thank God for Mrs Richards, as she was the knight in shining armour who came and rescued Kelly from the piranhas. "Kelly, darling, are you okay?" she asked soothingly. "Mr Lunateri and I noticed that you looked a little green, off-colour. You okay?"

Kelly took a deep breath, swallowed the bile that was rising in her throat, and finally answered the question. "I feel tired, Mrs Richards, but I'm okay."

"Are you sure, darling? Do you want me to call your mum to come and get you?"

"No, no, no need for that," Kelly added quickly. "I am okay for now." She reassured her teacher. Everyone in class was still staring at her and she felt horrible as a result.

"Why don't you see how you go in period one and two and take it from there, darling, okay?" said Mrs Richards with a great big, warm smile that soothed right to the soul.

Kelly just smiled back at her wonderful homeroom teacher and nodded her head in acknowledgement. "Yeah, let's see how it goes," she said under her breath. Everyone slowly turned to face the front as the last of the names were read out for roll call.

"Have a great day, girls," yelled out Mrs Richards over the sudden eruption of chitchat and squeals when the bell rang, indicating the end of homeroom.

Kelly just sat at her desk, feeling queasy. She wasn't in the mood to socialise and she certainly didn't care what anyone did on their weekend. Babushka popped into her mind and she felt incredibly sad. Kelly wondered how her fairy godmother was doing. Was she out of her coma? She grabbed her phone out of her bag and checked to see if there were any missed calls. Nothing. No calls and no messages. She was hoping the doctor would have contacted her by now with some good news. Feeling disappointed, she placed the phone back into her bag and stared out the window.

"Baba, if you can hear me, please come back. Please," Kelly whispered, hoping that somehow the message would find its way to her.

Ding, ding, ding went the bell for period one and Mrs Martin promptly walked through the door, placing her belongings on the desk in front of the class.

"Good morning, ladies. How are we today?"

Mrs Martin was a middle-aged woman who dressed like a banker. She loved to wear tailored suits and silk shirts with a pussy bow. To be honest, she oozed class and sophistication and she was highly intelligent. Mind you, the woman also had a photographic memory and never ever forgot a word spoken in conversation. The girls thought she was better suited running the country rather than English class.

She was very fair and incredibly encouraging. She never embarrassed you in front of your peers and always help you if you asked. She was a tiptop boss lady and very admired at school, not just by students but also by her colleagues. Oh, and did I mention she loved to wear pearls? Drop pearl earrings that were incredibly divine. An exquisite top-of-the-range pearl necklace that probably cost a small fortune was worn around her delicate neck, and a to-die-for pearl bracelet with a diamond clasp was always worn on her right wrist. She was so stunning yet elegant.

"Let's get down to business," said Mrs Martin, casually

leaning against the teacher's desk at the front of the class. "We have a lot to cover but, like always, not enough time." And she clapped her hands together, signalling that she was ready for business and there was no room for negotiations. Similar to a judge slamming down his gavel as the final verdict was delivered. The room was quiet and order was in the house, as everyone always listened to Mrs Martin when she spoke. "Who would like to go first?"

First? thought Kelly, poking her head up. *First for what?* She looked around the class, hoping someone would know what the teacher was asking or at least volunteer... But no one budged and no one uttered a word, too afraid to find out what "first" meant.

"Anyone?" asked Mrs Martin. Her eyes scanned the room and found no willing volunteers. "Come on, girls, this is your chance to practise your poem in front of an audience. Better to take this opportunity now, before you go in front of the school assembly on Friday if you are chosen." A murmur instantly erupted within the room. "Now, now, girls, you knew about this. I'm just giving you an opportunity to practise before assembly." She frowned. "So..." Clapping her hands together once again, she pressed, "Who would like to go first?" And once again, everyone stayed mute and didn't move a muscle. "Have you all completed your assignment, may I ask?" She questioned the class with concern while hoping the answer was a yes.

"Ehem." All of a sudden, a pristine voice sounded in the middle of the back row. It was Sandra, the most popular girl in school. "Mrs Martin, I'm not sure about all the other students in the class, but I certainly did my homework as you requested." Sandra batted her eyelashes at the teacher and then lifted her poem to show it off to everyone in class—Miss Goody Two-Shoes.

"Well done, Miss Jenkins. You are a star," said the teacher in response.

"You're welcome and you can always count on me, miss," said the brown-noser, batting her lashes some more and feeling all high and mighty.

Kelly rolled her eyes. *God, Sandra, you are such a brown-noser. Go wipe your nose, you dirty girl,* she thought. She giggled to herself as she sat there, picturing Sandra with poo on her face. If only such a thing would actually happen…

"God, that would be so funny," Kelly murmured to herself.

"Well, since you displayed such great leadership, Miss Jenkins, I would like to invite you up to the front to show the class how it's done." Mrs Martin stood aside and gestured for Sandra to take the floor, a big smile beaming across her face.

"Of course." Sandra got up and took the opportunity at hand. There was never a moment where Miss Goody Two-Shoes did not like the spotlight. Everything had to be about her, and only her. No one else was allowed to have the spotlight, let alone share it with her.

God, here we go, thought Kelly as she watched Sandra make her way to the front of the class. She had a big grin on her face and she was loving the attention.

Sandra adjusted her uniform and flicked her perfect, long, straight hair back over her shoulder. Then she cleared her throat and began her poem. "My one true love, by Sandra Jenkins." She paused for dramatic effect. "Johnny, my one and only." She breathed heavily and emphasised the word *only*. "You are my heart and you are my soul." Sandra touched her heart space and closed her eyes, visualising her true love. "You are with me wherever I go…"

Oh my God, thought Kelly. She covered her face with the palm of her hands, embarrassed for Sandra and embarrassed by what she was hearing. The poem was unsettling her stomach and she was starting to feel nauseous.

"Stay with me forever," continued Sandra, pleading to her audience. "Guide me and leave me never… Protect me with your manly arms…"

"Oh," said Kelly, removing her hands from her mouth and sitting straight. She quickly looked for a bag or a container, but it was all too late and all too sudden. There was nothing that could have stopped it, nothing that could have prevented it.

Bleurgh! The spew flew right out of Kelly's mouth. Luckily, it didn't land on the girl sitting in front of her. It just dropped on the table, forming a great big puddle of smelly green bile.

The girls closest to her screamed while the girl sitting next to Kelly shouted, "Oh my God," and jumped out of her seat and away from the spew. The girl directly in front of Kelly turned around to see what all the commotion was about, and when she did, she screamed at the top of her lungs. And didn't stop screaming. She just stood there and screamed and screamed and screamed. Everyone in the room stopped and turned their attention to the piercing sound, and this of course angered Sandra.

"What are you doing?" she hissed. Sandra walked up to the screaming girl and grabbed her by the arm, pulling her so that she faced her when she spoke. "Don't you have any

RESP—oh my God!" Sandra screamed when she realised what was going on.

Kelly just sat there and continued to spew all over her desk. *Erp, erp, erp. Splat, splat, splat.*

"Mrs Martin!" yelled Sandra.

"On it," she replied. Mrs Martin grabbed the bin and brought it to Kelly. By this stage, the puddle was so big that the smelly green bile was overflowing down the sides of the desk and onto the carpet. "Here, spew into the bin, Kelly," she ordered as she covered her nose and mouth, shielding herself from the horrific smell. Everyone else started to dry retch as the smell travelled throughout the room. "Open all the windows nice and wide," instructed Mrs Martin. "And someone please open the door."

"Errrp," continued Kelly. She convulsed on the spot where she sat. Her stomach was empty. Empty of food, empty of bile, and there was nothing left to bring up. Her body shook and her hands trembled. Mrs Martin handed Kelly a tissue so that she could at least wipe her mouth. Kelly grabbed it and dabbed at her face. When the dry retching had ceased and the trembling had stopped, Kelly wiped her eyes with the back of her hands and looked up at the class. All the chairs were empty, and Kelly couldn't help but wonder where everyone went.

"Kelly, you okay?" asked Mrs Martin, her eyebrows knitted with concern.

"No, miss, I have a really bad headache and I don't feel good," she said, rubbing her stomach.

"Grab your bag and go home and have a rest. There is no point in you being here if you don't feel well, and clearly you don't," she instructed, pointing to the vomit.

"Okay, miss." Kelly grabbed her bag, which had (by divine intervention) come out unscathed and clean of any vomit, and headed to the door. "Oh, miss, before I forget…" She dug into her schoolbag and pulled out her poem. "Here, this is my poem."

"Oh, thank you, Kelly," said Mrs Martin. "Now go straight home. Do you want me to call your parents?"

"No, no need, miss," said Kelly quickly. "Home is ten minutes away and I will call my parents when I get there." She waved to her teacher and left the room and the mess for someone else to deal with.

On her way out of the corridor, Kelly realised where all the girls went. They were all sitting outside in the shade, fanning themselves. Some looked a little worse for wear while others were lying down on the cool grass. But poor Sandra was sobbing, completely distraught after being rudely interrupted while she was reciting her poem. There was a cluster of girls huddled around her. Her *yes* crowd, her entourage. All comforting her, stroking her hair, and telling her not to cry as she was too beautiful for that.

Kelly just continued to walk and strode right past them and out the school gates, feeling much better already.

～

Bing went the elevator, signalling it was about to arrive on the ground floor and startling Kelly out of her daydream.

After she had left school, her legs took over while her mind wandered and they brought her to the hospital. Her heart was telling her to go see Baba and this time her legs listened. The elevator doors opened and Kelly stepped inside. She quickly pressed number four, followed by the *close doors* button. She was growing impatient, and everything felt like it was moving at a snail's pace.

"Come on," she muttered while breathing out her frustration. Not long after. *Bing!* And she arrived at her chosen destination. There was no one else in the elevator and no one else waiting to board from a different level, so it was a quick, straight run. Kelly didn't know what room Baba was in on level four, so she decided to ask at reception. "Excuse me, nurse, can you help me find my godmother? Her name is Lilliana."

The nurse looked up at Kelly. She'd been deep in thought, concentrating on the file in front of her. "Sorry, miss, I didn't catch what you were saying. Who were you looking for?"

Maybe it was the fatigue that made Kelly more irritable than normal. "I said I'm looking for my godmother Lilliana. Please take me to her." And the girl started to tear up, fighting back the waterworks and not wanting to embarrass herself in front of a stranger.

Apart from looking pale and slightly green around the edges, the pain Kelly was carrying was also palpable and the nurse seemed to sense it. So, instead of giving her a piece of her mind, the woman decided to give her a piece of her heart. "Sure, sweetheart, come with me." She got up off her chair and held her hand out to Kelly. "I will show you the way, hun. It's not far at all, bed number ten."

Kelly eagerly grabbed the nurse's hand—deep down, the girl needed some sort of comfort. The weekend was a disaster, and right now it seemed as if the awfulness was seeping into the new week. The last thing she wanted and needed were more problems on top of what she already had.

It didn't take long to navigate through the busy corridors of level four. Even though it was visiting hours, not many people were actually visiting. The nurse stopped abruptly at the entrance to bed ten. She turned around and grabbed both of Kelly's hands. "Now, darling, before we go inside, I want you to prepare yourself. Lilliana is in a deep coma, and she looks a little pale." Kelly flinched at the news. The nurse gently rocked her hands from side to side, trying to soothe her and lift her spirits. She looked Kelly right in the eyes. "Rest assured, hun, Lilliana is receiving great care from everyone here on level four, okay?"

Kelly nodded in response and offered the kind nurse a smile. "Thank you for your help. I really appreciate it." The nurse gave Kelly's hands a final squeeze before she walked back to her desk. Kelly stood at the entrance for a second longer, gearing herself up before she walked in. She heaved in a breath. "Here we go." And opened the door.

Babushka was alone in that small room at the hospital; she didn't share it with anyone. There were no flowers, no get-well cards, and no balloons. She was lying very still with an oxygen mask on her face and a monitor attached to her body, constantly measuring medical indicators of health such as: temperature, pulse, breathing, and blood pressure. It broke Kelly's heart to see her fairy godmother like this.

"Oh, Baba," she whispered.

Kelly noticed a chair next to Baba's bed. Before she went to sit down, she rearranged it slightly, bringing the seat closer to Baba so that she could hold her hand while she sat. There was not much else to do but sit, hope, and wait. She discarded her bag in the corner of the room and made herself comfortable in the chair. Kelly knew she didn't need her phone, as no one would be calling her, and left it in her bag. The teachers weren't going to call her parents and her parents knew she was going to visit Baba after school to get her ointment. Which meant she was going to have peace for the next few hours and that made her feel a little lighter.

Kelly turned to her godmother and looked at her, really looked at her. She appeared older for some reason. Before all this happened the 'old' wasn't noticeable. All you saw was her strong spirit, her humour, her love to help, and her love for everyone. Kelly was confused. Why was this happening? Why was her fairy godmother so sick?

She hugged herself, not knowing what to do or how to deal with the pain she was feeling, and gently rocked herself in her seat, fighting back the tears.

The door to Babushka's room suddenly flew open and a nurse walked in. It was the same nurse from before. "Hi, hun, just doing a quick check. So sorry to disturb you."

Kelly didn't say anything. She just smiled and continued to rock herself on the spot; some tears escaped and started to roll down her cheeks. She quickly wiped them away, not wanting anyone to see.

The nice nurse scribbled some notes in Babushka's file. "Okay, everything seems to be in order," she said out loud and turned to Kelly. "Can I get you something, hun? A tea or a water perhaps?"

"No, thank you. I'm okay."

The nurse nodded. "You know, they say they can hear you. Why don't you hold her hand and talk to her. See if she responds?" And with that final remark, the nice nurse turned on her heel and walked out the door, leaving Kelly with some food for thought.

"Hmmm, not such a bad idea. I hope they can hear us

and feel our presence." She grabbed Babushka's hand and gently kissed it.

Electricity ran through Babushka's body as she lay in the black nothingness. "Oh!" she screamed and her voice echoed, yet her eyes stayed shut—she was far too afraid to open them.

"Baba, it's me, Kelly. Can you hear me?" the teenager asked, holding Babushka's hand close to her lips like a microphone. Perhaps the closer it got to her mouth, the easier it would be for Baba to hear and recognise her voice.

"That voice," mumbled Baba to the void. "I know that voice."

"I miss you, Baba, and I'm sorry that you are in pain." Kelly wept and her tears trickled down her face, onto Baba's hand, and into her palm.

Baba clasped her fist into a ball, feeling the moisture but not understanding where it had come from.

"Please come back to us," cried Kelly. "Please, we need you. I need you, Baba."

"You don't need an old hag," Baba replied to the void. "I'm finished. There is nothing more I can give." Tears flowed down her cheeks. Lightning seemed to crack in the distance, lighting up Baba's world for a split-second. She shook and yelled out in fright. The winds picked up from nowhere and began to toss her about like a rag doll. Something was coming. Babushka breathed in and out, trying to slow her heart rate and prevent a panic attack. Crack went the thunder even louder than before. The pulsing noise returned right above where she was lying.

Doop, doop, doop, doop.

"Baba, can you hear me?" pleaded Kelly. "Come back to us."

Doop, doop, doop, doop. The sound intensified.

Babushka screamed. "Stop this madness!" And grabbed at her tormented head.

Crack, bang went the thunder, electricity flying through the nothingness.

"Wake up, Lilliana," echoed the voice, the same voice as before. "Wake up and rise."

Babushka continued to cry out in agony, the electricity growing stronger by the minute.

"Baba, if you are there and you can hear me, please give me a sign. Please, Baba," continued Kelly.

Everything was too much. Babushka just wanted to sleep and sleep forever. But, for some reason, it was not her time to go. She opened her eyes ever so slowly. And there, hovering above her once more, was the beautiful woman clad in white robes with the magnificent staff.

"Who are you?"

But the woman didn't answer, simply hovering above Baba, with her silver hair glowing bright and her robes flapping against the breeze.

"Baba, please come back to us," Kelly repeated over and over again.

"Wake up and rise, Lilliana," boomed the voice. "Wake up, rise, and take your place."

Babushka screamed and covered her ears with her palms. "But what is my place?" pleaded Babushka. "What is my place, my lord? Show me, please. I don't understand!"

The beautiful woman hovering above Babushka grabbed her staff with both hands, turned it onto its head—the orb now facing the ground—and touched Babushka gently on the chest. Electricity erupted throughout the nothingness, like a huge firework going off at the stroke of midnight on New Year's Day.

Kazam!

Bolts raced through Babushka, passing through every cell, every nerve, and every tissue. Limb after limb, organ after organ, received this bombardment of pure-white energy. It coursed through her veins, through her legs, up her torso, to her chest, neck, and head. Along her arms and out through her fingertips.

Zap!

"Ouch!" Kelly screamed, releasing Babushka's hand immediately. She looked at her fingers. The tingling was strong and it lingered, travelling up her forearm before fading away.

God, what the hell was that? she wondered, rubbing her hands together and massaging her forearms. She got up off the chair and had a quick look around the bed. Everything seemed in order. *What caused that shock?* she wondered. *That zap?*

Without dwelling further, Kelly grabbed her bag and left the room, heading straight for the nurse's desk while hoping to catch that nice nurse to inform her of the electric shock she received. Babushka could be in danger because her bed may be faulty. Or worse, something could be wrong with the equipment. That thought was terrifying. Kelly loved her fairy godmother, and she didn't want to lose her.

18

KELLY OPENED THE front door to her house. She was drained and her head felt warped. "God, what a day," she murmured to herself, leaning against the door. She took a deep breath to steady her mind.

Oh, that smells good. What is it? she wondered.

She inhaled again and closed her eyes, searching for the answer as the smell was so familiar. A delicious fragrance engulfed her nostrils. It entered her nasal passages and travelled right down into her lungs. She could taste it, it was scrumptious, and it was her favourite. Homemade shepherd's pie.

Kelly loved shepherd's pie. To be honest, it didn't matter what type it was. As long as there was the word *pie* in the name of the dish, she would eat it and enjoy it thoroughly.

There was one rule in life—mind you, it was a rule that should be made into law. Pie goes with sauce and sauce goes with pie. Those two should never be separated, and if they were, then a penalty should be handed out so that it never happens again. It was sacrilege, a sin, and a big fat NO.

"Hey, Mum," said Kelly as she strolled into the kitchen. "What you cooking, good looking?" she added, trying to see if the pie was ready.

"Hi, hun," said Joyce. She walked up to her daughter and gave her a big hug, rubbing her back.

Kelly flinched and pulled away. "Sorry, Mum, but my back is tender from the rash and it flares up when it is rubbed." The teenager quickly side-stepped her mother to sit down at the kitchen table.

Joyce didn't say anything; she bit her tongue because she was worried that saying something would cause tension. "How was school, hun?" she asked instead, busying herself in the kitchen and keeping her eyes averted.

"Yeah, it was okay. Usual stuff, different day," Kelly replied, though that was a lie.

"Aha… So what did you learn today?"

"Nothing." Kelly shrugged in response.

If only you knew what I had been up to, she thought to herself, *you'd probably skin me and hang my bones up to dry.* The teenager shivered at the imagery.

Joyce opened the oven door and pulled out the tray, checking to see if the mashed potatoes on top were nice, golden, and crispy—the way they all liked it. "Hmmm, just a little bit more and we will be ready."

"Smells awesome," piped up Kelly.

Joyce closed the stove and grabbed a couple of plates from the cupboard. "So, tell me, how is Babushka?"

Kelly suddenly jumped up in her chair as if she was stung by a bee on her bum. "Ahem, ahem, ahem," she stuttered. "Babushka," she attempted to stall. "Why do you want to know about Babushka, Mum?" She fidgeted in her chair and pulled at her collar. It was really hot in the kitchen all of a sudden.

Joyce continued to set the table as she gave her daughter a worried glare. "You mentioned yesterday that you were going to see Babushka after school." She walked to the fridge and took out a large bottle of cold water.

Oh my God, thought Kelly. *I'm so busted. What am I going to say?*

A little angel playing a harp suddenly popped up on her right shoulder. "Always remember, Kelly, the truth will set you free."

The truth, smirked Kelly to herself. *The truth, in this case, will have me locked up in the looney bin with the keys thrown away.*

"That's exactly what will happen," piped up the little red devil who appeared on her left. Now this guy was cheeky, and Kelly knew it. He was smoking a cigar and blowing rings right into her face. Kelly sneezed. "If I were you, kiddo, I would not listen to sparky over there. What would he know?" He tapped his cigar and gave Kelly the biggest, most mischievous grin possible.

"Tell your mother the truth," sang the angel in his melodious voice.

"Lie," said the devil, in contrast.

"You can trust your mother. She will help you," pressed the angel.

"Yeah, you can trust her to throw you right into the looney bin, like you said," spat the devil. The looney bin was not where Kelly wanted to go right now. And if she told her mother the truth and nothing but the truth, so help her God, her mother wouldn't be her only concern.

Because her father would throw her into a padded room himself and flush the keys down the toilet, making sure she stayed there forever.

"Yeah, Mum, I did go see Babushka today after school." And she said no more about that, glued to her chair while hoping the questions about Baba would stop.

Please change the subject. Please, please, please, she thought, crossing her fingers under the table.

Her mother pulled the tray out of the stove and brought the pie to the table. It was golden brown, steaming hot, and absolutely perfect. It looked so good and incredibly yummy. Joyce sat next to Kelly and served the pie. The teenager grabbed her fork and dived in. She ate her meal like a hungry wild wolf. *Num, num, num.* She barely chewed, swallowing some pieces whole. *Gulp.* It tasted so good and her belly loved it. Besides it was nice to eat food for a change today.

"Slow down, Kel," said Joyce. "You will make yourself sick."

Kelly didn't listen. She just kept on shovelling the pie into her mouth, one forkful after another until it was all gone. *Belch!* "Oh, sorry, Mum," she said, covering her mouth. "Where did that come from?" She attempted to act surprised.

"So, how is Babushka?" pressed her mum again.

Kelly grabbed her glass of water and took a long swig. *Gulp, gulp, gulp.* "Baba is okay, Mum, and she sends her regards," she lied.

"Oh, wonderful. Thank you," said Joyce while she slowly enjoyed her meal. "Did she give you that ointment for your back? "

"Um, no. She, um, she's missing some sort of ingredient and said she would get it to me in the next couple of days, maybe earlier," added Kelly quickly, trying to act normal.

"Oh, that's a shame. How is the rash feeling? Has it spread any farther?" asked Joyce, her eyebrows knitted in concern for her daughter's health and well-being.

"No, Mum, it's still the same, just very frustrating."

Joyce stopped eating her pie and looked at her daughter. "Do you want me to make an appointment, hun, to see the doctor?"

"No, no, Mum," said Kelly, her hands raised in protest. "I really don't want to take my clothes off in front of a perfect stranger." She rolled her eyes at her mother.

"Kelly, we can book a female doctor. It's okay. Besides, I'm worried about you and I think seeing a doctor about your back will ease a little of the burden you are carrying." She reached out her hand and clasped Kelly's, squeezing it gently.

"Mum, I am not carrying any burdens. I am not a donkey.

Joyce grabbed her forehead with her index finger and her thumb, pinching it to release some pressure. "Darling, I didn't call you a donkey. All I said was that it would be good to see a doctor. That's all." Joyce was irritated that nothing was going smoothly lately, especially when it had to do with her daughter. She was at her wit's end, and most of all, she didn't understand why all this was happening when her daughter was normally a good kid.

They sat there in silence at the kitchen table, neither wanting to say a word. Joyce continued to eat her scrumptious pie at a steady pace, enjoying each juicy morsel even though the atmosphere in the room was incredibly sour, while Kelly remained silent. For some reason, silence worked for her lately. As soon as the heat was on, shutting her mouth and keeping it shut proved to work in her favour, as everyone else also shut their mouths too.

"Mmm," said Joyce, trying to break the ice and bring some warmth back into a freezing-cold room. "That was amazing. I really enjoyed it." She wiped her mouth with a napkin.

"When is Dad coming home?" asked Kelly abruptly.

Joyce pushed the plate aside and clasped her hands together. "Dad is working late tonight. He rang and said he had to catch up on paperwork. He's been on the road a lot lately, rescuing animals, but hasn't had the time to do all the admin stuff." Joyce smiled.

"Oh," said Kelly, and she looked in the opposite direction, waiting patiently to be dismissed from the table.

Joyce took a deep breath and exhaled. She twiddled her thumbs, trying to think of a topic of conversation. She didn't want to end dinner on such a terrible note, with her daughter even more distant. "So, Kel, what would you like to do for your birthday?" she asked sheepishly. "Do you have any plans with your friends?"

Here we go again, thought Kelly. *More annoying questions.*

She turned her head slowly towards her mother. It was clear she wasn't in the mood, but she had to take her hat off to her mother for trying. "No, nothing planned," said Kelly, her tone blunt.

"*Okay*, do you want me to organise a dinner with your friends somewhere? Perhaps at a wood fire pizza place or something?"

Kelly couldn't believe what she was hearing. *A wood fire pizza restaurant for a 16th birthday? Oh. My. God.* She opened her mouth and tried to speak but her lips just wouldn't work, stalled by a full-system malfunction. Due to shock and the sheer absurdity of her mother's idea, she looked up to the ceiling and shook her head instead.

"What, Kel?" piped up her mum. "What did I say now to upset you again?" Joyce threw her hands up in frustration and did the sign of the cross, hoping for some divine intervention or perhaps a lightning bolt from the heavens to strike her down where she sat. Enough was enough, and Joyce had more than ENOUGH. So she got up from her chair, grabbed her plate, and placed it into the sink.

Kelly didn't bother speaking nor helping to clean up after dinner. She just pushed to her feet and went upstairs to her bedroom. End of conversation and stupid questions.

~

"Da da daa…" went the lyrics of another one of Vlad's favourite songs of all time, and this one was a doozy. He had his favourite T2 sunglasses on and he was with his most trusted creation, cruising down the passageways of the burrow and heading down to his best friend's house, for a hot chocolate and marshmallows. "Da da daa…" continued the lyrics through Bee's speakers, and Vlad smiled, pressing the pedal to the metal. If others saw what he was doing, and how fast he was travelling, they would definitely think that he was on the highway.

"Da da daaa…" Vlad sang along this time, bopping his head and thumping the steering wheel with his paw to the beat, dreaming of adventure. Adventure was definitely something he craved; it was brewing in his blood.

Life in the burrow was tough, and it was getting tougher as each day passed. The constant quarrelling, the constant headaches, the annoying bickering, and annoying badgering. Everyone was at their wits' end with each other, and it felt like there was never any peace. Peace only came when Vlad was knee-deep in his latest project, or zooming around in Bee with one of his favourite songs blaring through the speakers. And right now, he felt at ease and at peace.

"Da da daaaaaa" Vlad sang out during the final lyrics, raising his right hand, displaying the shaka sign to the universe, and gesturing that everything was okay. He certainly felt okay. He was happy in that moment and incredibly carefree. He was on his way to Babushka's house.

What could possibly go wrong? he thought.

He accelerated along the final stretch, flew up the ramp, and *pop*—out he came through the trapdoor under the fireplace. *Sherrrt!* went Bee's tyres as he steered her to a stop. He was gentle, of course. Rational Vlad would never do anything to deliberately hurt his favourite creation. Though it was tempting to let loose.

"Woohoo!" the little rat screamed. "That was crazyyyy, Bee."

Beep, beep, boop. "Yes, it was," replied Bee, agreeing with her sidekick. Vlad jumped out, looked down at his wristwatch, pressed a button, and watched his car transform into a robot.

"High-five," said Vlad, holding up his palm. Without thinking twice, the robot high-fived her maker, pivoted on her heel, and made her way towards the couches. Bee loved sitting on the couches, as they were so cosy. The pillows engulfed and suffocated you, and Bee loved that sensation. It was like lying right in the middle of a soft, fluffy, white marshmallow. Or being cocooned like a caterpillar in layers of soft tissue, protected from the elements and predators. And it was sheer bliss.

"Honey, I'm home," sang Vlad out loud, making his presence known. But there was complete silence. No one within the house stirred and nothing made a noise.

Oh, thought Vlad, scratching his head and looking around. *This is odd.*

The house felt cold. Empty. It had no life. He made his way through the kitchen, listening for any clues to the whereabouts of Babushka.

"Ah, I have a hunch!" Vlad walked up to the kitchen drawers and started to climb. He found that being a rat was a big advantage. His abilities were far greater now than when he was a human on Saphira. For example, he could scale a wall, or any surface really, with the utmost ease—thanks to his big paws. His long, hooked claws had tremendous grip and could easily latch on to anything. It made climbing these drawers an absolute treat. Oh, and his tail! The tail of a rat was long, nearly twenty-three centimetres, and a very *handy* appendage. It helped rats balance when they were moving, especially when they were climbing. Vlad had no problem scaling the kitchen cupboards at Babushka's house. In fact, he did it with grace. And, most of all, he made it look easy.

When he reached the top, he pulled himself up and gasped. "Ohhhh!"

There, lying on a cooling rack, were loads and loads of muffins. But these muffins were not hot. These muffins didn't even let off an incredible scent, which you could deeply inhale and get lost in. No, these muffins looked dry and they were starting to grow mould, with little puffs of hair growing from the centres—just like old Nana's big, brown, wet mole that always had one long hair sprouting from the middle. And it was one of those moles that was always smack-bang either right next to Nana's nose or right above her lip. You could never miss it, and you could never keep your eyes off it. If you were *super lucky*, Nana would give you a kiss on the lips and rub that mole all over your mouth and face. *YUCK*. Bonus points if Nana had bad breath.

"What is going on?" asked Vlad out loud. "This isn't like Lilliana." He stood there, on top of the kitchen bench, and stared at the muffins. A tear trickled down his face at the thought of all those scrumptious desserts going to waste. The taste would have been mind-blowing. Vlad shook his head, to snap himself out of it. There was a crisis at hand, and it had nothing to do with the lost muffins. "Get a hold of yourself," he muttered under his breath. "Lilliana!" he yelled out. "Lilliana, where are you?"

He held up one enormous ear, listening intently for a response, any clues as to the whereabouts of his dear friend. But only silence seemed to reply.

"Hmmm," he said to himself.

Vlad clasped his hands behind his back and started to pace. Babushka's kitchen had an L-shaped layout. It had a stainless-steel sink positioned right under a set of windows with cupboards on each side. When Vlad scaled the kitchen cabinets to reach the benchtop, he used the set of drawers in front of the sink, the long side of the L-shape as opposed to the short side, missing a very vital clue to the whereabouts of Babushka. If by fate or chance he'd chosen the shorter side, he would have stumbled upon the note left by Kelly, explaining the whereabouts of Babushka. He paced past the stale muffins and away from the sink, his eyes glued to the benchtop as he went.

Hmm, where are you Babushka? he thought. All sorts of images rushed through his mind as his imagination ran wild. *Perhaps someone broke into the house and kidnapped her?* he considered. *No, no, that's not possible.* He shook his head. *There would be signs of a struggle, and I haven't seen a hint of that.*

He continued to walk back and forth across the benchtop. "Besides, everyone loves Lilliana. Who would want to hurt a beautiful old lady?" he wondered aloud. "Oh!" He stopped dead in his tracks and placed his paws over his snout, shocked at his realisation. "No," he whispered. "No," he repeated with a whimper. He started to tremble, a sick sensation travelling to the pit of his stomach. "What if it was her condition? Oh, what if she deteriorated even more or had an episode and forgot where she was?"

His little paws were shaking, his forehead sweaty, as images of a hurt Babushka flooded his mind.

"Bee, Bee!" he yelled out from the benchtop. Vlad rushed forward and didn't turn back again, waving his hands in the air while trying to grab Bee's attention from the couch. "Bee, Bee!" he continued, the edge drawing nearer. "Bee, Bee, Babushka is hurt and we need to find her!" But Bee was cocooned in a pillow and couldn't hear anything.

Damn, why can't she hear me? Suddenly, a piece of paper caught his eye. *Aha! I know what I will do with that. I will scrunch it up and throw it at Bee to get her attention.* Vlad's spirits lifted at the thought.

He gripped the paper with his paws and started to crumble it. But his gut was nagging at him for some reason.

Stop what you're doing! He ignored his gut instinct and continued.. His stomach dropped and gurgled.

"God, what is going on?"

Crumble, crumble, crumble went his little paws. *Niggle, niggle, niggle* went his gut. The feeling was getting stronger and stronger the more he scrunched his paper.

"Ah, okay!" he yelled out. "What is this paper? It's probably trash or some sort of pamphlet that Babushka doesn't need anyway." He rolled his eyes, unscrunched the paper, smoothed it out flat, and started to read.

Babushka is sick. She fainted and couldn't
be revived...

"Revived?" squeaked the little brown rat. His gut had been right after all. This piece of paper was important. And right now, even though the note was scaring him to bits, he was also thanking his lucky stars. "I called the ambulance to have her taken to hospital," he read the words aloud.

Oh, hospital! thought Vlad. He knew this new information was bad, but it was good at the same time. The hospital would help her and give her the best possible care. He continued to read the note, hoping for more answers.

"If you need more information, please call Kelly at 0408 123 456." Vlad looked up and smiled. "I know where she is!" he shouted. "Bee, Bee, I know where Babushka is! We have to go back and tell the others." Vlad placed the note back on the bench where he'd found it. He ran to the edge and started climbing down steadily. He was a rat on a mission, and nothing was going to stop him.

It didn't take long to reach the floor, and when he did, he bolted. *BAM.* If you remember Speedy Gonzales, well, this was the rat version of that very same mouse. And if there were any witnesses that day, they too would have seen dust forming behind Vlad as he sped his way towards the lounge area. He was fast and he was determined. Without thinking, Vlad scaled the coffee table and reached the top. He jumped up and down repeatedly until he finally got Bee's attention.

Beep, beep, burp went Bee.

"That's okay, Bee," said Vlad. "I would cocoon myself in those pillows too. They are super soft." He gave her a wink. "But guess what? I know where she is," he announced excitedly.

Beep, beep, beep. Bee sat up and prepared herself, sensing that it was time for action and that playtime was over.

Vlad pointed to the kitchen bench and filled Bee in on what he'd uncovered. "We have to go back to the burrow and inform the clan. Emergency meeting!"

Beep, beep, burp said Bee.

Vlad looked at his trusted sidekick and scratched his head. "What do you mean we have to find Wymann? I don't understand?" he said.

Beep, burp, beep, gurt continued Bee. And, this time, she pointed to something peculiar on the coffee table—something Vlad would surely like to see.

"Necklace? What do you mean necklace?" questioned the rat. "Why in God's name would Wymann leave his necklace here?" He turned his head in the direction Bee was pointing. And there, right on the corner of the coffee table, was Wymann's legendary necklace of truth. Vlad's eyes nearly bulged out of his head at the sight. "Wymann never takes that necklace off," he muttered to himself. Like a zombie, he stomped closer, racking his brain for answers.

What is going on? he thought. *First Babushka and now Wymann.*

He stopped in front of the necklace and stared at it. He'd never been this close to it. EVER. And, my God, was it stunning. The blue jewels were the most gorgeous shade imaginable and they looked perfect.

How could anyone cut jewels to such perfection? thought Vlad. They were flawless and the gold that held it all together... *Wow, wow, wow.* The craftsmanship was beyond spectacular.

Vlad's mouth was beginning to salivate, and his heart was racing a million beats per hour. He held out his paw. The desire to touch it was great, and the allure was pulling him forward, near impossible to resist. The necklace of truth was shrouded in mystery. No one but the bearer knew its power. NO ONE. There were stories, of course, rumours of what this very necklace could do. The power it could yield. But those were just that. *Stories and rumours.* Vlad desperately wanted to touch it, to feel its power. And in that moment, he wished he were human once again. He hadn't felt this desire to be human for a very, very long time. But with the necklace now lying within arm's reach, that latent want was amplified.

Beep, beep, burp said Bee, interrupting Vlad's thoughts.

He quickly tugged his hand back, his face glowing a bright-crimson hue, a colour that could have rivalled the blue glow of the necklace at any given time.

Beep, beep, gurt continued Bee.

"Yes, you are right, my dear friend," said Vlad, turning his back to the necklace and to temptation. He took a deep breath to calm his nerves. "Are you ready?" he asked the robot.

Bee jumped over the edge of the couch and did a perfect

pin drop. Ten points! A perfect score for perfect symmetry. About halfway through the descent, a compartment opened up and out popped two glorious wings. They adjusted automatically and realigned into a large glider, steadily and gently lowering the occupant to the ground in one piece. Bee landed, and her glider instantly folded up and pop back into place. Vlad watched with such pride at his glorious creation. He created this marvellous robot with his own hands and imagination—with a little influence, of course, from the *Transformers* cartoon.

Beep, beep, beep said Bee to her creator, taking him away from his thoughts yet again.

Vlad looked at his wristwatch, flicked the switch, and Bee transformed back into his sleek, beautiful, yet powerful car. He scurried down the side of the coffee table, not daring to throw a glance at the necklace, fearing that this time he would definitely touch it. Bee opened her car door and waited for Vlad to jump in. *Kerplunk* went the rat. He grabbed the walkie-talkie and immediately pressed the push-to-talk button.

"Cat, this is rat, over," said Vlad, and he waited.

"Rat, this is cat, receiving transmission loud and clear," said Tira on the other end.

Vlad continued immediately, "We have an emergency clan meeting situation. Please assemble the tribe and meet in the Great Hall in ten minutes."

Without asking questions, Tira simply replied, "Affirmative, see you back at the burrow." For this call to come through, it meant things were bad, something was up, and precautions needed to be put into place. Tira stood there for a split-second and wondered what it could possibly be.

Before she had set off on her nightly patrol, everyone was safe in the burrow. They all might have been feeling frustrated and agitated with one another, but they were well nonetheless.

She gently played with her whiskers, twirling them around her paw. *This means something's wrong with either Babushka or Wymann,* she thought.

Tira wasn't scared, at least not for herself. However, this extra problem might be enough to tip some of the members right off the edge, causing anarchy. And that was the last thing any of them needed right now. So off she darted, straight back to the burrow while blending in with all the shadows of the world.

Vlad placed his walkie-talkie into its designated slot, slapped his favourite T2 sunglasses on, and grabbed the steering wheel. It was time for some serious business. "You know what to do, Bee," he whispered, preparing himself for the rush. Bee slammed her door shut, winked at her creator from the screen on the dashboard, and set off in a cloud of dust and fury—back towards the fireplace and beyond.

~

Vlad left his quarters and made his way towards the Great Hall. He could already hear all the commotion, each of the companions yelling over the top of the other and not allowing anyone to finish what they were trying to say. He slapped a palm to his face, trying to hide from the chaos.

This was going to be a hard night, he thought to himself. But, in all seriousness, it had to be done.

Vlad took a deep breath, steadied his resolve, and pushed open the door abruptly. "Quiet!" he hollered, as he made his presence known in the Great Hall with his arms outstretched.

Everyone immediately stopped midargument, their full attention focused on the rodent. Vlad ignored the stares and snarls coming from some of the familiar faces in the room—well, some being one, and that one was none other than Tovah. Vlad knew tonight was going to be a challenge but he was hoping it wasn't going to be hell, so he crossed his fingers as he took a seat at the table. Still not looking at his audience, Vlad began to speak, "My dear friends…"

"Prrr," said Tovah, crossing his arms in disgust. Vlad lifted his gaze up and straight at Tovah. If looks could kill, the big, fat, *rude* owl would be toast. Sensing the tension, Tovah quickly shut his beak and listened for a change.

"My dear friends, we have a problem on our hands. Lilliana is in hospital."

The chamber erupted into chaos, each companion trying to get their point across, the reasons to why it had happened and what must be done next in order to secure the safety of all.

Vlad looked upon them all in utter shock. *Had everyone gone mad?*

Even the princess was yelling, screaming at the top of her lungs in her attempt to be heard—someone who always found a way to restore the peace within the burrow was now part of the chaos. Vlad couldn't believe what he was seeing. Surely all this was just a very bad dream, a nightmare, and he was certain he was going to wake up any minute.

"We leave the witch in hospital," said Tovah, snarling at the crowd.

"We can't leave her there. She needs us," said the princess, smiling back at the priest.

"We never leave anyone behind, damn ye," growled the toad, slapping the table so hard that it shook; several of the companions gasped at the force of the knock. "Lilliana never left anyone behind when we entered the portal. We sure as hell don't start now," he continued to grumble, pointing his dirty, little, webbed finger at everyone as he stared at them, one after another. "Besides, she saved us and we owe her."

"What do we owe that witch?" piped up Tovah as he stood up from his chair and started to pace around the hall, making his case with each back-and-forth step. "We don't owe her anything. We've been trapped here, on this godforsaken planet, for so very long. We don't owe her anything. Not even a thanks," he spat.

"*You*, sit right down and shut ye beak, ye stupid fat bird," hissed the toad. He was so angry at what the owl was saying. So incredibly angry that it made his blood boil to the point that steam appeared to be rising from his ears. "Ye would be food for the maggots and worms if it weren't for her and her magic."

"Her magic?" stated Tovah, stopping dead in his tracks. He turned to the toad. "Her magic does not work, and it probably didn't work from the beginning, otherwise we wouldn't be stuck here."

The toad screamed in frustration, hitting the table yet again, this time harder, causing the table to crack slightly. Vlad watched them in silence. He watched Tovah and Dylan attack each other. Round after round after round. And with each insult flung, the toad hit the table with his fist, causing the crack to slowly travel to the centre—the wood was going to break and it was going to break hard. And just like this crisis with Lilliana, it had the potential to break the clan along with it. But Vlad was not going to allow that to happen.

"STOP!" he yelled. "Just stop and look at what you all are doing to one another." Silence finally fell upon the hall.

"Stop this madness," he pleaded, holding his paws together in prayer. "Stop fighting each other." He looked straight at Tovah, "Whether we like it or not, we are in this together, all of us, including Lilliana."

Tova rolled his eyes at Vlad's comment and snorted. "Leave the witch to rot," he spat.

Tovah just couldn't help himself. He always had to have the final say in everything. And being a man of God, he believed his word was final and the only one that truly mattered. But not today. Enough was enough. Push had come to shove.

"Be quiet!" yelled Vlad, pointing his finger right at Tovah. "For a man of the cloth, you sure are mean, my dear priest." His tone was calm, controlled, and he surprised even himself. "You haven't taught us anything but hate, how to bicker, and how to stir," he continued, his eyes focused on the owl as he spoke. Tovah just stood there, frozen to the spot and not believing what he was hearing. "Hate will not get us anywhere," said Vlad, addressing everyone in the hall. "We need to work together to stay safe." Several companions nodded their heads. "We came here together. And, mark my words, we will leave here together too."

"Hear, hear!" sang out the princess in agreement.

"Aye," bellowed the toad. And everyone clapped and stomped in unison. Almost everyone...

Vlad continued to address the clan that night. He informed them, in great detail, about the note he'd found at Babushka's house and the name and number of the person who'd written it. It was decided unanimously—well, almost unanimously, as Tovah remained mute and fixed in his spot—that the best approach moving forward would be to contact

Wymann and get him to call the number. The clan believed that this "Kelly" person was the key.

Little did they know that Kelly was not just the *key* but the *solution* to reopening the portal.

19

WYMANN UNLOCKED THE front door to his house and turned the knob. It was late in the evening and he was exhausted and somewhat sad. Exhausted from running the bookshop all day and sorting through fifteen large boxes filled with all sorts of books donated by the community. And sad from feeling helpless and like a failure. He placed his hand on his chest right about where the magical necklace used to hang. A part of him missed having it there, a very small part. He was angry and felt slightly betrayed by the magic. He remembered how much comfort and reassurance it used to give him. It helped him believe and hope that one day they would go home. But now he had no hope left.

"Damn you," he muttered to himself. "Another pointless day." He released a heavy exhale as he walked into his house.

There was no one to greet Wymann when he came home from work. No one to ask him how his day had been. No one to eat dinner beside or to share a cup of tea with.

Wymann lived alone, and to be honest, he preferred it that way. Even now, when he'd lost all hope.

He lived in a small, two-bedroom, wooden house not far from Babushka and not far from his shop or the park either. He lived on Blight Street, which ran parallel to Babushka's house. Upon first glance, the house appeared rundown and decrepit. Some areas could use a good lick of paint, along with some clever carpentry work to make it not just safe to inhabit but also inviting. No one ever came over to visit— no one wanted to. Even though the whole community knew who Wymann was, they were afraid of the house. It looked too scary, like it belonged in a horror movie.

However, the scary part wasn't on the outside; it was on the inside. And, no, there weren't any dead bodies, or brains pickled in jars. No torture devices lying about, or demon dogs walking the property line. Believe it or not, the most terrifying things in Wymann's home were his books. There were thousands upon thousands of books. Books everywhere. There were more books than furniture. Every wall was covered. Old books, ancient books, priceless books, small books, thick books, thin books, and so on.

One room was filled so high that all the furniture was removed so that more books could be placed inside. Books lined the hallway. Books filled the kitchen cupboards and drawers. They were stacked up so high in the lounge room that they blocked the view of the TV. It didn't matter anyway because there was nowhere to sit—the couch was covered in books too. Even the bathtub was packed to the brim. Showering wasn't a problem for Wymann, as he didn't like to shower anyway, at least not the conventional way. He preferred to jump into a lake or a river to rinse himself off. The natural water was beautiful and felt incredibly fresh against his skin. It invigorated him and he swore black and blue that was what kept him young.

In the early days, when they'd first arrived through the portal, the companions who'd transformed into animals had found solitude in the abandoned burrow under the old oak tree. Whereas Wymann and Babushka lived amongst the trees and bushes of the parkland. They created shelter with whatever material they could find. And on more than one occasion, when the weather was bad, they'd spend the night in the public toilet. To most, that would seem absolutely putrid and filthy, as everyone knew how dirty and unhygienic those public toilets could be, but that is all they had and they needed to survive.

And a shower wasn't one from a running hot water system either, mind you. It was a dip in the local pond and Wymann loved it. It reminded him of the good old days back in Saphira. Of the cold water cleansing his skin and the warm sun radiating on his back—that was paradise. But Babushka didn't mind the pond acting as her ginormous bathtub. In fact, she would dive right in there, swimming and frolicking with all the fish and the turtles. The pond helped to cheer her up on those days when she was really, really sad.

But that all changed when the police came and took them to the homeless shelter ran by the local church. No one complained about Wymann or Babushka living at the park. The community was just worried about their health and well-being, as the wintertime could be harsh and unforgiving. The Bureau of Meteorology would even refer to the weather as The Big FREEZE—that's how cold and danger-ous it actually was.

The council ordered all animals to be kept indoors at night as temperatures plummeted well below negative ten degrees. It was a shift in the weather pattern, and some-thing that had never been seen before in the history of the community. The church was a godsend that year, because it helped hundreds of homeless people stay safe and most of all *warm*. The community Church, Saint Mary's, was situated about a ten-minute drive west of the park. It was a very old church, which had been built a very long time ago.

It was a special place, where all were welcome and no one was ever turned away. The doors were always open, along with everyone's arms. People didn't sleep within the church; there was no need. The property was vast, with dozens upon dozens of buildings, where the homeless could sleep, be fed, and showered. They were allowed to stay as long as they needed, until more permanent accommoda-tions were found, including suitable employment.

Wymann was very grateful for the help the church had given so long ago. It certainly changed his life and allowed him and the entire clan to survive. There was a time where it may have crossed his mind that they were stuck on this planet, but that realisation was quickly changed to the feel-ing of being incredibly lucky. Lady Luck was on their side when they came through the portal. If it weren't for this planet, and the community that welcomed them on the other side, they surely would have perished.

"Honies, I am home," yelled out Wymann as he closed the door behind him. His *honies* were his books and they greeted him with silence as he walked through the packed hallway towards the kitchen. Every room he passed was filled with his honies. He knew exactly where he left each book, which shelf, and in what pile. He had an incredible ability to store information and an incredible memory for learning. Some would say that he was a genius, as everything seemed to come easily to him.

He spent hours reading about chemistry, days reading about physics, and weeks reading about astronomy. And between, he somehow found the time to read about folklore, about mythical heroes, beasts, and magic. All sorts of magic, from all corners of the earth. He knew somewhere amongst the pages lay the answer on how to get back home.

"Ahh!" Plunking himself onto his favourite arm chair and reclining the seat, Wymann kicked off his old, raggedy shoes and stretched out his tired, old legs on a makeshift pouffe—a stack of books he didn't enjoy reading at all, so he didn't care if his sweat-soaked socks and smelly feet rested upon them.

He closed his eyes, just for a moment. All he wanted was some peace. For his mind to stop thinking and analysing. He was tired of it. He'd spent so many nights reading, learning, and thinking.

So many wasted nights, he thought, shaking his head as he remembered. Surely, by now, he would have stumbled upon the answer. Surely, by now, they would have found the boy. Surely, by now, they would have been back home.

A tear rolled down his cheek. His heart hurt. Not from any health problems, but because of the decision he'd made when the police arrived on that dreaded night when they came through the portal and got separated from Millard's son. Perhaps if he'd run faster, or even claimed the boy as his own, things would have turned out differently. They would still be here—stuck—but at least they would all be together.

Wymann kicked his legs in frustration. If he could, he would certainly kick himself instead. Right in the butt. "Damn you!" he screamed. "Damn you, books!" He shook a fist at his honies. "And damn you, Lilliana," he spat, his rage diminishing to a gentle sob. It was all too much for Wymann. The feelings that had been bottled up for years and years—brewing, bubbling, and brewing some more— were now overwhelming.

If only Lilliana could see the magic, he thought. *If only the threads could lead them to where Millard's son was taken, he could at least be free of this burden.*

The burden had taken its toll and it weighed a hefty sum, slowly beating Wymann down over time. Day by day, hour by hour. It wasn't like he didn't try. Wymann definitely tried to find him. He checked every available police record, looking into adoptions and foster homes, and nothing came up. Years later, he approached the front desk at the police station and asked numerous questions about "that night," wanting to know if an abandoned child was found during a great storm at All Nations Park. But the police said that it was not ethical, or legal, to discuss cases that were both private and confidential. Wymann was pressed on why he wanted to know and simply responded that he heard many rumours and wanted to put those rumours to bed. The police politely told him to stop listening to those rumours.

"Damn you, Lilliana," he spat again, hitting both armrests this time and kicking his legs like a small child having a fit in a toy shop.

"Now that's not a nice way to speak about a lady," purred the cat.

Wymann screamed, instinctively grabbing a book and throwing it behind him, in the direction of the speaker. It may not have been a sword but a book could do some damage too.

Luckily, the cat was none other than Tira, who was super smooth and incredibly intelligent. She could foresee a player's next move before the game actually began, analysing her opponent from afar and understanding how they ticked. She quickly ducked and sprang out of the way, allowing the book to collide into the side of the kitchen bench, missing her by a longshot.

"Pfft, I don't understand how you were ever a master swordsman, my lord," she teased.

"Oh, damn you too, you feral cat!"

"Damn me too?" she repeated. Tira placed a paw innocently on her chest and batted her lashes with a cheeky smirk. "I don't even know what I've done to receive such a beratement."

Wymann sat upright in his arm chair and turned to face her, his expression and voice equally stern. "You came into my house unwelcomed. That's what you did." He pointed a finger at her.

"I came here to bring you some news. Besides, what happened to your face? Oh my, did you fall over in your bookshop, dear lord?" Tira's smirk widened.

"No, I didn't! What is it with you all always thinking I've fallen over at the bookshop. It's clearly none of your business, and I don't care what you have to say," Wymann hollered. "Now get out!"

"*Clearly*, I can see that, my lord, but I have a message and the clan needs your help." Tira sat on her hindlegs and looked at Wymann in silence, waiting patiently to gain his full attention.

He was getting more and more agitated by the minute as all he wanted was some peace, and peace was not what he was getting. He was so fed up that he didn't turn around to speak to his unwanted visitor; he just remained seated in his armchair, refusing to look at her.

"Didn't you hear what I said? Get out of my house, you dirty feline," he spat.

"Babushka is in hospital, Wymann," said Tira sincerely.

And that's what it took. Five words to make Wymann change his demeanour instantly. He sat up, turned around, and stared Tira right in the eyes. "Lilliana is in hospital? What trickery is this? You are playing tricks on me," he insisted, narrowing his eyes at her.

Tira knew that the news had unsettled him. She could see that his hands were shaking. "I am not playing any tricks on you, my lord. I promise." She lifted her paws in reassurance.

"No, this can't be," he whispered. "I just saw her a couple of days ago, and she seemed fine," he stated. "She was doing her usual thing…" He trailed off into his thoughts. Wymann could not believe what he was hearing. His friend was in hospital. His friend, who helped everyone in many ways. His friend, who was always there for everyone. His friend, who had been through thick and thin with him, was in hospital.

He felt guilty. And childish. For his misdirected anger towards Lilliana. It wasn't her fault that they were here on earth. And it wasn't her fault that her magic wasn't working on this planet. None of it was her fault.

"How… how did it happen?" he whispered.

"Unfortunately, we don't know much, my lord," answered the cat. "Vlad went over one night and found her house abandoned. She must have been baking when it happened, because he found a few dozen mouldy muffins sitting on cooling racks."

"Was the front door broken in?" asked Wymann in alarm.

"No, they came in the usual way, through the fireplace. Nothing seemed out of sorts, like a robbery took place or anything," Tira explained patiently.

Wymann slapped himself on the head. "Oh, yes, yes, that's right. I totally forgot." His face was turning red.

Tira continued to explain what Vlad had found: the note sitting on the kitchen bench and the contact details of a person named Kelly scribbled upon it.

Wymann remained silent, trying to absorb every detail. At times, he secretly pinched himself, not believing what he was hearing and partially hoping he would wake up from this nightmare—if he truly was in one.

"We must call the hospital then," said Wymann, nodding his head in agreement. He turned to Tira. "The hospital will be able to tell us everything that we need to know and maybe we can go in and see her." He got up on his feet, feeling a sudden spring in his step while his heart released some of the pain. He felt lighter for a change. He was determined to find out more about his friend. Lilliana needed him and he wasn't going to let her down. Wymann stormed right over to his telephone, which was hidden, well, behind a stack of books of course. He grabbed the cordless handset, clicked a few buttons, and started searching through his internal digital phone book.

"What are you doing?" quizzed Tira, her ears perking up.

"I am going to call the hospital, and I bet my bottom dollar they took her to Saint Francis Memorial." He continued to search for the number.

"Maybe we should call the number left on the note instead, and see what they have to say about it all," suggested the cat. "The clan agreed it would be best to take that approach," she quickly added.

"Ah! Here we go," Wymann said out loud, feeling victorious, and he dialled the number, ignoring the cat's pleas. However, he did click on the speaker function so that Tira could hear too.

Brrt, brrt, brrt, brrt went the phone before it connected.

"Good evening, Saint Francis Memorial, how can I help you?" said a friendly voice on the other end.

"Ah, ahem, excuse me. Can you please help me find a patient admitted a couple of days ago? Her name is Lilliana."

"Lilliana, do you have more information please? Such as date of birth or a surname?"

"No, sorry, I don't have any more information. Would it be possible for you to please check the emergency department for a little old lady with grey hair," said Wymann, sounding anxious. He stood up and started to pace, dodging books here, there, and everywhere. Tira watched him and waited patiently to see what news he could find out about their friend.

"Sorry, sir, but we need more information as we're not told who is transported into the emergency department. Without identifying details, I won't be able to locate the person you are looking for. I am so sorry." The speaker sounded sympathetic.

"Oh, please, please, can you please help me find my friend? All I know is that she was taken to the emergency department a couple of days ago. Can you at least call the emergency department and see if she was there?" pleaded Wymann, his hope clearly dwindling.

The kind voice hesitated. "Look, sir, I can't do that type of thing. I need more information to find your friend. I really am so sorry."

"Oh, please, please, please! I beg you. Can you please give them a call, just this once? I have no one else but this friend. Please, please help me," begged Wymann.

His pleas for help pulled at the heartstrings of the phone operator, and she caved. "Okay, I will give them a quick call and see what I can find. Just one moment please." And she placed him on hold.

"What is going on?" asked the cat curiously. She'd been too busy navigating the various piles of books as Wymann paced back and forth to overhear the entire exchange.

Wymann covered the phone with his palm and answered Tira's question. "The phone operator is calling the emergency department to see if they can locate Lilliana. Fingers crossed, she comes back with some great news."

Click. "Hello, sir, are you there?" whispered the operator.

"Yes, yes, I am here," he answered.

"Yes, there was a Lilliana in the emergency department a couple of days ago, and she matches your description: little old lady with grey hair."

"Woohoo!" Wymann punched the air with one fist, doing a small skip on the spot while the anxiety dissipated momentarily. "Can you tell me what happened please?" he pressed.

"Unfortunately, sir, I can't tell you anything."

Wymann's heart sank at the sound, the temporary elation bursting like a bubble. *POP.*

"But you can call back tomorrow and the switchboard attendant can transfer you to building A, level four—that's where she's been admitted." You could hear the woman's smile through the receiver as she attempted to cheer up her despondent caller.

"Can I talk to them now?" asked Wymann, crossing his fingers, his toes, and his eyes for luck.

"Unfortunately, sir, it's too late and no one will be able to answer your call. I'm very sorry for the inconvenience."

Inconvenience? Damn straight it's an inconvenience, thought Wymann.

He was about to lose control of his manners and give this poor lady a piece of his mind when he heard Tira shriek. She could sense his frustration but she also understood that when you are told it's too late, it's literally too late and nothing—absolutely nothing—was going to change it. "Mind your manners," she whispered, her ears pointing down and the fur on her back pointing up.

"Uh, uh, er, th-thank you for your help," Wymann said sheepishly and quickly hung up. Tira continued to glare, not appreciating how he'd spoken to the kind lady. He might run a bookshop by day, but as soon as the doors were closed, you didn't get to toss your manners out with the trash.

"Be nice," she reminded him. "Always be nice to people as they are the ones assisting you. Now, that may not be the news we are after, but it certainly helps." Wymann nodded his head in agreement, even though he wasn't fully satisfied with the outcome. "I will go and tell the others of our progress. Thank you for all your help, my lord." Tira bowed and immediately set upon her way. The cat was never one to dawdle. If there was a task at hand, she would carry on until it was done. The clan came first and this new piece of information should lift everyone's spirits, especially Vlad's.

"Wait!" yelled Wymann. "How did you get inside my house?" He wanted to know the answer. But she was gone in a flash, nowhere to be seen.

Damn that cat, he thought.

⁓

Vlad sat in his laboratory, staring at the plans for his latest project. Hours had gone by without much progress. All he could think about was his dear friend. He was so worried about her and the worry was making his little head start to hurt.

"Ugh!" He threw the pencil across the room and it ricocheted off the wall. It was just too hard to concentrate. He needed answers and they were taking too long to reach him. "Come on, Vlad, concentrate," he muttered to himself, rubbing his throbbing temples. He picked up the plans with his paws, took a deep breath, exhaled his frustration, and focused.

The plans were a rough blueprint of his latest idea for a new type of robot, bigger and better than anything else he'd ever created or thought of in the past. Of course, he never told Bee about his plan as he didn't want her to think that she was old tech. His projects were always kept a secret until something went wrong, such as an explosion that shook the whole burrow. That was when certain clansmen like Tovah would stick their nosey beaks into his business, inform the whole burrow, and blow everything right out of proportion—making Vlad look like the bad guy. Granted, it wasn't just the owl's fault, seeing as the explosion didn't help.

"Damn," Vlad cursed and threw the plans aside. He felt bad for yelling at Tovah and for saying nasty things to him in front of everyone. He'd embarrassed the priest, made him a spectacle. "But what else was I supposed to do?" Vlad asked the imaginary jury. He jumped off his chair and paced his quarters. Up and down, up and down, like an animal in a cage. "I didn't mean to embarrass him. I-I-I just had enough. Yes, that's it!" He shook his head. "I just had enough of Tovah and his nosiness, sticky beak, and crazy old bird brain—awww!" Vlad stopped midtrack and raised his balled-up fists. The memories of all the times Tovah had made his life, and everyone else's, hard came rushing back. Bombarding his brain.

"You need to meditate, dear rat," spoke a voice from the shadows.

"Oh, stop trying to scare me, you smelly feline. I knew you were there," said Vlad in response, still fired up.

"Oh?" purred Tira. She remained in the shadows, enjoying the mind games she always played with Vlad. "How long have I been watching you then, dear rat?" she teased.

Vlad heaved an irritated breath. He wasn't in the mood for anyone's crap tonight, not even Tira's. He looked at his wrist and pressed a few buttons on his watch. Holding the straightest poker face he could muster, he replied, "Twelve minutes and fourteen seconds… fifteen seconds… sixteen… Shall I go on?" he asked.

"Ah, very clever, dear rat," said Tira as she emerged from her hiding place. "Very clever."

"Well, put it this way, feline… I was sick of interruptions, so I installed motion detectors and cameras." He pointed to a couple of spots in his quarters. Tira looked but she couldn't see the sensors; they were camouflaged and hidden from plain view.

"I trust you have placed the same sensors in the tunnel, leading to your chamber?" she asked curiously.

"Absolutely," replied Vlad. He had to do it, to give himself some warning before an onslaught of busybodies.

"Nice," said Tira, staring at Vlad, her cat eyes widened with both surprise and slight shock. She knew Vlad loved to invent but she never imagined he would be this creative. "Looks like all those countless nights watching *MacGyver* have truly paid off."

Part of her understood why he had done it and she should have seen this coming. The poor rat was always ridiculed by Tovah for the things he created. Though it probably wasn't the gadgets that drew the owl's attention, but more the company with which the rat kept. Meaning Babushka. Tovah simply hated her and it became his passion. If Vlad was doing something the owl did not agree with, he would throw Babushka right in the middle, just to get a row out of him. The old priest enjoyed making trouble. He loved to stir, his actions always deliberate.

Now Vlad had a very soft spot for Babushka. He didn't like it when anybody—and I mean absolutely anybody—spoke poorly of his dear friend. Sure, he would ignore it most of the time. But, eventually, when the rumbling became too much and the gas build-up became too unbearable, the volcano had to explode. So to speak. And better it pour from his mouth than out the other end, if you know what I mean. That would be a horrible mess, which no one, not even Vlad, would want to clean. He'd rather build a new burrow than use a mop and bucket.

But the most mind-blowing thing of all was the fact that Tovah wasn't always like this. Before the portal, he was a very loving and caring priest, who did a lot for Saphira. As a result, the people of Saphira loved him back for it, including the king. But that all changed when they came to earth and no one knew exactly why and how it all began. It was a big mystery.

Vlad raised his hairy arm and showed Tira his watch; the time was still visible with the seconds ticking by. "See? If I flick this button…" Flick went Vlad's finger. "You can see directly into the tunnel outside my quarters." Tira grabbed his arm and Vlad yelped as the cat pulled him closer to her.

"Wow!" she purred as she watched the lights flicker in the tunnel. "This is amazing, Vlad! Wow…" She was completely mesmerised by what she was seeing. The technology was incredible.

"Um, can I have my arm back please?" said Vlad, trying to pull it out of Tira's hold.

"Oh, yes, of course. Ahem." She released him from her grip, feeling slightly foolish. Vlad straightened his clothes and rubbed at his nearly bruised arm. "Where can I get one of those?" asked Tira, pointing to the watch. "I would love to have eyes like that within the burrow. It would come in handy."

"You don't need one of these, you nosey feline," spat Vlad. "I only use it for peace. My peace of mind and no one else's." He pointed to his head, which was throbbing madly. "Now, what news do you have for me, feline?" he demanded. The conversation was frustrating.

Tira narrowed her eyes and pulled her ears back. She wanted one of those amazing watches and she was annoyed that Vlad wouldn't give her one.

But that's okay, she thought. *Good will come to those who wait.*

"I had a friendly chat with Wymann and explained the entire situation to him."

"Yes, go on," said Vlad, closing his eyes from the pain in his head.

"Instead of calling the number on the note, he called the hospital."

"*What*?" said Vlad, his voice raised and angry. "My instructions were simple!" He pummelled a fist on his palm. "Call the number on the note."

Tira held up her paw, signalling for the rat to calm down. "I understand what your instructions were, but I can't make him listen. You know Wymann. He does what he wants."

Vlad exhaled. "God Almighty." He turned his back to Tira, taking a moment to think things through.

"Even though we didn't find out any information regarding Babushka, as in her health status, we do know which hospital and exactly where she is located: the building and floor number," said Tira, hoping the news would bring Vlad some peace.

"Yes, yes, that is good news, Tira." The rodent spun to face her. "I will inform the burrow in the morning and I'm sure the news will be uplifting."

Tira nodded her head in agreement. "And if I hear anything further from Wymann, I certainly will inform the burrow immediately as well."

"Wonderful," said Vlad. "I bid you goodnight then."

Tira bowed to her companion, her eyes lingering on the watch sitting on Vlad's wrist. Vlad noticed the stare but dismissed it. Better to ignore the matter than provoke the feline's curiosity. This time, instead of waiting for her to disappear amongst the shadows, the rat turned, picked up the draft plan, and sat at his desk. He didn't wait to see if she had gone; he simply sat at his desk, his eyes fixed to what was in front of him.

The occasional onlooker would assume that he was studying. But, little would they know, he was actually eyeing all of his motion sensors and cameras—and that included the other ten he'd placed at various points within the burrow. Vlad smiled to himself as he watched Tira silently slip out of his quarters, venture through the tunnel, enter into the Great Hall, and then creep out through the exit at the pond.

No one, absolutely no one, was going to disturb his peace now, thanks to his latest invention.

20

KELLY SCREAMED, SITTING upright in her bed and clasping her hand. The pain was excruciating and it travelled right up to her elbow.

For a minute there, she had been standing in a beautiful green grove. Surrounded by luscious green oak trees. They were huge, their trunks were thick, and their branches stretched high into the blue sky. It seemed as if the tops could touch the white fluffy clouds and sway gently with the birds in flight.

Before her were thousands upon thousands of white daisies, scattered everywhere. The sun was shining and rays of light could be seen streaming into the grove. It was beautiful and incredibly peaceful. Kelly smiled to herself. She knew this grove. She'd been here before. Her heart felt lighter. Her mind finally at ease. Closing her eyes, Kelly inhaled the freshness of the grove, taking in all its magic. Breath after breath after breath.

She stood there for a while, enjoying the peace and the magic. Slowly, soft flecks of what seemed like snow drifted and landed on her face. First on her nose and then on her cheek and so forth. It tickled a little and she giggled like a schoolgirl. The flakes floated through the air one after another, gently disintegrating upon impact and not leaving a small wet patch where they once were. Kelly wiped her cheek and realised that there was no dampness. She opened one eye and peered down upon her hand.

Ash, she thought. *What is ash doing here?*

She opened her second eye, hoping that would give her a better understanding of what she was seeing, when she realised that her brain wasn't deceiving her. Ash was smudged all over her palm.

"What?" she gasped. Kelly looked around in a panic. The grove had vanished. No daisies, no oak trees, no sunshine, and no peace. All the magic was gone. "W-what is going on?" she muttered, spinning on the spot, feeling both lost and disorientated. There was nothing around her. Absolutely nothing. Just ash blowing through empty space and time.

Thump, thump, thump. Footsteps sounded throughout the nothing. *Thump, thump, thump.*

Where are they coming from? Kelly wondered to herself. She turned about, looking and searching for the source.

Thump, thump, thump.

They were getting closer. The hairs on her neck stood up on end. Something was coming, but what was it?

Woosh. A sword was drawn from its scabbard. *Thump, thump, thump* continued the footsteps. They were fast-approaching.

Kelly started to sweat and her heart began to race like a greyhound. She clutched her abdomen, giving herself a bear hug. "How is this happening again?" she mumbled to the air, her eyes frantically searching the space for whatever was about to jump out at her.

The swordsman cried out and the sound echoed throughout the void. Kelly jumped, startled by the sudden outburst.

Thump, thump, thump. The footsteps were so close and travelling at full speed.

The swordsman yelled again, this time clearly coming from Kelly's rear. She jumped abruptly. And, there, about one hundred metres away, was the silhouette of a man, his sword drawn and raised, his feet running straight towards her. Panic froze her mind and fear consumed her soul. She searched for a weapon but there was nothing to grab to defend herself.

"Deep breaths, Kel. Deep breaths, girl," she said to herself, trying to settle her nerves, and it worked. She stood her ground, waiting for the attack.

Thump, thump, thump. The silhouette was fifty metres away. *Thump, thump, thump.* Twenty metres.

Her attacker was now visible and Kelly recognised him. Her heart skipped a beat. It was the traitor who killed Millard. "No! No! Why are you here?" she screamed and her legs wobbled.

Thump, thump, thump. Ten metres and closing.

Oh, what am I going to do? she wondered. *I have no sword. Please, please, wake up, Kel.*

She slapped herself across the face, hoping that would do the trick. But all it did was deliver a nasty sting to her nose. "Ouch."

Five metres. *Thump, thump, thump.*

The traitor issued his battle cry, and Kelly closed her eyes, covering her chest with her arms in hopes that an imaginary shield would somehow protect her. She tensed, anticipating the deadly blow.

Four meters, three, two... The traitor swooped down with his sword. One metre. And slashed at his opponent. *Kablam.* The sword connected with her hand. The same hand that wore the golden glove. Sparks flew and a great white light engulfed the nothingness and all within it, like a giant supernova. *BAM! CHING!*

And then everything disappeared.

Kelly looked at her hand, flipping it over and examining each side while expecting to find a great big gash where the sword connected. "Oh, nothing there. This can't be...?"

Kelly grabbed her hand and squeezed it. There may have been no open wound, no blood, but the pain was immense. She massaged her palm, rubbing gently and pulling each finger slightly. She remembered a massage therapist doing this once and the result was soothing. She continued up to her forearm, rubbing and pushing down slightly here and there, manipulating the muscle all the way up to her elbow where she stopped.

That should be enough, she thought, slowly stretching out her arm, wary of the pain. The last thing she wanted was to go to the hospital.

"Hospital... Baba," she whispered. "Oh, Baba, I hope today is a better day. Please come back to us." Kelly sat quietly in her bed, reflecting on her fairy godmother and momentarily forgetting about her pain. Her heart hurt and it yearned for her Baba.

She exhaled and rubbed at her face. Tuesday, another day. Kelly didn't feel like going to school today. She was embarrassed and anxious. She patted her belly to soothe it. It was rumbling like a truck speeding down a rocky dirt path, and it wasn't from the lack of food. She just had a very bad feeling something was going to go wrong.

Kelly looked at her clock and yelped. "Oh damn!" She jumped out of bed and quickly got dressed. She didn't care if she was late for school. She just cared that her parents would hassle her and she wasn't in the mood. Her gut was giving her strong signals that her parents, in particular her mum, would be at her door any second now.

"Quick, quick, quick," she muttered to herself, running her fingers through her messy, sticky hair like a makeshift brush before tying it up into a ponytail. She grabbed her schoolbag and left her room.

Psst, psst, psst. "I don't know what to do anymore," whispered Joyce in the kitchen. Kelly stopped abruptly at the top of the stairs. Her mum was whispering about something, and when she whispered, it meant she didn't want Kelly to hear.

"But how in God's name can I hear it?" the teenager wondered out loud.

Psst, psst, psst. "What happened?" whispered Mark in concern.

"W-what? Dad?" Kelly said to herself. "M-mum? Are you guys here?" She was shocked as she looked around. She didn't understand how she could hear her parents so loudly and so clearly when they weren't even in the room.

Psst, psst, psst. "She's been so rude to me lately, Mark. I'm so furious with her," continued Joyce, trying to explain the tension between her and their daughter.

Kelly couldn't believe what she was hearing. She scanned the second floor and noticed the door to her parents' bedroom was wide open. "Oh, the nerve," she muttered under her breath. She pivoted on her heel and walked directly to her parents' bedroom, getting ready to give her mother a piece of her mind. "Rude? I've been rude? Well, who is being rude now?"

Kelly snorted, entering the room without knocking. Her blood pressure was rising and she was about to explode. However, the moment she crossed the threshold, she noticed that no one was there. The bed was perfectly made as always and their robes were lying neatly on the armchair in the corner.

"Is this some sick joke?" Kelly asked herself. She quickly took a walk around her parents' bedroom, contemplating whether or not what she'd heard had been real. "Hmph. It must be the broken sleep. I'm going crazy."

There was nothing more to say and there was nothing more to think about. Already, things weren't going right and she hadn't even walked through the gates at school.

Psst, psst, psst. "How about we call the school and get them involved," said Mark. "Schools can be very helpful, Joyce. They have psychologists available onsite, who can sit and talk to the students."

Standing at the top of the stairs again, Kelly froze like a deer in headlights. "Psychologists? What would I need a psychologist for?" She balled her fists and puffed out her chest, like an angry gorilla.

Psst, psst, psst. "I'm worried that will make her rebel even more, Mark. Oh, I don't know what to do anymore."

Joyce's eyes welled up and she sobbed softly. "I just want my girl back."

"That's all I want too, darls." Mark wrapped his wife in a huge hug. "Come on, darling, come to Papa Bear and give me some honey." He held her there in his arms, rubbing her back in a soothing motion. *Psst, psst, psst.* "Everything will be okay. You'll see. I'll call the school and see what we can do to help our girl. She will never know, darling, okay?"

"Help. I don't need help." Kelly snorted, rolling her eyes at the conversation she'd overheard between her mum and dad. She stomped all the way down the stairs. "God, how rude!" Kelly burst into the kitchen without warning. She saw Joyce in tears, while Mark embraced his wife. Normally she would have stopped and asked, like a good daughter, if everything was okay, but not today. Not after what she'd heard.

Her parents were startled by the commotion. "Oh, good morning, Kel," said Mark in the cheeriest voice he could muster at the moment.

"Good morning? *Good morning?* Is that all you can say?" Kelly hissed in response. Mark just stared at his daughter in confusion while Joyce sobbed in his arms, too upset to even speak. This lack of response frustrated Kelly even more. "Oh, of course!" She slapped her hands together in realisation. "You don't have anything more to say because *you*…" She pointed a finger at her father. "…have already used up all your words. Haven't you, Dad?" she screamed.

Mark continued to stare at his daughter. *What is going on with you?* he thought.

His heart broke at the sight of his beloved little girl. This wasn't like her. He always believed that he and Joyce were 110% approachable. Always available for a chat. They drummed that into Kelly when she was a toddler, teaching her to always speak and confide in them when something was bothering her. And something was definitely bothering her now. Mark just wished he knew sooner so that he could help her better.

"Darling, what is wrong?" he asked gently.

"Don't call me *darling*!" yelled Kelly. "Why don't you both call me crazy instead? Because, apparently…" Kelly gestured quotation marks as she repeated her father's words. "*I need help.*"

"No one said you needed help," countered Mark.

"Oh, yes you did." Kelly pointed a finger at him. "I heard you."

"Ah, ah, ah… We are only trying to be here for you, Kelly. Clearly something is wrong." Mark's heart was racing at a rate of one hundred miles an hour, and he was beginning to sweat like a pig. What he really wanted to say to his daughter wouldn't come out. He couldn't find the right words and it hurt. It was like his brain stopped working and his tongue didn't want to function like it should. "How did you hear us? We were whispering," he asked instead. "There was no way you could have heard us, unless you were being rude and eavesdropping."

"Oh!" Kelly rolled her hands into fists and shook them vigorously. "I was not eavesdropping. You were both so loud I bet the neighbours heard you too!" She stomped her foot, not knowing what else to do.

Kelly's blood was now pulsating in her veins. Her breathing was so deep and laboured that her face changed colour. She was so angry at her parents that she decided it was best to just leave before she regretted what she would do or say next.

"Ahhh!" And out she ran, but before she slammed the door behind her, she yelled at the top of her lungs, "STOP TALKING about me!"

SLAM! She was gone, leaving two people bewildered in the kitchen, each trying to understand how their daughter had heard their whispers in the first place.

Shuffle, shuffle, shuffle. Stomp, stomp, stomp. Rattle, rattle, rattle went Kelly's schoolbag as she bolted to school.

She looked down at her wristwatch, checking the time. 8:55 AM. She had exactly five minutes to run through the gate before they padlocked it. Traverse the corridor, dodging every Tom, Dick and Harry and their schoolbags. And jump into her homeroom seat before the teachers arrived.

"God, I'm going to be so late," she muttered to herself.

Psst, psst, psst. "Okay, time to chain and lock the gate," said Barry, the gardener, to the last few students stepping onto the grounds.

"Oh!" yelled Kelly. The school gates where one block away, and she could already hear the jiggling and jangling of the brass chain. Her heart raced as she pushed her legs harder. The stress and anxiety were far too great for her to even contemplate how she could hear the brass chain from such a distance.

Barry unhinged the large gate and began to swing it shut. *Screech* went the hinges, crying out for oil.

"Come on, feet!" yelled Kelly, egging herself on. "Barry is closing the gate."

Heho, heho, heho. Kelly heaved, pushing harder and

harder and moving as fast as she could. But with broken sleep, hardly any food, and plenty of stress and drama, her energy levels were low and depleting fast.

Screech continued the gate. The gap separating the outside world and the school grounds was getting smaller and smaller by the second. Time was of the essence and Kelly was desperate. If she didn't step through the gates on time, she would not just be extremely late and locked out, she would be in deep trouble. Kelly would have to go to the office, sign in at reception, and give a reason. Then, her parents would be notified and that right there meant a whole lot of extra trouble at home, which she didn't need, especially after this morning. The tension in the house was astronomical and her parents were both at their wits' end.

Heho, heho, heho. Stomp, stomp, stomp. Screech.

Heho, heho, heho. Stomp, stomp, stomp. Screech. Smack!

Kelly flew, elbow-first, into the gate and knocked Barry over. "Well, wow, wow!" He flew backwards and landed hard on his bum, his chain flying out of his hand and landing in a heap on the floor not far from him.

Kelly continued to run while she shouted out her apologies to Barry. "Oh, so sorry, Mr Barry. So sorry!" She elbowed the door at the corridor entrance, not caring if anyone was standing in the way.

Kablam went the door as it was flung wide open. *Stomp, stomp, stomp* went her feet.

One minute to go. Before her life got even more complicated. She had to make it to homeroom before her teachers arrived.

Psst, psst, psst. "Look, it's barf girl," whispered one student to another. They both glanced at Kelly and giggled, like it was the best joke ever.

Psst, psst, psst. "Oh, she's going to be murdered by Sandra today," quickly murmured another girl when Kelly ran by.

"Hey, Jenny," whispered Connie. "Look, it's barf girl. Oh my God, do you think she will throw up again in English?"

The whispers continued as Kelly ran through the corridor, comments coming from all directions. Kelly couldn't comprehend what she was hearing. Everyone was snickering at her, laughing and teasing her. The remarks may have been whispered, but to Kelly, they were loud and clear. In stereo. The worst part of all was the fact that the words hurt because they came from some people she thought were her friends.

Psst, psst, psst. "I know. How dare barf face ruin my poetry recital. She is going to pay for what she did yesterday. Mark my words, girls..." whispered Miss Popularity to her posse of minions.

Kelly jumped into her homeroom, heaving like a bull who'd just rumbled and tumbled in a rodeo. *Heho, heho.* She bent over at the entrance, trying to catch her breath while her head raced. She didn't want to look up because she could feel all eyes on her. And one set in particular belonged to Sandra. After what she heard in the corridor, all Kelly wanted to do was disappear like the Invisible Man. Her morning started horribly, and it wasn't going to get better anytime soon. It felt like the whole year-level was against her.

"All right, all right, ladies. Get to your seats quickly, please," said Mrs Richards. "We have a tonne of things to get through before the bell goes." She placed her folders on the desk and waited patiently for everyone to be seated.

"Good morning, ladies," greeted Mr Lunateri as he

entered the room, fashionably late today. "You heard what Mrs Richards said. Now get a move on, please," he added.

Kelly waddled to her desk and avoided making eye contact. She even hummed to herself to block out the so-called whispers. "Hmmm, hmmm, hmmm," she hummed the tune to her latest favourite song and today it was "No Shelter" by Broken Edge.

Kelly felt all alone. She didn't understand why everyone had suddenly turned against her overnight. All the comments just didn't add up. It didn't make sense. She didn't mean to disrupt Sandra's poetry recital yesterday. It was just one of those freak things that happened once in a million years. An incident nobody had any control over. In fact, it could have happened to anyone. Absolutely anyone, at any time. It was just bad luck that it happened to Kelly, and even worse luck that it had to happen when Miss Priss had the spotlight on her.

Double whammy.

"Hmm, hmm, hmm," continued Kelly. She dumped her bag on the floor when she reached her desk. "Phew," she muttered to herself. The cleaners had been here yesterday and they thoroughly sanitised her seat. There were no traces of vomit anywhere and the desk itself looked better and brighter than it had before, almost like new. Even the graffiti was wiped away, along with the numerous marks left by ink and highlighter pens. She pulled out her chair and quickly sat down, looking straight at Mrs Richards.

Psst, psst, psst. "Barf head," whispered one student to another and they giggled. Mrs Richards ignored the snickering and continue to address the class, reading out the morning's newsletter.

"Hey, Sandra, throw this at barf face," whispered one of her minions sitting beside her.

"Stop it, Amy. I'm trying to listen to the teacher," Sandra hissed under her breath.

"Oh, sorry, sorry," replied the minion to her master— her embarrassment evident by the pink tint to her cheeks.

Kelly sat incredibly still at her desk, not because she wanted to listen to what her homeroom teacher was saying, but because she was shocked by what she was hearing being said about her.

Why isn't Mrs Richards doing anything about it? And why isn't anyone in the class standing up for me? she thought to herself, feeling more alone and broken-hearted than ever.

Yesterday was an accident. It wasn't something Kelly went out of her way to do; she wasn't that type of person. She drifted off in thought while she sat at her desk. When her name was called out during attendance, she automatically responded, "Here!"

It was a good thing that she was so deep in thought too. Because the whispers and the snickering comments in the background would have really set her right off and pushed her over the edge. Her life had been turned upside down, jiggled all around, then shaken and finally stirred. She didn't understand why it all was happening. Did she do something so bad in her past life that now was the time to pay for her sins? It just didn't make sense.

Ding, ding, ding went the bell, and Kelly snapped out of her daydream.

"Okay, girls, have a great day and see you all later," shouted Mrs Richards above the commotion that spontaneously erupted as soon as the bell rang. Kelly didn't want to hang around to listen to anymore foul comments about her. So she grabbed her bag and bolted out of the room in a flash, humming her way to her first class, which also happened to be her favourite. Art.

~

Kelly loved art. It was her escape from stress and her sanctuary from the real world. It was her happy place, where there were no limitations, no barriers, and free reign. She could do whatever her heart desired in art, and the teacher never judged anyone. Every student was encouraged to explore their imagination, and whatever they created was always applauded. The school was lucky to have Miss Davies as a teacher, and Kelly loved her dearly.

"Good morning, Miss Davies," said Kelly as she stepped into her class.

"Oh, good morning, HB. How are you today?" Even Miss Davies called Kelly *HB*. She liked the name and thought it suited her well.

"I am okay," said Kelly, her voice flat and her eyes teary.

"You sure?" asked Miss Davies in response. "You know you can talk to me anytime, about anything."

Kelly smiled at her favourite teacher. "Yes, I know but believe me I am okay."

Psst, psst, psst. "Let's see how much brown-nosing barf face does today," said one of the minions as they approached the art room. Kelly overheard the nasty comment and looked at Miss Davies sternly for just a split-second.

Why are you just staring at me? she thought. *Can't you hear that?*

She was about to take Miss Davies up on her offer and question her about the nasty comment her classmate had just made, but thought better of it. And good thing she did, as heaps of students started filing inside a second later. It would have been extremely embarrassing, not just for Miss Davies but also for Kelly.

Kelly went to her usual seat and sat down. She gave Miss Davies a quick glance and their eyes connected. The art teacher smiled at the teenager and gave her a wink, and that helped Kelly relax a little while some of the pain and anxiety from this morning melted away.

Perhaps she didn't hear it, Kelly thought.

"Good morning, artists," said Miss Davies to the class.

"Good morning, Miss Davies," everyone replied cheerfully.

"We're going to continue our lesson on mediaeval art today. So I would like you all to take out your sketchbooks and continue brainstorming about your idea for your major piece."

"Oh," everyone murmured in unison.

"Come on, guys. Just one more class and then, if you have your idea ready, we can make a start," explained Miss Davies.

Everyone shuffled in their chairs and took out there A4 sketchbooks from their bags. A couple of students opted for large butchers' paper instead, preferring more room to do the doodle while they brainstormed.

"If you need any assistance, come and see me please," said Miss Davies before she sat at her desk to do some work.

Kelly opened up her sketchbook and took out her tin of grey led pencils. These were new and she felt like a new tin would bring forth new ideas. She was excited as she peeled off the plastic.

I wonder what new ideas will come to mind, she thought.

Psst, psst, psst. "Oh look, barf face has new pencils," whispered a minion to her sidekick on the other side of the room.

Kelly overheard the comment and froze immediately, scrunching her lips into a snarl. "No, not here," she murmured to herself. "You will not disturb my peace in my happy place." So Kelly decided to hum her favourite song. "Hmmm, hmmm, hmmm." And it worked. The nasty comments were blocked instantly.

Grabbing her knew HB pencil, she wrote the heading *Mediaeval Major Ideas* at the top of her page and started to think. Mediaeval art meant many things to Kelly. It was a painting of a funny court jester, or a king's crown made of clay and beautifully decorated with jewels and other objects found at the local haberdashery store. Or perhaps a costume of a witch…

A mediaeval witch. Now that would be interesting, Kelly thought as her heart skipped a beat from the excitement that was starting to bubble deep inside her.

Kelly could incorporate her love of sewing and design with what she thought a mediaeval witch would wear. She could even create a magical staff with an orb at the top, using clay or even paper mâché. "Oh, oh, oh," said Kelly out loud as she frantically scribbled her ideas down. She could ask her dad to help her make a light to sit inside the orb, which they could connect to an ON/OFF button located farther down the staff—placing it were your palm would go and making it virtually invisible when held. As quickly as the idea came to Kelly, it dawned on her that it would be impossible to fulfil. Impossible because her relationship with her dad at the moment wasn't a good one. Kelly huffed in frustration.

Psst, psst. "Oh my God, no way you kissed him last night? Come on, give me details," muttered a minion to her friend, who was glowing with pride.

"No, I don't kiss and tell," said the friend, batting her eyelashes.

"Like hell you don't," reminded the minion, and they both giggled together.

Kelly was sickened by the conversation she was hearing. *God, sad cases,* she thought. *Get a life.*

She placed her pencil on top of her sketchbook and clasped her hands together. Sometimes, if she sat silently and just looked at her sketchbook, ideas would pop up in her head.

"*Psst, psst.* Look, barf face is meditating. Maybe we should go over there and show her how to meditate, if you know what I mean," snickered the minion.

"Oh, yeah, let's do that," giggled her sidekick, then she raised her hand for a high-five.

Kelly couldn't take it anymore. Her stomach did somersaults from the rude comments and her anxiety bubbled right to the surface. All the words she'd been hearing throughout the day cut like a knife, deep in her heart, penetrating right into the soul. They severed her happiness and sliced through her confidence. Words were more powerful than any punch. *Any.*

If this was a prediction of what the whole day would bring… Kelly thought. *No, I can't take a whole day of this bullying.*

She swiftly placed her sketchbook and pencils into her bag and approached her teacher. "Excuse me, Miss Davies," she said in a hushed voice. The art teacher looked up at her student and immediately noticed the sadness in the teenager's eyes.

"Kelly, you okay, hun?" she asked, holding out a concerned hand.

Kelly ignored the gesture. She just wanted to get out of class and fast. "I don't feel good, miss. Can I please go home?" No matter how hard she tried, the tears were welling up more.

"Sure, HB. Do you want me to call your parents to come and get you?"

Kelly jumped. "No, no, I can do that when I get home," she was quick to reply. "They will be in meetings all day and hard to catch. I will shoot them a message to tell them I am okay."

The explanation sounded reasonable to Miss Davies, so there was nothing further to discuss. "Okay then." She smiled. "I will see you next week." Kelly nodded at her teacher and walked out of the classroom.

Kelly didn't smile and she didn't say thank you. The only thing she did do was keep repeating in her mind: *Babushka, Babushka, Babushka.* That helped to drown out the comments she knew the students were saying behind her back and it also helped her not explode at a teacher for not doing a single thing about it.

~

"Hello, my beautiful fairy godmother," said Kelly as she sat next to her Baba. Kelly wanted to grab her hand and poor her heart out but she hesitated. The last time she held it, she received a vicious shock.

Would that happen again? she wondered.

The nice nurse did reassure her that all the equipment was thoroughly checked by a technician and there was no short-circuit nor glitch. Besides, it would have showed up in the readings and the readings showed no signs of abnormalities.

"Well, here goes nothing," Kelly murmured to herself, squinting her eyes and scrunching up her face as she reached out for Baba's hand. There was no shock, just tears, and they flowed down her cheeks as she sat there holding her fairy godmother's open palm. "Oh, Baba, please wake up. Please," she pleaded, forgetting all about the previous shock. Kelly felt so alone. She felt like the whole world was against her and everyone else was laughing at her. Even the people she thought she could trust or confide in, like Miss Davies. She felt her teacher was against her, not helping when Kelly desperately needed the support. Kelly sobbed into her godmother's arm. "Oh, Baba, I need you." Tears flowed down her face, and some trickled down on to Baba's hand where Kelly kissed it occasionally and ever so tenderly.

"Ohhh." Baba opened her eyes and raised her hand to examine it. "Water," she said out loud. "Where did water come from?" she asked the void. Using her index finger, she dabbed at the droplet and brought it to her lips. She gave her finger a hesitant lick. "Oh, saltwater. Where did this come from?"

For two days now, Babushka had been lying in a coma at Saint Francis Memorial, attached to a machine that constantly read her vital signs. *Chiga, chiga, beep* went the machines day and night. The nurses visited her often, monitoring the machines and checking on the patient. They wrote notes in their charts at every visit and then quickly left, not staying too long. During this time, Babushka lay still, suspended in a space, with nothing but her hospital bed to keep her company. Within the space, the void, there was no ground and no sky. There were no trees and no grass. There was no life and there was no air, yet Babushka could breathe. There was absolutely nothing but a sea of black space, and in the middle of that space was Babushka.

She examined the salt water on her fingers a little more, rubbing the tips together, spreading the droplets, and allowing her skin to absorb it. Babushka lay there, confused. "Why am I still here, and why are there traces of salt water on my hand now? Hmpf, I'm not thirsty," she said out loud and her voice echoed throughout the nothingness. "Besides, you can't drink saltwater."

"It is not for you to drink," boomed a voice suddenly.

Baba shrieked in response, not realising that someone was there watching her. But the voice was familiar; she recognised it. "Oh, the Sage of Light! He is here."

She moved slightly and shuffled her body on the hospital bed, looking from side to side while trying to find the source of the voice. She screamed and grabbed at her chest. It was sore, tender to the touch, and she placed her hand right where the pain was coming from. Baba remembered. It was the spot where the bolt had struck her, where the beautiful lady had zapped her with her staff. Baba shivered from the memory, and something deep within her chest began to stir. She sat up in her bed, the energy slowly returning to her body. The lack of movement had made her back ache and her legs twitch, her muscles eager to hit the ground running again.

"It must be the bolt," she said to herself, trying to explain the sudden change of heart. "But why?" she asked, secretly hoping the voice was listening.

The renewed feeling pulsed through her, starting at the very centre of her being and travelling outwards. Like a ripple in a pond. Growing bigger and bigger until it faded away. In this very instant, she felt physically stronger. A foreign sensation that added to her confusion. Babushka looked over the rail of her bed and saw nothing. There was no ground to step upon, yet the hospital bed somehow seemed to be supported by solid ground. She hesitated and clutched her heart, hoping for more strength to come her way.

"Believe and you shall see," boomed the voice soothingly.

The sound had Baba gasping for air and holding her breath. "Yes, you are listening," she spoke aloud, though she wasn't surprised. Taking a few deep breaths to psych herself up before she took the leap, Baba tossed her legs over the edge, closed her eyes, and jumped. Letting go of the bed quickly before she regretted her decision.

SPLAT. STOMP. Her feet landed on solid ground within the void, and ever so slowly, Babushka opened her eyes in bewilderment. She lifted her feet one at a time and examined each sole, not believing what she was seeing. She wasn't free-falling, a realization that blew her mind. "What is this place?" she asked no one in particular.

Twitch, twitch, twitch. A small light flickered at her feet. *Twitch, twitch, twitch.* It flickered again, showing sparks like that of a matchstick being scraped against powdered glass, but the friction didn't create enough heat to ignite the flame. *Twitch, twitch, twitch* continued the spark.

"What is this?" Baba asked the light, speaking to it as if it were alive. It didn't answer with anything but another twitch.

"Believe and you shall see," said the voice.

Babushka grabbed at her chest, placing a palm over her heart. It was racing a million miles per hour but she wasn't afraid. Fear didn't exist, as excitement spread throughout her body. "What do I do?" she asked herself and also the spark. But there was no answer, so she fidgeted on the spot, rubbing her hands together and shuffling her feet. She wanted to know what this spark was and why it was here. Slowly, hesitantly, Babushka reached out a hand towards the spark as it twitched, edging closer and closer, and finally…

BANG! They touched. The spark exploded into an enormous fireball. *BOOM!* It shot up into the air, whizzed around like a balloon blowing out all its air, until it dropped straight to the ground. *SPLAT.* Five metres away from where Babushka was standing.

"Oh, that's odd," she said to herself, scratching her head. She looked side to side and behind her back, wondering if she had missed something. But there was only the hospital bed, the deflated spark, and herself within the void. "Hmpf, now what?"

Kelly continued to cry while she held her fairy godmother's hand. "Everything is falling apart, Baba. Please come back. I need you. Please believe that we all need you," pleaded Kelly.

"Oh, that voice, I know that voice," said Babushka upon hearing the muffled cries of a distressed young girl. "But where are you? Can you hear me? Can you see me because I cannot see you," she continued, straining her eyes to see well into the distance, past the spark, while hoping something was beyond it and that it would give her the answers.

"Go and you shall see," boomed the voice, encouraging Baba to leave her spot.

"Go? Go where? There is nothing here but blackness." Babushka looked around again, hoping for another clue but the voice did not speak and nothing more happened. She exhaled, realising that the only way to find the answers was to seek them, and standing dormant wasn't going to solve anything. Without thinking twice, Babushka walked. She walked the whole five metres to the spark and she didn't look back. Not even once.

The spark had stopped twitching. It simply lay on the spot, unmoving and completely dull. Baba's heart sank at the sight. Before, it had been a beautiful light show, an uplifting and glorious fireworks display, and now it was a dimming flame, kindling that was extinguishing fast.

"Please, Baba, I love you. Please come back," pleaded Kelly.

"Oh," said Babushka, looking into the void.

Love was a very powerful word. It was one that she hadn't heard nor said in a long time. "Love hurts," she whispered to herself, remembering the love she once had for her king. Babushka closed her eyes as the memories rushed back. She remembered the good king, images, and emotions that had been locked up. Deep down and buried. Memories of his kindness and his love for all the people of Saphira. She smiled at the thought. He loved everyone and what made him good was that he gave everyone the chance to be heard, because a thief mattered just as much as a duke or a lord. Everyone mattered, regardless of their status in life, but not everyone loved the king back.

Tears flowed down Babushka's cheeks as she remembered what happened on that gruesome day and her heart sank. She'd never forgiven herself. "It's all my fault," she whispered to the memories, the pain returning tenfold.

"Go and you shall see," reminded the voice soothingly.

Tears continued to flow down Babushka's cheeks and they felt heavy, as did the pain. There had been a weight on her shoulders for an incredibly long time and she could not continue to carry it for a second longer. For the first time, in a long time, she felt the need to see. This beautiful woman was here for a reason and she had to find out what that reason was.

There was something out there in a nothing. Babushka didn't know why or what it was, but she felt the pull. It was strong and it tugged at her heart. She raised her hand and wiped the tears from her cheeks, using the sleeve of her blouse as a makeshift hanky.

Blurp, blurp, chug, chug, chug. She choked on her spit, steadied herself, took a deep breath, and whispered to the voice, "Show me."

And with those words, the spark dissolved into the void, disappearing forever. But, in its place, like switching on a light, a path materialised. Leading right into the unknown. It was this unknown that held the answers for Babushka, and it was the same path of light that would take her to them. So off she went.

21

WEDNESDAY MORNING ARRIVED so quickly. Too quickly for Kelly. She lay awake in her bed, staring at the ceiling, and felt exhausted. She rubbed her temples gently, trying to get rid of the bad headache that had made an appearance, uninvited, yet again.

"Ah, go away," she muttered.

She rolled onto her side, hoping it would help, but it seemed to only increase the throbbing.

Psst, psst, psst. "Go see if your lovely daughter is going to come out of her room today to go to school," Joyce said sarcastically to Mark as she poured herself a cup of hot black coffee. Today was already not a good day. Having not slept well last night, butting heads with her daughter was the last thing Joyce wanted to do.

Mark stopped eating midchew and looked at his wife from the corner of his eye. He could sense she wasn't in a good mood from the moment she walked into the kitchen.

And he dared not speak to her, let alone kiss her good morning, before she had her coffee. He quickly calculated that the lack of sleep equalled a set of full-on spiky horns, so it should take at least ten good sips of coffee before the horns started to recede and she became approachable. He smirked to himself, but karma was always watching and the universe made him choke on his mouth full of breakfast.

Hack, hack, hack, phew. He sent half-chewed muesli into his bowl, cursing himself for his cheeky thoughts. Not stopping to look at his wife or answer her question, he preceded straight out of the kitchen and up the stairs to Kelly's bedroom.

Better just leave, he thought before he got himself into more mischief.

Kelly yelled, having heard the conversation between her parents. She quickly grabbed her doona and covered herself. All the way up and over her head. "Please go away," she whispered, hoping to avoid yet another clash. "And why in God's name do you need to speak so loudly," she muttered.

Knock, knock, knock went the door. Mark grabbed the knob and turned it slowly, holding his breath, worried that what was coming next wasn't going to be good. Gently, he pushed the door ajar, allowing himself to see ever so slightly into the bedroom.

"Ah, Kelly, just seeing if you are all right," he stammered for a second but continued. "It's getting late and we… *I*," he corrected, hoping to avoid a clash, "was wondering if you are going to school today?" Mark strained his eyes, trying to see into Kelly's room from a tiny crack through the door. He was looking to get a glimmer of his beloved daughter as he hadn't seen her since yesterday morning. Besides, they had left things on bad terms and he hated it when she was mad at him. Thankfully that seldom happened—at least it used to. For some reason or another, lately, it was occurring a bit too often and it hurt him.

Kelly remained covered under her doona and didn't flinch. She was annoyed and frustrated at her dad for coming up to her room and bothering her. But she was angrier at her mum for speaking about her in a nasty way yet again. Behind her back. Kelly heard the sarcasm in her mother's voice and it cut her like a knife.

"Kel, are you awake?" asked Mark when she didn't answer his question. Mark strained again, but his efforts were useless. He decided to place his ear into the opening of the doorway, trying to hear her breathing. If he could hear her breathing, then he could tell if she was asleep or not. Nope, not only could he not see a damn thing but he also couldn't hear a damn thing. He exhaled in frustration.

Come on, kid. Talk to me please, he thought.

Kelly could sense that he was still standing at the foot of her door. She figured he wasn't going to budge until he got some sort of answer from her and her gut instincts were telling her to respond ASAP, before the wrath of Mother Dear was released upon her.

"Ehem." She cleared her throat. "Not right now, Dad, but later. I have a very bad headache," she whispered under her doona cover. The answer came out muffled but Mark heard it and felt a little relieved. If he didn't come downstairs with an answer, he knew that his wife was going to devour him for breakfast. So, this was something. Joyce may not like it but it was an answer.

"Okay, Kel," said Mark sympathetically. "Can I get you some aspirin or maybe some food to help your stomach?"

"No thanks, Dad. Just let me rest, *please*," she emphasised.

Mark hesitated at the door, wanting to fling it wide open, go to his daughter, and hug her. But he thought better of it. He gently closed her door and went back downstairs to report to Mrs Godzilla.

"Phew," Kelly exhaled and uncovered her face and head. She was sweating like a pig under the doona and her headache was starting to feel worse from the lack of fresh air. Thank God her dad left when he did, because she was definitely about to lose it. And bad. She balled her fists and hit her mattress again and again and again.

Why can't anyone just leave me in peace? she thought.

There was absolutely nowhere Kelly could go to find peace lately. Besides home, school had become her new personal hell. Everyone was sniggering behind her back, saying nasty things about her and no one (including her teachers) was doing anything about it. She wasn't imagining things, and she knew she wasn't the slightest bit crazy. If she could hear everyone's nasty comments at school, then so could the teachers. However, they all seemed to ignore the bullying.

"Why?" she wondered aloud. All Kelly wanted was for everyone, including her parents, to stop talking about her behind her back—and in her presence—as if she weren't in the room. "STOP," she muttered to herself and hit the mattress one more time. Her eyes welled up with tears and she quickly looked up at the ceiling, blinking the moisture away. "No, no more tears. I've cried enough. Get a grip, Kel," she breathed.

She closed her eyes for a couple of seconds, looking for a space to escape the hurt and the pain she couldn't shake off lately. She growled. Even closing her eyes no longer brought her solitude. Peace. It only brought more bad dreams and they were getting worse.

Last night's was horrific. She was back at the grove. Surrounded by thick, luscious, green oak trees. They were mighty and absolutely magnificent, just like the one at All Nations Park. Kelly noticed that the thousands upon thousands of daisies had returned, and in that moment, it reminded her of her father. The better days at least. When she was a little girl and there were no problems between them. The memory made her smile—how much she missed her dad. But just like before, the ash floated down. At first, it was subtle but then it felt like the pits of hell had opened up and rained down upon her in all its fury. *Swoosh, swoosh, swoosh.* The force of the ash was so strong and treacherous that it knocked her across the grove. Pushing her this way and tossing her that way, like a pair of dice being jiggled in the palm of her hands, and then abruptly thrown. Not caring how hard or where they landed.

Kelly screamed out in fear. "What is going on…?"

When the dust had settled and she lay flat on her back on the cold, burnt floor, Kelly thought the worst was over. If only…

"Ah!" The same ear-piercing, evil shriek erupted within the nothingness. Kelly jumped to her feet instantly. "No, no," she hollered, frantically looking for the swordsman. "Where is he?" She was beginning to panic.

Stomp, stomp, stomp echoed his feet. He was coming for

her. And fast. But from which direction? She looked about, turning on the spot, but she couldn't see anything.

"*You* will be forgotten," the traitorous swordsman hissed, his voice echoing around her.

Kelly was confused, scared, not understanding the message. "Why will I be forgotten? What have I done?" she called out between gritted teeth. She shook her fists and stomped her feet, her anger growing by the second.

Stomp, stomp, stomp. He was near but not.

"Your name and the names of those who have come before you will be forgotten," boomed the swordsman.

Immediately, Kelly thought of her parents, her mum and dad, and she started to whimper. "Why? Why do you want to hurt them? What have they ever done to *you*?" she screamed at the top of her lungs and fell to her knees. Devastated. Things of late had not been well between her and her parents. And now, the mention of something terrible happening to them brought on a powerful realisation. The fighting and the arguing wasn't worth it. Let bygones be bygones. It was time to forgive and forget.

Stomp, stomp, stomp echoed his fast feet within the nothingness. And then, suddenly, they stopped. Silence.

Kelly wiped her tears and looked around. "What the… where is the traitor?" she wondered. She stood and looked around.

He should be upon me, this very second, she contemplated. Kelly took a couple of steps forward, listening intently and looking sharply, but still nothing. She stopped and scratched her head. *What is going on?*

She decided to take a few more steps. Something didn't feel right. Something was out of whack. But what was it?

Again, she felt uneasy within her skin. The hairs on her neck stood on end and her eyes bulged at the realisation that, of course, she couldn't see anything. It wasn't in front of her but… behind her. Kelly started to tremble and her hands began to shake. Her heart raced a million miles an hour, occasionally skipping a beat.

"Please wake up," she pled to herself. "Please." She whimpered and closed her eyes, hoping that by doing so, she would be back in her bed. In her room. Seconds passed but nothing happened. The hairs on her neck fluttered slightly from a breeze, which somehow made its way into the nothing. Kelly had the urge to grab her neck and scratch it. But fought it for a bit longer.

Tick, tick, tick. The seconds went by, pulling at her, the realisation calling out to her. She flinched and shivered all over.

Slowly, she turned her body. Kelly was reluctant but the need to see what was standing behind her was stronger than anything else. She turned around. "Hmpf, nothing's here." She looked about. Left and then right. There was nothing within the nothing. And her fear faded. She smirked at herself for being so chicken. "Seriously, Kel, come on."

Annoyed by her self-imposed anxiety, Kelly decided to turn back and face the other direction… *BAM!* She screamed as she came face to face with a pair of bloodshot eyes. They penetrated right through her gaze, peering deep into her soul. She convulsed at the horror, at the evil emanating from the being standing in her midst.

But only momentarily. Then the darkness took her, and she finally noticed the object protruding from the centre of the traitor's forehead. It was a glorious red diamond and it pulsed with power, bright-red hues glowing within the nothingness. And Kelly realized that this must have been the horror Millard had witnessed.

Now, lying on her bed, the teenager analysed her dream—the one were Millard had seen the exact same object. She remembered the sheer terror written all over his face at the sight of this diamond. His fear was palpable but why?

What was the significance of this diamond? thought Kelly. *It's only a diamond.*

She exhaled an exhausted breath. Analysing and thinking, trying to put all the pieces together without having all the actual parts, was becoming too hard. It was like trying to solve an elaborate algebra equation without knowing how. "Damn," said Kelly out loud. "If only I didn't miss Mr Zang's algebra lesson on Monday, then perhaps I'd be one step closer to figuring out these strange dreams... And this diamond definitely doesn't make more sense than the rest."

Kelly remained in her bed, staring at the ceiling for a long while. The urge to move was nonexistent, and the thought of going to school today was extremely off-putting. But she knew that she couldn't stay here for much longer. The jitteriness and the frustrations were starting to kick in. She was beginning to feel a major case of ants in her pants and didn't know what to do with herself.

Fling, flop went her doona onto the floor. It was time to get out of bed.

But do what? she thought. Babushka entered her mind immediately but her heart just couldn't do it. Kelly couldn't spend another day sitting beside her fairy godmother, holding her hand and hoping for her to wake up. She just couldn't and she felt incredibly guilty.

"I am sorry, Baba," she whispered. Kelly looked around her room, wondering how to occupy her time. Reading wasn't an option, even though she loved it. Because in the state that she was in, she definitely couldn't focus nor absorb a word. She looked back at her bed and cringed. "No, I can't lie back down. No," she demanded and quickly turned away before she changed her mind.

Her eyes fell onto the chest of drawers beside her bed and she froze. Kelly knew exactly what was buried beneath all her bras and undies in the bottom drawer. The golden glove. She started to sweat, even though she wasn't doing anything but standing there staring at the chest of drawers. The last time she had seen it was Monday morning when she'd woken up from a bad dream. A dream where a robed shepherd had attacked her with his crook, for no apparent reason. And the glove, the same golden glove that now resided in the bottom of her chest of drawers, was the very thing that had saved her life.

Kelly remembered waking up that morning and feeling utter horror but then sheer relief, realising that it was only a dream. However, all that changed when she felt the golden glove under her pillow. What at first seemed like a dream, now turned into a nightmare that kept getting worse as the nights went by.

"No, I can't do this," said Kelly, throwing her arms up in defeat. No matter what way she turned in her room, there was always something standing in her way of feeling peace. She did the only thing she knew how to do and that was get dressed and go to school. School was the lesser evil, seeing as there was one good thing left about it, and that was her best friend Pi. If she hurried, she would be there by lunchtime, and it would give her a chance to talk and hopefully laugh.

~

Gemma sat on the basketball court at lunchtime. All alone. She didn't mind being alone, as the solitude allowed her to do what she wanted, and today that was reading her new science book she'd purchased online from Amazon. After what had happened at Wymann's bookstore on Saturday morning, the last thing she wanted to do was set foot into another bookstore ever again. She still got the shakes when she thought about it, and cursed herself for even wasting a minute's worth of her energy analysing what she'd seen.

How could Wymann attack HB? she wondered.

He was the gentlest of souls she'd ever met. He was so kind to her that day when she'd first walked into the bookstore with her mum. It just didn't make any sense. Gemma looked down at the book sitting on her lap and cringed, because she had to wait a whole two weeks to get her hands on it. Normally, it would only take a short walk to the shops after school or on weekends. But now, because of the incident and the resulting anxiety, it took two weeks.

"Grrrr," she muttered to herself.

"Hey, Pi, why so angry, best friend?" piped up a familiar voice.

"HB!" screamed Gemma. "Oh my *God*," she squealed in delight, throwing her book onto the ground and springing up to give her best friend a ginormous hug. "Where have you been? I've missed you so much and was getting worried about you," said Gemma, while holding Kelly's hands.

Kelly blushed. "I haven't felt well these past few days, babes, so I've been at home resting."

"Oh," said Gemma, concern lacing her voice. "What's going on, HB? You feeling any better today? You're here. That's a good sign."

Gemma gestured for Kelly to sit, so she dropped her bag and claimed a piece of the concrete next to her best friend. "Ha, yeah, you're right, Pi. It's a good sign, but I doubt it will be a good day, my friend."

"What do you mean? What's going on?" Gemma grabbed her lunchbox out of her bag and removed her sandwich. She unwrapped it and offered some to her friend, noticing that she wasn't eating anything.

"No thanks, babes. I'm not feeling hungry. Hmpf, I haven't had much of an appetite for a few days now." Kelly went quiet, staring into space.

Gemma noticed something big was worrying her friend. It didn't take a rocket scientist or much smarts to figure that out. She placed her sandwich back into her lunchbox and turned her full attention on her dear friend, having lost her appetite too. "What's wrong, Kelly?" she asked very gently.

"Everything, Pi, absolutely everything." Kelly burst into tears. The floodgates opened and she couldn't stop the flow. Gemma grabbed her friend and held her tight.

"Is it about what everyone is saying, HB? You know they all can just go get stuffed."

But Kelly just shook her head and continued to cry.

If it wasn't about the gossip around the school, then what could it be? thought Gemma. That gossip was so nasty and cruel. It was wrong that the teachers, including the principal, weren't doing anything to discipline Sandra. It just showed how large donations could make a lot of eyes look in the opposite direction, at times.

"Then what is it, HB?" Gemma pressed again.

Kelly didn't answer, feeling embarrassed. The truth was hard to believe and she worried her best friend would think she was a fruit loop and a crazy one at that.

Gemma could feel Kelly's reluctance to speak and it bothered her. She always thought they could approach each other and talk about anything, without any judgement.

So why was she hesitating? she wondered. She loved Kelly like a sister and thought Kelly knew that.

Gemma shook her friend gently, trying to grab her attention and bring her back from her daydream. "Come on, you can tell me, HB. You know I have your back."

Kelly heard her soothing words, which gave her the courage to find her own to speak. "I-I-I've been having bad dreams lately, Pi. But these bad dreams..." She hesitated for a second. "...feel... feel real." Kelly was embarrassed and didn't look at her friend when she spoke.

"Oh, HB, it's okay," said Gemma in response. "Dreams are only dreams. They aren't real, babes." She tried to soothe her friend while she held her, and continued her explanation. "During our hot mocha on Saturday when you first mentioned your bad dreams, I decided to do some research. You know me, HB." Gemma nudged Kelly gently and winked, trying to make her friend smile but all Kelly did was stare down at the concrete beneath them. Gemma cleared her throat, feeling defeated, but carried on. "I bought a spiritual book about dreams—in fact, I think you would love it, HB. It contains all this information, explaining the symbolism behind what you see in dreams. Yeah…" She nodded, hoping the news would brighten her friend's mood.

Kelly's stomach was doing somersaults and she felt really uneasy at the thought of what her best friend was saying about dreams. *How could it be possible for you to see a tomb and a golden knight in your dreams, but for it to mean something totally different from what it actually is?* she thought. Or what about a crazy shepherd running at you with the crook? *What does that mean? That you need to stay away from shepherds?* It just didn't make sense to Kelly. *And the biggest doozy of all: how do you explain the golden glove sitting in the bottom drawer of my chest of drawers in my bedroom? Surely the book of dreams wouldn't be able to explain that one…*

Kelly sat there and listened to Gemma speak some more about dreams and how they could be interpreted. She smiled at her best friend for trying, trying to help her see things in a different way, but it was no use. No matter what explanation Gemma gave, it just didn't clarify how Kelly had managed to pull the glove out of her dream and into her world. And the saddest part of all, Kelly felt that even if she did show the glove to Gemma, she couldn't prove that it actually *physically* came from one of her dreams. She knew it was a helpless situation, so she decided to just grin and bear it.

"Thanks, Pi, your research really helps," she lied and she gave her friend a squeeze.

"So, tell me what you want to do for your birthday?" asked Gemma with an excited squeal.

Kelly exhaled. She didn't want to keep talking about it and was hoping the conversation about her birthday would stop. But, at the same time, she was glad that they moved on to another topic. She shrugged. "I don't know, Pi. I don't feel like doing anything."

"But why?" said Gemma, surprised. "You're turning sixteen and it's a big deal."

"I understand it's a big deal, but my heart isn't in it. I don't know. I just can't explain it." She looked away from Gemma and checked the time on her watch. She noticed there were only minutes left of lunchtime.

Geez, that went too quick.

"Hey, Pi." Kelly perked up. "Let's get to PE early today. You know, take our time and enjoy the walk down to the gym. What do you say?" She hoped this would entice her best friend to end the conversation revolving around her birthday and talk about something different for a change.

"Yeah, sure, why not? Let's do just that."

The girls helped each other up off the ground and then slowly made their way towards the gym for the afternoon's last two classes of the day.

~

Shriek goes the whistle and everyone paused with the sudden blast of noise. "Oh!" muttered some of the girls, grabbing their ears to muffle the sound.

"Line up in a straight line, girls," ordered Mr Schaefer. The gym teacher was an ex-military veteran, who believed he'd never truly left the Armed Forces. Today, he was a strict PE teacher at Santa Lucia High School who stressed the importance of fitness and loved—and I mean *loved*—burpees. His love of burpees was not just to get his students super fit but to punish them when they stepped out of line. So disobeying orders, as he would put it, was a big fat NO.

After he blew that whistle, all twenty-four girls instantly

assembled in perfect formation: in a straight line, shoulders back, feet together, eyes front, hands by their sides, and ready for orders.

Mr Schaefer smiled as he walked the line to check his soldiers. "My, my, my, absolute badasses," he sang. "Okay, ladies, today we are playing a friendly game of basketball. We will be splitting into two teams and I'll be choosing those teams."

There was a sudden murmur of disappointment echoing throughout the line of neatly assembled students. Shoulders hunched instantly, while a couple of disappointed girls stood there, shaking their heads in defiance.

This did not anger Mr Schaefer. It only made him do what he did best. He blew his whistle hard and then barked out his punishment to the disobedient soldiers. Clicking his fingers, he pointed at each student who broke the formation and barked out, "Twenty burpees, *now*. Move it, move it, *move it*," he hollered.

And off they went, one burpee, two burpees, three burpees... *agony.*

Shriek went Mr Schaefer's whistle, and everyone stood back in perfect formation. He waited, watching them like a hawk ready to pounce on his prey. But no one moved, let alone breathed.

"We will be splitting into two teams, A and B. All even numbers will be Team A and all odd numbers will be Team B," he ordered. He started to pace as he spoke to the girls, always looking straight ahead, never at the ground, with his hands neatly clasped behind his back as he walked. "For those who don't understand, Kelly is at the beginning of the line, in position one, and therefore an odd: Team B." He continued to pace as he explained, "Gemma is in second place on the line and therefore an even: Team A. And so on." Mr Schaefer turned abruptly to face his students. "Now, get into your teams," he hollered. "Move it, move it, *move it!*"

And the girls quickly scrambled into two groups of twelve. Kelly huddled near her team and cringed. There were so many nasty girls—girls who were part of Sandra's entourage—within her team and they were snickering. She could hear their vile comments, and she was both sad and angry, all at the same time.

How am I going to survive this? she wondered, and searched for her best friend, who'd been assigned to the opposite team.

Team A was huddled together, and from what Kelly could tell, they were discussing strategies and who would be best suited for which position. She exhaled her frustrations. What I wouldn't do right now to be on that team…" Kelly muttered under her breath to herself, hoping for some sort of miracle.

As she continued to search for her best friend, her eyes fell on Sandra, who'd been standing there watching her for God only knows how long. And Sandra's stare looked sinister. She had a vendetta and Kelly felt like today, out of all the days, was the day she was going to pay for her sins. She gulped hard and spit, bile rising up into her throat. Instinctively, Kelly turned around and faced her team members, searching for support and comfort, trying to ease her anxiety and her racing heart. But all she found was Miss Priss's posse snickering and laughing at her even harder. They were enjoying the show and you could tell they were excited by the thought of what was to come.

"Okay, up first is Kelly, BG1 (bad girl 1), BG2, BG3, and BG4 on the court for round one," said the team captain, peering down at her clipboard.

Kelly turned to her in surprise. "No, Sarah, please," she pleaded. While Kelly was searching for her best friend, the girls had decided that Sarah, a particularly nice student who was also easily manipulated, would be their team captain.

Sarah was a very smart student but the girl lacked self-confidence and, sadly, friends as well. The *bad girls* convinced her to place Kelly and themselves on the court first. They said that they had a score to settle with Kelly, and if Sarah did as she was told, then maybe, just maybe, they'd let her have lunch with them sometimes. The sad part was… Sarah had agreed to it. She ignored Kelly's pleas and walked away to sit on the bench, ready for round one. Sarah didn't care about Kelly. All she wanted was to have cool friends, friends like Sandra, and it didn't matter what she had to do to get them.

Kelly watched Sarah walk away and wondered how someone could be so gutless and desperate to do vile things in exchange for popularity. She closed her eyes and shook her head in disgust.

Shriek went Mr Schaefer's whistle. It was time to get ready. Kelly walked towards the basketball court and took her position. She stood next to her opponent with a sense of dread bubbling in her gut. Her stomach was doing major somersaults, flipping this way and flopping that way. Kelly rubbed it, hoping to calm her discomfort but it was useless.

Shriek went Mr Schaefer's whistle again. "Okay, teams, the first to five points wins the round and then we swap players. Whoever loses gets fifty burpees." He chuckled aloud. "Got it?" he hollered. "So don't lose."

"Okay, you can do this, Kel," the teenager whispered to herself.

"Got it!" everyone screamed back.

Shriek! And it was game on. The ball was tossed in the air and quickly intercepted by BG1. She shoved her opponent out of the way and sped down towards the key, eager to slam-dunk the first point. Kelly and the rest of the girls ran in the same direction, either trying to provide assistance or snatch the ball from her. The opposition was closing in and they were closing in fast. BG1 had to make a decision: pass the ball or risk losing it. Kelly watched and waited.

Why weren't the other players, her posse, helping her? They were keeping well away from BG1, avoiding her. This didn't make sense. What's going on? Kelly wondered.

Without thinking, she decided to run in and help her team member, believing it was the right thing to do. Besides, she didn't want to be on the losing side and have to do fifty burpees. In Kelly went, treading closer and closer. When she was close enough to receive the ball, BG1 raised it high above her head and threw it hard and fast. Bullseye.

SMACK. BANG. The ball slammed right into Kelly's face with a loud thud. The impact sent her tumbling backwards. Kelly landed on her back, dazed. Sandra and her bad girls laughed hysterically, pointing and calling her names.

"Oh, barf girl fell over." They chuckled. "Stay on the floor, barf girl, where you belong."

Gemma ran to Kelly and knelt beside her best friend. "HB, HB, are you okay? HB!" she screamed, tugging at Kelly's arm.

"Oh, ow, ow, ow," the teenager whimpered in reply.

"Oh, Pi, my face hurts… bad." And she grabbed her nose and held it, her eyes clamped shut.

"Can you stand up, HB? I'll take you to the bench. Come on, babes, up you get," said Gemma pushing to her feet and holding out her hands.

Kelly lay on the cold floor, her eyes wide and her face slowly turning red from the impact of the basketball, while she grimaced from the pain. "Ow," she gasped and quickly looked at her hands, hoping her nose wasn't bleeding. "Phew." She was relieved there was no blood, but her cheek felt numb.

Why? Why would they do such a thing? Kelly wondered. *Why? All this because I interrupted her poem recital?* She shook her head, not understanding how people could be so cruel.

"Come on, HB," said Gemma again, clapping her hands together to catch her friend's attention and remind her that she was there to help.

Kelly grabbed Gemma's outstretched palms and her best friend heaved her up, grunting with the action. Kelly felt slightly dizzy standing on solid ground. She blinked her eyes and saw stars.

Mr Schaefer came up to the girls to see if everything was in order. "Is everything all right?" he demanded, rather coldly, clearly irritated that the basketball match had been put on hold.

"She's hurt, sir," said Gemma, pointing at her friend's face.

Mr Schaefer examined the girl, bending at the waist to examine her more closely. "How you feeling, Kelly?" he barked.

"I'm fine," she lied. "Just a scratch on the nose. Nothing more."

"Okay, then, play on!" he ordered. Before he turned and walked away, he gave Kelly a quick slap on the shoulder and added with a laugh, "What doesn't kill you only makes you stronger."

Kelly grimaced at the gesture, and her rash instantly kicked into overdrive and started to tingle—so much so that the skin on her back started to spasm. Kelly closed her eyes and tried to breathe it all out.

Gemma notice and gasped. "HB, what are you doing? You're in pain, babe!"

Kelly breathed in and out, then she opened one eye and whispered to her friend, "I'm okay, Pi."

"Like hell you are, Kelly," replied Gemma, her eyes narrowed. When Gemma used her friend's real name, it meant she was dead serious and deeply concerned.

"Listen, Pi, I can't sit on the sidelines, all defeated." Kelly gestured towards Sandra and her posse, who were all still snickering at her expense. Some even keeled over from laughter, with tears running down their faces.

"Yes, you can, Kelly," Gemma pleaded, her eyes welling up.

Kelly fluttered her lashes open and looked straight at Gemma. "I need to fight this and put an end to this bullying. If no one will stand up for me, then I need to stand my ground myself, okay?" She grabbed her hands and gave them a squeeze. "Now go back to the bench. Thanks for helping me, babes." Kelly walked away from her friend and took her place on the court. The bad girls giggled and winked at each other.

It was game on for a second time.

The whistle blew and the battle began. Just as before, BG1 secured the ball from her opponent with utmost ease and started to dribble towards the key. Kelly noticed how the other players were keeping their distance once again.

"Okay, so we're doing this again, hey?" the teenager muttered to herself. "We'll see about that." And she pivoted on her heel and set off. *Bam, woosh.* She flew like a speeding bullet straight towards BG1. She was so fast and smooth that no one saw her coming, not even her nasty team member. The rash on Kelly's back continued to tingle and her skin spasmed uncontrollably. "Woah," she gasped, wondering where the speed had come from.

BAM! Kelly grabbed the basketball off her team member and dribbled down towards the key. A couple more steps, a leap, and a jump and she slam-dunked the ball. *SCORE!* Everyone on the sidelines screamed, clapping and cheering at the sight. And at Kelly, who smiled and raised a hand in the air. A gesture of victory.

The bad girls stood there, shocked and paralysed to the spot, not believing what they'd just witnessed. They glanced over at their leader, hoping for some sort of explanation, but the look on Sandra's face was much the same. An expression of pure shock.

Kelly smirked at her rivals, enjoying the moment, and walked back to her position on the court with a new spring in her step. Sandra didn't like what she was seeing. The bully scratched her face and started to fume. She signalled to her posse, ordering them to attack harder, but it was pointless. Kelly single-handedly dominated that basketball court and continued to score, as if she'd been born to do it.

The whistle blew and Mr Schaefer piped up, "Kelly, my God, where did that come from?" He was super excited and didn't know how to contain himself. "Okay, round two. Quick change over, girls. Let's go!" he barked. "Move it, move it, *move it.*"

The girls rushed from the sidelines, while Kelly headed to the bench. She was beaming from ear to ear and felt good, even though her rash was incredibly irritating.

"Wow, Kelly, stay on the court and play again," called Mr Schaefer. "I want to see if that was just a fluke or not."

Kelly reclaimed her position on the court and waited for the new girls to join her. This time, Sandra was one of them. She looked at Kelly, straight in the eyes, and mouthed, "You're dead meat."

But, in that moment, Kelly didn't care what the bully had to say. She felt unstoppable. Powerful. Sandra narrowed her eyes and stared daggers at the girl she hated most in the whole wide world.

Shriek. The whistle blew and the game began. And what a game it was. Simply perfect gameplay from Kelly. She dribbled, she dodged, and she scored. Point after point after point. Slam-dunk after slam-dunk. The girls cheered from the sidelines, chanting Kelly's name and egging her on. At one point, they even created a short song with coordinated movements. "Kelly is hot to go. H-O-T T-O G-O. Awo, hot to go. Awo, hot to go." The girls clapped their hands and swung their hips as they cheered. Everyone was ecstatic, the atmosphere electric.

Well, almost everyone was happy. Sandra and her posse were mad as hell.

Shriek went Mr Schaefer's whistle, signalling the end of the game. The girls on the sidelines erupted into a loud roar, and the winning teams from each round danced and embraced each other—relieved they'd escaped the fifty burpees.

Gemma ran to Kelly and gave her a big hug. "Oh my

God, HB, you are amazing!" she squealed. They jumped on the spot like much younger schoolgirls. Others rushed over from the sidelines, creating a huge group hug, and together they hoisted Kelly up and chanted her name.

Kelly felt absolutely amazing. Hearing her name called out loud *positively* was the most exhilarating feeling of all time. Everyone loved her and she smiled brightly. Mr Schaefer came up to the group and signalled for Kelly to be brought down. The girls lowered their star player to the ground, and she approached her PE teacher.

"Kelly," he boomed. "You were amazing! Oh lordy, lordy, lordy!" He grabbed at his face in awe, losing his usually ironclad composure.

Kelly smiled at Mr Schaefer. She'd never seen this side of him. It was warm, instead of stone-cold, and she liked it very much. It also proved her suspicions that he definitely was a soft and caring teddy bear. Deep down, way down, inside.

"Now, Kelly, it would be an honour to have you on the school's basketball team," he said softly, holding his hands together. "I think the team, and me, would greatly benefit from it." He concluded with a smile.

Kelly couldn't believe what she was hearing. *This must be a dream*, she thought. Wow, wow, *wow*.

"Oh, yes, please, Mr Schaefer. I would love to," she sang.

And everyone, including the PE teacher, jumped for joy while screaming out a resounding, "YES!"

Ding, ding, ding went the bell. School had ended for the day. And it ended on an absolute high for some. The girls grabbed their bags and headed off to homeroom.

Shriek! Mr Schaefer blew his whistle abruptly, stopping everyone in their tracks. "The losing teams will meet me here straight after school." He glared. "We have some unfinished business to take care of." And he laughed his usual *I'm going to cause you great pain* laugh.

Sandra and her posse gulped, knowing that their punishment was going to be absolutely brutal. Fifty burpees would break them and probably even make them vomit like they'd never vomited before.

Sandra huffed in frustration and threw Kelly a glare as she walked out of the gym. "The score might be 0-1 in your favour, vomit girl, but I have more tricks up my sleeve," she murmured, her rage bubbling beneath the surface.

22

"*DAD, DAD!*" KELLY screamed as she ran through the back door of her house. The teenager was beaming. Beyond happy. She couldn't wait to get home to tell her dad what had happened in PE.

Finally, some good news to share.

She bypassed the kitchen, didn't even glance in, and went straight to her father's favourite chair in the lounge room. Only to find it empty. "Oh," she muttered to herself as she stared at the vacant leather recliner chair. She checked her watch instinctively, making sure it was the correct time.

Yep, 4:00 PM. He should be home from work by now, but where is he? she wondered.

"In here, Kel," yelled out a familiar voice. It was her dad. He was sitting in the kitchen.

Kelly pivoted on her heel and ran towards him. "Dad, Dad, Dad, guess what?" she sang.

Mark was shocked as his daughter zoomed into the

room, waving her hands frantically. Excitedly. Almost as if she were a different person, more like the girl he knew, and one he'd seen a lot less of these last few days. The girl standing before him right now was bubbly, cheerful, and had a beaming smile across her face—a smile he was happy to return. Placing the paperwork down on the table, Mark turned his full attention on his girl. "What, what, what?" he mimicked her, waving his hands in the air. God, how much Mark missed being a larrikin with his girl. She seemed to bring out the child within him, which helped him to look at life differently. Less stressfully. He always felt he could be himself to his daughter. Big and cuddly, but also Dad.

"Oh, Dad, you will never believe what happened in gym class today," she babbled.

"Tell me, tell me," he demanded. "Oh! And I bet it's awesome, Kelly Star." He slapped a hand on the table for effect.

Kelly dropped her bag on the floor and sat right next to her dad, like the good old days. "Oh, you will never believe it," she squealed.

Mark grabbed his face and pretended to squeal like a schoolgirl, stomping his feet under the table with the gesture. He was loving it. The here and now with his girl. Laughing and carrying on. It was sheer bliss. A part of him was still worried about her. Everything that had happened during these last few days was out of character. The yelling, the blunt answers, the attitude, the distance between them, the secrets, the lies. All of it. It wasn't his girl. But for now, Mark didn't want to say anything. He just wanted to revel in the moment, terrified it was fleeting.

"Today, at gym, we played basketball, Dad, and I kicked some serious butt," said Kelly, her palm raised for a high-five.

"No way, Jose!" Mark clapped her hand good and proper. *BANG*. Kelly giggled, propelling herself up and down on her chair and wiggling around the seat. "That's my girl, superstar," he added with a proud, giddy smile.

Kelly held up her hands. There was more she needed to say. The story wasn't over just yet. "Wait, wait, Dad," she demanded, smirking at him while covering her mouth with a palm. "But wait, there's more."

"*What?* But wait, there's *more!*" he bellowed.

"Oh God, stop," pleaded Kelly, grabbing her stomach. The continued laughter was causing her belly to ache.

Mark laughed, wiping the tears away from his eyes. *Hiccup!* "Oh!" He smirked.

Kelly looked away from her dad, trying to compose herself. She took a few deep breaths. "Well." She smiled, trying to hold back the next fit of giggles, before she told her dad the last bit of good news. "Today, Mr Schaefer asked me to join the school basketball team." Kelly grabbed her hair and screamed.

Mark mirrored his daughter's enthusiasm, reaching for his head and tugging. Together, they sat at the table, screaming with joy. He grabbed Kelly and gave her a huge hug. "I'm so proud of you, Kel, my superstar." He beamed.

Kelly hugged him back and felt so loved in that moment. So happy. She never imagined she would be a part of the school basketball team. This was a dream come true. Mark held his daughter and pulled her up to her feet. He took her hands and started to jump around the kitchen, squealing and laughing.

"Ahem," went a stern voice and both father and daughter stopped dead in their tracks. It was Mommy Dearest, staring at them in complete shock, not understanding what was going on.

Kelly released her dad's grip and danced away to her mum. "Oh, Mum, guess what?" She beamed.

Joyce looked at her daughter. "Errr, w-what," she murmured. It was more the change in character than anything else that had thrown her off. She looked at her husband, searching for answers. Luckily, Kelly's back was turned and she couldn't see what her dad did next.

Mark mouthed to his wife, "Play along," and then used his two index fingers to gently push the edges of his mouth up into a smile, signalling for his wife to do the same. Joyce understood straightaway and followed suit, grinning at her daughter.

"*Well*, Mum, come and sit down." Kelly gestured to the spare seat at the kitchen table. Joyce noticed how happy she was. It was like the old Kelly—the one who was bubbly, sweet, and always had the biggest smile on her face—had returned. Joyce stumbled to the chair and sat down, looking from husband to daughter and then back again. Mark winked, trying to reassure his wife that all was good.

"So, what do you want to tell me, hun?" said Joyce, her fake smile firmly in place. She was still very upset at Kelly and playing along was a challenge.

Kelly sat next to her mom. She rubbed her hands together with a slight squeal of excitement. "*Mum*, I have been asked to join the school basketball team. How awesome is that?" And the teenager started to scream again.

Joyce didn't feel excitement in that moment. The only thing ringing out in her mind was her daughter's rude behaviour over the last few days. Mark noticed, so he decided to jump in and scream and squeal with Kelly. He had his beloved daughter back, even if was only momentarily, and he didn't want anything (including his wife) ruining it.

Together, father and daughter danced around the kitchen, twirling each other around and around and around. Mark kept an eye on his wife, hoping her demeanour would change, but she continued to sit at the kitchen table with "I am still angry" written across her face. He didn't want Kelly to pick up on her mother's mood, so he stopped mid-twirl and gave his girl a big bear hug. He was so proud of her. He cocked one eye open, sensing the cold from the Ice Queen, looked up at his wife and mouthed, "Come on." But all she did was stare daggers in return, and this infuriated him even more. He pleaded, "Stop butting heads, *please*," and smashed his fists together, trying to show his wife what he meant, just in case she didn't understand his whispered words.

"Oh, Dad," said Kelly, suddenly looking up into his eyes. "Oh, Mum." And she turned to face her with an out-stretched hand. Joyce hesitated for a second, not wanting to reach out, but Mark's stern glare changed her mind and she got up and grasped Kelly's hand. "Mum, Dad, I am *so* happy right now." The girl smiled.

"And we are *so* happy for you, my darling," replied Mark, trying to keep the spirits high. "Aren't we, Mummy Dearest?" He nudged his wife, his smile wide.

"We sure are, darling girl. We are so happy for you," added Joyce, and to keep the momentum going in order to gain a little bit more normality in her life, Joyce grinned a great, big, fake smile.

Kelly jumped into bed that night, feeling happy and content. Happier and more content than she'd been in a while. She had a wonderful dinner with her parents, celebrating her most recent achievement. Joining the school's basketball team.

"Wow," she muttered to herself, still not believing what had happened during the day. She never saw herself as an athlete, and found that when it came down to running or any kind of ball sports, she was too clumsy, left-footed, and uncoordinated. She always stumbled and never scored a single point. Most of the time, no one ever wanted her on their team and that didn't help her confidence either. But today was different. Today, she somehow flew, she scored, and she didn't stumble. Not even once. "Wow, I never knew I had it in me." Kelly smiled.

And having her parents back, the way they were before all this craziness ever happened, before the thousand questions started, and before all the bad dreams began, felt really nice and warm. Kelly felt loved. She fluffed up her pillow and switched off her lamp, closing her eyes and looking forward to reliving her basketball glory in her dreams.

Crunch, crunch, crunch went her feet on the beautiful, lush, green grass.

Kelly noticed the daisies. But this time, she didn't smile. She knew where she was and she didn't like it. Her immediate fear turned to anger. "Why? Why again?" she screamed to the grove. "I don't want this," she whispered, tears filling her eyes and rolling down her cheeks. Kelly thought the bad dreams were over, as good things were starting to happen in her life. She stood up to the bullies today. And won. A good thing. She became a part of the school's basketball team. An awesome thing. Her parents were acting normal towards her for a change. A miracle!

So why more bad dreams? Why not some good ones? she wondered.

BOOM. Clashing swords sounded somewhere in the distance. The noise was deafening and Kelly jumped. She looked around, frantically searching for the traitor.

Where is he? she wondered. This evil and grotesque man wanted her and also her parents dead, for no reason at all.

His warning "you will be forgotten" rang loudly in her ears and she could still hear the hatred spoken in each word. Kelly shivered at the thought.

BOOM, CLASH continued the swords. Feet shuffling, dancing, and sidestepping in the deadly duel. Voices grunting, bodies being pushed beyond their breaking points, fatigue setting in.

Kelly turned and screamed, looking in every direction. But there was nothing within the grove. The traitor and his counterpart were nowhere to be seen, even though they could be heard. Loud and clear. "What is going on?" she muttered, hugging herself for comfort and wishing she was back on the basketball court. But instead, she was here. In the grove. Yet again. Silence descended. Even the great oak trees stopped swaying in the wind. Not a sound could be heard.

Then, suddenly… *BOOM!*

"You will be forgotten," echoed the traitor's voice, and his footsteps could be heard rushing through the grass. Rushing straight towards her…

Fearing the worst, Kelly panicked and started to run. She ran like mad, breathing fast and hard, her chest heaving.

Where? Where can I hide? she wondered, her eyes searching her surroundings, but all she saw was more grass. And more daisies.

"Your name and the names of those who came before you will be *forgotten*," bellowed the villain, his laughter echoing throughout the grove.

Kelly breathed in and out as she ran. With each step she took, she hoped to get farther and farther away, but the evil was all around her and it felt like it had penetrated her soul, leaving an unimaginable fear behind. *"Please* leave me alone," she pleaded, tears flowing down her cheeks.

The traitor laughed in response, and Kelly ran until her legs could not carry her any longer. She slumped to the ground, gasping for air and holding her chest, her hand trembling and her pulse racing. The coolness of the grass offered some comfort, so she closed her eyes, not caring anymore while hoping for the agony to end.

"Please stop, please stop, please stop," she chanted. Inhaling through the nose and exhaling through the mouth, breathing deeply and slowly. Her heartbeat fell back into a steady rhythm and her arms ceased shaking. "Please stop, please stop, please stop," she continued to repeat. A soft breeze flowed through the grove, and with it came a sweet, fresh scent. "Oh!" Kelly said, opening her eyes and recognising the herb. "Rosemary!"

She stood up abruptly, shocked by not just the smell but also by the presence of many, many silhouettes. Instinct had Kelly turning and looking behind her, and there were even more. Each figure was holding the hand of the figure beside them and so on, creating a circle around Kelly. She rubbed her eyes, clearing away the tears and the dried sleep and not believing what she was seeing before her.

"What is this?" she wondered out loud, slowly pivoting to each silhouette, one at a time. Standing before her, and around her, were the shimmering knights clad in golden armour. Each knight wore the same intricately designed armour as that of its counterpart, yet each was different in shape and size. And they were all staring at her. "Oh!" said Kelly, realising the armour matched that of the knight in the tomb. She fidgeted with her hands, fumbling her thumbs and not knowing what to do next. "Transparent figures… you must all be ghosts," said Kelly to herself, trying to make sense of what she was seeing. "Are you ghosts?" Her eyes darted here, there, and everywhere as she searched for an answer but there were none. The silhouettes remained in their spots, unflinching and silent.

A cool breeze flowed through the grove yet again, bringing the sweet scent of rosemary and peace, the aroma soothing and inviting. Kelly inhaled deeply.

"We are everything that you are."

"We are everything that you will be."

"We all flow through you and within you always," whispered the knights together.

Kelly jumped, not expecting to hear the chorus of voices. Their sound was melodious and calm. She tried to absorb their cryptic message but it didn't make any sense.

"Damn it, I was never good at riddles," she muttered under her breath. "What does that mean?" Her frustrations were growing to their boiling point. "I've been given pieces upon pieces of a puzzle, which don't fit well together at all.

And now some riddles. What's next?" She growled as her patience waned.

BOOM! The ground shook, knocking Kelly off her feet. She stumbled and landed on her bum. *Kablam.*

The villain laughed, the sick and delirious sound echoing as it went. Kelly was frightened, the fear rushing through her in great big waves. He'd found her...

Fast feet crunched through the grass. *Crunch, crunch, crunch.*

"No, *no!*" Kelly screamed. She lay on the floor in a foetal position, hugging herself, trying to disappear, and trembling.

"You will be forgotten." The traitor laughed hysterically at Kelly. "Your name will be forgotten," he rasped, and the ground continued to shake.

Kelly grabbed her stomach to steady herself, her teeth clattering with the force of the rattling. "Why?" she whispered. "Why?" She looked to the silhouettes and reached out for their hands, begging for help, but none of them moved. "Please, please, someone help me!" she screamed, buried her face into the ground, and sobbed.

Out of nowhere, a strong hand grabbed her shoulder. "Kelly, Kelly, darling, it's okay. You're dreaming." Mark had gone upstairs to check on his daughter after he realised how late it was. He was eating breakfast on his own and reading the newspaper and had lost track of time. Joyce wasn't there to remind him as she had gone into work early for the day— she had a very important meeting with the CEO. Hearing his daughter's screams for help had startled him, concerned that someone had broken into the house and attacked Kelly.

Thank God it was only a bad dream, he thought as he held his girl and rocked her gently.

"D-dad, w-what happened?" Kelly opened her eyes and looked up. Mark smiled down on her, his eyes slightly watery. "Where did the silhouettes go?" she questioned.

"Errr, what silhouettes?" asked Mark. "There's nothing here." He looked around Kelly's room as best he could. Holding a teenager on his lap made it a bit hard to move.

"Oh, it must be nothing then," Kelly replied. She was still shaken up by what she had seen and didn't want to discuss it with her dad. She burrowed her head deep into Mark's armpit, remembering how warm and comforting it was when she was a little girl. And now, as a young adult, it was just as comforting.

Mark sat on Kelly's bed and held her for what felt like an eternity. He closed his eyes and reminisced about all the times she'd hurt herself as a child. He was always there to pick her up off the ground and comfort her. His heart hurt when she hurt, but he was glad that he could hold her. Even now.

"Oh, oh," he said all of a sudden. "What time is it?" He tried to look at his wristwatch but couldn't managed to get a glimpse of it. And then he spotted Kelly's clock radio. "Lordy, lordy, lordy!" His eyes bulged right out of his head. "Is that the time? Kelly, come on, hun. You'll be late if you don't get dressed." He gently shook his daughter to wake her up.

"I wasn't sleeping, Dad, just relaxing, and it was so nice." She snuggled back into his armpit.

"Yeah, I know, hun, it *is* nice to just sit here, but you have school and I have work. So come on, darling. Time to get ready." Mark gently placed his daughter on her bed, but he didn't recover her with her doona. Because everyone knew what would happen if you cover yourself with the doona again: you'd go back to sleep and not wake up for ages and ages. Before he shut the door to her room to give her privacy, Mark reminded Kelly that he would be leaving in fifteen minutes. "Time is of the essence, Kelly Bear, and the Dad Express leaves in fifteen minutes."

KERPLUNK. And the door closed, leaving Kelly lying uncovered and cold on top of her bed.

~

"Okay, Kelly Bear, here we are! Front-door service," said Mark as he pulled to a stop outside the school gates.

"Oh, Dad, can't I stay home, *please*? I feel so tired and worn out," said Kelly, looking at the gates. Because of the bad night's sleep, she didn't feel like going to school today. She wasn't anxious or afraid about people talking about her behind her back anymore. And she wasn't afraid of the bullies. Yesterday proved to her that she could take them on and win.

"Look, hun, I know you're tired. I get that, but you're now on the school's basketball team and you need to lead by example," said Mark, pointing out a few good facts.

"Yeah, I know, Dad. I'm just tired. Besides, I'm sure they'll all understand." Kelly was trying her luck at a reasonable rebuttal.

"Absolutely, dear girl." Mark nodded his head. "But from what you're telling me, your PE teacher is a nasty drill sergeant, who has the capacity to eat you alive, yeah?" he asked.

"Yeah, so, Dad?" Kelly shrugged.

"Then, if you want to be on his good side and remain there, you go to school—even if you're dying," explained

Mark. "That way, he will always keep you on the team. You get me, hun?"

Kelly knew she'd lost the battle. Her dad was spot on. The last thing she needed was to upset her PE teacher, because he was definitely more than capable of eating someone alive and spitting their bones out when he was done. Kelly huffed, grabbed her schoolbag, and gave her dad a big kiss on the cheek. "Okay, Dad, I'll see you guys tonight, after school." And she reluctantly pulled the handle of the car door and stepped out.

"Okay, hun, go knock them dead," Mark called out before he drove off to work.

"See you, Dad." Kelly waved goodbye, looked at the gates, and hesitated for just a second. "Oh, Thursday morning," she said to herself. "I can't be bothered. Why can't it be Friday? Damn it." She took a deep breath and headed inside. Friday wasn't that far, but when she was tired, it felt as though she would have to wait a lifetime.

Kelly walked through the corridor of her school building and noticed how faces lit up as she went by—some people even waved. She could still hear the whispers, but this time, they were warm and encouraging. She couldn't believe it, and all this was as a result of being asked to join the school's basketball team. Some girls even gave her a passing high-five as she walked by.

Wow. Kelly smiled. *That has never happened to me before*, she thought. But she loved it. The attention and this new-found fame brought all sorts of amazing feelings with it. She was more confident, incredibly happy, and she loved being popular.

"So, this is what it feels like to be Sandra," Kelly muttered under her breath. She reached her homeroom and realised she had ten minutes till the bell. Plenty of time to freshen up, so she decided to go to the toilet. Because the Dad Express left the station (their house) so quickly, she hadn't had enough time to properly brush her hair or put on any mascara et cetera. Luckily the toilets were in the same building, so she didn't have far to go.

SWOOSH went the door as she gently elbowed her way inside. Kelly dropped her bag in front of one of the basins and took a good look in the mirror. "Oh, you look hideous." She scowled at herself. Using her hands, she tried to pin down the frizzy stray hairs but it was no use. They just popped right back up and stuck out even more. "Ugh, let's try brushing it out." Kelly squatted down and unzipped her bag. She searched for her hair brush, but couldn't seem to find it anywhere.

God, did I even pack it this morning? she wondered, trying desperately to retrace her steps in her head.

BANG went the door suddenly. Kelly jumped and shifted her gaze to the exit.

"Looky, looky what the cat dragged in this morning," said Sandra with her hands resting on her hips. She glared at Kelly with her eyes narrowed and her jaw set tight. "Barf face is here, girls," continued Sandra, and her entourage of two very solid, muscular minions smirked at her remark.

Kelly stood her ground. She didn't flinch. She wasn't going to allow Miss Priss to intimidate her today. "Haha, Sandra, *soooooo* funny." Kelly rolled her eyes at her antagonist. "So, how did you guys pull up with the burpees?" She smirked.

Sandra scrunched up her face—clearly, she wasn't happy

with the idea of someone making fun of her. Deep down, Kelly was laughing at the fact Miss Priss and her minions had to suffer at the hands of Mr Schaefer and his love of burpees.

Suffer, you slimy slugs, thought Kelly to herself.

"So? We pulled up fine," said Sandra. "Didn't we, girls?"

And, on cue, her minions barked unanimously, "We sure did, hmm."

"In fact, we smashed them and did all fifty burpees in record time," said Miss Priss as she snaked her way closer to Kelly, inch by inch.

Kelly maintained her cool, calm poker face. "Well, that's great news. Good for you, and congratulations," she added, smiling. But she was still laughing on the inside.

"Oh, thanks, and I thought it would be very appropriate to return the gesture. After all, you did get chosen for the school's basketball team," sneered Sandra, evil written all over her face.

The girls were all standing very close to one another, about a metre and a half apart. Kelly had a bad feeling in the pit of her stomach and the rash on her shoulder kicked in hardcore, causing her back to twitch and spasm. Silence fell upon the room as Sandra continued to leer at her prey. Click went her fingers and her minions rushed towards Kelly as their leader stepped aside to admire herself in the mirror. Kelly screamed as her arms and legs were grasped and she was hoisted into the air and turned upside down, her head facing the floor.

"Stop!" Kelly screamed. "What are you doing?" The blood was rushing to her head.

"What do you want us to do, Sandra?" said one of the minions, holding on tight to Kelly's legs.

"Let's proceed, shall we? We still have a few minutes before the bell rings," replied Sandra. She walked up to Kelly and bent over. Grabbing her by the chin, making sure her prey was looking straight into her eyes, she spoke, "I have a little something for you, just to say thanks for the burpees yesterday." And she winked for good measure.

Kelly wiggled as hard as she could but there was no use fighting. She was stuck. "Please, Sandra, you don't have to do this," she pleaded.

"Oh no, I insist," she sneered. "Besides, it's the least I can do…" Sandra gestured for the girls to proceed. "Now, I hope you enjoy the dunk. Your hair does look oily and in need of a wash." She laughed at her own joke.

The minions headed towards the first toilet cubical with Kelly in tow. "No, no, no!" she screamed in protest. The rash spasmed even more, causing Kelly's back to twitch.

Spasm, spasm, spasm, twitch, twitch, twitch. But the minions proceeded. The upside-down position had Kelly's face turning a bright red and her temples pulsing. "Oh, stop!" she screamed, the pressure in her head intensifying with each passing second. She closed her eyes, hoping it would help, and exhaled a deep breath.

"We are everything that you are."

"We are everything that you will be."

"We all flow through you and within you always," echoed the silhouettes.

Kelly's rash throbbed and her back spasmed as she listened to the voices in her head. She screamed and screamed as the silhouettes repeated their chant over and over again.

Her body shook and convulsed and then, suddenly, a huge spike of energy flowed right through her. From the top of her head to the tip of her toes.

SHAZAM! It pulsated as the silhouettes finished their chant.

Kelly opened her eyes. "Oh no, you don't," she spat at her assailants. She ripped her hands out of the minion's grasp with ease, outstretched her arms, and landed on the floor in a perfect handstand, her ankles clutched tight by her would-be attackers.

"Huh, w-what?" said the girls, shocked by what they were seeing.

How can this be? they thought, looking at each other questioningly.

The two minions were stronger than Kelly and way more muscular. Solid-built. A skimpy little thing like Kelly wouldn't have the same horsepower, let alone the stamina, to take on two sumo wrestlers, so to speak. But all the spasming and twitching seemed to somehow work in her favour. Maintaining her handstand pose, Kelly kicked with all her might and her right leg connected with minion number one (AKA sumo girl) hitting her right in the face.

SMACK, BANG. The girl flew so high and so fast, right through the opposite cubicle, smashing the door to pieces and landing against the toilet wall. *SMACK!* She was knocked-out cold. Her body slithered down onto the toilet seat, not budging or moving. From a distance, Kelly could make out a small indent on the girl's face where her shoe had connected.

A flip and a bounce later, Kelly was back on her feet. In a fighting stance. Ready for a fight. And, boy, was she angry. Minion number two (AKA sumo girl two) looked at her friend and growled. The sound was horrific, like that of a wild beast. Seeing her friend so easily beaten and slumped on top of a toilet like a rag doll by the hands of a toothpick of a girl was just too difficult to fathom.

"How? How can this be?" She pointed at her unconscious friend. "How could you?" she grunted at Kelly and screamed as she pivoted on her heel all of a sudden and ran towards her prey, her claws outstretched. Kelly sidestepped at the last minute, grabbed her antagonist's hands by the wrists and threw her across the room. Sumo number two flew like a paper aeroplane and landed right on top of the basin—headfirst—the action knocking her out cold.

KERPLUNK.

Sandra screamed at the sight, not understanding what had just transpired. "W-what?" she mumbled.

Kelly noticed how Sandra remained fixed to her spot, staring down at her knocked-out minion.

What are you going to do now? thought Kelly. Silently, she walked up to Miss Priss, spun her around, and grabbed her by the collar with both hands.

"I did nothing to you, Sandra, to deserve this," she rasped, spittle flying all over Sandra's face. "I did absolutely nothing!" She'd had enough. This bullying would end here and now. Kelly trembled as she stared into Sandra's eyes. Not from the fear, but from all the pain this girl had caused her over the years. Today was the final straw. Enough was enough.

"What on earth is going on in here?" yelled Mr Lunateri. Both girls turned their attention to their homeroom teacher, equally shocked by the sudden interruption.

"Oh, please, please help me, Mr Lunateri. She's hurting me," lied Sandra, bursting out in full-on tears and squealing hysterically. Mr Lunateri pounced at once and grabbed Kelly by the scruff of her dress. Sandra fell to the floor and covered her face, pretending to be hurt.

"You are coming with me, young lady, straight to the principal's office," he ordered.

"But I didn't do anything," protested Kelly. "They attacked me first!"

"You liar!" yelled her teacher, and he dragged her out of the toilets and all the way to the principal's office. In front of all of her peers. Humiliated.

⁓

"Sit down," yelled Joyce as she, Mark, and Kelly stepped through the back door and into the kitchen. Kelly did as she was told, peering at her hands in her lap. Mark sat opposite his daughter with a very concerned look on his face. He was surprised when he received a phone call from the school and gobsmacked when the principal told him what had happened.

This can't be true, he thought after the phone call had ended. *My daughter caught fighting? My girl…?*

Joyce, on the other hand, had been in the middle of a very, very important meeting with the CEO of the company she worked for. A meeting that included a very important and potential client. If this client were persuaded to jump on board, the resulting revenue alone would generate 30% of the yearly total revenue. Which meant awesome possibilities for the CEO and also for Joyce. But the urgent phone call from Kelly's school had, had a negative effect on Joyce, which threw her off her game. In the end, the client decided to seek expertise elsewhere, and as a result, the CEO was extremely unhappy. And so was Joyce.

She paced the floor of the kitchen, rubbing her hands together. Anxious, angry and about to pop. "How could you?" she whispered at first, while Kelly kept her eyes on her lap. "How could you?" spat Joyce a second time, the fire within her rising and fast. She stopped dead in her tracks and turned to Kelly. "Look at me when I speak to you. You have embarrassed us, the family. You have created this mess!" She pointed at her daughter.

"B-but," squeaked Kelly, trying to explain what happened. She felt as small as a mouse.

"Do. Not. Speak. Young lady!" yelled Joyce with all her might. Kelly looked at her father for support, but all she got in return was a cold, hard stare. "Oh," whispered Joyce, rubbing her face with her hands. Mark didn't say a peep. His wife was so angry and interrupting her now was only going to cause more issues. "You will go to counselling and you will write a letter of apology to each of those girls," she demanded.

"Mum!" Kelly slammed her fist on top of the table. "That's not fair!"

"Not fair? *Not fair?*" repeated Joyce, calmly walking up to her daughter. "I will tell you what's not fair. Getting an urgent phone call in the middle of a very important meeting and then being told that your nearly sixteen-year-old daughter was caught fighting. Now, tell me, how is that fair?" she questioned. Kelly remained silent while her mother gawked at her with disgust.

The war is over, thought Kelly and her heart sank.

Nothing, absolutely nothing, could change things now.

Nor make them any better. Sandra got what she wanted in the end and that was for Kelly to pay. To pay for interrupting her poem recital, for beating her in basketball, and for making her suffer the dreaded fifty burpees as a result. And now Kelly was in deep, deep trouble. Not only was she suspended for a week, but she was immediately taken off the basketball team too. The principal advised Kelly's parents that it was unclear if the teenager would be suspended indefinitely. It all depended on the school committee and the other families involved.

This is an absolute nightmare, she thought. *A living, breathing nightmare.* Much worse than the strange dreams she'd been having as of late.

"Go to your room. *Go!*" screamed Joyce as she broke into tears. She sat down on a chair and turned her back to Kelly, unable to look at her daughter. Mark got up from his chair, tapped Kelly's shoulder, and pointed to the stairs. No words were exchanged, but his daughter understood his instructions and followed suit. She bolted to her room, heartbroken.

Mark grabbed his wife and held her while she sobbed. He knew no amount of words would help. The pain and humiliation she was feeling was incomprehensible, so he just held her tight and rocked her gently.

Kelly ran into her bedroom and slammed the door shut. She leaned against it. Defeated and deflated. "Oh my God," she mumbled to herself, her heart racing.

Psst, psst, psst. "It's okay, darling," whispered Mark. "It's okay…" And Kelly's heart broke at the sound of her father's voice. The one person who would always support her had now turned his back on her. She felt so alone.

"I-I-I've had enough of that kid," murmured Joyce. "I am so humiliated. How? How could she, Mark? How could *she*?" And she cried some more.

Kelly was angry. Angry at her mother for not believing her side of the story. She tried to explain what had happened as they sat in the principal's office, but Joyce didn't want a bar of it. And now, hearing her mother speak about her own *humiliation*—like that was what all this was about—angered Kelly even more. She balled her right hand into a fist and slammed it into her pillow. *BAM!*

Kelly huffed and puffed and screamed, threw herself onto her bed, and started to pummel her pillow. She kicked her legs, trying to release the frustration. *BAM, KICK, BAM, KICK, BAM.* Until it left her breathless and her pulse racing. She lay on her back, staring at the ceiling, analysing everything that have happened over the last several days, and trying to understand how it had got her to this point. To this nightmare of a roller coaster ride.

Her rash started to tingle and she balled her fist yet again. "No, *no*," she mumbled under her breath. Sitting upright, she reached behind her shoulder and pulled and pushed her body beyond its limits, contorting it so she could get a better reach. Off she went, scratching and clawing at her rash. She went hell for leather, not caring if she drew blood. If she clawed off a piece of skin, good. That meant the rash was gone and new skin would heal in its place.

Scratch, scratch, scratch she went. *Claw, claw, claw.* And suddenly Kelly stopped and sat at the edge of her bed, her breathing deep, rapid, intense. She was bubbling beneath the surface and something was going to explode. She exhaled as her eyes landed on the chest of drawers. Or rather, on one drawer in particular. The one containing the source of her dreams.

"Enough," she spat, leaping to the drawer and pulling it open. She grasped all the panties and bras, throwing them across her room like confetti, and then she stopped. The golden glove was there, staring right at her. "It's all your fault," she muttered, tears rolling down her cheeks and blurring her vision. She quickly wiped them away with her sleeve. "It's all your fault," she spat again, chastising the glove as if it could hear her. Then an idea popped into her head.

Get rid of it.

"Damn," she cursed. "Why hadn't I thought of that earlier?" Kelly snatched up the glove and, instantly, a bolt of energy ran from the tip of her fingers, through her palm, and up her arm. Moving and charging as it went. She didn't feel it, numbed by her rage.

Throw it out the window. It was her first thought, her instinct, but her parents would find it on the lawn. *And then what?* she wondered. That could make her sentence worse. She looked around the room. *Put it in the closet,* said her gut. But what was the difference between the closet and the drawer. *Nothing,* she concluded. *Wrap it up and throw it in the trash,* piped up her mind. But, once again, her parents would find it and think she stole it from somewhere. *No, I can't do that either,* she decided.

No matter which way she turned in her room, her heart knew there was nothing she could do. The glove could not be hidden and it couldn't be thrown out. She was stuck with it. Kelly slumped to the floor, feeling defeated and worn out. Her tanks were empty. The end was near. She dropped her head into her hands and sobbed hard. The tears were like a waterfall, the salty drops thick and heavy. Without thinking, Kelly closed her eyes and used the glove to wipe at her face. One golden fingertip gently brushed her temple—*SHAZAM*—and she vanished from her room.

When Kelly opened her eyes again, the glow of the shield in the tomb caught her gaze. *W-what? I'm not dreaming. How can this be?* she wondered. Kelly jumped to her feet, worried that the shepherd might attack her. But he was nowhere to be seen. The tomb was deserted.

"Why am I here?" she mumbled to herself, looking at the glove in her hand. She was vibrating with rage. She closed her eyes and bared her teeth. "Grrr, ENOUGH!" she screamed, and her voice echoed around her.

"We are everything that you are."

"We are everything that you will be."

"We all flow through you and within you always," chanted the silhouettes.

Their song travelled into the tomb, growing louder and louder. Kelly spun in her spot, searching for the source, and slowly they appeared all around her. First, as tiny white lights that seemed to grow brighter as they chanted.

She watched them, mesmerised by the sight. "Who are you all?" she asked. The chanting continued, and when it reached its crescendo, the golden knight upon the altar moved. The man, clad in this magnificent and intricately made armour, sat up, manoeuvred his legs over the edge, and jump down. When his feet hit the ground, the chanting stopped. Kelly's mouth was wide open and her eyes bulged out of her head. She could not believe what she was seeing. The armour didn't make a sound. Nothing squeaked for oil and nothing rattled. It was as if the armour itself became a part of the wearer, a second skin.

The golden knight walked between two silhouettes, entered the circle, and stepped in front of Kelly. She did not flinch nor blink. Kelly yearned to touch the shiny armour now that it was so close. It compelled her, so she reached out an arm. The golden knight lifted his hands, not in protest but to remove his helmet, and Kelly flinched at the sudden movement.

"It's you!" she gasped, recognizing the face and the eyes. "You are Millard!"

He held out his gloveless hand, and Kelly looked into his eyes, unsure whether to grasp his palm or simply return his missing piece of armour. His eyes were warm and kind, much like her father's as well as her own. Her brain didn't know what to do next and her gut was numb, but her heart sang out. *Hold his hand*, it told her, so she did. The connection was electric, and images instantly bombarded her mind. Images of Millard's life, images of the Great War, images of Babushka, the oak tree, the clan, the missing babe—*her father…?*

Everything suddenly made sense. All the pieces finally fitted together. The puzzle was complete.

Kelly fell to her knees, gasping for air. All of this was so intense. She touched the floor with one hand to steady herself, and the coolness of the rock gave her some comfort. She peered up. Millard was still standing before her, looking straight at her, and he nodded.

"Go to Babushka," he whispered. "She is the key."

Kelly's heart leapt at the sound of his gentle voice. This golden knight was her grandfather and, like her dad, she was the descendant of a mighty family—a family from another world, a different planet, in the far reaches of the universe...

23

KELLY WOKE LATE that morning. It was Friday, her favourite day of the week, as at exactly 3:30 PM, the weekend would begin. And who didn't like the weekend? No school, no homework, no uniforms. It was utter freedom. But not for Kelly. Not today. She was suspended and trapped at home for only God knew how long.

She looked at the clock. It was 9:00 AM. Time to get up. Her stomach rumbled and she felt a little queasy from the lack of food. Food had not been her friend of late; she just didn't have a desire or an appetite for it. And who could blame her? With all the strange things happening in her life, the last thing on anyone's mind would be food. Today, it was different, though. Because she was hungry.

Kelly sat up and placed her legs over the edge of her bed. She took a deep breath and exhaled. "God, last night… last night was incredible," she murmured to herself, shaking her head in denial.

Was it real? she thought, smirking to herself.

"Of course, it was real!" And she verified as much, by lifting her pillow, looking straight at the golden glove—her grandfather's glove. From the first moment she'd laid eyes on Millard when she fell asleep under the old oak tree, she felt a connection, a familiarity, like they'd met before somehow. And now, seeing him in person, within the tomb, it confirmed her realisation. He truly was a part of her and she of him.

Kelly couldn't believe it. The golden knight was her grandfather. Even though all the pieces now fit together, it sure as hell opened the floodgates to another million and one questions.

What happened to him? How did they come here to earth? What was the Great War? What was so special about her family? The list was endless.

She picked up the glove and held it in her hands, no longer angry or afraid, as the meeting had changed everything. She now looked at the glove as a good omen, not a bad one—it had finally brought her some much-needed peace. The dreams over the last few nights had turned her world upside down, bringing with them so much fear and anxiety. But there truly was nothing to fear; they were simply an avenue used to send messages to her, and one of those messages was for her to go see Babushka.

"Babushka," thought Kelly out loud. She stood up immediately. "Oh, I need to go see my fairy godmother." Kelly remembered Millard's request. She placed her hands on her cheeks, shocked at the realisation. Babushka was connected to Millard and to the Great War.

But how is she the key? she wondered. *What is the key anyway?*

Without thinking twice and forgetting that she was suspended, Kelly got dressed and went downstairs. She stopped at the bottom landing, unsure if anyone was around. She was worried she would cross paths with her mother, who felt humiliated by her daughter's actions at the moment.

"Well, there's only one way to find out," Kelly mumbled under her breath. Mustering all the courage she could find, she stepped into the kitchen.

"Oh, good morning, sleepyhead," said Mark as he watched his daughter step into view.

"G-good morning, D-dad," Kelly stammered back, looking apprehensively around the room.

Mark quickly realised what she was doing. "It's okay, Kel. Mum has gone into work today and I chose to work from home." He smiled.

"You mean watch me," she said sarcastically as she helped herself to a box of cereal.

Mark shrugged at her remark. His daughter wasn't wrong. "Yeah, true that. I decided to stay home and watch you." He saw the disappointment spread across Kelly's face and quickly added, "Better me than your mother, hey." He winked.

Kelly sat down next to her dad. "So what are you working on?"

Mark shuffled some paperwork aside to give her more space. The last thing he needed was for her to spill her breakfast all over his work—*explain that one to the boss.* "I'm doing admin work today. You know, catching up on paperwork, which I don't normally get to do when I'm out on location."

"Ah," said Kelly in response. She stopped eating and looked at her father, like really looked at him. For the first time EVER, she had noticed how similar his eyes were to Millard's. The same vibrant blue, along with the same type of sparkle. "Errr…" A shiver shook Kelly and her body gently convulsed, including her head and her hands, sending some milk and muesli flying up and out of her bowl, luckily missing her dad's paperwork by a longshot.

"Hey, kiddo, did someone walk on your grave," said Mark, noticing the shiver.

"No, Dad," said Kelly in response.

No one walked on my grave, but I definitely walked into your father's tomb, she thought to herself. *Many times at that.*

Kelly desperately wanted to tell her dad about everything. About the dreams and messages, the tomb, and most of all, the golden knight. Her dad needed to know about Millard, his father. It was important.

But how? she wondered.

It wasn't every day that you found out your grandfather was a knight and it wasn't every day that you learnt your bloodline was incredibly important, even if you didn't know what that importance meant.

Kelly fidgeted at the table, tapping her bowl with her spoon and swinging her legs. *God, what do I do?* She racked her brain for an answer. *I have to find a way to tell him.*

A few mouthfuls later and some really loud slurping, Kelly still didn't know how to approach the subject with her dad. She was worried bringing up her grandparents might make him sad. Kelly had never met her paternal grandparents. They had passed away a long time ago and way before she was born. Mark never spoke about them because it hurt and he always cried when their names were mentioned. All she knew was that they loved him dearly and gave him a good life. One day, Kelly's mother told her a big, dark family secret. Mark had been adopted as a baby. The news shocked her right to the core and it got the teenager thinking…

Were there other uncles or aunties out there somewhere in the world? And who were her real grandparents anyway? At the top of her list was: why did they give him away?

Kelly was incredibly sad for her dad. She never knew any of the answers and desperately wanted to know more. Besides, it also concerned *her*, much more than her mum, as it was her family history too. Joyce told her daughter not to ever question her dad about it, that he would tell her in his own time, when he was ready. Kelly respected that wish. Until now.

Boy, did she have some amazing news for him, she thought.

"Kelly can you please stop tapping your bowl and swinging your legs. You are shaking the table, darls," said Mark, trying to hide his frustrations.

"Oh, so sorry, Dad," she said pausing her movements immediately. She shuffled on her seat, sitting straighter than before, and clasped her hands neatly together. Like an attentive student in a classroom giving her full attention to the teacher. She took a deep breath and braced herself, "Dad…?" said Kelly gently.

"Hmmm? Yes, Kel, what is it?" Mark responded, only paying half attention to his daughter.

"Um, um, err, Dad, um, um, um," she mumbled, unable to find the right words. It sounded right in her head but her mouth just couldn't do what she needed it to do.

"What is it, Kelly?" Mark looked at her from the corner of his eye. "You know, while I work at home, I need to actually do some work. So, tell me what you need, kiddo."

He placed his paperwork on the table and turned towards his daughter.

"Oh, oh, oh," continued Kelly, slightly embarrassed and taken aback. She looked down to her hands and then up to her dad. Her heart wanted to tell him about Millard but her gut argued otherwise. "CAN I PLEASEEEE GO SEE BABUSHKA?" she blurted out quickly before she regretted bringing up any sensitive topics.

Mark stared at his daughter. "Oh," he said, surprised at the question *and* the delivery. "Why?"

"Oh, oh, oh, you know, why not?" said Kelly, not knowing how to answer the question.

Her father's mood shifted yet again, appearing too serious. "Kelly, you know you are suspended, right? You remember that, yeah?"

Kelly looked at her dad and then at the floor, cursing herself for being stupid. She should have just eaten her breakfast and gone back upstairs to her room. "Yes, Dad, I know I'm suspended. I haven't forgotten."

"Okay, then that means you have to stay home until that suspension ends," he said as a matter of fact.

"I know, Dad, but, but, but..." She started shaking her hands, trying to come up with some sort of reasonable answer.

By now, Mark had had enough horsing around. He glanced at his watch and grunted, "Look, Kelly, I have a lot of work to get through. Go to Babushka's house and make sure you get back before 4:00 PM. Your mother should be home by then, and if she catches you not in your room, we..." He pointed between them. "...are both D-E-A-D. Do you understand me?"

Kelly looked at her dad and smiled. He was the best ever. Even though he was mad at her, that thankfully hadn't lasted too long. She jumped out of her seat and gave him a great, big bear hug. "Thanks, Dad, you rock," said Kelly, holding him tight.

Mark embraced his daughter and held her just as tightly. He was still mad at her but she was his girl and staying mad just wasn't an option. He believed anger never solved anything, and it only brought on more arguments and discomfort for all parties involved. And that wasn't worth it at all. "How is your rash going?" he asked suddenly.

"Oh, my rash," said Kelly, surprised by the question. "It's… it's… still the same."

"Did she give you the ointment she promised to make?" Mark pressed, curious.

Kelly was kicking herself for not thinking of the ointment—it would have been the perfect excuse to use to go to see Babushka. Besides, her parents didn't know that she was still in a coma in hospital. Good thing the hospital wasn't far from home. Kelly could get there, visit Baba, and be back in no time at all, under the pretence of picking up some special ointment as promised by Babushka herself.

"Actually, Dad, I'm going to pick it up today," lied Kelly. "I haven't heard from her, so I thought since I'm home, why not just mosey on over." She smiled, fidgeting slightly with her hands.

"Okay then, sounds good. You go do that and don't forget to say hi to her from me," said Mark as he turned his full attention back to his paperwork.

Deep down, Kelly was doing somersaults and jumping jacks. She was so happy that her dad had agreed to her plan.

Millard told her to go see Babushka, that she was the key, and Kelly had to know what that meant…

~

Babushka stared at the path ahead, within the nothing. It was so bright and vibrant. Like a ray of sunshine travelling into the distance.

"Oh," she said suddenly. Upon closer inspection, she realised the light was in fact the cords of energy connecting us to every living thing. Be it a tree, beast, person, earth, ocean, soul, heart, or gesture. It was the same spiderweb-like cords she'd seen back at Saphira when she was a child. But, for some reason, it had vanished when she'd come through the portal in the oak tree. Now, seeing it for the first time in forty years, it caught her a little off guard.

Babushka ran her hands through the cord and instantly felt the energy. It was so powerful she gasped. She hadn't felt the spark in a very long time but remembered the sensation at first touch. Her fingertips tingled as she played around with the cord. And memories flooded back of a childhood, of the days of playing hide and seek and using the cords to find her fellow hiders with the utmost ease. She smirked at the thought but then frowned, as in the beginning, not all of the people of Saphira were heartened by her powers. It was The Sage of Light who reassured her and encouraged her to embrace her gift and let it flow through her. Indeed, it had. Over the years, as she grew, her magic and her powers grew too. People from all over the realm came to see Baba, asking for her help—not just by way of magic but also with herbs. The knowledge she attained of her home planet's natural flora was outstanding.

You may wonder *why herbs?* Well, just like the children in

the village, not everyone believed in magic. They saw magic as trickery, an abomination, which brought more evil along with it. People feared magic and preferred to avoid it. So, Babushka found a way to help the people of the realm by looking into plant life and all the wonders contained within it. Her herbs, ointments, and concoctions could heal many diseases and ailments. And the most amazing part of all was the fact she never asked for payment. Nothing whatsoever. Babushka believed in kindness and generosity, hoping perhaps the same would be passed on to someone else and so on, making the world a better place. Sadly, it didn't work all the time, due to greed and power.

"Oh my," sighed Babushka, exhausted. She remembered what it had felt like to sense the energy, to have the magic flow through her. It was special and powerful. But now, as she stood in front of her cord, she felt like a shrivelled-up old sack, falling apart and full of moth holes.

What on earth could be at the end of the cord? she thought.

The winds suddenly picked up. Tangible but gentle. It didn't blow onto her face nor whisp across it. It nudged her from behind, like a hand encouraging her, pushing her to move forward. "Oh my!" squealed Babushka. She tried digging her feet into the ground but it was no use. The invisible hand continued to nudge her to move. "W-what?" she squealed again. "W-what's the hurry?" she yelled out in frustration.

"Come," echoed a voice within the nothingness and the invisible hand ceased its push. "Come and you shall see."

"Ha!" Babushka exhaled. "I'm too old for this." She looked at her feet, her old and shrivelled feet. The same feet that had travelled many miles. *Light-years.* "What would another short walk hurt?" She placed one foot after the other and moved along the cord—her cord.

One step led to two and so on. Slowly, she moved. A little anxious at first but determined. *Pitter-patter, pitter-patter, pitter-patter* went her feet within the void. With each step she took, she felt her energy growing, as if her body was absorbing the cord itself as she travelled. *Crunch, crunch, crunch.* Babushka stopped and looked down. Grass. There was grass everywhere. Beautiful, luscious, green grass. It felt cool and wet to the touch, just like the dew from the morning mist. It was soothing and calming, and it made her giggle as the water tickled her feet.

When Babushka looked up, the nothingness was gone. "Oh, w-w-what?" she mumbled, covering her face with her hands. It was the forest, her forest, at the edge of the village. The same forest she'd explored and hid inside when she was but a girl. Babushka's face lit up and joy filled her heart "Oh, oh my…" Tears of happiness streamed down her face in currents.

This must be a dream, she thought. *How could this be? Am I finally home?*

She lifted her arms and danced, danced right around the forest. Twirling and toiling and twirling some more. She kept her eyes open, watching the world spin, afraid it would disappear as quickly as it appeared. Vibrant colours from wild flowers, from magical mushrooms, and toadstools mixed together, created a rainbow as she spun. It was magical and it was beautiful. She twirled and twirled until it all got to be too much, the vertigo sending Baba crashing to the ground.

SPLAT! Babushka landed on a luscious bed of fairy moss. She exhaled, feeling light and content, sprawled out on her bed of vegetation, and enjoyed the peace and solitude. The earth was soft and the rays of the sun were warm.

Let me stay here forever, she thought.

"This is where I yearn to be," she told the forest.

"But you can't, Lilliana," whispered a gentle voice.

Babushka cocked one eye slightly open, trying to look upon her visitor. It was no one. She couldn't see a thing. *No, could it be…?* she wondered.

"It is okay, child. I won't harm you," whispered the voice again, reassuring her, just like he'd done long ago.

"Yes, yes, it is *you*!" screamed Babushka and she jumped to her feet—*SPRING*—running right up to the Sage of Light. She embraced him with all the love she could muster. "My lord, it is you," she whispered. "It is… You have brought me back, back to my home." She looked him straight in the eyes as she spoke, happiness written all over her face. Unfortunately, it was short-lived.

The Sage of Light gestured for Lilliana to sit next to him on the trunk of a fallen tree, and she did so. He took her hands and held them tenderly. "Lilliana, all this is an illusion. The forest is not real, and we are not within its shelter." Confusion replaced Baba's happiness and elation, as he spoke to her. "Lilliana, listen to me. A great evil has destroyed our homeland and the only way to stop it is for you to come back home," he explained.

"But, my lord, my powers are gone. I am weak and I'm old," she pleaded. "My magic has abandoned me. I cannot open the portal." Her hands began to tremble and she shivered.

He looked at her and his heart ached. "The magic never abandoned you, child. You just stopped believing in it."

Babushka released his hands and stood. She walked a

few paces from the trunk, her back facing the sage. Silence fell upon them. She needed the distance. She didn't want the sage to see her cry. The memory of the king's death stabbed right through her heart and her soul, and she wailed.

"How can I believe when my magic did not save him? How?" she asked.

"You did save me, Lilliana. You did," whispered the king.

"Oh! W-what?" Babushka quickly pivoted on her heel, facing the king for the first time since that dreaded day. "What? What is going on?" she shouted to the forest, not believing what she was seeing. Babushka spun in every direction, searching for answers amongst the trees and foliage, and looked back to the king. "You are not real. You are dead. *Dead!*" she screamed and dropped to her knees in agony.

"I am real, Lilliana, and I'm here with the Sage of Light," he whispered. "Have no fear."

"No, *no!*" screamed Babushka more forcefully, while grabbing her head and pulling at her hair. "You, you *died*. You cannot be real," she spat, breathing heavily.

The king walked up to her and laid his hand on her shoulder, squeezing it. "Shh, shh." Slowly, her breathing returned to normal. "Babushka, calm down. You did not kill me, Lilliana. You saved me," he whispered again.

As she listened to his words, memories bombarded her mind, image after image after image of the king dying. "How could I have possibly saved you, my lord? I know what I saw."

He squeezed her shoulder even more, trying to reassure her, to take away the pain she'd been carrying all these years. "You saved me by saving my daughter from the great evil, and now Saphira needs you to come home to save us all," he explained.

"But I can't," she cried out, sobbing like a child.

"Yes, you can, Lilliana. You can," he whispered. "Unburden yourself of this pain, once and for all. Forgive yourself."

The sage reappeared beside the king and added, "Yes, forgive yourself and rise from the ashes, your ashes. The day has come. Your day has come."

Babushka remained kneeling in front of them, truly listening to their words and absorbing them. They were right. It was time to let go. Forty years had gone by. Forty long years, during which she'd felt responsible for his death.

On cue, and as if he'd been reading her mind, the king added, "You couldn't have saved my life from this great evil. I knew that, but by whisking my daughter away to a safe place, you saved her. She is everything that I am and my memory lives on within her." His words rang true as they echoed in her mind and in her heart. She looked up to the king with tear-soaked eyes and lips trembling. He clasped her face in his hands and bent over, kissing her forehead. "Thank you for saving me," he whispered.

In that moment, suspended in time, Babushka's broken heart healed and the burden vanished. The weight fell right off her shoulders. Gone. She stood and closed her eyes, holding the king's hands. One then the other, she raised them to her lips and kiss them gently. "Thank you, my lord." As she enjoyed the moment of peace, a gentle wind started to pick up within the forest. The grass swayed, the flowers bobbed, and the leaves rustled. Something was coming.

"Lilliana," boomed the sage, and she turned her full attention onto him. However, when she opened her eyes, the king and the sage were gone. The forest disappeared, leaving her alone in the void, except for the cord of energy protruding from her belly and leading into the distance.

BOOM! Thunder crackled and lightning flashed ever so brightly. Babushka shivered and all the hairs on her neck stood on end. The wind blew more forcefully, wisping strands of hair wildly across her face. *Smack, smack, smack. Crack* went the thunder again. It was getting closer. *Crack, crack, crack.*

Babushka looked down at her hand and droplets of water stained her fingers. "W-what?" she mumbled. But as she looked back up, a figure appeared in the distance, attached to her cord. She shook her head, not believing that someone else was within the nothingness with her.

W-what is this? she wondered.

There was nothing left to stop her. The guilt was gone. The sadness had dissipated, and all that remained—which once was forgotten—was passion and love. Passion for magic and pure, unrelenting love drove her forward. As she took each step, the figure became clearer and clearer, until…

"Oh!" they each gasped when they realised who was standing in front of them.

"Baba," whispered Kelly.

"Kelly," whispered Babushka. They ran to each other and embraced.

KABAM! An enormous fireball lit up the nothingness, blinding them. The light was so bright and intense, engulfing everything it touched.

"The prophecy," boomed the Sage of Light from within the fireball, "speaks of a warrior of pure blood, who will return and bring order and balance to chaos. Their name will be Saskia, meaning Protector of Mankind."

Slowly, Babushka's and Kelly's eyes adjusted to the light and they uncovered their faces. Before them stood the sage and Millard, the knight clad from head to toe in his golden armour. Both women were gobsmacked. Unflinching.

"Lilliana," continued the sage, "I once told you that you were special. My child, you certainly are special and now the time has come for you to shine even brighter than the largest and most powerful stars in all the universe. Now is the time to unite with Saskia, return home, and destroy this evil."

Kelly stood, glued to her spot, and listened. Her heart was racing a million miles an hour. "I am part of this prophecy," she whispered. "I am Saskia…" She shook her head. It was all so surreal.

"Babushka, this is your destiny," boomed the sage.

"Yes, my lord," she answered with the utmost confidence, not even thinking twice about the matter. When the king had been alive, her duty was to help the people with or without magic. She'd spent forty long years without her powers, yet Baba still felt her purpose was to continue to help—even though the people of earth were from another galaxy far, far away. Especially now that her heart was healed and unburdened.

"Help Saskia, guide her to channel her abilities of speed, strength, hearing, and sight. Help her to reach her full potential," he declared solemnly.

Babushka nodded her head and bowed down to her lord, accepting his wishes.

Millard stood silent and watched Kelly as the sage spoke. He noticed the effect the whole thing had on her. And who could blame her? It was a lot to take in. He turned to Babushka and spoke, "Lilliana, look after my granddaughter, tell her about her bloodline, teach her about the past, and prepare her for the future." His voice was so gentle and soothing it brought a smile to Babushka's face.

Kelly's head swirled and she felt slightly dizzy. "Bloodline, past, future," she mumbled under her breath.

I have so many questions, she thought.

"And Babushka will give you everything you need," assured Millard, this time speaking directly and gently to Kelly. His words eased Kelly's mind ever so slightly and it was enough to stop the dizziness.

"Now step forward, Lilliana, and accept my light," boomed the sage, and Babushka complied. "Close your eyes and clasp my hands," he continued, and she did as she was directed. As their palms joined, the fireball of light began to pulse.

Doop, doop, doop. The illumination was near blinding, as the pulsing sound intensified. *Doop, doop, doop.* Kelly covered her eyes and screamed. The light was too much. Too radiant and too brilliant.

Doop, doop, doop. Brighter and brighter it grew, and when it reached its peak... *KABOOM!*

The fireball of light exploded into a supernova and vanished. Kelly jumped, jerking Babushka's hand abruptly, and screamed, her legs flying here and there and her hands touching herself everywhere. Checking to see that all the pieces were still where they were meant to be.

"Oh, thank God," she whispered in relief, slumping back in her chair and wiping the sweat from her brow. "Phew. Oh, Baba." She grabbed Baba's palm once again—this time feeling for a pulse.

"I'm fine, Kelly," whispered Babushka as she opened her eyes and looked up. "I'm fine."

Kelly babbled some incoherent words, which sounded like baby talk, trying to get something across but she couldn't.

However, Babushka knew what it was and she sat upright in her bed, grabbing both of Kelly's hands, "Shh, shh, child, all is good," she soothed.

She uncovered herself and jumped out of bed. The cold floor was refreshing beneath her feet. Kelly just continued to stare, mumbling like a baby. Before her, in all her glory, stood a beautiful woman with the whitest of hair. She wore a golden crown of ivy upon her head. A delicate white robe of silk adorned her body, covering her from head to toe. She was radiant, and within the sun's rays, she glowed ever so brightly.

The woman was Babushka. She'd risen from the ashes just like the vision said she would.

24

"B-BABUSHKA," SAID KELLY, pointing at her fairy godmother. She looked at the old woman from head to toe, taking in all that she'd become. It was amazing. It was like a butterfly had emerged out of its cocoon after it had metamorphosised, its beautiful wings glorious in the sunshine. Babushka was glorious and her magic and energy exuded for all to see. "W-what h-happened to you?" Kelly mumbled, blinking continuously and not believing her eyes.

Babushka walked around her hospital bed and stood in front of Kelly. She smiled down on the teenager and held out her hands. Kelly paused for a moment, unsure whether to clasp them or not. Seeming to notice the girl's hesitancy, Baba whispered, "It is all right, child. Ever since you were a babe, I've only ever loved you, and nothing has changed, not even now."

Kelly exhaled a long breath and looked at her fairy godmother. Baba's face might now be that of a glowing, vibrant woman but her eyes were still the same. Warm and loving. All the memories of her fairy godmother were beautiful and happy. How could she doubt her now? So Kelly took a leap of faith and clasped Babushka's outstretched palms.

KACHOO. Memories, all her memories from when she was a babe up until this very moment flashed before her eyes, like a projector showing slides on a wall.

"Huh? W-what is happening?" squeaked Kelly, not understanding and worried that her brain was going to get fried.

"We are dream feasting, sharing our memories and our lives together in the here and the now," said Babushka, trying to soothe the girl and not scare her with the strange experience.

"B-but why?" questioned Kelly.

"So your questions can be answered, and all your doubts doused away. So you can see the life I've lived and the life I was forced to choose to survive," whispered Babushka. "Now open your mind, relax, and trust the wonders of the magic. Allow my memories to flow through you too."

Kelly closed her eyes, steadied her breathing, and allowed the magic into her heart and soul. At first, the feeling was strange yet familiar as the energy travelled through her. It felt sort of similar to the energy that flowed through her hand and up her arm when she touched the golden glove. It tickled at times too and she smiled. But as she continued to steady her breathing, her body relaxed and the whole experience became more enjoyable and fascinating.

The memories of Babushka's life were extraordinary, and what made the experience even more breathtaking was the realisation that she felt exactly what Baba felt in each moment. If it was pain, Kelly felt that pain. If it was sadness, Kelly felt her sadness. If it was elation, Kelly revelled in it too. It was as if, by holding hands, Kelly not only lived her own life but also walked the footsteps of another simultaneously.

Suddenly Babushka let go and Kelly dropped to her knees. *Kerplunk.* "Oh! Oh, oh, oh my," she mumbled, placing both of her hands on the floor to steady herself. Her head was slightly dizzy after the sudden break from dream feasting.

Babushka knelt beside her and placed a hand on Kelly's shoulder. "Breathe, breathe slowly, my child. Breathe," she whispered. The dizziness was making her nauseous so Kelly decided to close her eyes, hoping it would help. "Shh, breathe, it's all right and it's normal to feel dizzy during your first dream feast. The same thing happened to me." The old woman smiled.

Kelly opened her eyes and looked at her fairy godmother. "Baba," she whispered, "I felt your pain. I truly felt it. The pain you carried after the king's death. I-I-I wish I knew, so I could have helped you and held you like you did with me." Tears welled up in Kelly's eyes as she recalled her godmother's pain. It was excruciating and she had no idea how her Baba had carried it for so long.

Baba wiped her tears away by using the soft silk sleeve of her robe, the touch as light as a feather. "My child, all is good now. There is nothing to cry about. Now is a time of joy. We've found you. We've found *you*..." she whispered as she stroked Kelly's face.

"The babe." Kelly perked up suddenly. "The babe in my dreams. Is Millard's son—my grandfather's son—my father?" Kelly pulled herself up from the floor and started pacing the hospital room. "You came here with the babe, but the babe was found by the police that night. Yes, yes, that's what happened. I saw it. It happened in the park. In the park where the old oak tree is." She stopped and turned to face Babushka. "That same oak tree is where I would often sit and look at the world, sometimes even meditate. And that's where I saw glimpses of a great war, of Millard, and those incredible blue eyes…" said Kelly, drifting off as she was immersed in the memory of those bright-blue eyes, now etched in her brain forever. The same blue that shown within her eyes and that of her father's. "Oh," she gasped as each of her questions was answered by the dream feasting.

Babushka just watched Kelly and allowed her to speak. It was important that all this information was properly absorbed and understood.

"Why couldn't you find him?" the teenager finally questioned. "Why didn't you look harder?" She knew the answers but wanted to hear them in Babushka's own words.

"The energy cords were severed the minute I stepped foot on this planet. The magic was gone, even my powerful staff came out this end shrivelled and dried up like an old branch from a dead tree," explained Babushka. "I could not follow the cords to find him, and every turn we took, led us to a dead end. There was nothing we could have done…"

Kelly turned away and looked out the hospital window at a world that now felt strange. All her life she had known this planet as her home, when in fact she was a visitor, some sort of tourist here on a holiday.

Babushka whispered, "Kelly, Kelly, are you okay?" She stood and watched the girl stare out the window. It was understandable that all this would be very overwhelming. Besides, it wasn't every day you were told you're from another planet.

God, this is just incredible, thought Kelly. *What am I meant to feel?*

She pivoted on her heel, confused as to why this was happening to her. Only her. "Babushka why doesn't my father see what I see? You know, I mean, oh, um…" It was hard to find the right words. In her mind, it made sense, but for some reason, when her mouth moved, it all got lost in translation.

"It's okay, child. Take your time," assured Babushka.

Kelly took another long breath. "Why isn't my father like me? He's the son of Millard, yet his father didn't come to him in his dreams." Kelly was saddened by the thought. She knew very little about her father's past because he never spoke of it.

Where did the magic go? she wondered.

"Your father would have been just as powerful as your grandfather, had he stayed in Saphira," explained Babushka. "When we went through the portal, the magic vanished. Some of us were transformed into animals, whereas others were protected one last time by the mystical objects in our possession, keeping us human in this world before the magic disappeared. I was carrying a powerful staff, which is now an old broomstick locked away in my cupboard at home. However, the grief I carried with me severed the cords of energy. Because I could not save the king, I lost faith not just in myself but also in the magic and it vanished completely." Babushka decided to keep pushing, to keep searching for the right words to help Kelly understand all the pieces of the puzzle. "When you and I were dream feasting, I saw a memory. It was of your father and the snake."

"Oh yes, I remember! He was so shaken up that day," added Kelly.

"He was shaken up because he saw something, something that didn't make sense to him but it makes perfect sense to me." Babushka took a few steps towards the windows, towards Kelly. "You see, child, he mentioned that he saw the snake bow to him, and let me tell you… he wasn't imagining it."

"W-what!" Kelly gasped. "How? How can this be?" she questioned.

Babushka gestured to the bed. "Please come and sit down. It will help you if you sit."

"No, no, thank you," said Kelly, holding up her hands in protest. "I can't sit. To be honest, I don't know what I want. Just please continue."

Babushka nodded her head in acknowledgement. "Snakes are part of the reptile family; they are vertebrates. Other creatures—such as lizards, turtles, crocodilians, and birds—are reptiles." Baba ticked off each animal on her hands as she spoke. "All these amazing modern-day beings are branches on a tree, and at the top of that tree are prehistoric beasts, known as dinosaurs, their descendants.

Kelly stared at Babushka, as the old woman pleaded her case. The teenager didn't understand what dinosaurs had to do with snakes and her dad.

"But on my home planet, we too have such beasts." Holding up her hands and gesturing with quotation marks, Baba said, "But we call them dragons."

"Dragons!" Kelly gasped for a second time. "Dragons? Real, winged, flying, fire-breathing dragons? The type you see in the movies?"

"Yes, real dragons but some are made of gold, some silver, some bronze, some of fire, and some of ice," explained Babushka.

Kelly could not believe what she was hearing. *Dragons, alive and real. Wow*, she thought.

"But wait," the teenager screamed aloud. "What do dragons have to do with my father and the snake?"

"The snake bowed because it sensed your father's long-lost power: dragon whispering," echoed Babushka's voice within the hospital room. "As you were starting to experience the dreams and the transformation, some of it—the magic—must have brushed on to your father and reawakened his abilities. The similarities between this planet's creatures, dinosaurs, and that of my home world, namely dragons, are uncanny. And as snakes are a relative of dinosaurs, your father has the ability to communicate with them."

"Dragon whisperer," mumbled Kelly. "Reawakening of powers. Dreams and transformation… *What?*" The teenager rubbed her face with her palms and massaged her forehead. A headache was coming on.

Babushka walked right up to Kelly and placed her hands on her shoulders. "I know this is all hard to believe, my child, and there is a lot to absorb, but I'm here to help you on your journey." Kelly did not look at her Baba as she spoke. The girl felt numb. Her fairy godmother gently lifted her chin so that their eyes met. "I'm here for you and beside you always," she whispered.

Hearing those words brought no comfort to Kelly. She stepped away and went back to staring out the hospital room window. Below, cars zoomed by, buses carried passengers to their destinations, and some people could be seen walking their dog in parklands next to the hospital. All were oblivious to what was happening within these walls. For days, Kelly's world was turned upside down and now it was being shaken all about. Like a snow globe with its fake snow particles swirling around and around and around. Her head felt shaken and her soul rattled.

"So, what happens now?" asked Kelly, her eyes still locked on the window. "What am I meant to do?"

"We leave here and go inform the others. I'm sure they would like to know that you have been found," answered Babushka.

"We just leave? Simply walk out the door? The doctors won't let that happen," said Kelly, her voice laced with concern. "They will keep you here, lock you up, and perform lots of tests on you like a lab rat." She turned around and faced Babushka. "I don't know how they will ever believe that a little old lady, who was in a coma, woke up to be a beautiful and radiant version of herself. They will think we're both mad."

Babushka smiled at Kelly, listening to the girl and her concerns. "Well, then, we don't walk out that door." She pointed to the only reasonable escape route, and Kelly's eyes popped out of her head.

"Then how do you suggest we leave? Through the window?" Kelly added sarcastically.

Babushka shook her head. "No, child, through the use of magic." And the old woman winked. "Come, hold my hand as we travel through space and time."

Kelly did not budge. She remained fixed to her spot by the window. *If we leave, what's going to happen?* she thought.

Babushka held out her hand and smiled. "If we leave, we start our journey of discovery, of destiny, of adventure, of magic…"

Kelly wasn't sure what that sort of journey looked like, but she was certain she had to get out of this room, one way or another. And if the method was magic, well, why not try it? Besides, it wasn't the strangest thing she'd ever done.

So why stop now?

Kelly clasped Babushka's hand ever so tightly, closed her eyes for comfort, and listened to the melody of an ancient chant. As the song rang through the room, their bodies slowly faded and twinkled away, travelling through threads of energy, far from level four and bed ten.

~

Vlad and Bee ended up spending the night on Babushka's couch. Even though his intention was only to come by for a quick visit, he missed his friend deeply, to the point it was becoming unbearable. He thought by being in her home, her special space, and seeing all the familiar things, it might boost his spirits. But it did not.

Everything within the house of his beloved friend, including its exterior, was now dull and tarnished. She was the shine that made everything glow and sparkle. Her absence could definitely be felt. So Vlad had curled up on the couch. He was just too sad to leave and preferred to remain there instead. The thought of going home, back to the burrow, was not any more appealing either. And since it was very late, and also to prevent any further noise within the burrow itself, Vlad decided to remain here. He felt safe, as he had his trusty sidekick watching over him at all times.

Bee remained vigilant throughout the night, watching TV and keeping one eye on the rat. She could afford to do so, as she was capable of motion tracking, motion analysis, and night vision. She was so advanced that she could fully watch and absorb through one eye, while the other was set on security alert, monitoring their surroundings for up to

500 metres. Walls and solid obstacles would not be a problem. Bee had the capabilities of looking straight through it all. If so much as a pin was dropped 499 metres away, Bee would not just see it. She would have calculated its height, mass, and density before it ever hit the ground. Yep, kid you not. Anyone would feel safe with Bee watching over them.

Click, click, click went the remote control as Bee flicked through the channels on the television. She was frustrated at the inactivity, as this was all she'd been doing now for the past forty-five minutes. Everything on TV was boring. It was all news, news, and more news.

Where are the cartoons? she thought.

Ever so slowly, Vlad began to stir. "Hmm," he moaned. He scratched his furry snout and rolled over onto his side, facing the TV.

Bee continued to click away on the remote control. *Click, click, click.* Still finding nothing decent to watch.

Even though Vlad's eyes were closed, the bright light flicking from each channel change was starting to rouse him. It was as if someone was shining an incredibly bright torch onto his face and then quickly switching it off. The split-second shine lured him out of his dreams and back to reality. "Hmm," mumbled Vlad, and he instinctively raised his paw and covered his eyes. But it was no use. The light always found a way to get through, be it a large or a small crack. "Hmm, God, w-what… what time is it?" grumbled the rat.

Immediately, Bee flicked a couple of buttons and found a news channel. And, there, situated on the bottom left-hand corner, next to the channels logo, was the time. She read it out to Vlad, "It's 11:49 AM, nearly midday."

Vlad's eyelids suddenly flung open, like a roller blind

flinging up to the top of the window. *KAFLING.* Luckily for him, his eyes were attached to his brain; otherwise they would have sprung right out of their sockets and flung right across the room, hitting the TV screen.

"Midday!" he screamed and jumped up on the couch. "Why didn't you wake me?"

Beep, beep, burp. "You needed to sleep, Vlad," said Bee. "You were exhausted. Besides, you had bad dreams overnight, yelling out for Babushka," she explained.

Vlad turned to his companion in alarm. "Really? What was I saying?"

Bee continued to click away on her remote control, preferring anything but the news. "You said something like: *We love you. Come back. We need to go home, all of us together.* You whimpered a little but that was all. Then your sleep finally became restful."

Vlad's cheeks turned red. He couldn't believe what he was hearing. "God, how embarrassing."

"Nothing to be embarrassed about. We all have nightmares from time to time," said Bee, trying to offer some comfort.

Vlad stretched his arms and reached for the sky. "Oh, ah, that's easy for you to say, Bee. You don't dream."

Beep, beep, beep, burp. "I am aware of that. Don't you worry," said the droid in response, but Vlad ignored her and continued to stretch. He ruffled the fur on top of his head, running his claws through his hair and sort of combing it at the same time. No matter what position he slept in, his hair always ended up looking like a dried-up floor mop. Shaggy and out of control.

Click, click, click continued the remote control. The

flashes of light coming from the TV were more and more bearable as Vlad's eyes adjusted.

Beep, beep, beep sprang an internal alarm within Bee. She dropped the control and turned away from the TV. She stood up on the couch and looked over the backrest. Something was coming. Vlad noticed straightaway that something was awry, stopped grooming himself, and watched Bee. "What is it?" he questioned her.

Beep, beep, burp. "My sensory indicator said something big is about to happen."

"Big? What do you mean by big?" asked Vlad, now up, standing on the couch next to his droid, and looking over the backrest. His gut kicked in and all the hairs on the back of his neck popped on end, telling him something was slightly out of whack. He scratched his neck, feeling uneasy, and looked beyond. Into the kitchen.

Beep, beep, burb. "My indicators are telling me that the temperature within this room is dropping rapidly. Yet, outside, the temperature has not changed and matches the weather forecast on the news. This means that we have something incoming," explained Bee, her voice cool and calm.

Vlad jerked his head in concern, looking right at the droid. "Incoming? Incoming from where!" he screamed, scanning the room and trying to work out the location.

"*That*, I am not entirely sure, but we will soon find out," she replied.

Vlad couldn't contain himself. He jumped off the couch, crawled under it, and covered his eyes. He was scared.

Beep, beep, burp. "It's all right, Vlad. This isn't anything bad. Nothing is going to happen to us," she tried to console him. "You can come out from there."

"Nooo, thank *you*," he squeaked. "I am not moving." The temperature continued to drop within the room, Vlad shivered, and his breath came out all smoky when he exhaled, but he refused to budge from underneath the couch.

Small sparks of light began to tingle here and there in front of the kitchen. "Oh!" yelled Bee. "It's coming. My senses can now see it. Vlad, look! There are flickers of light flying everywhere." Bee was getting excited. She'd never seen this type of light show, ever. "Come, have a look, Vlad," she begged. The lights grew in size and changed in colour. Flicks of reds, yellows, blues, and greens appeared, flowing all around and forming a giant circular rainbow. It was spectacular. "Oh, Vlad, look, look, *look!*" she screamed. "It is *so* beautiful."

Better than fireworks on New Year's Eve.

Bee was mesmerised by the light show and her senses suggested that it was about to reach its climax. Vlad made sure his eyes were shut throughout the whole ordeal. He heard every single word about the beautiful light show but he just couldn't find it in himself to look, not even peek with one eye open. The colours began to swirl. Round and round they went. Faster and faster they travelled, mixing with each other. And then, *BOOM*, like a firecracker going off, sparks exploded and formed into two silhouettes. Bee's jaw dropped as she looked upon two figures standing in the centre of Babushka's kitchen.

"Ah, we are back. Welcome," said Babushka.

Slowly and surely, Kelly opened her eyes. "Oh, oh, *oh my!*" she gasped. She released Babushka's hand and started patting her own body, making sure that everything was still where it was meant to be.

Bee just stood there, fixed to her spot, staring at the newly arrived visitors. She didn't recognise the younger lass but the older one looked familiar…

Babushka scanned the room. Everything was the same. Even the muffins and the pots were sitting in the exact same spot she'd left them on the day Kelly had first come to visit.

If only, she thought. *If only her magic worked, none of this would have happened the way it had. Perhaps they would have all gone home sooner. Many, many years sooner. Or perhaps not. Things always happen for a reason, even if the reason cannot be explained.*

Babushka glared at her pots and pans and scrunched up her face. "Ew."

The leftover muffin ingredients had dried up so much that no amount of soaking nor chiselling would remove it. She dry retched when her eyes landed on her once beautiful and soft muffins. Their sweet aroma had faded long ago and in their place was decay, which resembled the odour of the dirt collected under your big toe nail. It was revolting, the remnants extremely hairy. Hairier than a dog's bum.

"Hmpf, I know what to do," Baba said out loud and she closed her eyes and chanted a sweet melody. All the filthy pots and pans vanished in an instant and reappeared back in their rightful places, clean and shining. The muffins also disappeared, along with the hair and the smelly toenail residue. The kitchen was back to the way it should have been. Neat and tidy, spick and span. "Ah! My work is done," said Babushka, with a big grin across her face. She turned back to Kelly, who was fixated on the droid on the couch. "Oh, silly me," Baba sniggered. "Let me introduce you to Bee." She walked up to her goddaughter. "Kelly this is Bee, Vlad's amazing friend and creation. She is a super intelligent robot that has the ability to transform."

Beep, beep, burp. "Babushka," said Bee. "Is that really you?" The droid climbed up onto the back of the chair, trying to grab a better look. She stared into Babushka's eyes, those same beautiful and friendly eyes, and realised it truly was her. The robot screamed for joy.

The noise was so loud and high-pitched that it made poor Vlad crawl out from underneath the couch. "W-what is going on? What is this racket?" he yelled. He was huffing and puffing and waving his hands in the air. Kelly looked down at the commotion, her gaze dropping to the talking rat.

"W-what? A talking rat," she said aloud. She rubbed her eyes vigorously, thinking there must be a little leftover magic playing games with her. But when she looked back down at the rat and refocused, nothing had changed. It definitely was no magic show. So, she did what any person would have done in a similar situation. She started to scream.

Vlad jumped so high at the sudden sound that he somersaulted on the way back to the ground. And when he landed, he fixed his eyes on Kelly and screamed back just as loudly.

So now, instead of kisses and hugs and tears of utter joy, Babushka came home to a room full of screaming guests—animal, human, and robot alike.

What a day! she thought. *Never ever a dull moment, even after you wake up from a coma.*

Instead of using magic, Babushka decided to get calm and order the old-fashioned way. So, she pressed her index finger and thumb together, placing it into her mouth and taking a deep breath. Then she blew as hard as she could. The result was spectacular. A whistle so loud and piercing it echoed right through the room—*BOOM, BANG*—and silenced everyone at once. They all turned to her.

"Stop!" Baba demanded. She spread her hands and arms open wide. "We are all friends. Calm yourselves." And the silence surged. "Kelly, use your gift of sight. Look into Vlad's eyes and see that he is good and now your friend," Babushka explained gently, while pointing to the rat.

Kelly mimicked the gesture, with her arm raised and her finger out. "*You*, at the pond, you..." She searched Vlad's eyes, looked beyond the brown-coloured irises, and deep within the pupil. And as she dug deeper, the middle of her forehead began to tingle.

"Look with your third eye, and feel with your heart. Let the magic of love and light guide you, child," whispered Babushka. "Tell me what you see."

Kelly stared at the rat. She looked beyond his physical form and into his soul. And, boy, did it radiate goodness. "I... I see a kind heart, a genuine heart, a lover of all things robotic and... *MacGyver*," she yelled in surprise, breaking the connection. "Oh!" she gasped, her head spinning. Kelly grabbed the back of the couch, grounding herself and taking in deep breaths of air. But a lightbulb did go off and, as others would say, a penny did fall. "You took my bread and you waved to me," she whispered. "I didn't imagine it. I didn't!" Now she truly believed what she'd seen that day at the pond.

"This is Vlad, and you are right. He is an inventor and *loves* MacGyver, as do I." Babushka beamed. Kelly was no longer afraid. The girl knelt down in front of Vlad and extended a palm, he didn't hesitate to accept it, and they both shook hands in the name of peace and friendship.

"Nice to meet you, Kelly," said the rat, bowing his head before pointing to Bee. "And, er, yes, I love to invent. My biggest inspiration is MacGyver and my greatest creation is Bee." He didn't allow Kelly to speak, his excitement suddenly overwhelming. He'd found someone new to show all of his toys to. "Bee, Bee, come here for a sec," he shouted out, waving to his robot, who was still standing on the backrest of the couch watching everyone. Bee did as she was asked. With grace and precision, she leapt, repositioned her body into a pike position, and rotated forward all the way until her head was pointing up to the ceiling, before she straightened her body and gracefully landed on her feet beside Vlad. "Kelly, this is Bee." With one paw pointing upright, the rat gestured towards his greatest creation.

"Wow," said Kelly, blinking her eyes several times. She extended a palm and shook hands with the droid. "How? How do you control your droid," asked Kelly.

"Well…" said Vlad but Bee stepped in and decided to explain for herself.

Beep, beep, beep. "I am not controlled by my creator. Yes, he can monitor me and my power source via the device upon his wrist, namely for battery purposes, but I was built to be self-aware," explained Bee.

"Self-aware," echoed Kelly, a little startled. "Self-aware, like Skynet, you mean? You can think for yourself, which means you can learn and emulate your source?" The movie *Terminator* flashed into her mind, and in particular, images of her favourite character Sarah Connor. Kelly loved Sarah Connor in the Terminator and then later on in T2. The teenager loved how she started off as this shy and quiet lady who then became all brawn, a woman who was strong, confident, and in charge. Deep down, Kelly wished she could also be like Sarah Connor.

This time, Vlad stepped in to answer her question. "Yes, Bee is self-aware, artificial intelligence. However, she is not connected to the worldwide military communications network, so there will be no Judgement Day on August 29th."

"Phew," said Kelly, exhaling a breath she'd been holding for about fifteen seconds now. Even though the Terminator and T2 were mega Hollywood blockbusters, they weren't based on real events. However, today's technology was developing at a rapid pace, and it was scary to think what could happen. The nuclear war and the battle against the machines wasn't that absurd of a possibility. And now, as Kelly looked upon Bee, a self-aware droid just like a T-100, she realised the future wasn't that distant. "Vlad, this creation is extraordinary. Wow, wow, wow…" Kelly was in awe.

Vlad blushed at Kelly's kind words. It had been a very long time since anyone, besides Babushka, complimented him on his work. He liked it and it made him feel good. Vlad smiled at Kelly. "Thank you very much. I love to invent and I love all things droids and Transformers," he explained.

Kelly got excited at the mention of Transformers. "Oh! Me too! I love, love, love the *Transformers* and *Terminator* movies," she said with a new lilt to her voice.

"Oh, no way," said Vlad in return, as he squeaked with joy and jumped up and down on the spot. He was so happy. He loved this new person already, as they had many things in common. Things they could talk and talk about for hours.

Bee and Babushka watched on as the pair shared their

favourite scenes from the *Terminator* movies and discussed and debated over the semantics of each of the Transformers. Babushka smiled. She was happy that the pair got along so well and she wondered how the rest of the clan would take to Kelly. Would they be mad or would they feel relief that she was finally found? She may not be Millard's son but she certainly was a descendant. A dragon whisperer, just like Millard himself.

Only time would tell how all this pans out, Baba thought to herself.

"What is this?" boomed a voice suddenly, and everyone turned around. Startled. It was Wymann and he'd arrived unannounced through the back door. Babushka screamed with joy, so happy to see her friend again. "Wymann!" She ran towards him with her arms open wide.

"B-babushka, what? This can't be…" He embraced her in a great, big bear hug. "Oh. Babushka," he cried, tears running down his cheeks. He was so happy. His wish had come true. His friend had come home. Wymann looked at Babushka. "Oh my, you look so different. What happened?" he asked, grabbing her hands and holding them tight, afraid that she would be whisked away again.

"I have so much to tell you, my dear friend," she said. "But first, I want you to meet someone." She gestured to her side. Before the bookshop owner could turn towards where Babushka was pointing, he felt something tugging at his trousers.

TUG, TUG, TUG. He looked down and saw Bee standing next to him, holding his magical necklace, which was glowing a bright-blue colour. Wymann's jaw dropped immediately, and he grabbed the necklace out of Bee's hand.

"W-what the hell?" he mumbled. As he looked up from the necklace, his eyes landed on none other than Kelly. "*You!*" he snarled.

"Oh, I am sorry, Wymann," mouthed Kelly. "Sorry for punching you," she added rather sheepishly. Silence fell upon them and everyone looked at Wymann, to the necklace, and then back to Kelly.

"So," said Wymann, abruptly turning to Babushka. "Do you believe me now?"

"Well, yes, you didn't fall down at the bookshop after all," she replied with a grin, her cheeks a bright shade of red.

25

EVERYONE WAS EITHER seated on the couch or on the armchairs in Babushka's living room, staring at Kelly, at Wymann, and then at the magical necklace—which was back where it belonged. Around the neck of its original owner and still glowing its magnificent, iridescent blue hue.

Wymann stared hard at Kelly, not in anger or in a sinister way, but in utter disbelief. *How could you ever doubt yourself? The magical necklace never ever let you down*, he thought, and he shook his head.

"Why are you shaking your head, Wymann?" asked Babushka.

He took a deep breath and exhaled his frustrations, along with his fatigue, and rubbed his face. "I just can't believe it, Lilliana. I just can't… She's here." He pointed to Kelly. "And I was right from the very first day I laid eyes on her," he stated, abruptly turning to Babushka and touching her hand, his eyebrows drawn in concern. "But where is the missing babe? This doesn't make any sense to me."

Babushka looked into Wymann's eyes and saw the confusion and dread. Yes, he was worried about the whereabouts and the safety of Millard's son, as he still felt responsible for what happened that night. But Babushka patted his hand a couple of times and grasped it tenderly. "Allow me to explain." She smiled, and he nodded in acknowledgement. "Kelly and I dream feasted, and I saw and felt her memories. Her father, Millard's son, was found by police that very first night, as you already know, but then he was taken to an orphanage. I didn't see it firsthand, as I could only access the memory of Kelly's mother telling her about her father's childhood—the little that she knew," explained Babushka.

"My father never spoke about his adoptive parents," added Kelly, trying to help the situation.

Wymann and Babushka turned and looked at her. "Why?" asked the king's hand. "Was his childhood difficult?" he added, tears welling in his eyes. If the babe's upbringing was difficult, then it would be all his fault. He could have searched harder or perhaps looked farther, in order to find him and reunite him with the clan.

Kelly shook her head. "I don't know the details, but my mother told me that he was loved dearly by his adoptive parents." She looked at Wymann and smiled. Her gift of sight into the man's heart and soul showed her that he carried a lot of guilt for what happened the night of their arrival. Kelly didn't resent or blame him. She saw that the old man had tried his hardest to find her dad.

Wymann exhaled heavily and ran his hands through his

hair, feeling frustrated and agitated all at once. After a while, he addressed Babushka. "So your magic works now, yes?"

Babushka flinched at his sudden abruptness and chose not to answer him, nodding instead, afraid that spoken words would irritate her friend and he'd explode like a firecracker. Their last conversation ended with Wymann walking out the door. Broken, numb, and his faith in magic shattered. She didn't want to go hard on him and thought it wise to let everything slowly seep in. To let the dust settle, as it had been one hell of a storm lately.

"Can you see the cords again?" he asked, not looking at Babushka when he spoke.

"Yes, I can. They've returned. The magic has returned."

Hearing those words made him want to cry and laugh, all at the same time. It was an odd mixture of emotions. "Hmpf, fancy that, hey?" said Wymann.

The king's hand was having a hard time processing all this new information. For a very, very long time, all he'd done was spend every single spare minute reading and researching and then reading some more, trying to find a way back for the clan. And now it felt like a complete utter waste of time. Time that could have been better spent.

What did he get out of it?

Absolutely nothing beneficial, or so it seemed. He lost his eyesight from all the reading, and his back and shoulders were constantly sore and stiff from his bad posture, as he was always hunched over a book. And now he was an old man, who had nothing more than an old decrepit house, filled wall to wall with books. There were no picture frames filled with lifelong memories. No friends, no children, and no wife. Just books, books, and more books.

Wymann was angry. He stood, walked away from the lounge room, and stepped into the entrance of the kitchen, leaning on the bench and looking away from everyone. Silence fell upon the space as everyone looked at each other in concern, not knowing what was going to happen next.

Is Wymann about to leave? they all seemed to wonder.

He stared down at his balled fists atop the kitchen bench. The frustration and anger were bubbling to the surface, and he couldn't shake the sensation. He slowly started to tap one fist. *Tap, tap, tap,* hoping it would help soothe him. He had so many questions and he didn't know where to start. Questions he wanted to ask Kelly, questions he wanted to ask Babushka, just more and more questions.

"Does the babe feel the magic or did it vanish from him too?" asked Wymann.

There, that's a good place to start, he thought.

Softly, Babushka answered, "No, the magic within him vanished when he stepped through the portal. For some reason or another, the magic protected him one last time and prevented him from turning into an animal, and then it vanished." She took in a breath and quickly added, "With the cords being severed, I would not have had a chance to find him. Even as an adult when he walked into my house, I would not have known that he was Millard's long-lost son."

Wymann turned around, unsatisfied, his anger still bubbling deep within. "Then why did the necklace glow for the girl?" he blurted out. "She isn't the lost babe, the one we brought through the portal." He pointed right at Kelly, his eyes starting to glare, and she gulped down the tension she was feeling, and shifted in her seat. The teenager looked away from Wymann and turned to Babushka, seeking her godmother's help.

"Ah, erm, Wymann, no one could have foretold what was going to happen after we stepped through the portal. *No one*. I didn't know my faith in magic would be lost. I didn't know you would spend a lifetime reading and researching, or that our dear friends would live their lives as animals on this planet," pleaded Babushka. "No one knew."

He shook his head. He just couldn't accept these answers. They weren't fair. He balled his fists and trembled as he continued to absorb all the information. His face reddened, the tension bubbling and starting to rise. And he screamed, grabbing his hair and tugging at it with all his might.

The room filled with a collective gasp as everyone jumped in their seats. Babushka raised a palm, signalling for them to relax. Everything was going to be okay. He was just blowing off some much-needed steam. The king's hand continued to scream. He screamed and yelled so much that the glass shook in the windowsills. They rattled and rattled, and clanked and clanked, to the point they created their own mystical musical melody. Eventually, Wymann had worn himself out and plopped onto the floor in a heap, like a whimpering sack of potatoes. He covered his face with his hands, gently rocking back and forth while trying to soothe the pain in his chest.

Babushka lowered herself down beside him. She hugged his shoulders and brought him closer to her, resting his head on her bosom. "There, there, my dear friend," she whispered, stroking his head. "There, there." They sat in silence, one friend comforting the other, gently rocking on the floor together. "When the sage found me while I was in a coma, he showed me many things," Babushka explained in a hushed, even tone. "He showed me that I would rise from my ashes and become what I was always destined to be."

She pulled Wymann out of her embrace and gently lifted his chin so she could see his eyes.

"You too have done what you were destined to do," she assured him, but he didn't respond or acknowledge anything she was saying. He was numb. Babushka continued anyway. "The sage showed me that a prophecy was foretold long ago. The chosen one would return and restore peace where evil had risen. Kelly is the chosen one, and so was the babe, and Millard before them and so on. The chosen one is each member of the Drakon lineage. They have the power to destroy the greatest evil and send it back to where it came from." Baba grabbed Wymann by the face and held it, gently wiping away his tears with her robe. "Your life has not been a waste, my dear friend. You have been doing what was destined to be done. You helped save the bloodline."

He looked right into Babushka's beautiful eyes and held her gaze.

"And we all have helped save each other," Babushka added with a smile. "We could not have come this far without each other and that includes the clan at the burrow." Standing up abruptly, Baba realised something in that moment. "Which needs to be notified." She marched right up to the lounge room and spoke directly to her friend, the rat. "Vlad, we need to notify the others at once and tell them that we have found Kelly. Preparations need to be made for our return home immediately," she ordered.

"Immediately...?" repeated Kelly, her confusion evident. "Immediately," she said again to everyone, to whomever was listening. But they continued to chat amongst themselves, planning their return and ignoring the teenager. "STOP!" she screamed. "*STOP!*" She raised her hands in the air, and all eyes turned towards her. "Immediately…? No, I can't go anywhere *immediately*," she protested. Kelly then turned to Babushka. "This is my life. I have a life here. How can I leave immediately? I can't leave my family…"

A great sadness engulfed the girl and her heart shattered into a million pieces. How was she supposed to leave her parents? Her friends and her life? How? Over a stupid prophecy. Which had been foretold many, many years ago. On a planet she did not know existed. In a galaxy far, far away.

This is just crazy, she thought to herself.

"I can't do this, Babushka," she pleaded yet again. "I just can't…"

But her fairy godmother remained stern. "We must return, child. We must restore peace. It's your destiny," she explained.

"God, that word again, Baba. *Destiny*," she said sarcastically, rubbing her hands together, frustrated that no one was hearing her. "What guarantee is there that we will win against this evil? WHAT guarantee?" she bellowed. "We could all be killed, then what? Reset the game and play again?"

Babushka felt Kelly's fear and also her disbelief as it weighed heavily on the girl's words. "I cannot, and I don't know what is waiting for us when we return. But we must fight, together." She took Kelly's hand and held it tightly. "The evil will reign forever if we do nothing, and only you can stop it." Baba squeezed Kelly's hand even more this time. "Take your rightful place as a Drakon and come home with us."

The words rang through the teenager's ears and echoed in her head. She gasped, tearing her hand out of her fairy godmother's grasp, balling it into a fist, and shaking it. "W-what do I know about fighting?" she asked. "I-I don't know anything. All my life, I have only known HB pencils and sewing machines, and now you want me to go into battle?" Her body was trembling. "I-I-I can't do this."

And Kelly ran. She jumped over the coffee table, sprang across the couch, dodged Vlad and Bee, bypassed Wymann who remained on the floor, and ran out the back door. In a flash. Her legs did not stop and she did not slow down. She ran and ran, right up to her house, through the back door, skipped and jumped over a few steps up the stairs, and barged into her room before slamming the door behind her and leaning against it. Kelly was breathless as the tears cascaded down her cheeks.

"I can't do this," she mumbled and dropped onto her bed, her face buried in her pillow.

Luckily, Mark was on a Zoom meeting in the kitchen when Kelly had *zoomed* by. He didn't hear or see a single thing—that's how fast she ran. Her gift of speed certainly made her trip home a very, very quick one. If the ability were to be considered normal on earth, she definitely would have broken every world record, won every Olympic medal, during that run home. How amazing would that have been?

Mark, however, did in fact look up at one point, to see what was going on as he felt the house shake from the impact of Kelly closing her door—strength had been another gift bestowed upon her. Thank God the tremor didn't last long, and nothing got damaged in the process.

For what felt like ages, Kelly curled up on her pillow, emotionally and physically drained. Her tank was empty and she finally had enough of everything and everyone. "I can't do this," she mumbled to herself over and over again, refusing to lift her face. "I can't believe in something that is only words. Old words from long ago and a world I don't believe truly exists. And my parents… I can't leave my parents."

Even though things of late had not been well between Kelly and her mother, she still couldn't leave her. They could work through it and rebuild their relationship, Kelly was keen. She loved her mother and would do anything to win her trust back.

And her beloved dad… He was her hero and, my God, did she love him wholeheartedly. How could she leave her giant teddy bear? The one who gave her the best cuddles? How could she? The answer was simple. She just couldn't. It would be too heartbreaking. If she ever left earth to go back to a home she never knew, how would she manage to breathe without seeing her dad? She couldn't. It was impossible.

Kelly rolled over onto her back and stared at the ceiling once again. So much time had been spent staring at this very ceiling. It felt like that was all she had done lately in her room. She'd gotten to know every crack, every shadow, and all the spiders that lived within the cornices. She knew it like the back of her hand.

Psst, psst, psst. "Hi, darling," said Mark to his wife as she arrived home from work. "You look like you have had a hard day." He walked up to Joyce and gave her a quick peck on the cheek, then grabbed her hand and led her to a chair. "Here, darling, sit down."

"Oh, yeah, hard day. You are not wrong," she huffed as she pulled out another chair and rested her feet upon it.

Kelly sat up in bed. Her mum was home and she was in the kitchen with her dad. The teenager had this incredible urge to run downstairs and hug them. And that's exactly what she did. *ZOOM, FLASH.* She leapt over a few steps, and before she knew it, she found herself at the entrance of the kitchen, watching her parents. Her dad was giving her mum a massage, which seemed to be exactly what Joyce needed.

"Ehem," said Kelly, breaking the silence, and her parents turned and looked at her—well, her mum only peeked one eye a tiny bit open.

"Hi, Kelly," said Mark. But before he could utter another word, his daughter ran up and bear-hugged her parents. Tears flowed down her cheeks as she held them. The pain of leaving them behind was too great. She loved them very dearly.

"Hey, hey, hey," said Mark and Joyce together. "What's wrong, hun?"

Kelly stepped away from her parents and dried her eyes. "Nothing," she babbled. "I just want you to know that I love you both so much and that I am so sorry for the last week or so." And the tears started to fall down her cheeks again.

"Oh, Kel," said Joyce. She gestured for her daughter to come to her, tapping her lap, before adding, "Come here, hun."

Kelly smiled and jumped at the opportunity to sit on her mum's lap. It didn't matter what age she was. It didn't matter at all, as long as she had her mother.

Joyce hugged her daughter. "I'm so sorry, darling, for treating you harshly. I'm so sorry," she explained. "I had a lot of pressure from work and I took it out on you and that was wrong." She looked pleadingly into her daughter's eyes. "Can you forgive me?"

"Oh, Mum, it's okay. There is nothing to forgive. I understand." Kelly grabbed her mother and held her close.

Mark watched his girls hug. He was in awe and he had a big smile on his face. For days, he'd watched the tension between them grow and grow, until it became too unbearable. Even for him. Now, it was nice to finally see some love. He reached out for them both and hugged them tightly. His heart was singing. Mark revelled in the moment. It felt so good. He'd truly missed it. What felt like had been missing for so long had finally reared its head again. Love. Pure, unconditional love.

"Okay!" Clapping his hands together, his voice chipper, Mark asked, "Who's hungry?" Then he jumped up and down on the spot and raised a hand in the air. "Oh, oh, oh, I know! I know! How about we get a pizza, hey?"

Joyce and Kelly looked at each other and smiled. "Yeah, that sounds awesome," they replied in unison.

Mark did a happy dance, shaking his hips and wiggling his bum. The girls giggled. "Okay then, I will give Porky's a call," he said as he bowed and curtsied his way to the telephone in the kitchen.

Kelly slid off her mum's lap. "I will be back in a sec. Just want to take my jumper off. Feeling a little hot."

"Okay, hun, I will set the table." And Joyce set off busying herself in the kitchen. In the meantime, Kelly walked up the stairs with a renewed spring in her step, taking two at a time, her heart lighter and happier. Things were back on track with her mum and it felt good. There was still a very long way to go, but at least the ball was rolling and that was important.

Just before she reached her room, the teenager decided to tug at her jumper, trying to take it off before she made it to the door. She lifted the material over her head and blindly pushed her door open to step inside, grunting and struggling with the taut fabric. One pull here and one tug there, and finally she'd set herself free, only to stop dead in her tracks...

"Millard," she said the name with a gasp of surprise. "What are you doing here?" Instinctively, she took a couple more steps forward but her legs eventually halted. "How are you even here?" She stared at him in disbelief.

The dragon whisperer stood there, in her room, clad in his beautiful and intricate golden armour. God, he was a sight, his eyes ever so mesmerising. She looked at him and notice that he was missing his helmet, shield, sword, and a single glove. He looked so different without everything and, for the first time, Kelly noticed the resemblance between him and her father.

Wow... It was amazing how similar their features were. The same cheekbones, nose, hair—except her father wore his short—and definitely the same blue eyes. There was no doubt that Mark was a Drakon and that this was his father, Kelly's grandfather, Millard.

He spoke first. "I will always be with you. We will always be within you," he said. "Do not be afraid of your destiny."

Kelly shook her head. "Millard, I can't leave my parents.

I can't leave your *son*." She emphasised that last word before adding, "While I go into battle alone."

"But you won't be alone. You will have Babushka and the clan. You will have my spirit, your whole bloodline, within you and fighting beside you. Our strength, our sight, our speed, our hearing. All of it and all of us," he explained.

Kelly looked away, exhaling her frustrations. "This won't ever end, will it? The dreams, good and bad, the visits, the calling, it will never end?" she whispered. Deep down, she knew the answer. No matter where she went or what she did, it would follow her to the ends of the earth. And the only way to stop it—all this chaos, madness, and upheaval—was to accept who she was meant to become. The chosen one.

She would never be the same ever again. The girl who loved to draw and sew was no more. It was now time for Kelly to claim what was rightfully hers. And the only way to claim it, and become who she was always destined to be, was to return *home*. Kelly looked at her chest of drawers and knew what she had to do. She walked up, hunched down, and pulled open the very bottom drawer.

"What will happen to my parents and my friends?" she asked, her gaze focused on the items in front of her.

"Your parents and your friends will be all right," he explained softly. "Nothing will happen to them while you are gone."

Kelly stood with the golden glove in her hand. Sparks of electricity ran through her fingers and travelled up her arm. It tingled as it went, and she could feel the magic growing stronger.

"Put on my glove and then take my hand." Millard gestured. "I will take you to Babushka and, together, you will finally go home." He smiled.

She hesitated and glanced around her room one last

time. She took it all in, absorbed everything that had made her the person she was today. She saw her sketchbook and boxes of HB pencils. She looked upon her photos of her best friend Pi. How much she loved her...

Kelly noticed bits of fabric on her desk and recalled her love of sewing as her eyes jumped up to all the books on her bookshelf about vintage dresses. This is what she had become, and these were all the things she loved. They were a part of her. And now she'd been given an opportunity to learn a different part, a part she never knew existed, a part that was magical.

"Wow," she uttered aloud, realising the extent of the opportunity.

What does this magic hold? she thought. *I hope it brings peace and an end to all this chaos.*

"Take my hand, Kelly, and I will show you," answered Millard as he held out his one gloved hand.

If strength, speed, sight, and hearing were a mere taste of that magic, what would the rest bring? The curiosity was too great for Kelly to dismiss it, the wonder too tempting. But she also wanted everything to go back to normal, like it was before the dreams began. Was that even possible now?

Placing the glove on her hand, Kelly immediately felt the energy of the magic engulf her. *KAZAM*. It rushed through her body, causing her to gasp and her heart to skip a beat. The sensation was incredible. Thrilling. With her heart racing, and the excitement pumping, Kelly grasped Millard's palm and they both vanished...

∼੭

There was so much chatter in Babushka's house that evening. The entire clan had assembled and was now seated in the living room.

"Ar, this is a joke, ain't it?" grumbled Dyllon, shaking his fist at Vlad. "You brought me here to upset me and disrupt me sleep you stinkin' vermin."

"No, I didn't. For the love of God, you annoying old toad," spat the rat, feeling like he'd reached his max. "I told you we have found her and now we can all finally go home."

The toad looked around. "If you've found her, where is she then?" He gestured to the room before folding his arms in annoyance. "Besides, the last time I checked, the babe was a wee lad, not a gal."

"Hear, hear," shouted Tovah, perking up in his seat.

Dyllon stood from his chair and puffed out his chest, like a gorilla getting ready for battle. "This is trickery. Let's go back to the burrow, where it is safe. Enough for one day, I say," spat the toad. "Who's with me?" He scanned the room for supporters.

Tovah raised his feathered hand. "I am. Let's go back," he repeated.

"ENOUGH!" screamed the swan. "Enough from all of you." She pointed a finger at each member, one at a time. The princess was so angry and all her beautiful feathers were standing on end. She looked like a puffed-up turkey—*gobble, gobble*. Everyone stopped moving and even held their breath. This was a first for all, including the princess herself. "This has been the biggest shock of our lives, yes?" She directed the question to the crowd. "But we don't know the full story, the *whys* and the *hows*. So, if we don't know, why not ask!" she yelled at all her disobedient children, shaking her finger and trying to teach them the right way to go about things. "If we don't understand, we ask," she repeated.

The old toad and the owl looked away in embarrassment, their faces glowing crimson red. For the first time in her life, the princess felt the pull of the power and the buzz of confidence. Enough was enough, and enough had been bubbling deep within her for so very long. Watching and listening to their constant quarrelling, constant bickering, had finally reached its climax. It ended today.

"Babushka, it makes my heart sing to see you again and to have you back with us," explained Annie. "Tell us what has happened to bring us all here this night." The swan's newfound confidence was evident in her voice.

Babushka caught everyone's stare, each appearing confused. Some frightened, scared about what the gathering meant. It was up to her to settle these fears and to take away their confusion. "The sage has shown me the prophecy and also led me to Kelly. She is the chosen one, destined to destroy the evil." The explanation did not bring any comfort. The eyes remained confused, scared, and now some bulged out of their sockets. Babushka quickly pressed on. "Magic faded in this world but found a way to twinkle again. Just like death, eventually life finds a way to live on. The magic saved us as we went through the portal. Some…" She pointed to her furry and feathered friends. "…were forever transformed but others…" She pointed to herself and Wymann. "…remained true to form. That is the power of magic." The clan listened attentively. "I rose from my ashes, stronger than ever before. Love brought me here and now we must go back to save our homeland," she concluded.

"But it's been so long," piped up the toad.

"We don't know what is left," echoed the priest.

Babushka held up her hands, hearing their concerns. "Yes, we don't know what we will face, or what we will see, but we will be together. And just like we have survived here for so long together, we will survive there *together*."

The toad, perhaps old in his age, didn't understand what he was hearing. Or maybe, deep down, he was just scared like the rest of them. "But how will we survive?" he blurted out. "Where is the missing babe anyhow? Where is the chosen one? This Kelly?" He gestured. "She isn't here. She doesn't believe in it," he spat angrily.

The tension in the room was starting to get hot and supercharged again. No matter how many questions were answered, more and more arose as a result.

"Ba, to the seven hells with ye all," spat the toad. "I'm too old for this and I care no longer." He jumped off his chair and started heading towards the fireplace and the tunnel that led back to the burrow.

Beep, beep, burp. "Big disturbance, Vlad. My motion sensors are going haywire. Something big is coming," said Bee.

The rat jumped up suddenly. He flicked his watch and looked at the readings. "My God, Bee, you are right." He scanned the room to see if any sparks of light could be seen. Nothing yet.

Dyllon continued to flap his hands and wave his fists at the clan on the way out. "Ye all are crazy and should get your heads checked," he blurted, while pointing one finger at his temple.

Suddenly, the sparks flew across the room. *ZIP, ZOOP, ZOOM.* The atmosphere crackled ever so slightly, sending tiny bolts of electricity flying here, there, and everywhere.

"I am going back to bed," grumbled the old toad, more to himself than to anyone else. Everyone just watched as the geezer continued to babble.

Vlad and Bee, on the other hand, had different ideas. "Here it comes. Bee," shouted the rat to his trusty sidekick.

Beep, beep, burp. "It's a big one," she responded, watching her sensors and getting excited.

"I've had absolutely—"

KAZAM. ZAP. And a ball of light erupted right in front of Dyllon, sending him flying backwards in the direction he'd come from. *Tumble, tumble, roll.* And finally, *kerplunk.* The toad stopped falling and ended up next to Wymann on the floor, dazed and confused.

Everyone screamed, raising their hands and trying to block out the piercing bright light. The energy exploded within the room, sucking up some of the air. The illumination radiated and continued to glow. To the naked eye, it looked like a blinding light. But on Bee's sensors, it appeared to be a bright star. Iridescent, sparkly, and full of magic.

Beep, beep, burp. "Wow!" gasped the droid. What an incredible sight it truly was.

Ever so slowly, the light subsided. And, finally, when it was no longer too bright, the crowd of onlookers peered up. "Oohhh."

"What is the meaning of this?" blurted the old toad, rubbing his eyes.

"Magic," said Babushka.

And there, standing in the middle of the light, glowing in complete wonder, and wearing her grandfather's glove, stood Kelly. Beside her, Millard.

"She is here," sang Babushka. "This is Kelly, daughter of the lost babe and descendant of the Drakon family. Millard's granddaughter."

"Millard," whispered Wymann. "Is… is that really you,

my dear friend?" Wymann stared at the figure, tears filling his eyes. How he missed him. The pain was fresh. He took in the silhouette before him, looking at his glorious armour, his trademark, and then at the piercing blue eyes. Those mesmerising eyes. "Yes, it is you," he whispered.

Everyone pushed to their feet and walked up to Kelly and Millard, including Dyllon and Wymann. The sight was absolutely spectacular.

"I am here. I am here with you always," Millard spoke gently. He looked at them all, one at a time, and acknowledged them with a nod. "Thank you for looking after the bloodline. You are all the bravest of the brave. I bow down to you." And without hesitation, he bowed his head to the clan, showing them his love and gratitude.

And everyone returned the gesture, offering him their love. Including the princess, who was only ever told stories about this legendary dragon whisperer.

"The time has come, to go home, together," said Millard. "What once was broken will be whole yet again. Do not be afraid. The prophecy is true." Millard gestured to Babushka, and she nodded in response.

Silently, the old crone left the group and ventured to her broom cupboard. Opening it slowly, trying not to have all the contents spill out everywhere, Babushka peered inside. *Peep.* "Ah, there you are, just as I was shown." And she stuck one arm into the small crack of the door, pulling out her shrivelled walking stick, which had been restored to its original glory. And, boy, was she glowing bright. The orb radiating pure magic.

Babushka smiled. Her staff was back to normal. She could feel its power, and this time she understood it much better. More so than ever before.

"Everyone, everyone." She gestured. "Make a circle and hold hands."

Vlad grabbed Kelly's hand, his new friend and fellow lover of *Terminator* and *Transformers*.

What new adventures awaited them? he wondered. He gave her a gentle squeeze, assuring her that he was here for her, and she smiled down upon the rat.

The princess followed and led by example, showing them that they needed to be brave in this moment and in every moment to come. She took her place beside Vlad and smiled at everyone. "Come," she encouraged.

And they all complied, holding hands and forming a circle with Millard. Babushka took his hand and allowed his magic to enter her soul, her very being. *WOOSH*. It was powerful. She raised her hand, including the staff, high into the sky. The others mimicked the gesture. Kelly looked upon her fairy godmother. She was beautiful and magical and her aura glowed. She was goodness and love and there was never a reason to doubt her again.

Babushka closed her eyes and began to chant, and the words filled the room and made everything vibrate and pulse. An incredible wind picked up and travelled all around, grabbing everything in its path. Furniture, armchairs, ripping the TV off the wall, the pots and pans out of the kitchen, including the curtain from the windows. Everything was engulfed by the whirlwind. A super twister, destroying everything in its path.

The room continued to pulse while Babushka continued to chant, her words loud and clear. Some of the clan closed their eyes. And you couldn't blame them. The sight of the twister was frightening.

Bah-bum, bah-bum, bah-bum echoed the pulse. *Twirl, twirl, twirl* continued the twister.

Babushka started to glow. Kelly noticed the spark. At first, it flickered ever so slightly and then it grew as the old woman chanted. "Oh! It's the medallion," mumbled Kelly. The Medallion of Light. The same medallion the sage had gifted her. God, it was beautiful and incredibly powerful.

When it reached its climax, shining in its full glory, and the chanting had engulfed the room, the orb atop the staff shot out a bolt of pure-white magic. Ripping a hole, a portal, in the present. The twister twirled its way around the room, like a dancer coiling its tush. It gently engulfed each member of the clan before spinning its way into the open portal. Vanishing forever.

THE END

ABOUT THE AUTHOR

Anissa Papadakos is an author and artist based in Melbourne, Australia, where she lives with her husband and two cheeky children.

Anissa's love of drawing began at an incredibly young age, with her biggest influence at the time being Bart from 'The Simpsons'. Her passion is to make magic via writing and creating, and she does that through children's books, self help books for parents, young adult novels and her comic strip 'Chop Suey Mama'.

www.magicwallsandcanvas.com
www.instagram.com/magic_walls_and_canvas
www.facebook.com/MWCau

www.ingramcontent.com/pod-product-compliance
Lightning Source LLC
Chambersburg PA
CBHW020248120726
47904CB00001B/123